Had'st thou lived in days of old,
O, what wonders had been told
Of thy lively countenance,
And thy humid eyes that dance
In the midst of their own brightness,
In the very fane of lightness;
Over which thine eyebrows, leaning,
Picture out each lovely meaning;
In a dainty bend they lie
Like the streaks across the sky,
Or the feathers from a crow,
Fallen on a bed of snow.
KEATS

The village of Ashleigh is situated in one of the most lovely and romantic of the English counties; where mountains, valleys, woods and forest trees appear to vie with each other in stately magnificence. The village is literally embosomed amongst the trees. Lofty elms, majestic oaks, and wide-spreading beech trees grow in and around it. On one side, as far as the eye can reach, are mountains covered with verdure, with all their varied and lovely tints of green. On the other side the view is partially obstructed by a mass of forest trees growing in clumps, or forming an arch overhead, through which nevertheless may be gained a peep of the distant sea, with its blue waves, and sometimes the white sails of a ship; or, on a clear day, even the small fishermen's boats can be distinguished dotted here and there like small pearls.

Ashleigh has its country inn and ivy-mantled church, with the small house dignified as the Parsonage, close by. Other houses are sprinkled here and there down the green lanes, or along the road, shaded by its lofty elms, at the end of which, on a small eminence, stands the Manor or "Big House," as the villagers call it.

It is a large, brick building, but with nothing grand or imposing about it; in fact, but for the lovely grounds and plantations on a small scale around, the clematis, jasmine and other beautiful creepers, too numerous to mention, trained up its walls, and hanging in luxuriant festoons about the porch, and the dark ivy which almost covers the roof, the whole of one side, and part of the front itself, it would be an ugly, unwieldy-looking edifice; as it was, everything appeared bright and gladsome.

Before you reach the village, a bridge crosses a small stream which flows from the hill-side, and after winding gracefully and silently through the midst, passes by the mill and being just seen like a long thin thread of silver in the distance, is lost in the rich meadows beyond.

It was the beautiful spring time of the year:—

"The delicate-footed May,
With its slight fingers full of leaves and flowers."

The sun was just setting in all its regal splendour beneath the deep rich crimson sky, throwing long dim shadows from the stately trees which over-arched the road along which a young girl was slowly wending her way. Her figure was slight, yet her step—although she appeared very young—had none of the buoyancy or elasticity of youth. It was slow; almost mournful. But either the graceful figure or step itself had a certain dignified pride, neither stately, haughty, nor commanding; perhaps it combined all three. Her face was very lovely. Fair golden masses of hair waved under the broad straw hat she wore, while her eyes were shaded by long, dark silken lashes. She had a clear, high forehead, and a delicately fair complexion. Such was Amy Neville. She paused as she reached the bridge, and, leaning against the low masonry at the side, looked back. Nothing could be lovelier than the scene she gazed on. The sun, as we have said, was just setting, and the sea, distinctly seen from the bridge, looked like one large, broad mirror, its waves dashing here and there like glittering diamonds. Far off, touched by the last rays of the sun, the white cliffs stood out grandly, while birds chirped and warbled among the leafy branches; groups of merry, noisy children played in the village, under the shade of the elms, through which here and there long thin white wreaths of smoke curled gracefully and slowly upwards.

A cart, with its team of horses, roused Amy from her reverie, and she went into the lane where the hedge-rows were one mass of wild flowers. The delicate primrose, yellow cowslips, blue-bells, bryony, travellers' joy, and a number of others, almost rivalling in their loveliness the painted, petted ones in our own cultivated parterres, grew here in wild luxuriance, and as Amy sauntered slowly on, she filled the basket she carried on her arm with their beauty and fragrance. As she came in sight of one of the houses before mentioned, a child of about ten years of age came flying down the narrow garden-walk to meet her. Throwing her arms round her neck she upset Amy's basket of treasures, covering her dark hair with the lovely buds and blossoms. Leaving her to collect the scattered flowers, Amy passed into the cottage, her home.

"You are late, Amy," said a voice, as she entered the little sitting room, "or otherwise I have wished to see you more than usual, and am impatient. Sarah has been eagerly watching the road ever since her return from her walk. Poor child! I fear she misses her young school companions."

"I think I am rather later than usual, mamma, but old Mrs. Collins was more than usually talkative; so full of her ailments and griefs, I really was quite vexed with her at last, as if no one in the world suffers as she does. Then the evening was so lovely, I loitered at the bridge to watch the sun set; you can have no idea how beautiful it was; and the wild flowers in the lane, I could not resist gathering them," and throwing her hat carelessly on the table, Amy seated herself on a low stool at her mother's feet.

"And why have you wished to see me so much, and what makes you look so sad, dear mamma?" she asked, as Mrs. Neville laid her hand caressingly on the masses of golden hair.

Receiving no reply, she bent her eager, loving eyes on her mother's face. There was a sad, almost painful expression overshadowing the eyes, and compressing the lips, and it was some time ere Mrs. Neville met her gaze, and then tears had gathered under the long eyelashes, though none rested on her cheek.

"I have been for a drive with Mrs. Elrington, Amy."

Amy turned away her face; she dared not trust herself to meet those mournful eyes, expressing as they did all the grief she feared to encounter; so she turned away, lest she also should betray emotion which must be overcome, or be wanting in firmness to adhere to the plan she had formed, a plan she knew to be right, and therefore to be carried out; if the courage and resolution of which she had so boasted to Mrs. Elrington did not give way in the now wished for, yet half-dreaded conversation.

It May Be True by Mrs Henry Wood

COMPLETE IN THREE VOLUMES

Ellen Price was born on 17th January 1814 in Worcester.

In 1836 she married Henry Wood, whose career in banking and shipping meant living in Dauphiné, in the South of France, for two decades. During their time there they had four children.

Henry's business collapsed and he and Ellen together with their four children returned to England and settled in Upper Norwood near London.

Ellen now turned to writing and with her second book 'East Lynne' enjoyed remarkable popularity. This enabled her to support her family and to maintain a literary career.

It was a career in which she would write over 30 novels including 'Danesbury House', 'Oswald Cray', 'Mrs. Halliburton's Troubles', 'The Channings' and 'The Shadow of Ashlydyat'.

Sadly, her husband, Henry died in 1866.

Ellen though continued to strive on. In 1867, she purchased the magazine 'Argosy', founded two years previously by Alexander Strahan. She was a prolific writer and wrote much of the magazine herself although she had some very respected contributors, amongst them Hesba Stretton and Christina Rossetti. Although she would gradually pare down writing for the magazine she continued to write novel after novel. Such was her talent that for a time she was, in Australia, more popular than Charles Dickens.

Apart from novels she was an excellent translator and a writer of short stories. 'Reality or Delusion?' is a staple of supernatural anthologies to this day.

Ellen Wood died of bronchitis on 10th February 1887. He estate was valued at a very considerable £36,000.

She is buried in Highgate Cemetery, London.

A monument to her in Worcester Cathedral was unveiled in 1916.

Index of Contents

VOLUME I

CHAPTER I

"And she mentioned the letter to you, mamma?" asked Amy.

"She did. And much more beside. She tried to talk me over; tried to make me give my consent to parting with you, my dear child."

"And did you consent, dear mamma? Did Mrs. Elrington tell you how much I had set my heart upon going?"

"You wish to leave me, Amy?" asked Mrs. Neville reproachfully. "Think how lonely I should be. How I should miss the thousand kind things you do for me. And when I am sad, who will cheer me as you have done? I cannot part with you, my child. It is too hard a trial. I cannot bring myself to think of it!"

"But, mamma," replied Amy, pausing to stifle her rising emotion. "You have Sarah, and she is full of fun and spirits, and always laughing and merry, or singing about the house. And then, dear old Hannah will, I know, do her best to fill my place, so that after a while you will scarcely miss my sober face, and I am sure it is what I ought to do, dear mamma, instead of remaining here in idleness, and seeing you daily deprived of all the many comforts you have been accustomed to; and think of the pleasure it would give me to know and feel I am working for you, my own dear mother;" and Amy drew her mother's arm fondly round her neck.

"Slaving for me, Amy! A governess's life is a life of slavery, though to you it may appear all sunshine. A path of thorns; no bed of roses, such as your excited fancy may have sketched out."

"No, mamma; you are wrong. I have thought over all the discomforts, mortifications, slavery, if you will, and it does not alter my opinion. I am willing to bear them all; and Mrs. Elrington, whom you love so much and think so highly of, told me she thought if you gave your consent it was the very best thing I could do. Nearly a month ago the idea entered my head; and she offered then to write to a friend who she thought might want a governess for her children, and I have pondered upon it ever since. Do consent, dear mamma, pray do. Indeed you must let me have my way in this."

"Well, Amy dear, I will say no more; I half promised Mrs. Elrington before I came in; and now I give my consent; may I never have to regret it," and Mrs. Neville turned away and bent her head over her work that her daughter might not see the tears that were fast filling her eyes.

"Oh, thank you, again and again, dear mamma," said Amy, rising and kissing her pale cheek, "I will go at once and tell Mrs. Elrington; see it is not yet dusk, and I shall be back before Hannah has prepared the tea table; or if not, quite in time to make the tea."

Mrs. Neville, Amy's mother, was dressed in deep mourning, her once dark hair, now tinged with grey, smoothly braided beneath the close-fitting widow's cap. The large, dark mournful eyes, the small delicate features, the beautifully formed mouth, all told that Amy's mother must once have been gifted with no common share of beauty. Sorrow more than time had marked its ravages on her once fair face.

She had married early in life, and much against the wishes of her friends, who did not approve of the poor but handsome Captain Neville. Some years after their marriage, by the sudden and unlooked-for death of an uncle and cousin, he came into a large property; but whether this unexpected accession of wealth, with the temptations with which he was surrounded in his new sphere, changed his heart, or whether the seeds were there before, only requiring opportunity and circumstances to call them forth into action; who can tell? Suffice it to say, he ran a sad career of dissipation; and at his death little indeed remained for his widow and children. And now the once courted, flattered, and admired Sarah Barton, bred up and nurtured in the lap of luxury, with scarcely a wish ungratified; was living in a small cottage, and her beloved child on the eve of departing from her home, to be that poor despised being— a governess. Captain Neville had been dead about four months, and his widow mourned for him as the father of her children, thought of him as he had been to her in the first early days of their married life, the fond and loving husband.

Amy did not return till late. Mrs. Elrington had promised to write to the lady that evening; and less than three days might bring the answer.

As day after day passed, poor Amy's heart beat fast; and her slight form trembled whenever she heard the little gate opened, leading into the small garden before the house; yet day after day passed by, and still Mrs. Elrington came not; and Amy almost feared her kind old friend had forgotten her promise, or, what was still worse, her application to the lady had failed.

About ten days afterwards, one morning, as Amy sat with her mother in the little sitting room, working and listening to the exclamations of delight that fell from the lips of her little sister Sarah, who was wondering how dear dolly would look in the smart new dress Amy was making for her, the sound of approaching carriage wheels was dully heard coming down the road. Presently a pony chaise drew up before the gate. Amy could hardly draw her breath as she recognized from the window the slow and measured step, the tall and stately figure of her kind old friend; and gently pushing away her sister, who attempted to detain her, probably disappointed at the unfinished state of dolly's frock, and not daring to look at her mother, she went and met the old lady at the door.

"Dear Mrs. Elrington, I thought you would never come! Have you heard from the lady, and what does she say?"

"Yes, Amy, I have heard twice from the lady since I saw you; but I thought it best not to come until I had received a definite answer."

"It is very kind of you to come at all, dear Mrs. Elrington. But have you been successful? Is the answer favourable?"

"Yes, Amy. The lady has engaged you, but there are three little girls, not two, as I at first thought; however they are very young, and I hope your trouble will be slight."

Poor Amy! What she had so long sighed and wished for, now seemed in its stern reality the greatest calamity that could have befallen her. She thought of her mother, whose comfort, solace, and companion she was, how lonely she would be; what could or would she do without her? Must she, indeed, leave her and her home where, for the last few months she had been so happy, and live amongst strangers, who cared not for her? Must she leave her birds, her flowers, all the thousand attractions and associations of home? Yes, she must give up all, and only bear them closer in her heart, not see and feel them every day; and as these thoughts crossed her mind, tears she could not keep down welled up into her eyes; they would not be controlled, and looking up and meeting Mrs. Elrington's pitying gaze bent full on her, with a smothered sob she hid her face on her kind friend's shoulder.

Mrs. Elrington suffered her to weep on in silence, and some minutes elapsed ere Amy raised her head, and, smiling through her tears, took Mrs. Elrington's hand and led her to the door of the room she had just quitted and calling her sister, left the friends together.

An hour afterwards, when Amy entered the room, her mother was alone, Mrs. Elrington was gone.

The widow's head rested on her hand, and tears were falling fast upon a small miniature of Amy that her husband had had taken, for he had been proud of his daughter's beauty.

She heard not Amy's light step, and the daughter bent softly over her mother, and pressed her lips gently to her forehead. "My child." "My mother." And they were folded in one long, mournful embrace.

It was the first—the last time Amy ever gave way before her mother; she felt she must have strength for both; and nobly she bore up against her own sorrowful feelings, smothered every rising emotion of her heart, and prayed that her widowed mother might be comforted and supported during her absence, and her own steps guided aright in the new path which lay so gloomily before her.

Mrs. Elrington was now almost constantly with them; Amy had begged it as a favour, for she felt she could not do without the kind old lady, who was ever ready with her cheerful voice and pleasant, hopeful words to cheer her mother's drooping spirits.

How fast the days flew by! It was Amy's last evening at home; in a few short hours she would be far away from all those she loved.

A heavy cloud seemed to hang over the little party assembled round the tea table, and scarce a word was spoken.

As the tea things were being removed, Mrs. Elrington went softly out, and the widow, drawing her chair near her daughter's, clasped her hand in hers, and in a low voice spoke long and earnestly words of love and advice, such as only a mother knows how to speak.

Often in after years did Amy call to remembrance the sad, sweet smile, the gentle, earnest voice with which her mother's last words of love were uttered.

CHAPTER II

A PROUD LADYE

Spring by Spring the branches duly
Clothe themselves in tender flower;
And for her sweet sake as truly
All their fruit and fragrance shower:
But the stream with careless laughter,
Runs in merry beauty by,
And it leaves me, yearning after
Lorn to weep, and lone to die.

In my eyes the syren river
Sings and smiles up in my face;
But for ever and for ever,
Runs from my embrace.
MASSEY

As we shall have occasion to speak of Mrs. Elrington often in these pages, some description of her is necessary, though a very slight one will suffice.

She lived in the large house called the Manor, before described, and had lived there for years in lonely solitude. She was a widow, and although the widow's cap had long ago been laid aside, yet in other respects her dress had altered little since the day she had first worn widow's weeds; it was always black; even the bonnet was of the same sombre hue, the cap, collar, and cuffs alone offering any relief to it. Her features were very handsome, and her figure tall, upright, and stately. Her hair was perfectly snow white, drawn off the high broad forehead, under a simple cap; she was greatly beloved, as also held in some slight awe; her voice was peculiarly soft, and when she spoke a pleasant smile seemed to hover about her face which never failed to gladden the hearts of those whom she addressed; but in general the expression of her features when in repose was sad.

Mrs. Elrington and Mrs. Neville were old friends, which accounted perhaps for the latter's choice of Ashleigh as a home on her husband's death. They had both been severely tried with this world's sorrows; the one years ago, the other very recently, so that Amy's earnest entreaty that Mrs. Elrington would come and cheer her mother was comparatively an easy task to one who so well knew all the doubts, fears, and desponding feelings existing in the mind and harassing the thoughts of the widow, so lately afflicted, now so sorely tried.

Early in the morning of the day on which Amy was to leave her home, Mrs. Elrington was at the cottage, encouraging the daughter, and speaking hopefully to the mother; the *return*, not departure, being what she dwelt on to both, but it was a painful task after all, and everyone looked sad. As Mrs. Neville left the room to see if everything was satisfactorily prepared for the coming departure, Amy drew near her old friend, and said—

"Dear Mrs. Elrington, I do hope mamma will not fret much after I am gone; she seems very downhearted now, and full of sadness. I am keeping up as well as I can, but I dare not look in her tearful face."

"I make no doubt she will feel your absence much, Amy; but she knows all is for the best and as it should be, and that, in time will help to make her happy again. After all it is but a temporary parting from one she loves. How many have had to bear a more lengthened, and in this world an eternal separation! Your mother has still one child left to love. I lost my only one—all I had."

"It was a hard trial to you, and still harder to bear," replied Amy, as Mrs. Elrington's voice faltered—

"Very, very hard to bear: God alone knows how I did bear it. But He who dealt the blow alone gave the strength. I fear my stricken heart murmured sadly at first; it would not be comforted nor consoled. The thought of my poor boy's broken heart was dreadful. Amy, child, do not trust too soon in the man who seeks your love; and oh! be very wary of an ambitious one. Ambition sunders, breaks many hearts, the coveting either rank or riches, whichever leads on to the one darling object of life only to be obtained by possessing either one or both of these, and thereby sacrificing your love or perhaps breaking your heart in the act of stepping over it to reach the goal he longs for; and which, when attained, must, under these circumstances bear its sting, and make him look back regretfully to the time gone by for ever; or, perhaps worse still, to days too painful to recall.

"I would far rather it would be so; than that a man should love me for either my rank or riches, but having neither, perhaps no one will think me worth having, or take the trouble to fall in love with me."

Mrs. Elrington smiled as she looked at the lovely, almost scornful face now lifted to hers, and thought what a stumbling block it would prove in many a man's path in life.

"You are laughing at me," exclaimed Amy, as she caught the smile on the old lady's face. "Do let us talk of something else; of Mrs. Linchmore, for instance; I do so want to know what she is like, only you never will tell me."

"Because I cannot Amy; it is years since we met," replied Mrs. Elrington, in a hard tone; "so that what she is like now I cannot describe; you will have to do that when next we meet."

"But then," persisted Amy, "in that long ago time what was she like?"

"Very beautiful. A slight, tall, graceful figure, pliant as a reed. Eyes dark as jet, and hair like a raven's wing. Are you satisfied, Amy?"

"Not quite. I still want to know what her character was. I am quite satisfied that she must have been very beautiful."

"She was as a girl more than beautiful. There was a charm, a softness in her manner that never failed to allure to her side those she essayed to please. But in the end she grew vain of her loveliness, and paraded it as a snare, until it led her to commit a great sin."

"She may be altered now," exclaimed Amy, "altered for the better."

"She must be grievously altered. Grief and remorse must have done their work slowly but surely, for I never will believe that her heart has been untouched by them."

"I am afraid I shall not like her," replied Amy, "and I had so made up my mind that as your friend I should like her at once."

"We are not friends, Amy! Never can be now! Did we meet to-morrow it would be as strangers. Let us speak of her no more. I cannot bear it," exclaimed Mrs. Elrington in an agitated voice, but after a moment her face grew calm again, and she moved away looking more sorrowful than angry; but Amy could not help wishing with all her heart that her journey that day were miles away from Brampton Park; but there was scarcely time for thought, for in another moment the coach was at the door, and although bitter tears were shed when the last kiss was given, Amy tried to smile through her tears and to be sanguine as to the future, while Mrs. Neville was resigned, or apparently so, and little Sarah—the only one who gave way to her grief unrestrained—sobbed as if her heart would break, and when old Hannah took her by force almost, from her sister's arms, she burst into a perfect passion of tears, which lasted long after the coach was out of sight which conveyed Amy partly on her road to her future home.

The morning was hot and sultry, one of those warm spring days, when scarcely a breath of air disturbs the hum of the bee, or interrupts the song of the birds; not a leaf stirred, even the flowers in the garden scarcely lent their sweet perfume to the light wind; and the rippling noise the little stream made gently gliding over the pebbly ground could be distinctly heard from the cottage.

In the lane just outside the gate were collected a number of men, women, and children; some out of curiosity, but by far the greater number to bid farewell to, and to see the last of their beloved Miss Amy; for although so recent an inhabitant, she was a general favourite in the village, and numberless were the blessings she received as she stepped past them into the coach, and with a fervent "God bless you," from Mrs. Elrington, she was gone.

It was evening before she reached Brampton Park, her future home, and the avenue of trees under which she passed were dimly seen in the bright moonlight.

It was a long avenue, much longer than the elm tree road at Ashleigh, yet it bore some resemblance to it; the trees as large and stately, and the road as broad; but instead of the fragrant flowers in the little lane at one end, Amy could discern a spacious lawn stretching far away on one side, while the house, large, old fashioned, and gloomy rose darkly to view on the other; but within a bright lamp hung in the large, old handsome hall, illuminating a beautifully carved oak staircase. Pictures of lords and ladies, in old fashioned dresses, were hanging on the walls; Amy fancied they gazed sternly at her from out their time worn frames, as she passed by them, and entered a large handsome drawing-room, where easy couches, soft sofas, luxurious chairs of every size and shape, inviting to repose and ease, seemed scattered about in happy confusion. Crimson silk curtains hung in rich heavy folds before the windows; a carpet as soft as velvet covered the floor; alabaster vases and figures adorned the many tables; lamps hung from the ceiling; in short everything that taste suggested and money could buy, was there.

At the further end of this room, or rather an inner room beyond, connected by large folding doors, sat a lady reclining in a large arm chair; one hand rested on a book in her lap, the other languidly on the curly head of a little girl, kneeling at her feet; her dark hair lay in rich glossy bands, on either temple, and was gathered in a knot at the back of her small, beautifully shaped head, under a lace cap; a dark silk dress fitted tight to her almost faultless figure, and fell in graceful folds from her slender waist; a little lace collar, fastened by a pearl brooch (the only ornament she wore), completed her attire, which was elegant and simple. Her eyes were dark and piercing, the nose and chin well-shaped, but perhaps a little too pointed; and the mouth small and beautiful. Such was Mrs. Linchmore, the mother of two of Amy's pupils. She was generally considered handsome, though few admired her haughty manners, or the scornful expression of her face.

Mrs. Elrington had sent Mrs. Linchmore a slight sketch of Amy's history, and had also mentioned that she was very young; yet Mrs. Linchmore was scarcely prepared to see so delicate and fragile a being as the young girl before her. A feeling of compassion filled her heart as she gazed on Amy's sweet face, and her manner was less haughty than usual, and her voice almost kind as she spoke.

"I fear, Miss Neville, you must have had a very unpleasant journey; the weather to-day has been more than usually warm, and a coach—I believe you came part of the way in one—not a very agreeable conveyance."

"I was the only inside passenger," replied Amy, seating herself in a chair opposite Mrs. Linchmore, "so that I did not feel the heat much; but I am rather tired; the after journey in the train, and then the drive from the station here, has fatigued me greatly."

"You must indeed be very tired and depressed, one generally is after any unusual excitement, and this must have been a very trying day for you, Miss Neville, leaving your home and all those you love; but I trust ere long you will consider this house your home, and I hope become reconciled to the change, though I cannot expect it will ever compensate for the one you have lost."

"Oh, not lost!" exclaimed Amy, raising her tearful eyes, "not lost, only exchanged for a time; self-exiled, I ought to say."

"Self-exiled we will call it, if you like; a pleasant one I hope it will be. Mr. Linchmore and I have promised Mrs. Elrington we will do all we can to make it so. I hope we may not find it a difficult task to perform. The will will not be wanting on my part to insure success, if I find you such as Mrs. Elrington describes."

"She is a very kind person," murmured Amy.

"She was always fond of young people, and very kind to them, so long as they allowed her to have her own way; but she did not like being thwarted. Her will was a law not to be disobeyed by those she loved, unless they wished to incur her eternal displeasure. I suppose she is quite the old lady now. It is," continued Mrs. Linchmore, with a scarcely audible sigh, "nine long years since I saw her."

"She does not appear to me very old," replied Amy, "but nine years is a long time, and she may have altered greatly."

"Most likely not," replied Mrs. Linchmore, in a cold tone. "Life to her has been one bright sunshine. She has had few cares or troubles."

"Indeed, Mrs. Linchmore!" exclaimed Amy, forgetting in her haste her new dependent position. "I have heard Mamma say that the death of her husband early in life was a sore trial to her, as also that of her son, which occurred not so very long ago."

"You mistake me, Miss Neville," replied Mrs. Linchmore, more coldly and haughtily, "those may be trials, but were not the troubles I spoke of."

Amy was silenced, though she longed to ask what heavier trials there could be, but she dared not add more in her kind friend's defence; as it was, she fancied she detected an angry light in Mrs. Linchmore's dark eyes as they flashed on her while she was speaking, and a proud, almost defiant curl of the under lip.

Amy felt chilled as she recalled to mind Mrs. Elrington's words, that she and Mrs. Linchmore never could be friends; and wondered not as she gazed at the proud, haughty face before her, and then thought of the gentle, loving look of her old friend. No; they could not be friends, they could have nothing in common. How often had Mrs. Elrington expressed a hope that Amy would learn to love her pupils, but never a desire or wish that she might love their Mother also; and then the description which Amy had so often eagerly asked, and which only that morning had been granted her; how it had saddened her heart, and predisposed her to think harshly of Mrs. Linchmore.

There must be something hidden away from sight, something that had separated these two years ago. What was it? Had it anything to do with that dread sin Mrs. Elrington had lately touched upon, and of which Amy had longed, but dared not ask an explanation? If they had loved each other once, what had separated them now? Where was the charm and softness of manner which almost made the loveliness Mrs. Elrington had spoken of? Very beautiful Amy thought the lady before her, but there was nothing about her to win a girl's love, or draw her heart to her at first sight.

How strange all this seemed now. She had never thought of it before. It had never occurred to her. Her thoughts and feelings had been too engrossed, too much wrapt up in regret at leaving her home, and arranging for her Mother's comfort after her departure, to think of anything else; but now, the more she pondered, the more extraordinary it seemed, and the more difficult it was to arrive at any satisfactory conclusion, and the impression her mind was gradually assuming was a painful one.

A light, mocking laugh from her companion startled Amy; it grated harshly on her ears, and snapped the thread of her perplexing thoughts.

"I doubt," said Mrs. Linchmore, as the laugh faded away to an almost imperceptible curl of the lip; while her head was thrown haughtily back, and she proudly met Amy's astonished gaze; "I doubt if Mrs. Elrington would recognise me; nine years, as you wisely remark, may effect—though not always—a great change. It has on me; many may possibly think for the better; she will say for the worse. But time, however hateful it may be for many reasons, changing, as it does sadly, our outward appearance; yet what wonderful changes it effects inwardly. It has one very great advantage in my eyes, it brings forgetfulness; so that the longer we live the less annoying to us are the faults and follies of youth; they gradually fade from our vision. I could laugh now at Mrs. Elrington's bitter remarks and sarcastic words; they would not cause me one moment's uneasiness."

Amy was spared any reply by little Alice suddenly rising, and claiming her mother's attention.

"This is the youngest of your pupils, Miss Neville. Alice dear, put down my scissors, and go and speak to that lady."

The little girl, who had been staring at Amy ever since she entered, now looked sullenly on the floor, but paid no attention to her mother's request.

"Go, dear, go! Will you not make friends with your new governess?"

"No I won't!" she exclaimed, with flashing eyes. "Nurse says she is a naughty, cross woman, and I don't love her."

"Oh, fie! Nurse is very wrong to say such things. You see how much your services are required, Miss Neville. I fear you will find this little one sadly spoilt; she is a great pet of her papa's and mine."

"I trust," replied Amy, "we shall soon be good friends. Alice, dear, will you not try and love me? I am not cross or naughty," and she attempted to take the little hand Alice held obstinately beneath her dress.

"No, no! go away, go away. I won't love you!"

At this moment the door opened, and Mr. Linchmore entered. He was a fine, tall looking man, with a pleasing expression of countenance, and his manner was so kind as he welcomed Amy that he won her heart at once. "Hey-day!" he exclaimed, "was it Alice's voice I heard as I came downstairs? I am afraid, Isabella, you keep her up too late. It is high time she was in bed and asleep. We shall have little pale cheeks, instead of these round rosy ones," added he, as the little girl climbed his knee, and looked up fondly in his face.

"She was not in the least sleepy," replied his wife, "and begged so hard to be allowed to remain, that I indulged her for once."

"Ah! well," said he, smiling, and glancing at Amy. "We shall have a grand reformation soon. But where are Edith and Fanny?"

"They were so naughty I was obliged to send them away up stairs. Fanny broke the vase Charles gave me last winter."

"By-the-by, I have just heard from Charles; he has leave from his regiment for a month, and is going to Paris; but is coming down here for a few days before he starts, just to say good-bye."

"One of his 'flying visits,' as he calls them. How sorry I am!"

"Sorry! why so?"

"Because he promised to spend his leave with us. What shall we do without him? and how dull it will be here."

A cloud passed over her husband's face, but he made no reply; and a silence somewhat embarrassing ensued, only broken some minutes after by the nurse, who came to fetch Alice to bed, and Amy gladly availed herself of Mrs. Linchmore's permission to retire at the same time.

They went up a short flight of stairs, and down a long corridor, or gallery, then through another longer still, when nurse, half opening a door to the left, exclaimed,—

"This is to be the school-room, miss. I thought you might like to see it before you went to bed. Madam has ordered your tea to be got ready for you there, though I'm thinking it's little you'll eat and drink to-night, coming all alone to a strange place. However you'll may be like to see Miss Edith and Miss Fanny, and they're both in here, Miss Fanny at mischief I warrant."

Then catching up Alice in her arms, after a vain attempt on Amy's part to obtain a kiss, she marched off with her in triumph, and Amy entered the room.

On a low stool, drawn close to the open window, sat a fair-haired girl, her head bent low over the page she was reading, or trying to decipher, as the candles threw little light on the spot where she sat. Her long, fair curls, gently waved by the soft evening breeze, swept the pages, and quite concealed her face from Amy's gaze on the one side; while on the other they were held back by her hand, so as not to impede the light.

A scream of merry laughter arrested Amy's footsteps as she was advancing towards her, and turning round she saw a little girl, evidently younger than the one by the window, dancing about with wild delight, holding the two fore paws of a little black and white spaniel, which was dressed up in a doll's cap and frock, and evidently anything but pleased at the ludicrous figure he cut, although obliged to gambol about on his hind legs for the little girl's amusement. Presently a snap and a growl showed he was also inclined to resent his young mistress's liberties, when another peal of laughter rewarded him, while, bringing her face close to his, she exclaimed,—

"Oh, you dear naughty little doggie! you know you would not dare to bite me." Then, catching sight of Amy, she instantly released doggie, and springing up, rushed to the window, saying in a loud whisper—

"Oh, Edith, Edith! here's the horrid governess."

Edith instantly arose, and then stood somewhat abashed at seeing Amy so close to her; but Amy held out her hand, and said—

"I am sorry your sister thinks me so disagreeable; but I hope Edith will befriend me, and teach her in time to believe me kind and loving."

"She is not my sister, but my cousin," replied Edith, drooping her long eyelashes, and suffering her hand to remain in Amy's.

"Is Alice your sister?"

"No; she is my cousin, too. I have no sister."

The tone was sorrowful, and Amy fancied the little hand tightened its hold, while the eyes were timidly raised to hers.

Sitting down, she drew the child towards her, while Fanny stood silently by, gazing at her new friend. They chatted together some time, and when nurse came to fetch them to bed, Edith still kept her place by Amy's side, while Fanny, with Carlo in her lap, was seated at her feet, nor did either of the little girls refuse her proffered kiss as she bade them "good night."

How lonely Amy felt in that large long room.

Notwithstanding the evening was a warm one, the young girl drew her shawl closer round her shoulders, as she sat down to her solitary tea; and tears, the first she had shed that day, rolled slowly over her cheeks as she thought of her mother's calm, loving face, and her sister's merry prattle. How she missed them both! Although but a few short hours since they parted, since she felt the warm, silent pressure of her mother's hand, and Sarah's clinging embrace, yet the hours seemed long; and oh, how long the months would be! But youth is hopeful, and ere Amy went to bed, she had already begun to look forward to the holidays as nearer than they were, to image to herself the warm welcome home and the happy meeting hereafter with those she loved.

CHAPTER III

Alas!—how changed that mien!
How changed these timid looks have been,
Since years of guilt and of disguise,
Have steel'd her brow, and arm'd her eyes!
No more of virgin terror speaks
The blood that mantles in her cheeks;
Fierce and unfeminine are there
Frenzy for joy, for grief despair.
SCOTT

Mrs. Linchmore had married for money, yet money had not brought the happiness she expected. At its shrine she had sacrificed all she held dearest on earth, and with it her own self-esteem and self-respect. In the first few months she had tried to reconcile the false step to herself, had tried to hush the still, small voice within that was constantly rising to upbraid her. Was not wealth hers? and with it could she not purchase everything else? Alas! the "still, small voice" would be heard. She could not stifle it; it pursued her everywhere: in her pursuits abroad, in her occupations at home—Home! the name was a mockery. It was a gilded prison, in which her heart was becoming cold and hard, and all the best feelings of her woman's nature were being turned to stone.

Ten years had passed away since Mrs Linchmore stood at the altar as a bride; ten, to her, slow, miserable years. How changed she was! Her husband, he who ought to have been her first thought, she treated with cold indifference; yet he still loved her so passionately that not all her coldness had been able to root out his love. Her voice was music to him, her very step made his heart beat more quickly, and sometimes brought a quick flush to his face; all that she did was his delight, even her faults he looked on with patient forbearance. But although he loved her so devotedly, he rarely betrayed it; his face might brighten and flush when he heard her step, yet by the time she had drawn near, and stood, perhaps, close by his side as he wrote, it had paled again, and he would even look up and answer her coldly and calmly, while only the unsteadiness of his hand as he bent over the paper again, would show the tumult within; while she, his wife, all unconscious, would stand coldly by, and pass as coldly away out of his sight, never heeding, never seeing, the mournful longing and love in his eyes.

To her children Mrs. Linchmore appeared a cold, stern mother, but in reality she was not so. She loved them devotedly. All her love was centred in them. She was blind to their faults, and completely spoiled them, especially Alice the youngest, a wilful affectionate little creature, who insisted on having, if possible, her own way in everything. She managed it somehow completely, and was in consequence a kind of petty tyrant in the nursery. Nothing must go contrary to her will and wishes, or a violent burst of passion was the consequence. These paroxysms of temper were now of such common and frequent occurrence, that Nurse Hopkins was not sorry the young governess had arrived, and Alice been partially transferred to the school-room, where Amy found it a hard task to manage her, and at the same time win her love. Whenever she reproved, or even tried to reason, Alice thought it was because she disliked her. "Mamma," she would say, "loves me, and she never says I am naughty."

Her sister Fanny was the veriest little romp imaginable, almost always in mischief. Chasing the butterflies on the lawn, or sitting under the shade of the trees, with her doll in her lap, and Carlo by her side, was all she cared for, and Amy could scarcely gain her attention at all. She was a bright, merry little creature, full of laughter and fun, ready to help her young playmates out of any scrape, and yet, from utter thoughtlessness, perpetually falling into disgrace herself. Tearing her frock in climbing trees, and cutting her hair to make dolls' wigs of, were among her many misdemeanours, and a scolding was a common occurrence. But she was always so sorry for her faults, so ready to acknowledge them, and anxious to atone further. Amy's kind yet grave face could sober her in a moment, and, with her arms thrown round her neck, she would exclaim, "Oh, dear Miss Neville, I am so sorry—so sorry." She was a loveable little creature, and Amy found it one of her hardest trials to punish her. She hated books. Nothing pleased her so much, when the morning's task was done, as to put (so she said) the tiresome books to sleep on their shelves. She showed no disinclination to learn, and would sit down with the full determination of being industrious; but the slightest accident would distract her attention, and set her thoughts wandering, and Edith had generally nearly finished her lessons before Fanny had learnt her daily tasks.

Edith, a child of ten years old, was totally dissimilar, and of a reserved, shrinking nature, rendered still more so from her peculiar position. She was the orphan daughter of Mr. Linchmore's only sister, bequeathed to him as a sacred trust; and he had taken her to his house to be looked upon henceforth as his own child; but no kind voice greeted her there, no hands clasped the little trembling one in theirs, and bade her welcome; not a single word of encouragement or promise of future love was hers, only the cold, calm look of her new aunt; and then total indifference. Sad and silent, she would sit night after night in the twilight by the nursery window, her little thoughts wandering away in a world of her own, or more often still to her lost mother. None roused her from them; even Fanny, giddy as she was, never disturbed her then. Once nurse Hopkins said—

"Miss Edith, it isn't natural for you to be sitting here for all the world like a grown woman; do get up, miss, and go and play with your cousins."

But as nurse never insisted upon it, so Edith sat on, and would have remained for ever if she could in the bright world her fancy had created. It was well for her Amy had come, or the girl's very nature would have been changed by the cold atmosphere around her, so different from the home she had lost, where all seemed one long sunshine. It was long ere Amy understood her; so diligent, so attentive to her lessons, so cautious of offending, so mindful of every word during school hours, and yet never anxious to join Fanny in her play; but on a chair drawn close to the window, and with a book in her lap, or her hands clasped listlessly over the pages, and her eyes drooping under their long lashes—so she sat. But a new era was opening in the child's history.

Some few weeks after Amy's arrival, as she sat working very busily (Edith, as usual, had taken her seat at the window), she felt that the child, far from reading, was intently watching her. At length, without looking up, she said—

"Edith, dear, if you have done reading will you come and tidy my workbasket for me? My wools are in sad confusion. I suspect Alice's fingers have been very busy amongst them."

She came and busied herself with her task until it was completed. Then, still and silent, she remained at her governess' side.

"Who is this shawl for, Miss Neville, when it is finished?" asked she.

"For my mother."

Edith drew closer still.

"Ah!" said she, "that is the reason why you look so happy; because, though you are away from her, still you are trying to please her; and you know she loves you, though no one else does."

"Yes, Edith; but I should never think no one loved me, and if I were you I am sure I should be happy."

"Ah, no! It is impossible."

"Not so; I should be ever saying to myself would my dear mamma have liked this, or wished me to do that. Then I should love to think she might be watching over me, and that thought alone would, I am sure, keep me from idleness and folly."

"What is idleness?"

"Waste of time. Sitting doing nothing."

"And you think me idle, then?"

"Often, dear Edith. Almost every day, when you sit at the window so long."

"But no one minds it. No one loves me."

"I mind it, or I should not have noticed it; and I will love you if you will let me."

For an instant the child stood irresolute, then, with her head buried in Amy's lap, she sobbed out, "Oh! I never thought of that. I never thought you would love me—no one does. I will not be idle any more," and she was not; someone loved her, both the living and the dead; and the little craving heart was satisfied.

And so the days flew by. The summer months passed on, only interrupted by a visit from Charles Linchmore. He was very unlike his brother; full of fun and spirits, as fair as he was dark, and not so tall. He seemed to look upon Amy at once as one of the belongings of the house, was quite at home with her, chatted, sang duets, or turned the pages of the music while she sang. Sometimes he joined her in her morning's walk with the children. Once he insisted on rowing her on the lake; but as it was always "Come along, Edith, now for the walk we talked of," or, "Now then, Fanny, I'm ready for the promised lesson in rowing;" what could Amy say? she could only hesitate, and then follow the rest. She felt Mrs. Linchmore look coldly on her, and one evening, on the plea of a severe headache, she remained up stairs; but so much consideration was expressed by Mrs. Linchmore, such anxiety lest she should be unable to go down the next evening, that Amy fancied she must have been mistaken; the thought, nevertheless, haunted her all night. The next morning she had hardly commenced studies when Charles Linchmore's whistle sounded in the passage.

He opened the door, and insisted on the children having a holiday, and while Amy stood half surprised, half irresolute, sent them for their hats and a scamper on the lawn, then returned, and laughed at her discomfiture. He had scarcely gone when Mrs. Linchmore came in; she glanced round as Amy rose.

"Pray sit down, Miss Neville, but—surely I heard my brother here."

There was something in the tone Amy did not like, so she replied, somewhat proudly,

"He was here. Madam."

"Was here? Why did he come?"

"He came for the children, and I suppose he had your sanction for so doing."

"He never asked it. And I must beg, Miss Neville, that you will in future make him distinctly understand that this is the school-room, where he cannot possibly have any business whatever."

With flushed cheeks, for a while Amy stood near the window, just where Mrs. Linchmore had left her; and then, "Oh! I will not put up with it!" she said, half aloud, "I will go and tell her so." But on turning round there stood Nurse Hopkins.

"It's a lovely place, miss, isn't it? such a many trees; you were looking at it from the window, wern't you, miss? And then all those fields do look so green and beautiful; and the lake, too; I declare it looks every bit like silver shining among the trees."

"It is indeed lovely; but, Nurse, I was not thinking of that when you came."

"No, miss? Still it does not do to sit mopy like, it makes one dull. Now I've lived here many a year, and yet, when I think of my old home, I do get stupid like."

"Where is your home Nurse?"

"I've no home but this Miss, now."

"No home? But you said you had a home once."

"Yes Miss, so I had, but it's passed away long ago—some one else has it now; such a pleasant cottage as it was, with its sanded floor and neat garden; my husband always spent every spare hour in planting and laying it out, and all to please me. I was so fond of flowers. Ah! me," sighed she, "many's the time they've sent from the Park here to beg a nosegay—at least, John, the gardener has—when company was coming."

"Your cottage was near here, then?"

"Yes Miss, just down the lane; why you can see the top of it from here, right between those two tall trees yonder."

"Yes. I can just catch a far off glimpse of it."

"You've passed it often too, Miss. It's the farm as belongs to Farmer Rackland."

"I know it well. But why did you give it up?"

"My husband, or old man, as I used joke like to call him, died," and Nurse's voice trembled, "he was young and hearty looking too when he was took away; what a happy woman I was Miss, before that! and so proud of him and my children."

"How many children have you?"

"I had three Miss; two girls and a boy. I seem to see them now playing about on the cottage floor; but others play there now just every bit as happy, and I've lost them all. I'm all alone," and Nurse wiped her eyes with the corner of her white apron.

"Not all alone Nurse," said Amy, compassionately.

"True Miss; not all alone; I was wrong. Well, I sometimes wish those days would come again, but there, we never knows what's best for us. I'm getting an old woman now and no one left to care for me. But I wasn't going to tell you all about myself and my troubles when I began; but somehow or other it came out, and I shall like you—if I may be so bold to say so—all the better for knowing all about me; but I want, begging your pardon, Miss, to give you a piece of advice, if so be as you won't be too proud to take it from me; you see I know as well as you can tell me, that you and the Madam have fallen out; and if it's about Miss Alice, which I suppose it is, why don't be too strong handed over her at first; she will never abide by it, but'll scream till her Mamma hears her, and then Madam can't stand it no how; but'll be sure to pet her more than ever to quiet her."

"But Nurse, I do not mean to be strong-handed with Miss Alice, that is, if you mean severe; but she is at times naughty and must be punished."

"Well Miss, we should most of us be sorry to lose you: you are so quiet like, and never interferes with nobody, and they do all downstairs agree with me, that it ain't possible to cure Miss Alice altogether at first; you must begin by little and little, and that when Madam isn't by."

"But that would be wrong, and I cannot consent to punish Miss Alice without Mrs. Linchmore's free and full permission; neither can nor will I take charge of any of the children unless I am allowed to exercise my own judgment as to the course I am to pursue. I am not I hope, harsh or severe towards your late charge; but I must be firm."

"I see Miss, it's no use talking, and I hope Madam will consent to let you do as you wish; but I fear—I very much fear—" and nurse shook her head wisely as she walked away.

"Well, I've done all I could, Mary," said she to the under housemaid, as she went below, "and all to no purpose; there's no persuading Miss Neville, more's the pity; she thinks she's right about Miss Alice, and she'll stick to it. I wish I'd asked her not to go near Madam to-day. I'm positive sure she was going when I surprised her after passing Mrs. Linchmore in the passage. She came from the school-room too, I know, and vexed enough she was, or she'd never have had that hard look on her face. Well, I only hope the Master will be by when they do meet again, or there'll be mischief, mark me if there isn't."

"Law! Mrs. Hopkins, how you talk. I wouldn't wait for the master neither, if I were Miss Neville. I'd speak at once and have done with it, that's my plan; see if I would let Miss Alice come over me with her tantrums, if I was a lady!"

"She speaks every bit like that lady you were reading about in the book last night; she'd make you believe anything and love her too. Well, I hope no harm will come of it, but I don't like that look on Madam's face, nor on Miss Neville's, neither, for the matter of that."

But nurse was wrong. Perhaps Amy changed her mind, and never spoke to Mrs. Linchmore. At all events, things went on as they did before Charles Linchmore came—whose visit, by the way, was not quite such a flying one—and continued the same long after he had gone away.

CHAPTER IV

THE BOOK SHELVES

"O my swete mother, before all other
For you I have most drede:
But now adue! I must ensue,
Where fortune doth me lede.
All this make ye: now let us flee:
The day cometh fast upon;
For in my minde, of all mankynde
I love but you alone."
THE NUT BROWN MAID

Amy spent the summer holidays with her mother. Mrs. Neville had grown pale and thin, while a careworn expression had stolen over her face, supplanting the former sad one; and she had a certain nervous, restless manner unusual to her, which Amy could not fail to remark. Mrs. Elrington attributed it to anxiety on her daughter's account during her absence. It was a trying time for Mrs. Neville; she felt and thought often of what her child might suffer, all that one so sensitive might have to undergo from the neglect or taunts of the world; that world she knew so little of, and into the gay circles of which only two short years ago she had been introduced. How she had been admired and courted! Perhaps some of those very acquaintances she might now meet, and how would it be with her? How would they greet her? Not with the grasp of friendship, but as one they had never seen, or having seen, forgotten. She was no longer the rich heiress, but a governess working for her own and others' support. She was no longer in the same society as themselves, no longer worthy of a thought, and would be passed by and forgotten; or, if remembered, looked on as a stranger.

Mrs. Neville thought her daughter altered. She had grown quieter, more reserved, more womanly than before, and more forbearing with little, exacting Sarah.

Would Amy do this, or look at that? show her how to cut out this, or paint that—always something new; but Amy seldom expostulated or refused assistance, but was, as her mother told Mrs. Elrington, a perfect martyr to her sister's whims and fancies. She had changed. But why? Her mother watched her narrowly, and doubted her being happy, and this thought made her doubly anxious, and imprinted the careworn look more indelibly on her face. A few mornings before Amy returned to Brampton, at the close of the holidays, she went over to Mrs. Elrington's, and found her busy in the garden tying up the stray shrubs, and rooting up the weeds.

"I am afraid, Amy dear, you have come to say 'good-bye,' so I must finish my gardening to-morrow, and devote my time for the present to you."

"I shall be very glad, Mrs. Elrington, for indeed I have a great deal to say. I am so anxious about mamma."

"Anxious, Amy! Well, come in and sit down, and tell me all about it. Sit here close by me, and tell me what is the matter, or rather, what you fancy is; as I think the anxiety is all on your account."

"It's mamma, Mrs. Elrington. I am so dissatisfied about her; she is so changed."

"Changed! In what way?"

"In every way. She is not so strong, the least exertion tires her, and I so often notice the traces of tears on her face. Then she is so dull; and will sit for hours sometimes without saying a word, always busy with that everlasting knitting, which I hate; it is quite an event if she drops a stitch, as then her fingers are quiet for a little. If I look up suddenly, I find her eyes fixed on me so mournfully: at other times, when I speak she does not hear me, being evidently deep in her own thoughts. She is so different from what she used to be, so very different."

"I cannot say I have noticed any change, and I am constantly with her."

"Ah! that is just why you don't see it. Hannah does not."

"But, my dear, she never complains: I think she would if she felt ill."

"Mamma never complains, dear Mrs. Elrington; I wish she would, as then I might question her, now I feel it impossible. Does she seem happy when I am away?"

"Quite so; and always especially cheerful when she has your letters."

"I will write much oftener this time; and you will also, will you not? and tell me always exactly how she is, and do watch her, too, Mrs. Elrington, for I am sure she is not so strong as she was."

"I will, indeed," and Mrs. Elrington pressed Amy's hand, "but you must not fidget yourself unnecessarily, when there is not the least occasion for it. I assure you I see little change in your mother—I mean in bodily health, and I hope, please God, you will find her quite well when you come again, so do not be low-spirited, Amy."

And so they parted. Mrs. Elrington's words comforted without convincing Amy; and her face wore a more cheerful expression for some days after her return to Brampton.

Mr. Linchmore greeted her very kindly; even Mrs. Linchmore seemed pleased to see her; while the children, especially Fanny, were boisterous in their welcome, and buzzed about her like bees, recounting all the little events and accidents that had happened since she left, until they were fetched away; when Mrs. Linchmore and Amy were alone.

"I trust you enjoyed your visit home, Miss Neville?"

"Thank you, yes; it was a great treat being with my mother and sister again."

"We missed you sadly, and are not sorry to welcome you back again. Edith and Fanny have both grown weary of themselves and idleness; as for Alice, only yesterday, while I was dressing for dinner, having taken the child with me into my room, she amused herself by scrubbing the floor with my toothbrush, having managed to turn up a piece of the carpet in one of the corners; indeed, I should weary you, did I recount half she has been guilty of in the way of mischief."

Amy smiled, and Mrs. Linchmore continued,

"Did you ever leave home before for so long a time?"

"Never. My mother and I had never been parted until I came here."

"You must have felt it very much. I trust Mrs. Neville is well?"

"No. I regret to say I am not quite satisfied with my mother. I do not see any very material change, neither can I say she is ill, but I notice a difference somewhere. I fear she frets a great deal, she is so much alone."

"But your sister?"

"She is too young to be much of a companion to mamma, and I think tries her a great deal. She has been rather a spoilt child, being so much younger than I."

"Younger children always are spoilt. Have you no friends besides Mrs. Elrington?"

"Yes; several very kind ones: there are many nice people living near, but none like clear, good Mrs. Elrington; she is so true, so unselfish, so kind, and devotes a great deal of her time to mamma."

"Does she notice any change in your Mother?"

"She assured me not. But then they meet so constantly, she would not be likely to notice it so much as I, who only see her seldom. She has promised to let me know if she does see any alteration for the worse, so with that I must rest satisfied, and hope all is well, unless I hear to the contrary."

"How is Mrs. Elrington?"

"Quite well, thank you, and looks much the same."

"She asked about me, of course?" and Mrs. Linchmore half averted her face from Amy's gaze.

"Yes, often; and as she has not seen you for so many years, I had much to tell her. She seemed pleased to hear of the children, and asked a great many questions about them."

"You thought she seemed pleased to hear about them. I suspect curiosity had a great deal to do with it, if not all. You will grow wiser some day, Miss Neville, and learn to distinguish the true from the false—friends from foes," and Mrs. Linchmore's eyes flashed. "Did you give her my message, the kind remembrances I sent her, with the hope that—that she had not forgotten me? Did she send no message in return?"

The question was sternly asked; Amy hesitated what to say. What was the mysterious connection between the two? and why was it Mrs. Linchmore never spoke of Mrs. Elrington without a touch of anger or bitterness? even the latter, who seemed ever careful of wounding the feelings of others, never spoke of Mrs. Linchmore in a friendly manner, though she appeared to know or have known her well at some earlier period of life.

The question embarrassed Amy, "I was so hurried," said she, "in coming away that I forgot—I mean she forgot—."

Mrs. Linchmore rose haughtily, "I dislike equivocation, Miss Neville, and here there is not the slightest occasion for it. I did not expect a message in return; I think I told you so, if I remember aright, when I entrusted you with mine," and very proudly she walked across the room, seated herself at the piano and sang as if there was no such thing as woe in the world, while Amy sat, listened, and wondered, then softly rose and went upstairs to the school room.

"Here we are! so busy, Miss Neville," cried Fanny, "putting all the things to rights. It's so nice to have something to do, and I'm sorting all the books, although I do hate lessons so," with which assertion Fanny threw her arms round her governess' neck, while Alice begged for a kiss, and Edith pressed closer to her side and passed her small hand in hers.

Certainly the children were very fond of her; Fanny had been so from the first; it was natural for her to love everybody, she was so impulsive, but the other two she had won over by her own strong will and gentle but firm training. Carlo, Fanny's dog, seemed as overjoyed as any of them, leaping, barking, and jumping about until desired rather severely by his young mistress to be quiet. "You are making a shameful noise, sir," she said, giving him a pat, "will you please let somebody else's voice be heard; and do sit down, dear Miss Neville, and let us tell you all we have done since you have been away; we have lots of news, we have not told you half yet, have we, Edith?"

So they began all over again, totally forgetting what they had said or left unsaid, Amy patiently listening, pleased to think how glad they were to see her. Each tendered a small present, to show that their little fingers had not been quite unprofitably employed; half pleased, half frightened lest it should not be liked. They told her amongst other things that uncle Charles had been to Brampton again, but only for three days; he would not remain longer, although Mrs. Linchmore had wished him to; he had brought his dog "Bob" with him, such an ugly thing, who growled and showed his teeth; they were all afraid of it, and were glad when it went away.

"Bob used to come up here, Miss Neville, and sit in the window while uncle was at work."

"At work! what work, Edith?"

"The book shelves. Oh! have you not seen them? do come and look, they are so nice. See, he put them all up by himself, and worked so hard, and when they were done he made us bring all your books; then he set them up, and desired us not to meddle with them as they were only for you. Was it not kind of him? We told him it was just what you wanted."

"How could you? I did not want them at all."

"Yes, Miss Neville, indeed you did; you said long before you went away how much you should like some."

But Amy thought she neither wanted nor liked them, and felt vexed they had been put up.

"Ah!" said Fanny, catching the vexed expression, "you can thank him for them when he comes again; we were to tell you so, and that he would be here in November, and this is August Miss Neville, so it's only three months to wait."

"You can tell him Fanny when he comes, that I am much obliged to him, lest I should forget to do so."

And Amy turned away, feeling more vexed than she liked to acknowledge to herself; she had had nothing to do with putting up the shelves, but would Mrs. Linchmore think so if she knew it? And did she know it, and what had she thought? "Mamma was right," said she to her self. "It is very hard to be a governess; and he has misinterpreted and misjudged me."

A thorn had sprung up in Amy's path, which already wounded her slightly.

CHAPTER V

VISITORS ARRIVE

O! if in this great world of strife,
This mighty round of human life,
We had no friends to cheer,
O! then how cold the world would seem!
How desolate the ebbing stream
Of life from year to year!
J. B. KERRIDGE

Autumn passed away, and winter spread its icy mantle over the earth. Abroad all looked bleak, cold, and desolate. Trees had lost their leaves, flowers their blossoms, and the beautiful green fields were covered with snow; while here and there a snowdrop reared her drooping head from under its white veil, or a crocus feebly struggled to escape its cold embraces. Within doors, things wore a brighter aspect than they had done for some time past. Visitors had arrived at Brampton, who, it was hoped, would enliven the old Hall, and dissipate the dulness of its haughty mistress. Rooms long unoccupied had bright, cheerful fires blazing in the grates; footsteps hurried to and fro, echoing through the long, lofty passages, where all before had been so still and silent. The old, gloomy, melancholy look had totally disappeared, and the house teemed with life and mirth.

Mrs. Hopkins was no longer nurse, but had been installed as housekeeper in the room of one who had grown too old for the office; and was all smiles and importance, much to the disgust of Mason, the lady's maid, who, having always considered herself a grade above the Nurse, now found herself a mere cipher next to the all-important Housekeeper, who seemed to sweep everything before her as she walked grandly down the long corridor; Mason's pert toss of the head, and still perter replies, were met with cool disdain, much to her disappointment, as she tried to discomfort her; but all to no purpose, as Mrs. Hopkins' sway continued paramount; and she wielded her sceptre with undiminished power, notwithstanding all the arts used to dislodge her.

It was a half-holiday; Amy had fetched her hat, and was on her way out; in the corridor she met Mrs. Hopkins, who was always fond of a chat when she could find the opportunity; besides, she had long wished for some one to whom to unburden all Mason's impertinences. She immediately courtesied, and began—

"Good morning, Miss. Isn't the old house looking different? it does my heart good to see it, we havn't been so gay for many a year. I am so glad Madam has given up going to foreign parts; it ain't good for the young ladies, and I'm certain sure it ain't no good for servants, Mason's never been the same since she went; I havn't patience with her airs and graces!" Here she broke off abruptly, as Mason crossed the passage, her flowing skirts sweeping the floor, and a little coquettish cap just visible at the back of her head. "Only look at her, Miss, thinking herself somebody in her own opinion, when in most everybody's elses' she's a nobody. Why, Miss, a Duchess couldn't make more of herself," said Mrs. Hopkins, testily.

"Indeed, I do not believe she could," replied Amy, smiling, "and I am sure would not think more of herself."

"Think, Miss! Why, it's my belief she dreams at night she's found the hen with the golden egg, and so builds castles on the strength of it all day long; and airy ones she'll find them, I know," and Mrs. Hopkins laughed at the idea of Mason's supposed downfall.

"I suppose, Nurse, you have been very busy?"

"Yes, Miss, just what I like. I don't care to sit with my hands before me. I'm always happy when I'm busy. It isn't natural for me to be idle."

"How many strangers are here, Nurse? You must forgive me for calling you Nurse, but I am so accustomed to it."

"Forgive you, Miss! I'm Nurse to you and the children if you please, always, I'm proud of the title; but to Mason and the rest I'm Mrs. Hopkins," said she with firmness. "As to how many are here, why I can't exactly say; they're not all come yet, there are several empty rooms, but I suppose they'll be filled to-day or to-morrow at the latest; then the young Master's to come; but his room's always ready; he comes and goes when he likes. We call him the young Master, because he's to have the Hall by-and-by. He's a thorough good gentleman, is Mr. Charles, and will make a good master to them as lives to see it. But it is a pity, Madam has no son."

"Excuse me for interrupting you, Miss Neville," said Mrs. Linchmore's voice close behind, "but I wish, Mrs. Hopkins, another room prepared immediately; one of the smaller ones will do," and Mrs. Linchmore passed on. Amy followed; while nurse shrugged her shoulders, shook her head, and muttered, "Another man! Humph! I don't like so many of 'em roaming about the place; it ain't respectable."

Mrs. Linchmore, on reaching the hall, was turning off to the library, when Edith and Fanny ran past, closely pursued by a young girl, who stopped suddenly on perceiving them, and, addressing Mrs. Linchmore, exclaimed,

"Pray do not look at me, Isabella, I know my toilette is in dreadful disorder. I have had such a run that I really feel quite warm."

"Your face is certainly rather flushed," replied Mrs. Linchmore, as she looked at the young girl's red face, occasioned as much by the cold wind outside, as by her run with the children.

"I know I'm looking a perfect fright," she added, vainly endeavouring to smooth the dishevelled hair under her hat.

"Your run has certainly not improved your personal appearance. Allow me, Miss Bennet, to introduce you to Miss Neville, whom I fear you will find a sorry companion in such wild games."

"I don't know that!" and she gazed earnestly at Amy. "A romp is excusable in this weather, it is so cold outside."

"A greater reason why you should remain in the house, and employ your time more profitably;" so saying, Mrs. Linchmore walked away, leaving the two girls together.

"That is so like her," observed Miss Bennet, "she takes no pleasure in a little fun herself; consequently thinks it's wrong any one else should. Now, children, be off," she continued, looking round, but they were nowhere to be seen, having fled in dismay at the first sight of Mrs. Linchmore.

"Are you going out?" asked she, placing her hand on Amy's arm.

"Only for a short time."

"Then for that short time I will be your companion,—that is if you like."

Amy expressed her pleasure, and they were soon walking at a brisk pace round the shrubbery.

Julia Bennet had no pretensions to beauty, though not by any manner of means a plain girl. She had a very fair, almost transparent complexion, and small, fairy hands and feet. She was a good-natured, merry girl, one who seldom took any pains to disguise her faults or thoughts, and consequently was frequently in scrapes, from which she as often cleverly extricated herself. If she liked persons they soon found it out, or if she disliked them they did not long remain in ignorance of it; not that she made them acquainted with the fact point blank, but no trouble was taken to please; they were totally overlooked. Not being pretty, no envious belles were jealous of her, and young men were not obliged to pay her compliments. Nor, indeed, had she been pretty, would they have ventured to do what she most assuredly would have made them regret; yet she was a great favourite with most people, never wanted a partner at a ball, but would be sought out for a dance when many other girls with greater pretensions to beauty were neglected. She was a cousin of Mr. Linchmore's, the youngest of five sisters, only one of whom was married. Julia gazed over her shoulder at her companion's hat, dress, and shawl; nothing escaped her penetrating glance. She was rarely silent, but had always something to say, although not so inveterate a talker as her sister Anne. The latter, however, insisted that she was more so, and had resolutely transferred the name of "Magpie" or "Maggy," with which her elder sisters had nicknamed her, to Julia.

"I have quite spoilt Isabella's temper for to-day," began Julia. "She will remember that romp, as she calls it, for ages to come. I cannot help laughing either, when I think of the figure I must have been when I met her. Now confess, Miss Neville, did I not look a perfect fright?"

"You looked warm and tired, certainly,"

"Warm and tired! Now do not speak in that measured way, so exactly like Isabella, when I was as red as this," and she pointed to the scarlet feather in her hat, "and as for tired, I was panting for breath like that dreadful old pet dog of hers. Well, I am glad I have made you laugh; but do not, please, Miss Neville, if we are to be friends, speak so like Isabella again. I hate it, and that's the truth."

"I will not, if I know it, but will say yes or no, if you like it best, and wish it."

"And I do wish it, and that was not said a bit like Isabella, so I will forgive you, and we will make up and be friends, as the children say," and she gave her hand to Amy. "And now tell me, Miss Neville, by way of changing the subject, where, when, and how you became acquainted with my cousin."

"I am governess to her children," replied Amy, quietly.

Julia stopped suddenly, and looked at her in surprise.

"And are you really the governess of whom Edith and Fanny have talked to me so much? Why, you cannot be much older than I."

"Do you not consider yourself old enough to be a governess?"

"Well, yes, of course I do; but you are so different to what I always pictured to myself a governess ought to be. They should be ugly, cross old maids, odious creatures, in fact I know mine was."

"Why so?" asked Amy.

"Oh, she did a hundred disagreeable things. All people have manias for something, so there is, perhaps, nothing surprising in her being fond of bags. She had bags for everything; for her boots and shoes, thimble and scissors, brushes and combs, thread, buttons,—even to her india-rubber. A small piece of coloured calico made me literally sick, for it was sure to be converted into a bag, and a broken needle into a pin, with a piece of sealing-wax as the head."

"She was not wasteful," said Amy, who could not forbear laughing at the picture drawn.

"Wasteful! Truly not. It was 'waste not, want not,' with her; she had it printed and pasted on a board, and hung up in the school-room, and well she acted up to the motto."

"But I dare say she did you some good, notwithstanding her peculiarities."

"Well! 'the proof of the pudding is in the eating,' another of her wise sayings; and it is early days to ask you what you think of me, so I shall wait until we are better acquainted, which I hope will be soon. How glad I was to get rid of her! I actually pulled down one of the bells in ringing her out of the house, and would have had a large bonfire of all the backboards and stocks, if I had dared. I could not bear her, but I am sure I shall like you, and we will be friends, shall we not? do not say no."

"Why should I? I will gladly have you as my friend."

"That is right; you will want one if Frances Strickland is coming: how she will hate you. She likes me, so she says, so there is something to console me for not being born a beauty; so proud and conceited as she is too, everything she says and does is for effect. Her brother is as silly as she is proud, and as fond of me as he is of his whiskers and moustaches."

"I need not ask you if you like him."

"I shall certainly not break my heart if you are disposed to fall in love with him."

"Nay, your description has not prepossessed me in his favour. And who are the other guests?"

"I cannot tell you, for their name is legion, but you will be able to see them soon, and review them much better than I can," and Julia turned out of the shrubbery into one of the garden walks leading up to the house.

"Here is Anne," added she, in a tone of surprise, "all alone too, for a wonder. See!" and she pointed to a young girl seemingly intent on watching John the gardener, who was raking the gravel, and digging up a stray weed here and there.

"Look here, John," cried she, as they approached unperceived, "here is a weed you have overlooked. Give me the hoe, and let me dig it up. What fun it is!" added she, placing a tiny foot on the piece of iron, "I declare I would far rather do this than walk about all by myself. There! see! I have done it capitally; now I'll look for another, and just imagine they are men I am decapitating, and won't I go with a vengeance at some of them," and then turning she caught sight of Julia and Amy.

"Well, Maggie," said she, "here I am talking to John, in default of a better specimen of mankind, and really he is not so bad. I declare he is far more amusing than Frank Smythe, and has more brains than half the men I have danced with lately, and that's not saying much for John," and she pouted her lips with an air of disdain.

"This is my sister Anne, Miss Neville," said Julia, introducing them, "and so this," and she pointed to the hoe still in her sister's hand, "is your morning's amusement, Anne?"

"Yes," said she, carelessly, "I was thoroughly miserable at first, stalking about after John, and pretending to be amused with him, but all the time looking towards the house out of the corners of my eyes; I am sure they ache now," and she rubbed them, "but all to no purpose, not a vestige of a man have I seen, not even the coat tail of one of them. I was, as I say, miserable until I spied John's hoe, and then a bright thought struck me, and I have been acting upon it ever since, and should have cleared the walk by this time, if you had not interrupted me."

"Pray go on," said Julia, "it is very cold standing talking here, and I have no doubt John is delighted to have such efficient aid."

"Now Mag, that is a little piece of jealousy on your part, because perhaps you have not been spending the morning so pleasantly. But there is the gong sounding for luncheon, come away," and she threw down the hoe; "let us go and tidy ourselves; I am sure you want it," and she pointed to her sister's hair; then went with a bounding, elastic step towards the house.

"Good-bye, Miss Neville; I must not increase my cousin's bad temper by being late. My sister Anne is a strange girl, but I think you will like her by-and-by, she is so thoroughly good natured."

Amy watched Julia's light graceful figure as she went up the walk, then turned and retraced her steps round the Shrubbery.

CHAPTER VI

"GOODY GREY"

*"A poore widow, some deal stoop'n in age,
Was whilom dwelling in a narwe cottage
Beside a grove standing in a dale.
This widow which I tell you of my
Tale Since thilke day that she was last a wife
In patience led a full simple life;
For little was her cattle and her rent."*
CHAUCER

The country round Brampton was singularly beautiful and picturesque. A thick wood skirted the park on one side, and reached to the edge of the river that wound clearly, brightly, and silently through the valley beyond, and at length lost itself after many turnings behind a neighbouring hill, while hills and dales, meadows, rich pastures and fields were seen as far as the eye could reach, with here and there cottages scattered about, and lanes which in summer were scented with the fragrance of wild flowers growing beneath and in the hedges, their blossoms painting the sides with many colours, and were filled with groups of village children culling the tiny treasures, but now were cold and deserted.

To the right, in a shady nook, stood the village church, quiet and solemn, its spire just overtopping some tall trees near, and its church-yard dotted with cypress, yew, and willow trees, waving over graves old and new.

Further on was the village of Brampton, containing some two or three hundred houses, many of them very quaint and old-fashioned, but nearly all neat and tidy, the gardens rivalling one another in the fragrance and luxuriance of their flowers.

In the wood to the left, and almost hidden among the trees, stood a small thatched cottage with a look of peculiar desolate chilliness; not a vestige of cultivation was to be seen near it, although the ground round about was carefully swept clear of dead leaves and stray sticks, so that an appearance of neatness though not of comfort reigned around. It seemed as if no friendly hand ever opened the windows, no step ever crossed the threshold of the door, or cheerful voice sounded from within. Its walls were perfectly bare, no jasmine, no sweet scented clematis, no wild rose ever invaded them; even the ivy had passed them by, and crept up a friendly oak tree.

Within might generally be seen an old woman sitting and swaying herself backwards and forwards in a high-backed oak chair, and even appearing to keep time with the ticking of a large clock that stood on one side of the room, as ever and anon she sang the snatches of some old song, or turned to speak to a large parrot perched on a stand near: a strange inhabitant for such a cottage. Her face was very wrinkled and somewhat forbidding, from a frown or rather scowl that seemed habitual to it. Her hair was entirely grey, brushed up from the forehead and turned under an old fashioned mob cap, the band round the head being bound by a piece of broad black ribbon. A cheap cotton dress of a dark colour, and a little handkerchief pinned across the bosom completed her attire.

The floor of the room was partly covered with carpet; the boards round being beautifully clean and white. A small table stood in front of the fire-place, and a clothes' press on the opposite side of the clock, while on a peg behind the door hung a bonnet and grey cloak. The only ornaments in the room, if ornaments they could be called, were a feather fan on a shelf in one corner, and by its side a small, curiously-carved ivory box.

The owner of the cottage was the old woman just described. Little was known about her. The villagers called her "Goody Grey," probably on account of the faded grey cloak she invariably wore in winter, or the shawl of the same colour which formed part of her dress in summer. The cottage had been built by Mr. Linchmore's father, just before his death, and when completed, she came and took up her abode there; none knowing who she was or where she came from; although numberless were the villagers' conjectures as to who she could be; but their curiosity had never been satisfied; she kept entirely to herself, and baffled the wisest of them, until in time the curiosity as well as the interest she excited, gradually wore away, and they grew to regard her with superstitious awe; as one they would not vex or thwart for the world, believing she had the power of bringing down unmitigated evil on them and theirs; although they rarely said she exercised any such dark power. The children of the village were forbidden to wander in the wood, although "Goody Grey" had never been heard to say a harsh word to them, nor indeed any word at all, as she never noticed or spoke to them. The little creatures were not afraid of her, and seldom stopped their play on her approach as she went through the village, which was seldom. Unless spoken to, she rarely addressed a word to any one. Strangers passing through Brampton looked upon her—as indeed did the inmates at the Park—as a crazy, half-witted creature, and pitied and spoke to her as such, but she invariably gave sharp, angry replies, or else never answered at all, save by deepening if possible the frown on her brow.

As she finished the last verse of her song, the parrot as if aware it had come to an end flapped his wings, and gave a shrill cry. "Hush!" said she, "Be still!"

Almost at the same instant, the distant rumble of wheels was heard passing along the high road which wound though a part of the wood near. She rose up, went to the window, and opened it, and leaning her head half out listened intently. Her height was about the middle stature, and her figure gaunt and upright.

She could see nothing: the road was not distinguishable, but the sound of the carriage wheels was plainly heard above the breeze sighing among the leafless trees. She listened with an angry almost savage expression on her face.

"Aye, there they come!" she exclaimed, drawing herself up to her full height, "there they come! the beautiful, the rich, and the happy. Happy!" she laughed wildly, "how many will find happiness in that house? Woe to them! Woe! Woe! Woe!" and she waved her bony arms above her head, looking like some evil spirit, while, as if to add more horror to her words, the bird echoed her wild laugh.

"Ah, laugh!" she cried, "and so may you too, ye deluded ones, but only for awhile: by-and-by there will be weeping and mourning and woe, which, could ye but see as I see it, how loath would ye be to come here; but now ye are blindly running your necks into the noose," and again her half-crazed laugh rang through the cottage. "Woe to you!" she repeated, closing the window as she had opened it. "Woe to you! Woe! Woe!"

Ere long the excitement passed away, or her anger exhausted itself; and she gradually dropped her arms to her side and sank on a bench by the window; her head dropped on her bosom, and she might be said to have lost all consciousness but for the few unintelligible words she every now and again muttered to herself in low indistinct tones.

Presently she rose again, opened the clothes-press, and took out some boiled rice and sopped bread, which she gave to the parrot.

"Eat!" said she in a low, subdued tone, very different to her former wild excited one, "Eat, take your fill, and keep quiet, for I'm going out; and if I leave you idle you're sure to get into mischief before I come back."

The bird, as she placed the rice in a small tin attached to his perch, took hold of her finger with his beak, and tried to perch himself upon her hand. She pushed him gently back and smoothed his feathers, "No, no," said she. "It's too cold for you outside, you would wish yourself at home again, although you do love me, and are the only living thing that does." And another dark expression flitted across her face.

She put on the bonnet and grey cloak, and taking a thick staff in her hand, went out.

The air was cold and frosty. The snow of the day before had melted away, and the ground in consequence of the thaw and subsequent frost was very slippery; but she walked bravely and steadily on, with the help of her staff, scarcely ever making a false step. At the outskirts of the wood was a small gate leading on to a footpath which ran across the park, making a short cut from the valley to the village. Here she paused, and looked hastily about her.

Now Goody Grey had never been known or seen to enter the Park, yet she paused evidently undecided as to which path she should pursue, the long or the short one. At length she resolved upon taking the long one; and shaking her head she muttered, "No, no; may be I'll be in time the other way;" and on she went as steadily as before, on through the village and up by the church-yard; nor stayed, nor slackened her walk until she gained the large gates and lodge of Brampton Park; then she halted and gazed up the road.

Notwithstanding the time it had taken to come round, probably half an hour, yet the carriage she had heard approaching in the distance had only just reached the bottom of the hill, the road taking a long round after leaving the wood. It came on slowly, the coachman being evidently afraid to trust his horses over the slippery road. Slowly it approached, and eagerly was it scanned by the old woman at the gates. Presently it was quite close, and then came to a stand still, while the great lodge bell rang out; and Goody Grey advanced to the window, and looked in.

On one side sat two rather elderly ladies; on the other an effeminate looking young man and a girl. These were evidently not the people she expected to see, for a shade of vexation and disappointment crossed her face. After scanning the countenances of each, she fixed her eyes on the young girl with an angry, menacing look, difficult to define, which the latter bore for some moments without flinching; then turning her head away, she addressed one of the ladies sitting opposite her.

"Have you no pence, Mamma? Pray do give this wretched being some, and let us get rid of her."

"I do not think I have, Frances, nor indeed if I had would I give her any. I make a point of never encouraging vagrants; she ought to be in the Union, the proper place for people of her stamp. I have no doubt she is an impostor, she looks like it, there are so many about now; we are overrun with them."

"Well, Mamma, if you won't give her any, pray desire Porter to drive on. What is he waiting for?"

"My dear, they have not opened the gates. There goes the bell again."

"Really, Alfred," said the girl, turning towards the young man at her side, "one would think you were dumb, to see you sitting there so indifferent. I wonder you have not more politeness towards Miss Tremlow if you have none for your mother and sister. Do not you see?" continued she, taking the paper he was reading from his hand and holding it so as to partly screen her face. "Do not you see what an annoyance this dreadful old woman is to us?"

He yawned and stretched himself, giving at the same time a side glance at Goody Grey, as if it was too much trouble to turn his head. "Ha! yes. Can't say I admire her. What does she want?"

"Want! We want her sent away, but one might as well appeal to a post as you."

"I shall not exert my lungs in her behalf; but you are wrong as regards your polite comparison of 'post,'" and, putting down the window, he gave a few pence into the old woman's hand, intimating at the same time that he should be under the painful necessity of calling the porter;—and he pointed to the man at the gates—unless she moved away.

"Take my blessing," said she, in reply. "The blessing of an old woman—"

"There, that will do. I do not want thanks."

"And I do not thank you," replied she, putting both hands on the window so as to prevent its being closed. "I don't thank you. I give you my blessing, which is better than thanks. But I have a word for you;" she pointed her finger at Frances Strickland, "and mark well my words, for they are sure to come to pass. Pride must have a fall. Evil wishes are seldom fulfilled. Beware! you are forewarned. And now, drive on!" she screamed to the coachman, striking at the same moment one of the horses with the end of her staff; it plunged and reared violently, the other horse became restive, and they set off at full speed up the avenue. Fortunately, the road was a gradual ascent to the house, for had there been nothing to check their mad career, some serious accident might have happened; as it was, one of the windows was broken against the branch of a tree, the carriage narrowly escaping an upset on a small mound of earth thrown up at the side of the road.

The travellers were more or less alarmed. Miss Tremlow, who was seated opposite Alfred, seized hold of him, and frantically entreated him to save her, until he was thrown forward almost into her lap—"All of a heap," as that lady afterwards expressed herself—as the carriage swerved over against a tree, when she gradually released her hold, and sank back into a state of insensibility.

"I hope she is dead!" said Alfred, settling himself once more in his place by his sister, and rubbing his arm.

"Dead!" echoed his mother. "Who is dead?"

"Only that mad woman next you in the corner; there! let her alone, mother; don't, for Heaven's sake, bring her round again, whatever you do. I have had enough of her embraces to last me a precious long time."

The horses now slackened their speed, and were stopped by some of the Hall servants not far from the door.

Mr. Linchmore was at the steps of the Terrace, and helped to lift out Miss Tremlow, who was carried into the house still insensible; while Mrs. Strickland, who had been screaming incessantly for the last five minutes, now talked as excitedly about an old witch in a grey cloak; while Frances walked into the house scarcely deigning a word, good, bad, or indifferent to any one—her pale face strangely belying her apparent coolness—leaving her brother to relate the history of their misadventure.

CHAPTER VII

AMY GOES FOR A WALK

"Such is life then—changing ever,
Shadows flit we day by day;
Heedless of the fleeting seasons,
Pass we to our destinies."
THOMAS COX

All the visitors had now arrived at Brampton Park, and were amusing themselves as well as the inclement weather would allow of, the snow still covering the ground, and the cold so intense as to keep all the ladies within doors, with the exception of Julia Bennet, who went out every day, accompanied by the three children, as Amy's spare time was quite taken up with Miss Tremlow, who had continued since her fright too unwell to leave her room.

Julia Bennet often paid a visit to the school-room in the morning, and sadly interrupted the studies by her incessant talking. Often did Amy declare she would not allow her to come in until two o'clock, when the lessons were generally ended for the afternoon's walk; but still, the next morning, there she was, her merry face peeping from behind the half-opened door, with a laughing, "I know I may come in; may I not?" and Amy never refused. How could she?

One morning, after getting her pupils ready for an earlier walk than usual, and giving them into Julia's charge—who vainly tried to persuade her to go with them—she bent her steps, as usual, to Miss Tremlow's room. On entering, she was surprised to see that lady sitting up in a large arm chair propped with cushions and looking very comfortable by the side of the warm fire. On enquiry, she learnt that Julia had been busy with the invalid all the morning, and had insisted on her getting out of bed.

"I am so very glad to see you looking so much better, and really hope you will soon be able to go down stairs; it must be so dull for you being so much alone," began Amy, as she quietly took a seat near.

"Miss Bennet wished to persuade me to do so to-day; but I really did not feel equal to it, though I do not think she believed me; she has her own peculiar notions about most things, and especially about invalids; I dare say she means it all kindly, but I cannot help thinking her very odd and eccentric."

"She is a very kind-hearted girl, it is impossible not to help liking her."

"She is very different from you, my dear, in a sick room, very different."

And well might she say so. Amy was all gentleness, so quiet in her movements; there was something soft and amiable about her; you loved her you scarcely knew or asked yourself why. Julia was all roughness, bustling about, setting the room to rights—Miss Tremlow's,—whenever she entered it; talking and laughing the while, and endeavouring to persuade the unfortunate individual that it was not possible she could feel otherwise than ill, when she never exerted herself or tried to get better. Her too you loved, and loving her overlooked her faults; but she obliged you to love her, she did not gain a place in your heart at once as Amy did. Very different they were in temper and disposition; Julia hasty and passionate; Amy forbearing and rarely roused; but at times her father's proud, fiery spirit flashed forth, and then how beautiful she looked in her indignation.

"I think I read to the end of the sixth chapter," said Amy, taking up a book and opening it; "for I foolishly forgot to put in a mark."

Amy read every day to Miss Tremlow, and thus whiled away many a weary hour that would have passed wearily for the invalid.

"You need not read to-day, my dear, you will tire yourself; so never mind where we were. I hope myself to be able to read soon."

"I shall not be in the least tired; I like reading. Shall I begin?"

Miss Tremlow fidgeted and moved restlessly among the cushions, and then said wearily—

"Do you know, my dear, I think it will be too much for me; I feel so tired with the exertion of getting up."

The book was instantly closed, Miss Tremlow feeling quite relieved when it was laid down.

"You are not vexed, Miss Neville, I hope. Your reading has been such a treat to me, when otherwise I should have been so dull and stupid."

"Indeed, no, it has been quite a pleasure to me; but you do look weary and tired. Shall I pour you out a glass of wine?"

"No, my dear, no; there is not the slightest occasion for it. And now let us talk of something else; you shall tell me all about the visitors, so that they may not be quite strangers to me when we meet."

"I have not seen any of them, except Mrs. Bennet and her daughters, and Mrs. Strickland and hers."

"But you go down of an evening, and surely there are other visitors."

"I always used to spend my evenings with Mrs. Linchmore; but within the last week I have remained upstairs, thinking I should be sent for if wanted, and as no enquiries have been made, I conclude my absence is not noticed; or if noticed I am only doing what is usual in such cases."

"Mrs. Linchmore is very foolish, and ought to have you down; you are too pretty and young to be allowed to mope upstairs by yourself. You may smile, but youth does not last for ever; it too soon fades away, and then you will become a useless, fidgetty old maid, like myself; no one to love or care for you, and all those who ought to love and take care of you wishing you dead, that they may quarrel for the little money you leave behind."

"But I have very few distant relations, and those I have do not love or care for me."

"More reason why you should have a husband who would do both; but that will come soon enough, I have no doubt. In the meantime you seem very young to have the care of these three girls, the youngest a perfect torment, if I remember aright; so spoilt and humoured."

"I am nearly nineteen," replied Amy.

"Too young to be sent out into this cold world all alone; but your mother has, of course, advised you for the best."

"Yes, she gave me her advice; and love, and blessing, as well; the latter was highly prized, but the first I did not follow. She did not wish me to be a governess, but advised me strongly against it; still I cannot think I have done wrong," added Amy, answering the enquiring look Miss Tremlow bent on her. "Because—because—Oh! it would take too long a time to tell you all I think, and you are weary already."

"Not so," and she took Amy's hand in hers. "I am interested in my kind young friend, so shall prove a good listener, though perhaps I am too tired to talk; so tell me your history, and all about yourself and those you love."

Yet Amy sat silent, so that Miss Tremlow, who watched her, was troubled, and added hastily, "never mind, my dear, I am sorry I asked you. It was foolish and thoughtless of me."

"No, indeed, Miss Tremlow; it is I who am foolish; mine is but the history of an every day life. There is little to tell, but what happens, or might happen, to anyone; still less to conceal."

And Amy drew her chair closer still, and with faltering voice began the history of her earlier years. A sad tale it was though she glanced but slightly at her father's extravagance; but to speak of her mother's patience, long suffering, and forbearance through it all, she wearied not, forgetting that as she did so her father's conduct stood out in all its worst light, so that when she had finished Miss Tremlow exclaimed hastily—

"He must, nay, was a bold, bad man, not worthy of such a wife! It's a mercy he is dead, or worse might have happened."

"Do not say that, Miss Tremlow; my mother loved him so dearly."

"That is the very reason why I cannot excuse him; no woman would; but there now I have pained you again, and quite unintentionally; so please read to me, and then there will be no chance of my getting into another scrape, because I must hold my tongue, and I find that no very easy task now, I can assure you."

Amy silently took up the book she had previously laid down, but had scarcely read three pages when the door opened, and in walked Julia with a glass of jelly in her hand.

"I have been looking for you everywhere, Miss Tremlow," she said.

"Why did you not come here? Had you forgotten I was ill?"

"Certainly not, witness this glass of jelly; but your room was the last place in the world I thought of looking for you in, considering I made you promise you would rouse yourself, and go below."

"I wish I could rouse myself," sighed Miss Tremlow, "but I am not equal to it, or to go down stairs amongst so many strangers."

"Not equal to it? All stuff! You never will feel equal to either that, or anything else, if you remain much longer shut up in this close room; you will make yourself really ill; and now please to drink this glass of wine, but first eat the jelly, and see how you feel after that."

"I will drink the wine my dear, but I could not touch the jelly. I do really think it is the fourth glass you have brought me to-day, and—no, I could not touch it."

"Well, you must take your choice between this, and some beef tea. Will you toss up, as the boys do, which it shall be?"

"No, no; I'll have nothing to do with the tossing. I suppose I must take the jelly," and she sighed as she contemplated it.

"Yes, and eat it too, and hate me into the bargain; when I do it entirely for your good, because as long as you remain up here, and complain of weakness, you must be dosed, and treated as an invalid, and made to take strengthening things; so be thankful you have two such nurses as Miss Neville and myself; one to talk and recount your pains and aches to; and the other to insist upon rousing, and making you well, whether you will or no, by forcing you to take and eat what is good for you, and scolding you into the bargain when you require it, which is nearly every day. Now, I am sure you are better after the jelly?" continued she, taking the empty glass from her hand.

"It is of no use saying I am not," replied Miss Tremlow wearily.

"Not the slightest," said Julia, sitting down by Amy. "Why, you don't mean to say that Miss Neville has been reading to you?" and she took the book off Amy's lap, where it had lain forgotten. "After all my injunctions, and your promises."

Miss Tremlow looked somewhat abashed.

"You really ought to be ashamed of yourself; as for Miss Neville, she looks fagged to death; for goodness sake go out and take a walk, and try and get a little colour into your cheeks, or there will be jelly and beef tea for you to-morrow," and Julia laughed merrily. "And now," she added, addressing Miss Tremlow, as Amy left the room, "Why did you allow her to read? Did I not tell you it was bad for her; and that, not being strong, the air of this close, hot room, is too much for her."

"Do not scold, or go on at such a rate, my dear; I really am not strong enough to bear it. I did refuse to hear the reading; but in the course of conversation I made an unfortunate remark, and she looked so pained, that to get out of the scrape I asked her to read; but she had scarcely opened the book when you entered."

"Never mind how long she read, you disobeyed orders; so as a punishment, I shall put you to bed; and then I will read the whole book to you if you like."

Miss Tremlow was delighted; she really was beginning to feel sadly tired, and in no humour for Julia's chattering, so submitted without a murmur; fervently hoping Julia would not persevere in the reading, or that some one else in the house might be taken ill, and receive the half of Julia's attentions.

As Amy quitted Miss Tremlow's room, she almost fell over Fanny, who came bounding down the corridor, never heeding or looking where she went. Fanny never walked; her steps, like her spirits, were always elastic. Amy's lectures availed nothing in that respect. Her movements were never slow—never would be—everything she did was done hastily, and seldom well done; half a message would be forgotten, her lessons only imperfectly said, because never thoroughly learnt.

"Of course it is Fanny," said Amy, turning to help up the prostrate child. "Have you hurt yourself, and why will you always be in such a hurry?"

"I was right, though, this time, Miss Neville," said the child, rising, "because Miss Bennet told me you were going out as soon as she came in, and Mamma wants you; so you see I am only just in time to catch you, because you are going out, you know."

"You would have plenty of time had you walked, instead of running in that mad way. I am not yet dressed for walking. Are you hurt, child?"

"Oh, no, Miss Neville, not a bit. I think I have torn my frock, though. Isn't it tiresome? Only look!"—and she held up one of the flounces, nearly half off the skirt.

"I do not see how you could expect it to be otherwise. It must be mended before you go to bed, Fanny."

"Yes, Miss Neville; I suppose it must. Oh, dear! my fingers are always sewing and mending. I wish Mamma would not have my dresses made with flounces."

"You would still tear them, Fanny."

"Yes, I suppose I should; well, I have pinned it up as well as I can; and now shall we go to Mamma; she is in her room, and Mason is so busy there," said Fanny, forgetting all about her frock. "Do you know we are going to have such a grand dinner party to-night; mamma is to wear her pink silk dress, with black lace. I saw it on the bed; and such a lovely wreath beside it. How I do wish I was big enough to have one just like it!"

"And tear the flounce like this," replied Amy, laughing, and knocking at Mrs. Linchmore's door.

"Come in, Miss Neville; I am sorry to trouble you, but I heard from Fanny you were going out, and I wished to know if you would like to come down into the drawing-room this evening, after dinner, it is both Mr. Linchmore's wish and mine that you should do so; moreover, we shall be glad to see you. The children will come and you could come down with them, if you like."

"Thank you, but if I am allowed a choice, I would far rather remain away. I am so unaccustomed to strangers; still if you wish it I—"

"No, you are to do just as you like in the matter, we shall be very glad to see you if you should alter your mind, and I hope you will. And now what news of Miss Tremlow? Is she really getting better, or still thinking of Goody Grey?"

"She sat up to-day for the first time, and is I think decidedly improving, but her nerves have been sadly shaken. Miss Bennet tried to persuade her to go downstairs to-day; but I really must say she had not strength for the exertion."

"I miss Julia sadly this dull weather, and I wish she would think of others besides Miss Tremlow; she devotes nearly the whole day to her."

"Is not her sister as merry and cheerful?"

"Anne is all very well, but thinks only of pleasing herself, she never helps entertain; you will scarcely see her in Miss Tremlow's, or anybody else's sick room. And now if you are going out, I will not detain you any longer. Perhaps you will kindly look into the conservatory as you return, and bring me one or two flowers, and you, Fanny, can come with me," and taking Fanny's hand she left the room, as Amy went to put on her bonnet.

CHAPTER VIII

"I saw the light that made the glossy leaves
More glossy; the fair arm, the fairer cheek,
Warmed by the eye intent on its pursuit;
I saw the foot that, although half erect
From its grey slipper, could not lift her up
To what she wanted;
I held down a branch
And gathered her some blossoms."
LANDOR

Amy went for a walk in the grounds; there being plenty of time before the evening closed in, as Julia had purposely returned early. A solitary walk is not much calculated to raise and cheer the spirits, and Amy's, though not naturally dull or sad, were anything but cheerful during her ramble. Miss Tremlow's questions had recalled sad scenes and memories which she had tried to forget; but some things are never forgotten; out of sight or laid aside for a time they may be, until some accident, or circumstance slight and trivial perhaps in itself, recalls them; and then there they are as vivid and fresh as ever, holding the same place and clinging round the heart with the same weight and tightness as ever; until again they fade away into the shade; crossed out, as a pen does a wrong word, yet the writing is there, though faintly and imperfectly visible, whatever pains we take to erase it.

How Amy's thoughts wandered as she walked along over the frosty ground! Time was when she had been as gay as Julia, and as light-hearted; but she began to think those were by-gone days, such as would never come again, or if they did, she would no longer be the same as before, and therefore would not enjoy them as she once had. Then she sighed over the past, and tried to picture to herself the future; tried, because very mercifully the future of our lives, the foreseeing things that may happen, is denied us. What a dark future it appeared! To be all her life going over the self-same tasks, the same dull routine day by day; her pupils might dislike their lessons, but how much more distasteful they were to her. What a dull, dreary path lay before her! She passed into the conservatory as these thoughts filled her heart. It was getting dusk, and entering hastily, she gathered a few flowers, and was turning on her way out, when she was attracted by a beautiful white Camellia, ranged amongst a number of plants rather higher up than she could reach. She stretched her arm over those below—in vain, the flower was beyond her still. She made a second attempt, when an arm was suddenly passed across her, and it was severed from its stem by some one at her side.

"It was a thousand pities to have gathered it," said a tall, gentlemanly-looking man; "but I saw you were determined to have it," and he picked up the flower, which had fallen, and held it for her acceptance.

"Thank you," said Amy, nervously. He had startled her; his help had been so unexpected. She told him so.

"You did not perceive me? and yet I am by no means so small as to be easily overlooked. I wish I could be sometimes; but I regret I frightened you."

"Not exactly frightened; only, not seeing you or knowing you were there, it—" and Amy stopped short.

"Frightened you," said he, decidedly.

She did not contradict him. It was evident he did not intend she should, for he scarcely allowed her time to reply as he went on,

"There is another bud left on the same plant. Will you have it? I will gather it in a moment."

"Oh, no, by no means. Perhaps I ought not to have taken this; but John is not here to guide me; I am rather sorry I have it now."

"Never mind; it is I who am the culprit, not you. Will you have the other? Say the word, and it is yours. It is a pity to leave it neglected here, now its companion is gone," and he moved towards the flower.

"Indeed I would rather not. One will be quite enough for Mrs. Linchmore, and, besides, I have so many flowers now."

"They are not for yourself, then? I could almost quarrel with you for culling them for anyone else."

"I never wear flowers," replied Amy, somewhat chillingly, with a slight touch of hauteur, as she moved away.

But he would not have it so, and claimed her attention again.

"Why do you pass over this sweet flower? just in your path, too; I do not know its name, I am so little of a gardener, but I am sure it would grace your bouquet; see what delicate white blossoms it has."

"Yes it is very pretty, but I have enough flowers, thank you."

"You will not surely refuse to accept it," and at the same moment he severed it from its stem. "Will you give me the Camellia in exchange?"

"No. I would rather not have it."

"It is a pity I gathered it," and he threw it on the ground, and made as though he would have crushed it with his foot.

"Do not do that," said Amy hastily; "give it to me, and I will place it with the other flowers in my bouquet."

"But those flowers are for some one else, not for yourself. You said so; and I gathered this for you. Will you not have it?"

"You have no right to offer it," replied Amy, determined not to be conciliated, "and I will only accept it on the terms I have said; if you will pull it to pieces I cannot help it."

"No. I have not the heart to kill it so soon; I will keep it for some other fair lady less obdurate," and he opened the door to allow of her passing out. "I suppose we are both going the same way," said he, overtaking her, notwithstanding she had hurried on.

"I am going home," replied Amy, now obliged to slacken her steps, and hardly knowing whether to feel angry or not.

"So am I; if by home you mean Brampton House. How cold it is! are you not very lightly clad for such inclement weather? The cold is intense."

"This shawl is warmer than it looks. We feel it cold just leaving the conservatory; it was so very warm there."

"True; but we shall soon get not only warm, but out of breath if we hurry on at this pace."

Amy smiled, and slackened her steps again. She felt she had been hurrying on very fast.

"I think I saw you the day the Stricklands arrived?"

Then as Amy looked at him enquiringly; he added, "you were coming up the long walk with the children and helped Miss Tremlow upstairs when she was able to leave the library."

"I did," replied Amy, "but you? I do not remember you in the least. Oh! yes I do, you were at the horses' heads. Yes, I remember quite well now; it was you who first ran forward as they came up at that headlong pace and stopped them. How stupid of me not to recollect you again."

"Not at all. I scarcely expected you would."

"Yes, but I ought to have, because out of the number of men collected you were the only one who led the way; the only one it seemed to me who had any presence of mind; there were plenty who followed, but none who took the lead." Amy was quite eloquent and at home with him now, and he smiled to himself as she went on. "I had not patience with all those men, talking, screaming to one another, ordering here, calling there, none knowing what ought to be done, all talking at random as the horses dashed on, when suddenly you sprung from among them, the only one silent amongst all the noise; the horses were stopped; the carriage stood still; and the by-standers had nothing to do but cease talking, and follow the example you set them."

"Really you will make me out a hero; I only did a very simple action." Amy was silent, she was afraid she had said too much. "Do you know how Miss Tremlow is?" continued he; "poor lady, I fear she was seriously alarmed."

"She was indeed, but is now getting better, and I hope will soon make her appearance downstairs."

"I am not surprised she was frightened, my only wonder is the accident did not end more seriously. This Goody Grey, whoever she is, is greatly to blame; mad she undoubtedly must be, and I cannot understand Mr. Linchmore's allowing her to go at large."

"I believe she is quite harmless. I am going to see her some day; she lives in a cottage down in the wood yonder."

"This was no harmless action, it looks like malice prepense, unless indeed they excited her anger unintentionally."

"That is exactly what I have been thinking, and I intend finding out more about it when I see her."

"I should be cautious how I went to see her; she may not be so harmless as you imagine. At all events do not go alone; I will accompany you with pleasure if you will allow me?"

"Thank you, I am not afraid. What harm could she do me? and as for her foretelling future events I simply do not believe it, and should pay little or no heed to anything she told, whether for good or ill," said Amy, laughing as they reached the Terrace, when, wishing him good-bye, she went in.

"I hope you have had a pleasant walk with Miss Neville, Mr. Vavasour," said Anne Bennet, coming up just behind as Amy disappeared, "Mr. Hall and I have been close to you nearly all the way home, but you were too busily engaged to perceive us."

"I hope you also have had a pleasant walk. Have you been far?" asked Mr. Vavasour, evading a direct answer.

"An awful distance!" answered her companion, evidently a clergyman, by the cut of his coat and white neck band.

"You know nothing at all about it," exclaimed Anne, turning sharp round, "or I am sure you would not call it far; why we only went across the fields round by the church and so home again. I thought you said you enjoyed it extremely?"

"I am ready to take another this moment if you like. What say you? shall we make a start of it?"

"No, decidedly not, it is too dark; but I will hold you to your word to-morrow. I know of a lovely walk; only three or four hedges to scramble through, but that is a mere nothing, you know. The view when we do reach the hill is charming, you can form no idea of it until you have seen it," and laughing merrily at Mr. Hall's disconsolate look, Anne left him.

She peeped into the drawing-room; there was no one there but Mrs. Linchmore.

"What all alone! where's Julia?" asked she abruptly.

"I fancy in her own room, or with Miss Tremlow; she was here a few minutes ago, and was enquiring for you. Have you had a pleasant walk?"

"Oh! very. Everybody asks me that question, or insinuates it, so that I shall begin to imagine I have been in Paradise; here comes my Adam," added she sarcastically, as Mr. Hall entered, "and really I can stand him no longer, the character of Eve is odious to me. I cannot play it out another moment, so leave it for you if you like to assume it."

Away went Anne, her anger or ill temper increasing as she went up the stairs. Flinging the door of their room wide open, and then closing it as sharply, she quite astonished Julia, who sat with her feet on the fender before the fire reading.

"She's a flirt, Mag!" exclaimed she, throwing her hat on the table, and flinging herself into an arm chair, close to her sister. "Yes, you need not look at me in that way; I say she's a flirt; I am certain of it!"

Julia burst out laughing.

"You may laugh as much as you like, it will not annoy me. I shall hold to that opinion as long as I live, and you may deny it as much as you please; but I shall still say she's a flirt. Nothing will convince me to the contrary, and now I think I have exhausted my rage a little; I felt at fever heat when I came in," said she, putting her hair off her face.

"I cannot think what your rage is all about, Anne," said Julia. "Of course she is a flirt, no one ever asserts otherwise; it makes me laugh to hear you go on; when not a soul, and least of all I, would take the trouble of contradicting you."

"More shame to you then, that is all I can say, when you pretend to be so fond of her; I am sure I expected you to fly into a tremendous temper at my assertion of her being a flirt. If I had a friend I would stand up for her, no one should accuse her of sins in my presence."

"I fond of her! well I think your walk has turned your head. I fond of Isabella, indeed! You must be mad, when I begged mamma to leave me at home, because I so much dislike her goings on."

"Isabella! who talked of Isabella? I am sure I did not; I said as plain as possible, Miss Neville."

"Miss Neville! she is no flirt, and never will be," said Julia decidedly.

"Ah! there it is, I knew you would say so, although only a minute ago you said no one would take the trouble of contradicting me."

"Neither shall I. You can hold a solitary opinion if you like."

"Stuff and nonsense about solitary opinions! I shall just convince you."

"You will never do that."

"How can you tell, seeing I have not tried? but only listen to my story, and I am certain you will be convinced."

"I am all attention," and Julia closed her book.

"You must know then that after luncheon I asked Mr. Vavasour to chaperon me out walking, or rather I gave a hint he might go with me if he liked, and really I think it was the least he could do, considering Isabella being 'nowhere.' I had devoted myself to him all the morning, and positively went so far as to fetch the paper knife for him; when whom should I find awaiting me when I came down dressed for walking, but that dreadful Mr. Hall, his best hat and coat on. I felt just mad with vexation, and should have given him an answer that would have sent him flying; only I fortunately caught sight of that Vavasour's face at the window, watching our departure, with a smile at the corners of his mouth. I was in such a rage, but managed to wave him a smiling adieu, before I vented it out by walking my friend Hall through all the gaps in the hedges by way of finding short cuts; until he was in a thorough state of disgust and despair about his new coat, etc., and not anxious to take another walk in a hurry; when whom should I see in the distance, as we came home, but that wretch Vavasour and Miss Neville, laughing and talking together as thick as two peas. No wonder he would not go out with me, when he had a walk in perspective with her."

"Do stop Anne, you have talked yourself quite out of breath; and have not convinced me either, for I still think you are wrong, and that most likely he met her accidentally in the grounds. I sent her out myself; she was very loath to go, so could not have promised to walk with anyone."

"Accidental fiddlestick. I am a woman, and do you suppose I do not know a woman's ways. They looked as if they had known one another for years; she must be a desperate flirt if they are only recently acquainted."

"Perhaps they have met before. Suppose you ask her, instead of condemning her unheard."

"What a goose you are, Julia! You will never make your way in the world. Ask, indeed! and be laughed at by both her and Mr. Vavasour for my pains. I have not patience with you, Mag."

"I have not patience to listen to you; so I shall go on with my book, if you will let me."

"No, I will not, Mag! I feel desperately annoyed, and will talk, whether you like it or no, because if I do not, I shall feel in a rage all the evening, and I am determined Mr. Vavasour shall not see how he has disgusted me."

"I dare say he does not think about it. Had you asked him point blank, of course he would have walked with you; but most likely he never understood your hint."

"Upon my word, Julia, you are Job's comforter, and make me more vexed than ever. I feel inclined to do something desperate, and have half a mind to go down and torment that Mr. Hall afresh. I would if I thought I should find him in the drawing-room."

"Don't, Anne; stay where you are, and do try and leave that unfortunate Mr. Hall alone. I am sure you tease his very life out, poor man! I do not believe he is quite so stupid as he looks, and expect he will turn round upon you some day."

"I wish he would; there would be a little excitement in it; and as for teasing him, I am sure I do not care if I do. Men wear the very life out of us poor women."

"Not all of them, Anne."

"Yes, all of them; even Mr. Hall,—who is as simple as—as—I am sure I do not know anything half bad enough to compare him to—would tyrannise over a woman the moment he found out she loved him. Men are all alike in that respect. Even he has sense enough for that, or, rather, it is a man's nature, born in him, and he can no more get rid of it than he can fly."

"You will change your opinion some day, Anne."

"Never! If ever I fall in love, I shall make a fool of myself, as most women do, and be paid out the same; but my opinion will remain unaltered all the time I am allowing myself to be trodden on. But there, thank goodness, I am not in love, and not likely to be. My thraldom is far off, I hope. Besides, I am wiser than I was a few years back. 'A burnt child dreads the fire,' Mag. They will find it a hard task to entice me into mischief. I like to pay them out. No retaliation provokes me."

"Not Mr. Vavasour's?" laughed Julia.

"Oh, Mag," said Anne, rising, "how tiresome you are! You will be an old maid, I prophesy, you are so prosy, and then we will both live together and enjoy ourselves."

"I do not look forward to any such lot," replied Julia. "I should be miserable."

"Then I will live by myself. No nephews or nieces, mind, to torment me. That would be anything but enjoyment. How slowly the time goes! I declare it is only five o'clock. Just call me when it is time to dress, will you?" and she walked across the room and threw herself on the bed, first throwing a large warm railway wrapper on the top.

"There," said she, drawing it over her. "I am perfectly comfortable, and intend forgetting that wretched Miss Neville and Vavasour in the arms of Somnus, so you can go on with your book, Mag."

She remained perfectly still for a few moments, then sitting bolt upright, and throwing off the shawl, she exclaimed,—

"I have thought of a capital plan, Mag, of annoying that wretch, Vavasour. How glad I am I lay down; it might never have entered my head, sitting there by that cosy fire. Just watch his face, please, to-night, will you, towards the end of the evening? I say, Maggie, do you hear? or am I talking to a stone? Why don't you answer?"

"Yes, yes; I hear you, I thought you were asleep."

"Then do not think any such thing until you hear me snore; and now, good-night, or rather good-bye, until six o'clock. Just stir up the fire, it is awfully cold over here; do not forget we dine at seven, and I must have an hour to dress, as I intend making myself quite killing. And now for my bright idea again," and once more she drew the wrapper over her, and composed herself to sleep afresh.

CHAPTER IX

WHAT BECAME OF THE FLOWER

"A true good man there was there of religion,
Pious and poor, the parson of a town:
But rich he was in holy thought and work;
And thereto a right holy man; a clerk
That Christ's pure gospel would sincerely preach,
And his parishioners devoutly teach.

Benign he was, and wondrous diligent,
And in adversity full patient.

"Tho' holy in himself, and virtuous,
He still to sinful men was mild and piteous;
Not of reproach, imperious or malign;
But in his teaching soothing and benign.
To draw them on to heaven, by reason fair,
And good example was his daily care.
But were there one perverse and obstinate
Were he of lofty or of low estate,
Him would he sharply with reproof astound,
A better priest is nowhere to be found."
CHAUCER

Mrs. Linchmore was in the drawing-room, where she had been sitting ever since Anne went off so abruptly, leaving her with Mr. Vavasour and the curate.

The latter was awkward and ungainly; and we question much if he would have tyrannised over a wife: certainly not, unless some unforeseen event accidentally discovered to him that he might make a woman who loved also fear him, and jealous; this latter thought had never entered his head—perhaps it was to come.

As Mrs. Linchmore and Robert Vavasour sat chatting and laughing, he remained perfectly silent; sitting firmly upright in the chair he had drawn close by, his long legs drawn up under him, trying in vain to find an easy position for his hands; and those long arms, which he never seemed to know what to do with, they certainly were too long for his body, just like two sails of a windmill. He looked, as he sat, decidedly like a man who could be thoroughly and completely henpecked—notwithstanding the sometimes stern look on his brow—by any woman possessing only half the amount of Anne Bennet's spirit; and she would not have been edified had she returned to the drawing-room as she threatened, and as no doubt Mr. Hall wished she would, for he looked thoroughly uncomfortable and out of place; evidently in the way of the two that sat there, who never addressed a single syllable to him, but left him totally unnoticed, he all the time wishing to join in the conversation, yet not knowing how to set about it.

In the pulpit he was a different creature altogether. No longer the timid, awkward curate, but, to all intents and purposes, a straightforward, honest man, unswerving in exhorting to the right, unshrinking in pointing out the wrong. There, his long, ungainly legs hidden, his face lighted up, as he warmed with his subject, he became decidedly handsome; even taken at his worst, he could never be called plain.

He was much liked in his parish, a small country village some few miles distant from Brampton; smiles and kindly words greeting him whenever he passed by the cottages; and such deep courtsies! A clergyman can generally tell by the latter the kind of estimation in which he is held by his parishioners. If liked, a deep courtesy and friendly voice speaks to him. If otherwise, a slight reverence and scarcely a good morrow is vouchsafed. Friendly voices always greeted Mr. Hall, even the children ran to the doors to make a courtesy, and glance half slyly at his pleasant, good humoured face.

Whether he had fallen in love with Anne or no, was not quite certain; if he had, she took the most sure way of curing him, by laughing at him, and turning him into ridicule; not from ill nature, but simply because she had nothing better to do, and found the time hung heavy on her hands. Not an idea had she that he was pained by it, or indeed perceived it; but there she was wrong; he did see it, and inwardly vowed each time it happened should be the last; yet somehow or other he would be sure soon again to find himself either next her at table, or by her side out walking, or told off as her partner in a round game; and so his vow was broken, and would have been had he made twenty such.

Strange it was, that being a clever, well-read man, his powers of conversation were so limited, but as long as those about him talked, he did not appear to think it necessary to exert himself to amuse others, so he passed as a dull, stupid, slow man.

Perhaps his silent, reserved habits had grown upon him imperceptibly, from living so much alone as he had done for the last five years, with only an elderly woman to look after his house, and act as housekeeper; and a boy to wait on him.

The conversation of the two near him had sunk almost to a whisper, it was so low; but they were mistaken if they suspected he was a listener. He was not; his thoughts were with Anne, wondering at the time she took in taking off her hat, and expecting every moment to see the door open.

What would he have said, had he known she was then sound asleep, with no thought for anyone in the whole world, least of all for him. Still his eyes kept wandering towards the door, and at length it did open, but it was Frances Strickland who came in and seated herself on a sofa just behind him.

"You are doing nothing, Mr. Hall," said she presently, "so do come here, I want my skein of wool held."

Mr. Hall did not like the dictatorial manner in which this was said; still, having no excuse to offer, he advanced.

"Pray bring a chair and sit down. How can I wind it, with you towering above me in that way."

"I am tired of sitting," replied Mr. Hall, mildly resenting this speech, "so will stand if you will allow me."

"I should never have supposed you tired of sitting, after the hedges I saw you scrambling through with Anne Bennet."

Mr. Hall coughed uncomfortably. "I enjoyed my walk and am accustomed to the country. It would be well if all young ladies were as active as Miss Bennet."

"Or as masculine, which?"

"The former, certainly. I see nothing of the latter about her," replied he rather decidedly.

"How strange! Everybody else does. I suppose you will not attempt to deny she is a very fast girl."

"I am not sufficiently acquainted with Miss Bennet to be able to form, or rather give an opinion as to her character; most young ladies of the present day are fast, and perhaps your friend is not an exception to the general rule."

"Pray do not call her my friend. I am unlike the generality of girls in that respect, and am hand and glove with no one."

"Do you mean you have no friend?"

"None, I am happy to say."

"I pity you, Miss Strickland," replied Mr. Hall.

"Reserve your commiseration," she said proudly, "for those who require it. I should dislike having a friend even as active and fast as Miss Bennet, who, according to your idea," said Frances sarcastically, "should have been born a grade lower in life; a housemaid for instance; no amount of hard work would have been too much for her."

"She would have struggled bravely through it all, I make no doubt," replied he. "I have no mean opinion of Miss Anne's courage."

"Or have worked herself into a consumption, and so become a heroine, as she appears to be already in your estimation. Pray take care, Mr. Hall, you have let half a dozen threads drop off your fingers. How excessively careless!"

"Yes. I do not understand holding it; excuse me," and he laid the tangled mass in her lap.

Was he as stupid as Anne pictured him; or would she, as Julia said, some day find out her mistake.

"What hopeless confusion, Miss Strickland," said Mr. Vavasour, advancing a step, as he passed by. "Is this your doing, Hall?" and he laughed, while Frances's eyes flashed with mortification and anger.

"I am afraid so," replied he quietly. "The fact is Miss Strickland enlisted my services, without making the least enquiry as to my capabilities, hence this unfortunate failure. But I have resigned the post I have filled so badly; will you take my place and do better?"

"I am very sorry to refuse, but I have promised to have a game of billiards with Strickland, and the time's up," said he, looking at his watch. "Many thanks to you all the same, my dear fellow, for making me the offer of such a Penelope's web to unravel." And he passed on. Mr. Hall followed.

"Tiresome, abominable man!" exclaimed Frances, gathering up the wool apparently hopelessly entangled, and advancing towards the fire where still sat Mrs. Linchmore. "Is not that Mr. Hall too bad; just see what he has done—quite spoilt my skein."

"How was it managed?" asked Mrs. Linchmore carelessly.

"I asked him to hold it; of course I ought to have known better, such a stupid creature as he is; his fingers are as awkward as his legs. I cannot think how it is you invite him here, unless it is to be in the way and make himself disagreeable; as in this instance."

"Disagreeable! You are the first person, Frances, I ever heard apply that epithet to Mr. Hall; no one ever thinks of him, and had you left him alone, it would not have happened."

"I know that; but I took compassion on him; you and Mr. Vavasour were so deeply engaged," she said maliciously; "you never gave him a thought, and because I did, this is my thanks. I shall be wiser for the future."

"As most people are. Learn wisdom, and yet commit foolish actions every day of their lives."

"Perhaps I shall be different from most people," and she commenced trying to disentangle the wool.

"A hopeless task," said Mrs. Linchmore, "only waste of time and temper; better let it alone, there are plenty of wools upstairs in my work basket; I have no doubt Mason will find you a match for this, if you ask her, you are most welcome to any I have," and she took up the book she had laid down, as a hint to Frances she wished the conversation to end.

So at least Frances thought, and left her alone, after first putting away the wool in the sofa table drawer.

But Mrs. Linchmore did not read, she laid the book carelessly in her lap, and was soon, apparently, deep in thought, from which she was only aroused by her husband's entrance; drawing a half sigh at the interruption, she took up her book again, and gave no reply to his greeting.

"I am afraid I have disturbed you, Isabella; you were dozing, were you not? or very nearly so."

"Never mind. It is almost time to dress for dinner." She shut up the book, and was rising, when he said,

"Do not move yet, Isabella; I came here to seek you; wishing to have a few moments' conversation."

She looked at him enquiringly

"I have been thinking it would be as well if you wrote and invited Mrs. Elrington to come and spend this Christmas with us."

"Mrs. Elrington!" cried she, in astonishment.

"Yes, I think it would be the right thing to do; nay, I am sure of it, and wonder it has never struck either of us before."

"It would be the last thing I should think of; as I am sure there is not the slightest use in asking her."

"Why not?"

"She would never come; but would send a refusal, perhaps not couched in very civil terms."

"I think you may be wrong. I hope so, at least. It is true she held aloof when we married, why, or wherefore, I never knew; and has continued estranged ever since; but surely her sending Miss Neville is a proof she might be conciliated; at all events, there can be no harm in attempting it."

"She will never be conciliated, never! Besides, why should she be; you surely are not at all anxious about it?"

"She brought you up, Isabella; was as a mother to you when you lost your own; surely you are in her debt for that, and owe her some kindness for all she bestowed on you."

"She has never taken the slightest notice of me during my ten years of married life; therefore, however deep my debt of gratitude, I consider it to have been cancelled after so much neglect and coldness."

"But recollect the kindness that went before. You owe her some gratitude and kindly feeling for that; however misjudging, or mistaken, she may be; at least, I think so."

"I cannot see it."

"I am sorry you do not, Isabella, and that I have failed in convincing you; little as I know of Mrs. Elrington," continued he, rather decidedly, "I cannot believe she, or indeed any woman, would bear malice so long, and not be anxious at some time during their life to make amends; it is unlike their nature; besides, she is no longer young, years are creeping on her slowly, but surely; depend upon it she will take the invitation kindly."

"Never!" said his wife again; "she does not think herself in the wrong, and is so different from most women; she is sternness itself; and I hope, Robert, you will give up the idea of asking her."

"I cannot do that. You know, Isabella, I never speak, or express a wish, unless I have fully considered the question at stake. It is my wish you should write, and I cannot but think the reply will be different from what you seem to expect."

"Do not force me to write, Robert. It is disagreeable to me."

"Force you!" exclaimed he, in surprise. "Certainly not; but I wish it, Isabella, most decidedly."

"How can I write, or what can I say? when she has never addressed a line to me for such a length of time, or taken the slightest notice of me whatever," said she half pettishly, half mournfully, very different from Mrs. Linchmore's usual haughty tone.

He looked half irresolute as he noticed it; her anger and coldness would only have made him more stern; but one symptom of softness melted him at once.

"Isabella, dear," and he came near, and took her hand, "I am sorry to have to ask you to do anything disagreeable, and what is evidently so painful to you; you will forgive me, dear one, will you not?"

But she looked up coldly in his face, and drawing away her hand, returned not the pressure of his; and his irresolution faded away while he said,

"You must not forget, Isabella, she opened a correspondence with you, after her long neglect and silence, and sent us Miss Neville; surely that was a sign her coldness was giving way."

"She heard we wanted a governess through Mrs. Murchison. I never had a line from her on the subject; our correspondence was carried on entirely through a third person, from first to last."

"You forget the letter she wrote when Miss Neville came?"

"No; I remember that perfectly. A very cold, stiff letter, I thought it."

"A very cold one, certainly. Well, perhaps it would be better I should write; I will if you wish it; I am quite decided in my opinion that one of us ought to do so."

"No, no, by no means," replied Mrs. Linchmore, hurriedly. "I will do as you like about it; and write to-morrow morning, since you think I ought, and you wish it so much."

"Thank you, Isabella." He stooped down over her again, and kissed her forehead; but she received it coldly as before, her face half averted. "I fear," he added, "it will give you pain; but it is right."

"Pain! He little knows or even guesses how much," said Mrs. Linchmore half aloud when he was gone, "or how much misery he has raked up during the one short half-hour he has been here. I wish he had never come; or rather never thought about the invitation."

With a sigh she arose slowly, and went to dress for dinner. To be gay and light, with a secret woe gnawing and tearing at her heart strings.

Seated at the glass, Mason brushing and plaiting her hair, the book still in her hand, apparently Mrs. Linchmore read, but it was not so; her thoughts wandered; several times she turned back the pages, and re-read what had gone before.

Presently Amy came in, bringing the flowers she had gathered.

"Come in, Miss Neville. What a lovely bouquet you have brought me. I hope you have changed your mind about coming down this evening, and that we are to have the pleasure of seeing you after all."

"No indeed, Mrs. Linchmore, I have not. I should much prefer remaining away, unless, as I said before, you particularly wish me to go down."

"No, you must please yourself entirely, and do just as you like. But I think Mr. Linchmore will be disappointed if you do not. He wished it; as he said you must find it so especially dull all alone by yourself."

"I do not, I assure you; and have several letters to write to go by to-morrow's post. I am glad you like the flowers Mrs. Linchmore," and she laid them on the table with the Camellia.

"Thank you. How beautifully you have arranged them! But the Camellia, why not place it with the rest?"

"I thought you would wear it in your hair as you did the other evening. Is it not beautiful? so purely white."

"Mason has taken out this Italian spray," and she took up an elegant silver ornament of Maltese work, "but I do not intend wearing it, neither can I this lovely Camellia; kindly place it amongst the other flowers you have arranged so nicely," and she gave the bouquet into Amy's hand.

"What a thousand pities, Ma'am!" said Mason. "It would look beautiful; far better than the ornament."

"Tastes differ," replied her mistress. "Thank you, Miss Neville, that will do very nicely; I thought, or rather feared, you would have to take the bouquet to pieces, but you have managed it admirably."

"I had not secured the flowers so very tightly, or perhaps the string had become loose."

"How tiresome the weather is, keeping so very cold; everyone seems out of temper with it, and must find Brampton especially dull. I am sure I scarcely know what to suggest as an amusement by way of novelty. Can you think of anything, Miss Neville? for I have exhausted all my ideas."

"I cannot imagine how any one can find it dull here," replied Amy, "so many to talk to, and so much to do."

"Everyone is not so easily satisfied. I am quite weary of it, and think I must give a ball. That will afford a little excitement for some time to come, and please everybody except Mr. Hall; and he can go and look after his parishioners for that day."

Mason had now finished the last plait, and inquired what ornament her mistress intended wearing in her hair, as she must arrange it accordingly.

Mrs. Linchmore turned to Amy.

"Would you kindly bring the flowers on my work table yonder? and Mason wind the plaits round my head so as to hang rather low."

Amy crossed the room, and took the flower out of the tumbler. Could it be possible? She examined it closely. Yes, there was no mistaking it. It was the self-same spray Mr. Vavasour had gathered, and offered her an hour or two before; there were the delicate white blossoms he had so admired. A beautiful little flower, or rather spray, it was; but too small, too insignificant to be worn in that rich dark hair.

An unconscious smile hovered on her lips as she returned and gave it to Mason, who turned up her eyes on beholding it. That miserable little piece of green and white to adorn the plaits she had arranged? It was not worthy of a place there, but Mason dared not say so; she merely ventured on the enquiry as to whether Miss Neville had brought the right flower.

"Certainly," was the reply. "Place it on the left side, and almost as low down as the hair itself."

But Mason was cross, and pinned it in badly, she would not understand Mrs. Linchmore's directions.

"What are you doing! Mason; I never knew you so awkward. How badly you have arranged it; not in the least as I like."

"Mrs. Linchmore wishes the spray to hang a little lower," suggested Amy.

"Perhaps, Miss Neville, you will very kindly pin it; as Mason seems to be so excessively stupid."

"I never pinned in such a flower before Ma'am," replied Mason, shrugging her shoulders, while she made way for Amy to take her place, who soon arranged it to Mrs. Linchmore's satisfaction.

The dress was put on, its rich silk folds falling round her graceful figure. Her dark hair, almost throwing the black lace trimmings into the shade, wound round her small head in thick bands. Very beautiful she looked; and so Amy thought, as she stood gazing at her, while Mason fastened the bracelets round the fair white arms, and drew a shawl round the still fairer shoulders.

"You will find it cold, Ma'am, going down the corridor and stairs."

"I dare say. Good night, Miss Neville. I regret we are not to have the pleasure of seeing you," and with a proud, firm step, Mrs. Linchmore went out.

Would she have entered the drawing room so haughtily, had she known she was wearing a flower that had been offered; nay, gathered for her governess! The room was a blaze of light, as with a proud, yet graceful step, a slight, haughty movement, perceptible about the small beautiful head, Mrs. Linchmore bowed, and shook hands with her guests.

Even in that shake there was haughtiness. It was no cordial grasp of the hand, but a slight, very slight pressure, as the small taper fingers met yours, and they were withdrawn, while a smile just curled the corner of the lips, and she passed on; each tiny foot firmly, gracefully, yet proudly planted on the ground: the same mocking smile, the same haughty bend repeated, ere, gathering the rich silk dress in one hand, and dropping at the same moment the splendid Cashmere that had partially concealed her beautiful figure, she leant back, as if tired of the exertion, amongst the soft crimson cushions of the sofa.

"What a beautiful, cold-hearted creature she is," thought Robert Vavasour, as he watched her.

"What airs she gives herself," muttered Sotto Voce, a rather pretty woman, and a neighbour, "coming in as if she were an Empress, after we have all been assembled here the last ten minutes! For my part, I wonder she condescends to come at all."

How fortunate it is opinions differ, as well as tastes; but I am not so sure this lady was singular in hers; certain I am, it would not have caused Mrs. Linchmore one moment's uneasiness; she did not care a straw what women thought of either her pride or her looks; she knew well that by far the greater number envied her, therefore she could afford to laugh at such speeches; but it was a rule with her—perhaps a studied one—not to make her appearance until nearly all her guests were assembled.

She was never, even when an invited guest, early, but always amongst the late comers; never actually unpunctual, but generally last, when she would walk in as she had done now, haughty and graceful, the perfection of ease in every slow and measured movement, totally unmindful of, or apparently careless and unconcerned at the glances of admiration or the many eyes bent on her as she passed.

Few could have entered a room filled with company so calmly and gracefully, with the lady stamped in every step she took, every turn of the head, every bend of the swan-like throat, or easy, graceful figure: the pretty neighbour might have practised it for hours—nay, days, and failed. It was innate in Mrs. Linchmore: it was impossible to conceive her doing anything awkwardly, or out of place. Even now, as she leant amongst the soft cushions, she was grace itself; while a lady near, sat stiffly upright, looking most uncomfortable, though the self-same cushions were behind and around her, inviting to repose and ease.

"My flower is highly honoured," said Robert Vavasour, as he drew near, and partly leant over the back of the sofa.

"Your flower!" exclaimed Mrs. Linchmore, with a well-acted glance of astonishment.

"It is scarcely worthy of a place amongst those rich dark braids," added he, softly.

"Ah, yes," replied she, raising her hand to her head, "I had quite forgotten all about it. It is a lovely spray."

"It would have looked better in the bouquet. Those braids require no addition to set them off."

"So Miss Neville said when she pinned it in. I am sorry she has done it awkwardly, and that it does not please you," said she carelessly, "It is too late to remedy the defect now."

"Defect," said he, rather hastily, "the word is unwisely chosen; it is impossible to find fault. The only defect, since you will it so, is the unworthiness of the flower itself."

"Do you condemn my poor bouquet also?"

"It is exquisite," he said, taking it from her hand, "and a great deal of taste displayed in its arrangement; the colours harmonize so well. The flowers are lovely."

"I suppose they are lovely; everything that costs money is. I used to be just as well pleased once with the wild flowers growing in the hedges. Take care, Mr. Vavasour, you will crush my poor Camellia. See, it has fallen at your feet."

"Not for worlds!" replied he, stooping and raising it from the ground; "how loosely it was tied in; see, the stem is not broken, but has been cleverly fastened with a piece of thread. I may keep it, may I not?" asked he, as she stretched out her hand for it.

"It is not worth the keeping."

"Say not so, for I prize it highly. Is it to be mine?"

"Yes, if you wish it," replied Mrs. Linchmore, with a faint attempt at a smile, while the thought flashed across her mind that she wished she had thrown his flower away.

Then she rose and led the way in to dinner, anything but pleased with the result of her conversation either with Robert Vavasour or her husband, and it required a great effort on her part to fulfil her character of hostess for that evening; and many noticed how far more haughty she was than usual, and how absent and at random the answers she gave.

"So I have the Camellia at last," thought Mr. Vavasour, "and Miss Neville pinned in the flower I gathered, which she refused to accept; well, strange things happen sometimes; I am certain she never foresaw this."

And he too moved away and followed his hostess.

CHAPTER X

A PASSING GLANCE

"And what is life?—An hour glass on the run,
A mist retreating from the morning sun,
A busy, bustling, still-repeated dream,
Its length?—A minute's pause, a moment's thought;
And happiness?—A bubble on the stream,
That, in the act of seizing, shrinks to naught.
What is vain hope?—the puffing gale of morn,
That robs each flow'ret of its gem,—and dies;
A cobweb, hiding disappointment's thorn,
Which stings more keenly through the thin disguise."
JOHN CLARE

The eight o'clock train came whizzing and puffing into the Standale station; Standale was a large town about ten miles distant from Brampton, and the nearest railway station to the Park. Charles Linchmore had barely time to step on to the platform, ere it was off again and out of sight, puffing as hard and fast as ever.

"Tom has sent me a horse?" questioned he of the porter.

"Yes, Sir. Waiting for you the last ten minutes, Sir."

Charles Linchmore passed out, and was soon wending his way along the road to Brampton Park. The moon had not yet risen, and owing to the slippery state of the roads, on account of the heavy fall of snow and recent frost, he rode on leisurely enough.

"Come along, Bob," said he to a shaggy Scotch terrier, who kept close to the hind legs of the horse; "come along, old fellow, I'd give you a run after your pent-up journey, only the roads are so confoundedly slippery, and her majesty is determined to hide herself behind the clouds to-night."

The dog wagged his tail as though he understood his master, and kept on as before. He was not much of a companion, but what with an occasional puff at his cigar, and talk to his dog, Charles Linchmore went on comfortably enough. As the smoke curled about his handsome mouth, his thoughts wandered. What were they doing at the Hall? Was Miss Neville still there, or absent as when he last paid his visit? and if there, had any of the numerous visitors found out what a nice girl she was?

"Of course they think her pretty, of that there can be no doubt," thought he, "and I dare say she has found it out too by this time, and gives herself airs; unless such an example as my brother's wife before her eyes gives her timely warning, and she steers on another tack. There's no being up to the girls now-a-days; as to prying into their hearts it's impossible, and not to be imagined for a moment; they are growing too deep for us men, and beat us out-and-out in deceit and man[oe]uvring."

"She has magnificent hair," thought he after a pause, "I suppose it's all her own—just the colour I like, though she has a ridiculous fashion of binding it up about her head. Perhaps she thinks it makes her look like a Madonna;" here he took a long puff at his cigar. "Well, I could not fall in love with a Madonna, it's not my style, and I do not think she is like one either; an angel's eyes don't flash like hers do sometimes. Perhaps Robert thinks his wife an angel, there is no accounting for tastes, but if Miss Neville has grown one iota like her, I'll—" here he paused again, "I'll have a flirtation with her, and—and then go back to my regiment."

The idea made him savage, and throwing away his cigar, he halted until the groom who rode behind came up.

"You can ride on, home, Tom, I don't want you," said he, and then he listened to the clatter of the horse's hoofs on the hard frosty ground, until they faded away in the distance out of hearing.

"We are all selfish," mused he, "that man would have ridden more slowly and carefully had it been his own horse. I dare say though, I am just as selfish if I only knew it."

He lit another cigar, and rode on some miles without interruption, until stopped by the Brampton Turnpike Gate.

"Hulloa!" called he.

But no notice was taken of his repeated shouts, although a faint gleam of light shone partly across the road from a slight crack in one of the shutters, showing that some of the inmates were at least awake.

"Confound the fellow!" muttered Charles as he called again.

When the door suddenly opened, and the figure of a man stood in the doorway.

"I tell yer I can undo it very well myself, and will too, so just stand fast," said he in a thick voice, to somebody inside the cottage, while and with anything but a steady gait he managed somehow between a shuffle and scramble to get over the one step of the cottage,—lifting his legs at the same time, as if the steps was so many feet, instead of inches high,—and reach the gate. Here, steadying himself by leaning both arms across the top, he looked up to where Charles Linchmore stood.

"I say young, man!" exclaimed he. "What do yer mean by hollering and bawling in that way? Havn't yer any patience. If ye're in sich a mortal hurry, why don't yer take and jump the gate? Eh!"

"Open the gate, you blockhead, or I will make you," exclaimed Charles, angrily.

"Speak civil, can't yer? I ain't going to open the gate with them words for my pains."

Just then the moon emerged from behind a cloud, and shone full on Charles Linchmore's face. The man recognised him in a moment, notwithstanding his tipsy state.

"In course, Sir, I'll open, who says I shan't? Bless yer sir, I'll open it as wide as ever he'll go. Dang me! if I can though," muttered he, as he fumbled at the fastening.

"Bring a lanthorn, Jem, can't yer," called he, turning his face towards the cottage, the door of which still remained open. "Bring a light; yer was mighty anxious just now to come out when yer wasn't wanted, and now yer are, yer don't care to show yer face."

He had scarcely finished speaking when another man emerged from the cottage, a hand was placed on the lock, and with a clatter the gate swung back to the other side of the road.

"I've half a mind to give you a sound horsewhipping," said Charles, passing through, followed by Bob, the latter venting his displeasure in a low suppressed growl, "but I hope your wife will save me the trouble, so I shall reserve it for some future opportunity."

"Thank yer Sir. She takes to it kindly she do, and don't want no 'swading."

"I hope she will give you an extra dose of it at all events," said Charles. "Is that you, Grant?" he added, addressing the other man. "It's scarcely safe for you to be out so late, is it?"

"You've heard all about the trial then, Sir?" questioned Grant.

"I read an account of it in the papers, and was sorry enough for poor Tom."

"Most everybody was Sir, and the parson gave us a fine discourse the Sunday after his funeral; but somehow preaching don't heal a broken heart, and Susan do take on awful at times; she haven't forgotten him, and it's my belief never will."

"Poor thing! Her husband's was a sudden and sad death, shot down like a dog by the poachers. The gang are still prowling about, so they say."

"Yes, Sir, and will do more mischief yet, they're a bad, desperate set, the lot that's here this year."

"I suppose you are keeping this man company, or looking after him in his drunken state. You would scarcely be going home alone at this late hour of the evening?"

"No, Sir. I am going home. I've been up to the Hall, and stayed there longer than I ought."

"It is too late a great deal for you to be out, and the whole country round about swarming with poachers."

"True, Sir. But I shan't go before my time—"

"Nonsense!" interrupted Charles. "Come, I tell you what; I'll see you home, I have nothing better to do; but first get that man safely housed somewhere, do not leave him out here to be run over."

"Oh! I'll soon settle him, sir."

And while Charles Linchmore struck a light and lit another cigar, Grant went once more into the cottage.

Opening a door, he called up the stairs, "Mrs. Marks! Here's your husband. I've brought him home rather unsteady on his pins; you'd better come down and see after him at once afore he gets into mischief."

"He is! Is he?" screamed a shrill voice from the top. "I expected as much. I warrant I'll soon make him steady again!"

With which satisfactory reply Grant rejoined Charles Linchmore, and they left the 'pikeman singing a drunken song, and vainly trying to shut the gate, the opening of which had previously so baffled his endeavours.

Turning off the high road, they struck into a side path or narrow lane, the tall hedges towering above them on either side, while here and there a tree loomed like a giant overhead.

"So you have been gossiping up at the Hall, Grant?" began Charles, encouraging his companion to talk.

"Yes, Sir; and a sight of company there is there now; not a man or maid able or willing to talk to you; so it's not much in the way of a gossip I've had. No, sir, I went to see my daughter Mary, but she was busy with the young ladies, getting them ready for a big dinner. Sich a sight of carriages in the yard, and the dogs barking like mad. You'd scarce know the place again, Sir. It's so changed."

"I'm glad of it. It used to be as dull as ditch water."

"Lord love ye, Sir! You won't find it dull or lonesome now. Why afore the frost set in, the roads were all alive with ladies and gentlemen riding over them. Matthew the Pikeman hadn't no time scarce to eat his victuals, let alone take a drop. So there's some excuse, Sir, for him getting muddled a bit now, and he didn't forsee the party up at the Hall to-night."

"I see," replied Charles, smiling, "he was overworked, poor man, I've no doubt it is so."

"Well, as to that Sir, I can't say he's got much to worry himself about on that score. His wife says he's an idle dog; but then that's her way, she never says he's over-burthened with brains."

"A vixen, eh? It's a good thing all women don't resemble Mrs. Marks."

"Yes, Sir, it is. Which same is a comfort if you're thinking of taking a wife; I ask your pardon, Sir, for being so bold."

"I Grant! I take a wife! That is anything but a sensible speech of yours, and requires a great deal of thought."

"Well, Sir, I dare say when your time comes, you'll get one as'll suit you, as Mrs. Marks suits her husband, he'd be nothing without her, and though he brags and bullies about awful behind her back, he's like a tame cat afore her. To every word he gives, she lets fly more than a dozen. It's my belief she'd talk any man dumb in half an hour."

"A pleasant life for Marks, upon my soul! I no longer wonder he frequents the public house."

"He don't go there often, Sir, don't think it. No, he most allays manages to go on the sly, and it ain't so easy to 'scape her eyes. Sometimes when he thinks she's safe at the wash-tub, he sneaks off; but he darn't for the life of him go on if he hears her voice calling out after him behind. Then he's forced to turn tail, and go back home with it 'tween his legs, with scarce even a growl. But it 'grees with him, he don't get so very thin; most others would be worn to skin and bone afore this. And now I'm in sight of the cottage, sir, so I needn't trouble you to come any further, and I'm much beholden to you, Sir, for coming so far."

But Charles Linchmore saw him safe to the door, then turned his horse's head once more towards the Hall.

This time he had not long to wait at the Turnpike Gate. It was swung open by a tall, bony, masculine looking woman,—apparently quite a match for the thin, spare Pikeman—who wished him good night in a loud, shrill voice.

"Mrs. Marks," thought Charles. "Her voice sounds hoarse, as though she had been pitching into that unfortunate husband of hers pretty considerably. I hope there's no second Mrs. M. to be had, or reserved for me, as Grant half hinted, in some snug corner."

As he entered the Lodge gate, he wondered if Miss Neville had joined the guests at dinner; who had taken her in, sat next her, and talked to her; and whether he should find her the centre of an admiring circle, or flirting in some "snuggery," or on the "causeuse," where he had had such a desperate flirtation with his cousin, Frances Strickland, only a year ago.

But he had scarcely taken half-a-dozen steps in the Hall, before he saw her standing at the further end, by the large roaring Christmas fire.

He crossed at once to where she was; holding out his hand cordially, forgetting in a moment all his savage thoughts and suspicions.

"Good evening, Miss Neville. You have not forgotten an old friend?"

Amy gave him her hand, but not quite so eagerly as it was clasped in those strong fingers of his.

"The sight of the fire is quite cheering. I am half frozen with the cold," continued he, drawing nearer to it.

"It is a bleak drive from the station; and I always fancy colder on that road than any other."

"I rode it; and should have been warm enough if the frosty roads would have allowed of a gallop. I met Grant, the head Keeper, as I came along, and saw him home; it was too late for him to be out alone, and a price set on his head by those cowardly ruffians, the poachers."

"You heard about the fight then. What a sad affair it was from beginning to end. It has made us all nervous and fearful for Grant, as he gave the principal evidence against the unfortunate man who was hung; and they have vowed to be revenged on him; but Mr. Linchmore has doubled the number of Keepers nearly, so we hope that will intimidate them."

"I hope it may; and now suppose we talk about something more lively; the dinner for instance. How many people are here?"

"About thirty altogether. But they have all left the dining-room now some little time. You are late."

"I meant to be. I hate dinners," he said crossly, half inclined to be out of temper again, as of course she must be waiting for somebody out there; otherwise why all alone?

"Here Bob," said he aloud, "here's room for you, old fellow; come and warm your toes. He's no beauty, Miss Neville, is he?" and he glanced inquiringly in her face. "Would she think him a horror, as his Cousin Frances had done?

"Decidedly not," replied Amy, "but I like dogs."

"I am glad of it. I am very fond of Bob, I believe he is the only creature who cares for me. By-the-by how is my sister's fat pet? Poor beast, what a specimen of a dog he is! Bob and he never got on well together."

"He is as asthmatic as ever, and has not had a fit for an age. I cannot say what the sight of your dog may do, especially if he turns the right side of his face towards him."

"Yes. That eye is certainly rather so-so; and the lip uncomfortably short; but I am proud of those marks, and so is he; they are most honourable wounds, and show he has borne the brunt of many a battle without flinching."

While Amy and he both laughed, Frances Strickland came into the hall. She glanced at the two in surprise, and stood for a moment irresolute. Once she made as though she would have gone towards them, then turning, went swiftly into the music-room; came back as softly, and with another look re-entered the drawing-room.

Closing the door, her eyes wandered restlessly until they fixed their gaze on Mrs. Linchmore, who, seated on the music stool, was carelessly turning the pages of a book, while two or three young men seemed eagerly proffering their services, or selecting from among a number of songs the one she was to sing.

An expression of disappointment flitted over Frances' face while going towards the piano. One of the gentlemen had just moved away to another part of the room. So laying down the music she held in her hand, she advanced towards the vacant seat, and had nearly secured it, when it was filled by another, just as Mrs. Linchmore began one of the airs from "Lurline."

Again that vexed, baffled look, with a dimly perceptible frown. As she turned away, Anne Bennet rose and seated herself by Julia.

"Look at Frances, Maggie," whispered she, "and tell me what you see in her face."

"What should I see?" laughed Julia, "but pride. I have never been able to find any other expression."

"Then you are a greater simpleton than I; and if I had the stick the fool gave to the king on his death bed, you should have it; for I see a great deal more."

"Wise sister Anne. What do you see?"

"An angry, spiteful, vexed look; as if she had seen a ghost in the music-room, where I know she went just now."

"Nonsense! Even if she had it would not frighten her, she would think it had only made its appearance to fall down and worship her; and would spurn it with her foot."

"I am certain she saw something out there, and I am determined to see what it was."

"Of course," said Julia demurely, "and here comes Mr. Hall to help you."

"Always coming when he is not wanted," exclaimed Anne crossly. "I shall not say a word to him; or if I do, I will be abominably rude."

Quite unconscious of what was awaiting him Mr. Hall advanced, and said good humouredly,

"I have been thinking Miss Anne, where we shall go to-morrow for the walk you have so kindly threatened me with."

"It will most likely pour in torrents," replied she.

"I do not anticipate it, the glass is rising, so there is every prospect of our walk coming off; and if I might be allowed to choose, I know of a very lovely one, even in winter time."

"That is impossible," said she sharply, "everything looks cold and bleak."

"Not while the snow remains in the branches of the trees; even then the Oak Glen can never look ugly; the large rocks prevent that."

"The Oak Glen! Oh, pray do not trouble yourself to take me there; I will lead you blind-fold." That will settle him, thought she.

But no, Mr. Hall was not to be defeated in that style, and went on again quite unconcernedly.

"You have sketched it, perhaps. It would make a lovely painting."

"I do not paint; that is to say only caricatures of people that make themselves ridiculous." That must finish him, thought she, as Julia gave her dress a slight pull.

But Mr. Hall had not the slightest idea of leaving, and seemed as though he heard not; and quite out of temper Anne said;

"What are you pulling at my dress for, Julia? I think she has a secret to tell me Mr. Hall, so you really must go away."

"I dare say it will keep until to-morrow," replied the impenetrable Mr. Hall; "young ladies never have any very serious secrets."

"You are quite right, Mr. Hall," said Julia, "my secret will keep very well until to-morrow."

"What a wretch he is!" thought Anne, tapping her tiny foot impatiently on the ground; "Isabella will have finished that song soon, and then it will be too late. How tiresome I cannot get rid of him, when every moment is so precious."

"Mr. Hall," said she aloud, "If Julia's secret will keep, mine will not; and since you are determined to remain here, why you must be a sharer in it; there is no help for it."

"By all means," replied he, coolly, "I am all attention."

"You will only hear part of it; but men are so curious, I dare say you will soon ferret out the rest. Can I trust you?"

"Of course. It is only the fair sex that are not to be trusted."

"I have no time to quarrel with you, or I would resent such a rude speech. Now will you attend, please. I am going to ask you to help me—that is if you will."

"Certainly I will. I am all attention."

"I am desirous of leaving the room without Miss Strickland's knowledge; can you help me to manage it?"

"Is that all? You shall see."

He went over to where Frances still stood by the piano; with huge, ungainly strides, as though a newly ploughed field was under his feet, instead of the soft velvet carpet.

"What an awkward bear he is!" said Anne to her sister, as she watched him; "I shall give him a hint to get drilled, or become a volunteer parson, he would be sure to shoot himself the very first time he handled a rifle; do only look at him Mag, he is like a large tub rolling along."

"Do not abuse him Anne, see how quickly he has done what you wished; I am sure he deserves praise for that."

"I wish he always would do what I wish; and then I should not be tormented with him so often," replied Anne.

CHAPTER XI

THE MEETING IN THE SCHOOL-ROOM

Thus, when I felt the force of love,
When all the passion fill'd my breast,—
When, trembling, with the storm I strove,
And pray'd, but vainly pray'd, for rest;
'Twas tempest all, a dreadful strife
For ease, for joy, for more than life:
'Twas every hour to groan and sigh
In grief, in fear, in jealousy.
CRABBE

Frances did not look very well pleased when she saw Mr. Hall advancing; in fact turned away her head almost rudely, so that any very timid man would have taken the hint and retreated.

But Mr. Hall, however simple he looked, was not timid; he had a way of always carrying his point. That strong unflinching will of his would have subdued a much more formidable enemy than a proud, weak woman. I say weak, because when a woman gives way to or does not strive against any besetting sin, she lays herself open to attack, and is easily wounded when that most palpable fault is assailed. So it was with Frances.

Her mother and Mrs. Bennet were sisters, the first had married a rich merchant, the other a comparatively poor man, whose five daughters did not conduce to enrich him, however much they might his family fireside. Mrs. Linchmore's mother was an elder sister, she had died young leaving her only child to the care, as has been seen, of Mrs. Elrington. Frances and Mrs. Linchmore somewhat resembled one another. The same haughty look, and at times, scornful expression appeared in both, but with this difference, that the former could command hers at will almost, while the latter was either not so well versed in the art of concealment or scorned to use means to prevent its being visible.

They were both rich. Riches do not of necessity bring pride, although they in a great measure foster and increase it. They make the seeds bear fruit which otherwise would remain dormant for ever, and Frances being an only daughter had been early taught to believe she was a magnet, towards which all hearts would turn, and that wealth was necessary to happiness, while her cousins the Bennets were quoted as examples of poverty, until she thoroughly learnt to despise and pity them, believing in her ignorance that they and all must envy her and her parents wealth.

Mr. Hall, in her ideas, was a poor simpleton almost beneath her regard, and she would have taken no notice of him had it not been for his admiration of Anne. She could not bear another should receive worship while she was present. He was simply a being to be made useful, as in the instance of the skein of wool; though that little episode had in some slight measure induced her to think he was not quite such a Simon Pure as he looked, and although Mr. Hall on this occasion really exerted himself to be agreeable, the tangled mass lying in the sofa table drawer, was too recent an injury to be easily forgotten; and he only received monosyllables in reply to his remarks.

But he was not to be defeated. Anne had asked him to help her, and help her he would; so notwithstanding Frances' ungraciousness he talked on, and so engrossed her attention that he soon had the satisfaction of watching Anne's unobserved escape from the room, and of thinking that perhaps she would like him a little better for his clever management.

Alas! Anne had far too much curiosity to think of anything but gratifying that. Until that had been satisfied not a thought had she for anything else. Her inquisitiveness was as great almost as Frances' pride. There never was a plot concocted at home, or a pleasure planned as a surprise for her, but she had found out all about it before it was in a fair way of completion. Her sisters were constantly foreboding scrapes and troubles for her, but nothing as in this instance daunted her. She would not be baffled. She guessed from Frances' face that something had annoyed her; that trouble was in consequence in store for some one, and she was resolved to find out what that something was.

As she stood outside in the hall, she saw at a glance Frances' ghosts, and ever impulsive, was beside them in a moment.

"Good evening, Charles. There are at least a dozen cousins in there," and she pointed in the direction of the drawing-room, "waiting to say the same to you."

"Then let them wait, until I have warned and nerved myself to encounter such an immense array of females."

"Most men would have been roasted in less time; but you have had very pleasant company," and she glanced at Amy, "to perform your deed of martyrdom in."

"I had a cold ride," replied he drily, "and only arrived a short time ago from the Brampton Station."

"In these fast days even the clocks are somehow in the fashion, and go faster than they did formerly. I remember when I used to think half-an-hour an awful long time to wait for anybody, and I suspect Mrs. Linchmore's patience is fast evaporating."

"Nonsense! How should she know I have arrived?"

"Because all ill news travels fast."

"Do not be surprised, Miss Neville," said Charles, apologetically, "at any thing you hear fall from Miss Bennet's lips, she is—," he hesitated a moment, "rather peculiar."

Anne's laugh rang loud and clear through the hall; then coming close beside him, and standing on tiptoe, she whispered a few words in his ear, evidently by the sudden start he gave and the quick flush that succeeded it, something that annoyed him; for while Anne still laughed he wished Miss Neville good-night, and, whistling to his dog, went away upstairs.

Then Anne no longer laughed, but with a sigh turned suddenly to Miss Neville, and as she did so caught sight of Mr. Hall's face at the half-open drawing-room door.

"Is it possible!" exclaimed she, "that I caught sight of Mr. Hall's ugly phiz peeping through the door?"

"Yes; he was there not long ago; at least I saw him when you were whispering to Mr. Linchmore."

"Upon my word, I am losing all patience with that man. How I do wish Charles had been a little more cousinly; how astonished he would have been, and what a lecture he would have read me. Keep a secret, indeed! Not he. Why he is a thousand times worse that I. Good-bye, Miss Neville, I am sorry to have interrupted your cosy chat, but I could not possibly help it; you will forgive me, won't you."

Amy told her there was nothing to forgive. That she had promised the children she would take them upstairs, and was merely waiting for them.

"Then do not wait any longer," Anne said, "but take my advice, go to bed, and send Mary. You do not know Mrs. Linchmore as well as I do, she is peculiar in some things; and—now do not be angry—but I doubt if she would like your being here." And without waiting to see the effect of her speech, Anne went off.

"You cannot keep a secret, Mr. Hall," said she, stumbling upon him as she entered the drawing-room. "I have tried you, and you are not to be trusted in the very slightest."

"You forget, Miss Anne, you did not trust me, otherwise—"

"You would not have peeped," she said, finishing the sentence.

"True. I should not."

"But a secret is no secret when it is entrusted to a multitude. If you have found out mine—which, mind, I doubt—do not divulge it."

Ten minutes later Mrs. Linchmore herself left the room with the children, and Anne again enlisted Mr. Hall's services, asking him to see if Miss Neville was in the Hall. "Do not trouble to come and tell me, I do not wish it; but just shake your head, or nod as the case may be, yes or no; I shall understand you."

"I have found it all out, Mag," said she, crossing the room as Mr. Hall disappeared; and with no little pride Anne once more seated herself in the still vacant chair.

"I do not doubt you, Anne. Was it worth the trouble?"

"I should think so. There would have been a flame before now, the train was laid and the match all ready, but before it could be set fire to I dispersed it. So you see curiosity is not always a fault, but in some instances praiseworthy."

Julia laughed. "What reasoning," she said.

"It is sound, good reasoning though, Mag; and now do tell me if Mr. Hall is in the room?"

"Yes, and looking at you, Anne."

This should have satisfied her, and she should have given Mr. Hall the chance of making the promised signal; but no, she could not resist the pleasure of tormenting him a little, so went on talking to her sister and giving no heed.

Presently, a few minutes later, she again asked, "What is Mr. Hall doing Mag? Has he left off looking in this direction?"

"No, he is still looking," replied Julia, laughing.

"Oh what a wretch; and how foolish he is. I suppose he will go on looking until everybody in the room sees him," and slowly raising her eyes she received the promised shake, and really felt happy at having extricated Amy out of some trouble, though she hardly knew what. She remained where she was for the rest of the evening, expecting every moment to see her cousin Charles come in at the opposite door, but he never made his appearance. Frances' eyes were also constantly wandering in the same direction; perhaps she too expected him, but he disappointed them both. They saw no more of him until the next morning at breakfast, when approaching Anne as she stood at the window inwardly abusing the unpromising state of the weather—it was snowing fast—he asked who had told her of his arrival the evening before. "I am determined to know," said he, "so you had better make a clean breast of it at once, and tell me who acted as I am inclined to think so spitefully."

But Anne pretended not to understand him. He had been asleep and dreaming since. She had never even hinted that any one had been spiteful; it was a pure invention of his brain, and leaving him, she went to the table. There seeing Mr. Hall busy helping some cold fowl, she walked round and took a seat as far off from him as she possibly could. But what was her astonishment at seeing him, as she began cutting a piece of bread, deliberately walk round to where she was; and taking the knife from her hand, cut a slice which he put on her plate, and then seat himself beside her. She dared not look at her sister, knowing full well she was laughing, and that was sufficient to make her feel angry and indignant, so turning her face away, she vouchsafed him not one word, but listened to the conversation going on around.

"I am very glad to see you, Charles," Mrs. Linchmore was saying. "How early you must have arrived. Did you sleep at Standale? I believe the place does boast of an hotel of some kind."

"No. I arrived last night, but having indulged in a cigar as I came along, with Bob for a companion,—two of your abominations—I had to divest myself of my travelling costume lest you should detect the first; see Bob safely housed for the second, and take a glass of brandy and water for the third; and by the time I had finished that, I thought the bed looked uncommonly comfortable, so just tried it to see if it was, and suppose I was right, for I only awoke about twenty minutes ago, and have had a scramble to get down in time."

"Three very poor excuses. I did hear a whisper that you were here, but could not believe it, as I thought you would of course come and make yourself agreeable to my visitors, if not to myself and your cousins," said Mrs. Linchmore, with a slight symptom of annoyance in her tone, "however, Bob, if he was your only companion was, I have no doubt more pleasant company. By what train did you arrive?"

"By one of the late trains," replied he, catching a glimpse of Anne's face, the expression of which rather puzzled him, but he fancied it told him to be on his guard, so he added, "I was not in a fit state to be seen by any lady just from that dusty, smoky railway."

"I saw you," said Frances, quietly looking up, "but you were too busily engaged to perceive me."

"And—" Mr. Hall was on the point of adding "I—" and perhaps telling that he had seen Amy also; but before the latter word had escaped his lips Anne, turned round quickly and catching his arm whispered,

"My secret! Beware, beware!"

"Is that your secret?" asked Mr. Hall, "Remember I am still in ignorance; you only half trusted me. Pray forgive me."

Anne felt astonished and abashed. A great tall man like Mr. Hall ask her pardon so humbly; she thought she should like him a little better from that time forth. So full of wonderment was she, that she failed to notice the quick triumphant glance Charles flashed at her across the table, on hearing Frances' words.

It did not snow incessantly; some days were fine enough, and what with hunting, riding, shooting and skating, they passed pleasantly for the visitors, notwithstanding Mrs. Linchmore's fears that they were finding Brampton Hall dull and stupid.

The ball had not as yet been talked of, except in the housekeeper's room, where of course Mason carried the news, to the no small vexation of Mrs. Hopkins, who thought the place quite gay enough as it was; and sighed for the good old times, when she could walk about without being obliged to drop a courtesy at every step she took, as she encountered some fair girl, or man with fierce moustaches and whiskers; these latter she regarded as so many birds of prey, waiting for some unfortunate victim to pounce down upon and bear away in their fierce talons.

Charles Linchmore did not apparently care much for any of the gay party assembled, and often loitered away half the morning in the library, where setting the door ajar, and seating himself so that he could catch a glimpse of any one passing, he lounged impatiently until the gong sounded for luncheon. Then throwing down his book, with a gesture half of weariness, half of vexation, he either remained where he was, and took no notice of the summons, or went into the dining-room with anything but a happy or contented expression of face; feeling uncomfortably out of sorts and out of temper with himself and the whole world, and in no mood for Frances' soft smiles—who, proud as she was, could and did unbend to him—or for Anne's sharp retorts.

What had become of Miss Neville? Where was she? Did she never go out? It was an unheard-of piece of eccentricity, remaining so long shut up in the house; besides it was bad for the children. Surely a cold walk was better than none at all? These and many other questions Charles asked himself, until he grew tired and out of patience, and tried to think of other things, but it was useless; his thoughts always came back to the one starting point, Miss Neville; she was evidently uppermost in his mind; although he stood a good chance, or seemed to do so, of returning to his regiment, without even the flirtation he had threatened her with as a punishment, if he should find her at all resembling his brother's wife, or spoilt with mixing amongst the small world at Brampton.

Had he only wandered near the door leading out into the shrubbery from the flight of stairs in the wing appropriated to the children and Miss Neville, he would have seen her every day, and not wasted his mornings in vain wishes and surmises as to what had become of her.

One cold, raw day after a gallop with his cousin Frances, and almost a renewal of his old flirtation—she was a fearless horsewoman, and he could never help admiring a woman who rode well—he walked round to the stables to have a look at the horses.

As he passed in sight of the school-room window, he could not resist the temptation of looking up, and saw Amy, whom a few minutes ago he had almost forgotten, standing by the window. Scarcely knowing whether she noticed him or not, he raised his hat. She bowed slightly ere she moved away out of his sight.

Was it his fancy, or did he really detect a mocking smile on her lips? Was it possible she was glorying in having deluded him so successfully ever since the night of his arrival? The idea aroused him at once; he would no longer be inactive. The chase was becoming exciting, since she would not leave the citadel, he would storm it.

Instead of going to the stables, he turned back, and went to his own room, changed his thick, heavy riding boots, and then made for the school-room, passing Mrs. Linchmore's door on his way with a defiant, determined step; but he was uninterrupted in his journey; he met no one. He soon reached the corridor, stood before the school-room door and knocked. But the soft voice he had expected to hear in reply was silent.

Again he knocked. No reply still. He grew bolder, opened the door softly, and with Bob at his heels, walked in.

The room was tenantless. Amy and her pupils were nowhere.

So she had guessed his intention, perhaps seen him from the window turning back, and divining his motive, flown. He was angry, indignant, but his time was his own, he would wait where he was half the day; he would see her, she should not elude him thus.

Being in a bad temper, he vented it on unoffending Bob.

"How dare you follow me here, Sir?" The poor animal looked up wistfully, not knowing in what he had offended, since his master patted his head so caressingly as they stood outside the door together.

On the table was a half finished drawing, the paper still damp with the last touches, the brushes all scattered about; one had fallen on the edge of the paper; Charles took it up, carefully washed out the mark it had left, and laid it by carefully.

Amy's work-box stood invitingly open. He looked in, and turned over the contents: there was a piece of embroidery; small holes that had been cut out and sewn over, the "holy work," as he called it, that he hated so much.

Somehow this small piece appeared to have a curious interest in his eyes, he looked at it, put it down and then looked at it again. There was the needle still in the half finished flower, and a small mark as though the finger had been injured in the sewing. This decided him, and with a half frightened, guilty look he put it in his pocket, just as Bob, evidently with the view of making friends, rubbed against his legs.

"Ah! my friend," said Charles, looking down, "Your warning comes too late. The deed is done."

"What is too late?" asked Frances advancing into the room, "and what have you done?"

"You here," stammered Charles.

"Yes, why not? since Mr. Charles Linchmore designs to come."

"Then I came—, that is you forget," said he recovering himself, "I sometimes take my nieces for a walk."

"I forget nothing," replied she, "my memory serves me well."

"Why are you here?" asked he, "surely you can have no excuse for coming."

"It was chance directed my footsteps," replied she carelessly.

This was scarcely true. Ever since Frances had seen Amy talking with her cousin on the evening of his arrival, a strange fascination to speak with the governess had taken possession of her; why she hardly knew or questioned; but now at this moment, as she stood so unexpectedly face to face with Charles and marked his confusion, a jealous hatred crept slowly, yet surely over her heart, a jealousy that was to be the bane of her after life, to influence her every action, almost thought, and lead her to follow blindly all its revengeful promptings, undeterred either by the oft-times whispered voice of conscience, or the evident and consequent sufferings of others.

What woman is not jealous of the one she fears is supplanting her, or obtaining an interest in the heart of him she loves? but here Frances had barely reason for her jealousy, Charles never having given her sufficient cause to think he cared for her, beyond a cousinly regard; yet she loved him as much as her proud heart was capable of loving.

"This drawing is beautifully done," said she, advancing and examining it closely. "What have you done with the copy?"

The copy? What if she had named the "Holy Work?"

He cast a furtive glance at his pocket as he replied, "I have not seen it. I suppose Miss Neville draws without one."

"I have never heard Isabella say she was an artist."

"I suspect my 'brother's wife.'" This was a favourite term of Charles's; he generally spoke of Mrs. Linchmore as my 'brother's wife.' "I suspect my brother's wife knows very little about Miss Neville's accomplishments; she is not in her line; no two people could be more dissimilar."

"No. They are very different."

"Very."

"But you are wrong, Charles, in thinking Isabella does not trouble her head about her governess; she laughingly told me one day that she thought her rather inclined to flirt."

"Indeed!" said he, consciously. "When was that?"

"I almost forget—last month I think, she noticed it, so you see she must know something about her."

"Or next to nothing," replied he.

"I believe she thought that her only fault; and you know it did not look very well to see her come home so late with Mr. Vavasour."

"With Vavasour! When was that."

"Oh! I forget when; just a few days before you came."

"Flirting with Vavasour!" exclaimed Charles, thrown off his guard by the suddenness of the announcement. "I won't believe it!"

"You had better ask Anne, then; she can tell you all about it, as she and Mr. Hall walked home behind them, and talked about it afterwards; it made quite a stir at the time."

"I dare say. I don't doubt you," said Charles, whistling apparently quite unconcerned, when in reality he was infinitely disgusted.

"Well, if you do, you have only to come to the window," said Frances triumphantly, "and judge for yourself."

With quick, hasty footsteps he was by her side in a moment. Yes, there was Miss Neville, picking her way over the snow with Vavasour beside her, the children some few yards ahead, so that the two were alone. He had found out a way of meeting and joining her, though Charles had not; no doubt they had been carrying on this game for days, while he had been wasting his in hopeless guesses and surmises as to what had become of her, imagining her miserably dull, shut up in the school room.

Yes, the secret was out now. It was for him she had left the drawing so hastily, and all her things ruthlessly scattered about. For this he himself had waited so patiently, and had thought to wait half the day. He would have snatched the "Holy work" from his pocket and torn it into shreds if he could, but other eyes than Bob's were on him now, and without another word he strode away, passing through the door which separated these rooms from the large corridor, just as Amy's and the children's voices were heard on the stairs leading from the garden.

Frances watched his exit with a triumphant look; had she given him a bad opinion of Amy Neville? and had he believed her?

She remained where she was, still and silent, until the door opened and Amy came in, her face lighted up with smiles, and her cheeks glowing with a faint tinge of colour from her walk. Frances' face flushed hotly as she thought how beautiful she was; and passing by her with a scornful bend of the head in acknowledgment of the governess's greeting, she gained her own room, and bolted the door.

There throwing herself on her knees, she clasped her hands over her face as she murmured passionately, "I hate her! But he shall not love her! He shall not love her!"

CHAPTER XII

THE ACCIDENT

"All shod with steel,
We hissed along the polished ice, in games
Confederate, imitative of the chace
And woodland pleasures."
WORDSWORTH

"I will forget her! All dear recollections
Pressed in my heart, like flowers within a book,
Shall be torn out, and scattered to the winds!
I will forget her!"
LONGFELLOW

Alfred Strickland had chosen the breakfast-room as being the least likely to be visited by any one after the morning's meal had been despatched, and had made himself tolerably comfortable before the fire in a large easy chair with a book, where he remained undisturbed by the rustling of dresses and crinolines.

No two people were more dissimilar than Alfred and his sister. Their features were as unlike as their tastes, disposition, and temper. Indolence, not pride, was his failing; he seldom troubled his head about any one but himself, not that he was selfishly inclined; he was not, excepting on this one point of laziness, but would help any one out of a difficulty so long as it cost him little or no trouble, but if that "loomed in the distance," then his aid was very reluctantly given; advice you were welcome to, and might have plenty of it; it required no bodily exertion to talk, he could lie down and do that; but what inward sighs and groans if his legs were put into requisition!

Good-natured to a fault, his sister's taunts, and she gave him plenty of them—failed to rouse the lion within him, so he generally came off victorious in their pitched battles, and was just as friendly as ever the next time they met, whereas she would nurse her ill feeling for days.

He had been brought up to no profession. His father's hardly amassed wealth descended to him as only son, and perhaps the idea of having as much money at command as he could possibly want, first fostered his indolence and made him gradually sink into a state of quiet laziness which soon grew habitual, and from which as yet he had been roused but on one occasion.

If the book he happened to be reading accidentally fell to the ground, there it might remain until some one by chance saw it, and placed it on the table again. He was good looking, somewhat of a fop, and had rather a good opinion of himself, as most men of the present day have; and was always dressed with scrupulous regard as to taste and fashion.

The one occasion on which he had been aroused was, when returning home one day by the river side in his dog-cart, he saw a boy struggling in the water, evidently for life.

In a moment the reins were on the horse's neck, he had plunged in and brought him safe to land; then had to walk about a mile in his wet things, his horse having taken fright at the cries of the boy's companions.

Frances never believed this story, but always declared he had been thrown into the river by the jerk the horse gave when starting off.

Alfred Strickland was not the only one who had chosen the breakfast room as being the least likely to be interrupted by visitors. Julia had persuaded Miss Tremlow at last to come down stairs, and was even now advancing with the invalid on her arm to invade his fancied peace and quietness. As their voices sounded at the door, Alfred turned in dismay, and with no little disgust saw the two approach the fire near which he had made himself so comfortable, and as he thought secure from all invaders.

"We scarcely expected to find anyone here," Julia said, "but you will not interfere with my patient, being too lazy to move."

Alfred took the hint, and remained quiet, watching Julia as she first wheeled a chair nearer the fire, then placed some soft cushions, and a footstool and small table in readiness, all so nicely, and without the least exertion or trouble to the invalid, who seemed a mere puppet swayed about at the other's will; and he could not help thinking what a nice wife she would make.

"I don't mind having a cushion too, Julia," said he, "if you have one to spare."

"A cushion, you lazy creature. I've half a mind to throw it at your head. The idea of my waiting on you!"

"Thank you," replied Alfred, inwardly thinking what a vile temper she had, and how foolish it was to form hasty opinions.

"You will be paid out some day," said Julia. "I shall live to see you a perfect martyr to your wife's whims and fancies."

"God forbid that I should ever be so foolish as to marry at all, much less an invalid wife—of all things the most detestable."

"Well I will ask Goody Grey next time I see her what she prophecies."

"My dear," exclaimed Miss Tremlow, "pray do not mention that name; it sets me all of a tremble. I have not forgotten that dreadful day, and how the horses ran when she struck them. Have you, Mr. Strickland?"

"I? No indeed, I am not likely to forget it in a hurry, I shall be reminded of it for some time to come," and he rubbed his arm as though he still felt the grasp of her fingers.

"Let us talk of something else," said Julia; "this conversation is against orders, and strictly prohibited. I am going to fetch your port wine, Miss Tremlow, as I think you need it; now read your book, and do not think of anything else, least of all of that horrid old woman."

"She does it all out of kindness, I dare say," said Miss Tremlow as the door closed on Julia, "but I do so dislike being dosed."

"What an ungrateful being," said Alfred, "why, you ought to think yourself in luck at being so waited on. I wish I was."

"I wish you were, with all my heart."

"Here she comes," said Alfred, "armed to the teeth," as a few minutes after Julia returned with the wine in one hand and a shawl in the other.

"And your tormentor following in my train," laughed Julia, "my sister Anne, most anxious to persuade you to join the skaters."

There was no resisting Anne, who had made up her mind to stay and torment him, unless he gave up his book and went; so with many a sigh of reluctance, he slowly rose and prepared to accompany her.

"Here is your hat and coat," said she. "I do not mind getting them as a kind of preparatory recompense for fixing our skates, which you will have to do presently. Good bye, Miss Tremlow, I am glad to see you down again; how cosy you look! just like a dormouse wrapped up in flannel."

"Here's Charles," said Alfred, as they stumbled upon him in the passage. "Will not he do as well; he is partial to all these kind of amusements."

No; Charles was going for a ride, his horse already waiting for him at the door; besides he was in no mood for joining a party of pleasure; he had felt in a restless, dissatisfied mood ever since the day he had detected Amy walking with Mr. Vavasour, and he had carried away the piece of embroidery and gone to his own room so angrily; and while Frances was sobbing passionately he had thrown it on the fire, and paced up and down with hasty impatience.

Yet what right had he to be angry? He was not in love with her; no; he admired her, thought her different to most girls he had ever seen, inasmuch as she was no flirt; was agreeable, and did not give herself airs. It was her supposed flirtation with another that annoyed him. Had not his brother's wife given him black looks, smiling yet sharp hints about going into the school-room. What right had Vavasour to become acquainted with the governess? What right had he to walk and talk with her? perhaps visit her, where he had been forbidden to set foot, nay avoided.

Yet while he blamed and accused her, those soft, melancholy eyes pursued him, until in a softened mood he drew the work from the grate where it had lain scarcely singed, and locked it away in his desk. He could not return it, that was impossible; but he would never look at it, he would forget its existence, as well as Amy Neville's.

But was it so easy to forget her? As he rode slowly away from the Hall door, down the long avenue— avoiding the short cut by the stables, which would of necessity lead him past the school-room window,—he still thought of her, otherwise why go down the avenue? unless he feared Miss Neville might think he wished to see or watch her; he who had ceased to take any interest in her movements.

What was it to him where she went or who she walked with? His horses and dog were all he cared for in the whole world, and were worth a dozen women, who only existed in excitement, or a whirlwind of gaiety and pleasure. There was no such thing as a pretty, quiet girl to be met with; a score of plain ones; but if pretty, then flirts, coquettes; beings whose sole delight was angling for hearts, gaining and then breaking them.

But his was not to be lost in that way. The more he thought of Amy's supposed flirtation with Vavasour, the more bitter he grew. He was very sorry he had not joined the party on the ice. Why make himself miserable? It was not too late; he would ride round now, and if she were there, show her how little he cared for her.

He turned his horse's head, and cantered down the lane, nor slackened his speed until he came in sight of the lake, then dismounting and throwing the reins over his arm, he walked to a spot which commanded a view of almost the whole piece of water; but his eyes in vain sought Miss Neville, she was not amongst the skaters.

Many of the neighbouring gentry had come over to Brampton, and the lake presented a picturesque and lively scene. Conspicuous in the midst of the gay assemblage, on account of her tall and commanding figure, was Mrs. Linchmore, one hand rested on Mr. Vavasour's supporting arm, while seemingly with the utmost care and gentleness he guided her wavering and unsteady feet, as she glided over the slippery surface.

Frances Strickland, with a small coquettish-looking hat, white ermine boa and muff, was describing circles, semicircles, and all the most difficult and intricate man[oe]uvres known only to experienced skaters; now she approached so near as to make Mrs. Linchmore cling rather closer to the protecting arm of her companion, but just as a faint exclamation of alarm escaped her lips, with a smile Frances would take a sudden swerve to the right, and be almost at the other end of the lake before Vavasour had succeeded in quieting the fears of the haughty lady at his side.

It was strange, but Frances seemed to excel in everything. She was apparently as fearless a skater as horsewoman. Charles had seen her put her horse at a leap that even he, bold as he was, glanced at twice before following in her wake; yet she had never swerved, nay, scarcely moved in her saddle.

Now he gazed after her until the small hat with its waving scarlet feather was scarcely distinguishable in the distance; yet fearless as she was, he could not allow there was anything at all masculine about her; no, the proud bend of the head, the small pliant figure forbade that, yet still he was not altogether satisfied; there was a something wanting, something that did not please him; and then involuntarily, his thoughts wandered towards Miss Neville again.

"She takes the shine out of us all, does not she?" asked Julia, who had advanced unperceived to his side. "Is that what you were so deep in thought about?"

"Not exactly. She does skate admirably, it is true; but I was thinking if Lawless, a friend of mine could but see her, he would lose his heart in no time. She is just the sort of woman he is always raving about."

"Oh, ask him down by all means, and let him go mad if it pleases him, so long as we get rid of Frances."

"That speech savours of jealousy or rivalry. Which is it, Julia?"

"Neither the one nor the other."

"She is a girl many women would fear as a rival."

"Nonsense, Charles; she is so different to most women, so proud, and as cold as the ice she is skating on. If I were a man, I could not fall in love with Frances."

"Why not? She may be a little cold and proud perhaps, but that would only entail a little more trouble in winning her, and make her love the more valued when won."

"If she has any love to win. I doubt it; she is so utterly cold-hearted."

"I see nothing to find fault with on the score of coldness; few girls now-a-days—though not absolutely cold-hearted—have hearts worth the having, or wooing and winning."

"How bitter you are against us."

"Not more so than you were yourself. Did you not call Frances a petrifaction?" said he, laughing. "But, if Frances does not please you, who, may I ask, comes nearer perfection in your eyes?"

"Oh! lots of women. She and Miss Neville, for instance, ought not to be named in the same breath together."

Then, as Charles made no reply, she added, "I wonder if she skates?"

"Skates! Pshaw! she would be afraid to trust that dainty foot of hers on the slippery ice. I hate a woman with no nerve, afraid of her own shadow."

"If being an accomplished skater is the only proof of a woman's nerve and courage, what a set of cowards more than half our sex must be! I very much doubt if one in a dozen of us are acquainted with the art."

"Well, if not, you are well up in a dozen and one others wherewith to drive us poor men out of our seven senses at times."

"I know what is the matter with him now," thought Julia; "and why he is so cross, some girl he cares for has been paying him out. I hope it is not Frances. I cannot bear the idea of his having fallen in love with her, although I strongly suspected he was on the high road to it last night."

"Uncle Charles," said a small voice, while a tiny hand was laid on his arm, "I should so like to have a slide."

It was Fanny. Charles lifted his hat courteously but indifferently to Miss Neville's almost friendly greeting, and watched her furtively as she gazed over the lake.

What would she think of Vavasour's attentions to his brother's wife? Now she would find out that he could be as devoted to other women; could guide another's footsteps over the ice just as carefully as he had directed and picked her way for her over the snow; but whatever Amy thought she looked calm and unconcerned as she turned round and desired Fanny not to go so near the horse's feet. Charles assured her the horse was quiet enough; he had never known him indulge in the vicious propensity of kicking.

"He might disappoint you this time," suggested Julia, "and prove treacherous, there is no certainty about it."

"He might, but he will not," was the reply, "not that I place such implicit reliance in him as I would in Bob; a look is enough for him."

"I would not trust either of them," said Julia, "I have seen Bob's teeth, and heard his growl; and as for the horse, why it was as much as you could do to mount him yesterday, when you went out with Frances. I heard Mr. Hall say he would not insure your life for a pound."

"My thanks to Hall for his kind consideration in valuing my neck at so cheap a rate. Just assure him the next time you see him that I have not the very remotest idea of having it broken yet."

"He has not the very remotest idea of riding," laughed Julia; "only imagine those long legs of his dangling like ribbons on the side of a horse."

"Where is Hall? I do not see him among the skaters, though Anne is."

"No; he has gone over to see how they are getting on in that wretched little parish of his, and tried hard to persuade Anne and me to go with him, but my sister does not care for looking over churches, even if they were built in the time of Methuselah, and preferred the skating, much to his regret, and I must confess I was not at all sorry to do the same."

"Uncle Charles, do take me for a slide, please," pleaded Fanny, again undeterred by timid Edith, pulling at her sleeve and begging her not to go.

"I would take you with the greatest pleasure in life, Fanny; but what is to become of my horse?"

"Cousin Julia will hold him. Won't you, cousin?" asked the child, flying to her side.

"I hold him?" exclaimed Julia. "No, thank you, Fanny, I value my life too well; besides, child, I should be frightened."

"Miss Neville will, then, she is so fond of horses," cried Fanny, darting off to where her governess stood.

"A fruitless errand," muttered Charles, turning on his heels, "she has not a grain of courage. I wish she had."

But as if to shame him for this assertion, or to gratify his wish, when he looked up, there stood the governess.

"I shall be happy to hold your horse for you, Mr. Linchmore," she said, while Fanny clapped her hands and capered about with delight.

"You, Miss Neville!" he repeated incredulously. "Impossible!"

"And why not? he seems to stand very quietly. Is he inclined to be vicious?"

"Vicious! Far from it. But I am afraid—"

"I will hold him," interrupted Amy, decidedly, and without hesitation, "there is nothing to be afraid of."

"Charles thinks," said Julia, maliciously, "you have not the nerve for it."

"I see no occasion for any display of nerve," replied Amy, while, with little show of opposition on his part, she took the reins from his almost unwilling hand, and before he had well recovered from his surprise, he found himself on the ice with Fanny's hand fast locked in his.

And where was Frances all this time? Had she forgotten her determination—her newly-born hatred of Amy? Had she thought better of her secret machinations? No. Time only increased her dislike; more deeply rooted her jealousy, while molehills became mountains in her eyes.

Should she see herself supplanted by a governess, one so inferior to her in wealth and station, one whom he had known but a few hours. A few hours? Was it possible so short a time could have overthrown the power she fancied she had held in his heart for years. Impossible! It could not be, and again that bitter cry arose in her heart, and she inwardly exclaimed:

"He shall not love her!"

But Frances drove back the bitter feelings at her heart, and met him as he advanced on the ice with smiles and pleasant words, as though she knew not what sorrow or unhappiness was; but Charles, although he answered her courteously enough, was absent, and often gave random replies, wide of the mark.

Secretly angry, she was not baffled, and suddenly declared her intention of taking off her skates, she would then be better able to talk to Charles than flying round about him, and putting in a word here and there. She had had enough of the amusement for one morning, would Charles kindly come and help her? He was too polite to refuse, although it took him further away from the bank where Amy still held his horse. He gave one glance as he turned away—and yet another—the latter look betrayed him. Frances saw it, and a bitter remark rose to her lips, the only one she was guilty of that day; but it came angrily and vehemently; she could not help it, could not subdue it; she would have given worlds to have afterwards unsaid it.

"Miss Neville makes a capital groom. I suppose she has been accustomed to that sort of thing."

"I never heard Miss Neville say an unkind word of any one," was the severe rejoinder.

"I shall hate myself for that false move," thought Frances. "I must try and hide my feelings better," and she raised her foot to his knee, but even while she did so, a scream from Julia made him spring to his feet.

But he was too late; his horse was plunging and rearing violently, while Amy's weak arm seemed barely sufficient to curb and control him, although she was trying her utmost to pacify and quiet him.

Charles took it all in at a glance.

"I shall love that girl in spite of myself," he said, as he sprang across the frozen surface to her side.

How tenderly anxious he was, even his voice slightly trembled as he asked the question:

"Are you hurt?"

No, she was not. But her hand dropped helplessly to her side as he drew the reins from it.

"This is the wonderfully quiet horse," cried Julia. "I never saw such behaviour; astonishing in one of his meek temper, but of course this is the first time he has ever been guilty of such tricks."

"How did it happen?" asked Charles, of Amy.

"I scarcely know, it was all so sudden."

"But something must have frightened him?"

"Yes; I fancy the sound of a horse's feet galloping by excited him, and one of the hounds rushed to his side, and then he became almost beyond my control."

His sorrow was expressed on his face, and was more expressive than any words could be. His regrets— but before he could speak those, Amy had bowed, wished him good morning, and was gone.

The sorrow faded away from his face; a vexed look succeeded. Why had she left him so hastily? Could she not have spared him a few moments wherein to express his regret. Was she angry? No, he could not think so, her temper appeared unruffled, and her face wore its usual soft and sweet expression.

As Frances advanced to his side he impatiently sprang on his horse and cantered off, but Frances thought as she stood listening to his horse's receding steps on the hard frosty ground, that ere long the canter sounded in her ears far more like a gallop.

Some twenty minutes later, as Amy was returning home through the lane, her attention was drawn towards a horseman going at headlong speed across the distant fields. The children wondered who it could be, but Amy never wondered at all; she knew well enough.

"It is your uncle," she said.

CHAPTER XIII

"Still further on she crept with trembling feet,
With hope a friend, with fear a foe to meet;
And there was something fearful in the sight
And in the sound of what appear'd to-night;
For now, of night and nervous terror bred,
Arose a strong and superstitious dread;
She heard strange noises, and the shapes she saw
Of fancied beings bound her soul in awe."
CRABBE

But few of the party returned home in the very best of spirits, or appeared to have enjoyed their afternoon's pleasure on the ice. Charles scarcely raised his eyes during dinner, or addressed a word to any one. Anne was infinitely disgusted at his inattention and dulness, having made up her mind during Mr. Hall's absence to thoroughly enjoy herself, being in no fear of a look from those earnest eyes of his, as she rattled away almost heedless of what fell from her lips, or hazarded trifling, thoughtless remarks.

Frances' face, if possible, wore a more scornful expression than usual; she was inwardly chafing at her want of tact and judgment in giving way to temper, and allowing Charles to see that Amy was the cause of it. That thought vexed her proud spirit beyond measure, and although to all appearance she was calm and self-possessed, yet inwardly her heart trembled with angry passions, and her mind was filled with forebodings and dim shadowings of the future and what it would reveal to her.

Was it possible she could be supplanted by another, and that other no proud beauty like herself, but a governess! The thought was gall and wormwood to her. It was not only her pride that was touched. No; as I have said before, she loved her cousin with all the love of that proud, and to all appearance, cold heart. Should he not love her in return? Yes, he must. He should never be Amy's. Never! And she pressed her lips together and contracted the delicately-pencilled brows at the bare supposition. She would not believe—could not—that in so short a time his heart was another's. It was merely a liking, not love, and it must be her care to prevent the latter.

What right had he in the school-room? What was he doing there when she entered so inopportunely?

Ah! she had never guessed that secret yet, or found out the theft of the "Holy work," or her heart would have been even sorer than it was, and her thoughts more bitter and revengeful towards Amy.

Frances had never been thwarted; all had as yet gone smoothly with her; the bare possibility of the one great object in life—her love—being unvalued only made her the more determined to succeed. She had no softness, no gentleness of nature; her love was fierce and strong—headlong in its course; like a torrent it swept along, and carried away all and everything that impeded its course. There was no calm, no sunshine, no breaking of the heavy clouds; all was storm—would be until the end might be gained, and then—even then, there was a question if the troubled, angry spirit would be quiet, or at rest, or ever satisfied.

Charles did not re-enter the drawing room after dinner. "Gone for a smoke or prefers the company of Bob," was Alfred's ungracious rejoinder when his sister questioned him; so retiring to an ottoman in a far-off corner, Frances wrapt herself up in her thoughts, or, as Anne remarked, made herself as disagreeable as she could by refusing to join in any one game or amusement proposed. After fruitless attempts to strike up a flirtation with somebody, Anne walked off to bed, thinking a quiet chat with her sister was preferable to the dulness below.

As she reached the first landing on her way up stairs, a gust of cold wind from the sudden opening of the hall door made her pause and look round; and presently Mr. Hall's voice reached her: very pleasant and cheery she thought it sounded, and she could not resist the temptation of peeping over, just to see how he looked after his cold ride.

Yes, there he was, close by the fire, full in the light of the lamp, shaking himself like a large dog, his thick hair in a shocking tangled mass, but this was nothing unusual.

Anne smiled. "What a figure he is!" thought she, "such a great unwieldy creature!" and then half turned, as if to retrace her steps, but woman-like, fearful lest he should guess why she returned, magnanimously went on, but on reaching her own room, no Julia was there to unburden her vexations to, or talk herself into a more congenial mood with.

"She plays me this trick every night," said she, taking off her dress and throwing a shawl round her shoulders; then stirring up the fire into a blaze, she sat down and reviewed in her own mind the events of the day and the evening's dulness.

Some minutes slipped by; and then, whether she grew tired of being alone in that large room or vexed at her sister's prolonged absence she determined on going in quest of her.

Springing up, away she went to Miss Tremlow's room, and receiving no reply to her repeated knocks for admission, cautiously opened the door and went in, expecting to find her sister.

Miss Tremlow was disrobed for the night, and had tied a large yellow handkerchief round her head, the only symptom of a cap being the huge border overshadowing her small thin face like a pall; while one or two curl-papers—Miss Tremlow wore her hair in ringlets—made themselves guiltily perceptible here and there. Anne burst out laughing.

"My goodness, Miss Tremlow! how extraordinary you look," exclaimed she. "Do you always dress yourself out in this style when you have a cold?"

"A cold, Miss Anne? I have no cold."

"Then why on earth have you decked yourself out with that handkerchief. Oh! I know, you are afraid of thieves, and think the sight will frighten them. Well, you are not far wrong there."

"No such thing; I am subject to rheumatism, so take every precaution against it," replied Miss Tremlow stiffly, not exactly knowing whether to feel offended or not.

"Of course, quite right," replied Anne, not daring to raise her eyes until Miss Tremlow turned her back, and then the corner of the bright handkerchief stood out so oddly over the high-crowned cap, while a border almost as wide and stiffly starched as the front one drooped from under it, that the incentive to mirth was irresistible, and Anne laughed again.

"I cannot help it, indeed I cannot," said she, as the lady's now angry face met her gaze. "It is of no use looking so vexed, you should not make such a figure of yourself."

"You had better go to bed, Miss Anne," said Miss Tremlow sharply, opening the door.

And very submissively Anne went out of the room, but instead of going to bed, bent her steps towards the school-room, and there found the object of her search; her sister with Miss Neville.

"Such a scrape as you have led me into, Mag," began she, still laughing, and drawing a chair near the two round the fire. "Of course I thought you were in that queer sick creature's room. What a fright she has made of herself with her head tied up in that yellow handkerchief, enough to make any one laugh."

"I hope, Anne, you did not," replied her sister.

"Then hope no such thing, for I laughed outright, and so would Miss Neville, I am sure. I defy even that sober Mr. Hall to have stood it," and again Anne laughed at the bare recollection. "It's all your fault, Mag, had you gone quietly to bed as you ought, I should never like the Caliph have roamed abroad in search of adventure."

"Why did you come up to bed so soon?" asked Julia.

"So soon! I am sure I never spent so dull an evening; I suppose people's hearts were frozen as well as their toes with coming in contact with the ice. As to Frances, she behaved abominably, and turned the cold-shoulder to everybody. If it is to be like this every evening, I would far rather have the 'short commons' of home than the dainty fare here."

"For shame, Anne! What will Miss Neville think?"

"Think that I am in a bad temper, that's all. Isabella might have tried to amuse us a little; but no, she only thought of self, sitting so cosily flirting with Mr. Vavasour. How I do dislike that man! I am sure he is no good, and no one seems to know who he is. I do wish that handsome Captain Styles were here. Do you remember last year, what fun we used to have? We never had a dull evening then," and Anne sighed, and looked so comically sad that Julia and Amy both laughed.

"It is just as well he is not here," replied the former. "And as for Mr. Vavasour, everyone knows how intimate old Mr. Vavasour and Mr. Linchmore's father were."

"Yes; but that gives no clue as to who young Mr. Vavasour is."

Who Vavasour's parents were had never transpired. All he himself knew was, that he had been left an orphan at an early age, and entrusted to Mr. Vavasour. The utmost care had been bestowed on his education; no pains, no money had been spared.

Mr. Vavasour was an eccentric, passionate old bachelor, fond and proud of his adopted son, or, as some supposed, his own son; but this latter was mere idle surmise. He was certainly treated and regarded by the servants and even friends as such; and yet they had not a shadow of proof that he was so.

It must not be imagined that Robert rested calmly, or made no attempts to obtain a clue to his history, and clear up the doubt under which his proud, impatient spirit chafed. He did. He battled and waged war at times against the other's will, when the weight became more intolerable than he could bear; but only to meet with stern rebuffs, and a will as determined as his own. In that one particular, the two resembled each other; not otherwise. In outward form they were unlike.

It was after one of these battles, in which as usual Robert was vanquished, that wounded to the quick by the other's violence, and seeing the hopelessness of ever moving that iron will, Robert left the only home he had ever known, and went abroad.

After that nothing went right. The old man fretted, grew more and more exacting to those about him, and gave way more frequently to violent fits of rage. There was no Robert to act as mediator, or control and subdue him; and few were surprised to hear of his almost sudden death. He bequeathed not only his forgiveness but his wealth to Robert, who only returned in time to follow him to the grave.

He sought amongst the old man's papers for some document to throw a light on his birth. There was none. The only letter—if such it could be called—bearing at all on the subject was addressed to his lawyer, and ran thus—

"This is to certify that Robert Vavasour is not my son, as some fools as well as wise men suppose. The secret of his birth was never made known to me. He was entrusted to my care as a helpless orphan, under a solemn promise that I would never reveal by whom. That promise I have faithfully kept, and will, with God's help, keep to the end; believing it can answer no good purpose to reveal it, but only entail much unhappiness and sorrow."

He was not the old man's son then. There was comfort in that, small as it was: perhaps after all there was no shame attached to him. It was too late to remedy now his disbelief of Mr. Vavasour's word, and the angry manner in which they had parted, but it pained and grieved him deeply; until now that he was dead, Robert had never thought how much he had loved the only friend he had ever known.

Perhaps the person who had entrusted him to old Mr. Vavasour was still alive, perhaps even now watched over him. He thought it could not be his mother; she would not have left him so long without some token of her love. He would still hope that some day his birth might be no secret, but as clear as day: yet it weighed on his mind, and made him appear older than he was, and more reserved; and his manner at times was cold and distant, with no fancy for the light talk and every-day trifles passing around him.

No wonder Anne disliked him. Here was a something which checked her thoughtlessness far more decidedly than poor Mr. Hall's sober face. The one she had no fear of, while the other's sometimes sarcastic look annoyed and vexed her, and made her anxious to escape into a far corner away from him, whenever she saw that peculiar curl of the lip betokening so utter a contempt for what she was saying. No wonder she tried to prejudice Amy against him; her pride having been wounded ever since the day she thought he had neglected her so shamefully, and walked out with Miss Neville, leaving her to fare as best she could with Mr. Hall.

Seeing Julia determined on taking his part, she turned to Amy.

"You do not like him, do you, Miss Neville? I am sure Charles is worth twenty such men as Mr. Vavasour."

"I know so little of either."

"Oh, nonsense! It is a very safe reply, no doubt, but it will not do. My cousin was here half the summer."

"Only a fortnight the first time he came; and the second visit he made, I was at Ashleigh, at home."

"Quite long enough for you to find out what a good-for-nothing, kind-hearted creature he is. Besides, for the fortnight you had the field all to yourself, and after that advantage ought not to allow another to bowl you out."

"How you do talk, Anne; I am sure Miss Neville does not understand one half you are saying, you go on at such a rate."

"Of course I do; what is the use of sitting like this?" and she clasped her two hands together on her lap and twirled her thumbs. "Do tell me what you two say to one another when I am not here, for if Mag comes every night, and I suppose she does not go to that sick-body's room, seeing she dresses herself up in a style enough to frighten half a dozen children, with the belief she is the veritable 'Bogy,' you surely do not sit like two Quakeresses, without a word, waiting for the spirit to move you. Positively, Miss Neville, I look upon Mag's coming here as an invasion of my rights, since I am left shivering in bed, and frightened to death for fear of ghosts. They do say the house is haunted; and once I nearly fainted when a coal dropped out of the fire into the fender. I really thought the ghost had come, and durst not emerge from under the bedcloths until I was pretty nearly smothered."

"You surely are not afraid of ghosts, Miss Bennet?"

"Oh, but I am, though, ghosts, hobgoblins, thieves, and every other existing and non-existing horror; and if we are to talk of such things, I vote for the door being locked. Do stir the fire, and turn up the lamp. There, it does look rather less gloomy now. But how cold it is!"

"Cold?" said Julia, "I am as warm as a toast."

"No doubt of it Mag, so cosily as you are wrapped up in 'joint-stock property.' I wonder you are not ashamed to let me see you looking so comfortable, even your feet tucked up too. Would you believe it, Miss Neville, 'joint-stock property' is that dressing-gown, and belongs to both of us, hence its name, but Mag coolly walks off with it in this most shameful way every night."

"Perhaps she thinks you do not want it."

"I suppose she does; but having, as I say a share in it, I think I might be allowed to wear it sometimes."

"By all means, Anne. Why not?" said her sister.

"Why not? You shall hear, Miss Neville, and judge whether I complain without reason. You must know Mag and I have an allowance, and we found out we could not get on without a dressing-gown; so, as we are neither of us doomed to gruel and hot water at the same time, we agreed to club together and have a joint property one, since which the number of colds Miss Julia has had is quite unaccountable and shocking. I declare to goodness the gown—look when I will—is never on the peg, but for ever round her shoulders; however, it certainly will be my turn next, for I never felt so frozen in all my life. There!" said she, sneezing, or pretending to do so, "what do you think of that signal? does it not portend stormy weather ahead? And now cease laughing, and let us go to bed, for I am awfully sleepy, and tired into the bargain; quite done up."

"And no wonder," said Julia. "Did you ever hear anyone talk as she does? She never knows when to stop."

Amy thought she never had; but it was amusing and pleasant talk; there could be no dismals where Anne was. It was light talk, but still it was pleasant, and made everyone in a good mood, or at least cheerful.

"I shall see you early to-morrow, Miss Neville," said Julia. "I have so much to say to you."

"If you do not come to bed, Mag," said Anne, from the half-opened door, "I declare I will talk in my sleep to vex you."

Amy went with them as far as the baize door which separated this wing of the house from the other rooms, and then bid good-night to her visitors.

As the light from the candle Anne carried vanished, she was surprised at seeing a dim light glimmering through the key-hole of an unoccupied room opposite. It was but momentary, yet while it lasted it threw a long, thin, bright streak of light across the corridor, full against the wall close beside where she stood.

In some surprise, she retraced her steps, and drew aside the window curtain of her room and tried to look out. But there was no moon; it was one of those dark, pitchy nights, with not a star visible, betokening either rain or another fall of snow.

Full of conjecture as to whether her eyes had deceived her or not, and feeling too timid to venture out again, Amy went to bed, and tried to imagine all manner of solutions as to the cause of the light, all of which she in turn rejected as utterly improbable. She had satisfied herself it was not the moon's rays; then what could it be?

She recalled to memory the day Nurse Hopkins showed her over the house. The picture gallery, with its secret stairs leading into some quaint old unused rooms, with their old worn-out hangings and antique furniture; ghostly-looking, and certainly dismal and solitary, in being so far removed from that part of the house now teeming with life and gaiety; yet Nurse apparently had no fear, but walked boldly on, and appeared in no hurry to emerge into the life beyond, as she talked of the former greatness of the Hall. To Amy, however, the feeling of utter loneliness, the dull, dead sound of the opening and shutting of doors, as they passed through, sent a chill to her heart. Even the jingling of the ponderous bunch of keys Nurse carried jarred against her nerves, so that perhaps her own shadow might have startled and alarmed her.

But although Nurse, in a loud tone of voice, seemed never tired of recounting the by-gone grandeur, which had been handed down to her from the sayings of former housekeepers, yet her voice had sunk into a whisper, as in passing by that door, she stopped and said, "No one ever goes in there. It was old Mrs. Linchmore's room," as if the simple fact of its having been old Mrs. Linchmore's room forbade further enquiry, and was in itself sufficient to check all idle curiosity.

Amy passed by the door whenever she went into the long corridor. The room stood at one end, facing the entire length of the passage; but the door was at the side adjoining the door of another room, and opposite the baize door, so that Amy's dress almost brushed its panels in passing by, and never could she recollect having once seen the door standing open, or the signs of a housemaid's work near it.

Perhaps the room was held sacred by Mr. Linchmore as having been his mother's; perhaps he it was who was there now, although it did seem strange his going at such an hour, being past twelve o'clock by Anne's watch when they parted. Still, it might be his peculiar fancy to go, when secure from interruption and the remarks of others.

All people had strange fancies; perhaps this was his. And partly comforted and assured with the conclusion she had arrived at, and partly wearied with the effort, Amy fell asleep.

CHAPTER XIV

MEMORIES OF THE PAST

"And the hours of darkness and the days of gloom,
That shadow and shut out joys are come;
And there's a mist on the laughing sea,
And the flowers and leaves are nought to me;
And on my brow are furrows left,
And my lip of ease and smile is reft;
And the time of gray hairs and trembling limbs,
And the time when sorrow the bright eye dims,
And the time when death seems nought to fear,
So sad is life,—is here, is here!"
MARY ANNE BROWN

Amy passed a restless night, and awoke oppressed in spirit. It was yet early, but she arose and dressed hastily, determined on seeking the fresh air, hoping that, that, would in a measure restore her drooping spirits.

It was a bright, clear morning, and Amy felt some of its brightness creep over her as she picked her way across the hard, uneven ground towards the wood. Here the trees glistened with the frost, and birds chirped among the bare boughs, or hopped fearlessly about the path. She walked on heedlessly, striking deeper into the wood, and approached, almost before she was aware of it, Goody Grey's cottage. How bleak and desolate it looked now the branches of the tall trees stripped of their green foliage waved over it; while the dim, uncertain shadows streamed through them palely, and the wind whistled and moaned mournfully as it rushed past the spot where Amy stood deliberating whether she should continue her walk or not. A moment decided her on knocking lightly at the door, but receiving no reply, she lifted the latch and entered.

Goody Grey was seated in the high-backed arm chair, but no song issued from her lips; they were compressed together with some strong inward emotion, and she either did not see, or took no notice of Amy's entrance. The ivory box stood open on the table beside her, while in her hand she held some glittering object, seemingly a child's coral. On this Goody Grey's eyes were fixed with an expression of intense emotion. She clasped it in her hands, pressing it to her lips and bosom, while groans and sobs shook her frame, choking the words that now and then rose to her lips, and she seemed to Amy's pitying eyes to be suffering uncontrollable agony. How lovingly sometimes, in the midst of her anguish, she gazed at the toy! How she fondled and caressed it; rocking her body backwards and forwards in the extremity of her emotion. Amy stood quietly in the doorway, not venturing to speak, although she longed to utter the compassionate words that filled her heart. At length, feeling that under the present circumstances her visit would only be considered an intrusion, and could scarcely be a time to offer or attempt consolation, she turned to go. As she did so, the skirt of her dress became entangled in a chair close by, and overturned it. The noise roused Goody Grey; she hastily thrust the trinket into her bosom, and started up.

"Who are you?" she exclaimed fiercely. "What do you here? How dare you come?"

"I did not mean to disturb you," replied Amy, somewhat alarmed at her voice and manner.

Goody Grey paid no heed to her words, but walked up and down the small room with hasty steps, her excitement increasing every moment, while her features became convulsed with passion; some of her hair escaped from under her cap, and floated in long, loose locks down her shoulders, while her eyes looked so bright and piercing that Amy shrank within herself as the old woman approached her, and exclaimed passionately—

"Do you think it possible a woman could die with a lie on her lips, and revenge at her heart? with no repentance!—no remorse!—no pity for one breaking heart!—no thought of an hereafter!—no hope of heaven! Do you think it possible a woman could die so?"

"No. It is not possible," replied Amy; striving to speak calmly, "no woman could die so."

"True,—true; she was no woman, but a fiend! a very devil in her hate and revenge!"

"Ah, speak not so," replied Amy, as the first startling effect of her words and wild looks had passed away. "Say not such dreadful words. If any woman could have lived and died as you say, she deserves your pity, not your condemnation."

"Pity! she'll have none from me. I hated her! she wrecked my happiness when I was a young girl, and for what? but to gratify her insane jealousy. Do you see this?" said she, taking off her cap, and shaking down the thick masses of almost snow-white hair; "it was once golden, and as fair as yours, but a few short months of—of agony changed it to what you see, and drove me mad; she worked the wreck; she caused the—the madness, and gloried in it. And yet you wonder that I condemn her?"

Her hair was the silvered hair of an old woman, and as it fell from its concealment down her shoulders almost to her feet, throwing a pale, softened, mournful shadow over her excited features, Amy was struck with the beauty of her face; she must once have been very beautiful; while her face, lighted up as it now was, was not the face of an aged woman. No; it must have been, as she herself said, a sudden, severe sorrow years ago that had helped to change that once luxuriant golden hair to grey. Her figure, as she stood confronting Amy, was slight, and by no means ungraceful; that also bore no trace of age, and although she generally walked with the aid of a thick staff, it was more to steady the weakness of her steps than to support the tottering, uncertain ones of old age.

Who? and what had caused such a wreck? It must have been some terrible blow to have sent her mad in her youth, and to have left her even now, at times—whenever the dark remembrance of it swept over her—hardly sane in more mature age. Would the divulging of the secret remove the sad weight from her heart, or quiet the agony of her thoughts? It might in a measure do so, but Amy shrank from sustaining alone the frenzy that might ensue, and as Goody Grey repeated her last question of "Do you wonder that I condemn her?" Amy, with the view of soothing her, replied gently—

"She may have lived hardened in sin, but through the dark shadows remorse must have swept at times, and stung her deeply. Besides, her life and death were most wretched, and deserve your pity more than anger."

"Had she known remorse, she never could have died so revengefully. I don't believe she ever felt its sting, and as for pity, she would have scorned it!" and Goody Grey laughed a wild, bitter laugh at the thought.

"Did she injure you so very deeply?"

"How dare you ask me that question? Are not you afraid to? Don't you know it stirs up all my worst passions within me, and sends me mad,—mad do I say? No, no, I am not mad now; I was once, but that, like the rest, is past—past for ever!" and her voice changed suddenly from its fierceness to an almost mournful sadness.

"Did you know her well?" Amy ventured to ask, notwithstanding the rebuff her last question had met with.

"Aye, did I; too well—too well! Would to God I had never seen her, it would have been better had I died first: but I live, if such a life as mine can be called living. And she is dead and I haven't forgiven her; never will; unless," said she, correcting herself, "unless—oh God! I dare not think of that; does it not bring sorrow—deep, intense, despairing sorrow, sorrow that scorches my brain?" and either exhausted with her fierce excitement, or overwhelmed with the recollection of the cause of her grief, she sank down in a chair, and covering her face with her hands, moaned and rocked herself about afresh.

For the moment Amy felt half inclined to leave her—her strange words and wild manner had so unnerved her—but a glance at the sorrow-stricken face, as it was suddenly lifted away from the hands that had screened it, decided her upon remaining for at least a few minutes longer. Perhaps the compassionate feeling at her heart had something to do with the decision, or it might be she hoped to say a few words of comfort to the sorrowing creature so relentless in her bitter feelings towards one who had evidently been remorseless in her revenge, and unforgiving even in her death; one who had injured her, if not irreparably, at least deeply and lastingly.

As Amy stood deliberating how best to shape her words so as not to irritate her afresh, Goody Grey spoke, and her voice was no longer fierce or passionate, but mournfully sad.

"I am lonely," she said, "very lonely. There are days when the thoughts of my heart drive me wild, and are more than I can bear; there are days when I feel as if death would be welcome, were it not for one hope, one craving wish. Will this hope, this wish, ever be realised? Shall I ever be any other than a broken-hearted, despairing woman?"

"The clouds may clear—sunshine may burst forth when least expected."

"May! That's what I repeat to myself day and night—day and night. The two words, 'Hope on,' are ever beating to and fro in my brain, like the tickings of that clock, and sometimes I persuade myself that the time-piece says, 'Hope on, hope on.' But only the years roll on—the hope is never realised; and soon my heart will whisper, and the clock will tick, 'no hope, no hope.'"

"Do you never earnestly pray that God will lighten the heavy load that weighs on your spirits or that He will bring comfort to your sorrowing heart?"

"Do I ever cease to pray; or is there not one fervent prayer always on my lips and heart? Day after day I bewail my sins, and ask God's forgiveness and mercy for my poor, broken, contrite heart, and sometimes I rise from my knees, feeling at peace with—with even her. But then wild thoughts come back; thoughts that utterly distract me, and which I can neither control nor prevent, and then I go mad, and don't know what I say or think. But enough of my sufferings. You can neither heal nor cure them; even now you have seen too much, and betrayed me into saying more than I ought. Tell me what led you to my cottage so early?"

"I could not sleep last night," replied Amy, "and so strolled out, thinking the air would revive me."

"It is strange you could not sleep," replied Goody Grey, speaking as she usually did to strangers, in a half solemn, impressive manner. "You who have health, youth, and innocence to help you. I seldom sleep, but then I am old and careworn. Why could you not sleep?" and she looked as though she would pierce the inmost recesses of Amy's heart.

"I can scarcely tell you why, perhaps my fancy misled me; but whatever the cause, I would rather not speak of it."

"Well perhaps it were best so, and better still if the parent bird looked after her young, when the kite may find its way to her nest."

Amy looked up quickly.

"I scarcely understand your words," she replied, "or I am at a loss to understand their meaning."

"I meant you no harm, 'twas for your good I spoke. Others have thought like you and been deceived. Others have hoped like you, and been deceived. Others have been as loving and true as you may be, and been deceived. When you think yourself the safest, then remember my words, 'when you think that you stand, take heed lest you fall.'"

There was a tone of kindness lurking beneath her words, so that Amy regretted she had spoken so hastily, and felt half inclined to tell her so, when Goody Grey again spoke.

"Who is that tall, dark, fine-looking man; a Linchmore in his walk, and perhaps his manner and proud bearing, but there the resemblance ceases; the expression of the face is different, the eye has no cunning in it, but looks at you steadily, without fear? He is brave and noble-looking. Who is he?"

"I think you must mean Mr. Vavasour," replied Amy.

"Vavasour," repeated Goody Grey, thoughtfully, "the name is strange to me, yet—stay—a dim recollection floats across my brain that I have heard the name before; but my memory fails me sadly at times, and my thoughts grow confused as I strive to catch the thread of some long-forgotten, long-buried vision of the past. Well, perhaps it is best so. Life is but a span, and I am weary of it—very weary."

"We are all at times desponding," said Amy; "even I feel so sometimes at the Hall, and there you know the house is filled with visitors, and is one continued round of gaiety."

"Yes," said Goody Grey, as if speaking to herself. "Amidst the gayest scenes the heart is often the saddest. But," continued she, addressing Amy, "your sweet face looks as though no harsh wind had ever blown across it; may it be long before a cold word or look mars its sunshine. But there is a young girl at the Hall; one amongst the many visiting there who has a proud look that will work her no good. I have warned her, for I can trace her destiny clearly. But she has a spirit; a revengeful spirit, that will never bend till it breaks. She scorned my warning and thought me mad; yet evil will overtake her, and that, too, when least she expects it. Have nothing to do with her. Avoid her. Trust her not. And now go you away, and let the events of this morning be buried in your heart. I would not that all should know Goody Grey, as you know her; think of the old woman with pity; not with doubt and suspicion."

"I will. I do think of you with pity," replied Amy. "How can I do otherwise when I have seen the anguish of your heart."

"Hush! recall not thoughts that have passed almost as quickly as they came. And now farewell, I am tired and would be alone."

As Amy came in sight of the Hall on her way home, she met Mr. Vavasour.

"Where have you been to so early?" said he; "I have watched you more than an hour ago cross the park and make for the wood, but there I lost sight of you, and have been wandering about ever since in the vain hope of finding you. Where have you been?"

But Amy was in no mood for being questioned. She felt almost vexed at it, and answered crossly—

"I should have thought Mr. Vavasour might have found something better to do than to dog my footsteps. I had no idea my conduct was viewed with suspicion."

"You are mistaken, Miss Neville, if you think I view any conduct of yours with suspicion; such an unworthy thought never entered my head. If I have unwittingly offended, allow me to apologise for that and my unpardonable curiosity which has led me into this scrape."

"Where no offence is meant, no apology is required," said Amy, coldly. "It would have been better had Mr. Vavasour remained at home instead of venturing abroad to play the spy!"

"You compare me Miss Neville, to one of the most despicable of mankind, when I am far from deserving of the epithet."

"We judge men by their actions not by their words. I have yet to learn that Mr. Vavasour did not enact the spy, when both his actions and his words condemn him."

"Be it so," replied Robert Vavasour, almost as coldly as she had spoken. "But I would fain Miss Neville had conceived a different opinion of me."

Amy made no reply, and in silence they reached the house; his manner being kind, almost tender, as he bid her farewell.

CHAPTER XV

THE GALLERY WINDOW

"Know you not there is a power
Strong as death, which from above
Once was given—a fadeless dower,
Blessed with the name of love!
On it hangs how many a tale!
Tales of human joys and woes;
Fan it with an adverse gale,
Then it strong and stronger grows.
J. B. KERRIDGE

"Such a fuss about a piece of embroidery!" exclaimed Mason, entering the servants' hall; "one would think Miss Neville had lost half a fortune instead of a trumpery piece of needle-work. I'm sure she's welcome to any of mine," and she tossed over the contents of her work-box with a contemptuous nod of the head. "I don't suppose it was very much better than this—or this!" and she drew forth an elaborate strip of work; either a careless gift from her mistress, or one of her righteous cribbings, such as servants in places like hers think it no robbery to appropriate to themselves.

"Law! Mrs. Mason, however did you work it?" asked Mary, in her simplicity.

"It's one of Madam's cast-offs, I expect," said Mrs. Hopkins, with some asperity of manner.

"It don't much signify where I got it, or who it belonged to; it's mine now, and as good, I know, as the piece Miss Neville's turning the house upside down for. Governesses always make places disagreeable; they're sure to lose something or another, and then wonder who's taken it, and then make us out a pack of thieves. I've made up my mind never to take a situation again where there's a governess."

"Does Miss Neville accuse anybody of having taken it?" asked Mrs. Hopkins, more sternly than before, and certainly more sharply.

"Well; no, Mrs. Hopkins, she doesn't exactly do that, she wouldn't dare to; but a hint's as good as a plain-spoken word sometimes. I know I could scarcely stand quiet in Madam's room just now. I did say I was surprised she hadn't lost something more valuable, and should have spoken my mind more plainly than that, but you know Madam's temper as well as I do, Mrs. Hopkins; it isn't for me to tell you; and I can't always say what I wish. She had been put out, too, about that new violet silk dress; it's been cut a trifle too short waisted—a nasty fault—and doesn't fit as it ought, so it couldn't have happened at a more awkward time. Besides, I believe Madam thinks Miss Neville an angel, so quiet and 'mum;' for my part I dislike people that can't say 'bo' to a goose; and I don't think Miss Neville would jump if a thunderbolt fell at her feet."

This remark set Mary, and Jane, Frances Strickland's maid, laughing; but not a muscle of Mrs. Hopkin's face moved as she asked—

"How did you happen to hear of the loss of the piece of work?"

"Oh! Miss Fanny came in open-mouthed to tell her Mamma of it, and said 'wasn't it strange that though they had hunted high and low for it, they could not find it.' Miss Edith accused Carlo;—you know what a rampacious dog he is;—but then they would have found some of the shreds, but not a vestige of it could they see, rummage as they would. There's the school-room bell, Mary, that's for you to hear all about it, and be put on your trial, and be frightened to death." She added as Mary left the room, "She's no more spirit in her than the cat," and she glanced contemptuously at the sleepy tortoise-shell curled up before the fire.

"Mary's plenty of spirit when she's put to it," replied Mrs. Hopkins, "she's not like some people, ready to let fly at every word that's said."

"And quite right too, I say; when words are spoke that make one's heart leap up to one's throat; but there, servants ain't supposed to have hearts or tongues neither for the matter of that now-a-days; why if a man only looks at us, we're everything that's bad, when I'm sure I'd scorn to have the lots of 'followers' some young ladies have."

"Mrs. Mason," said Mrs. Hopkins, rising with dignity, "this talk does not become you to speak, nor me to listen to; leastways I won't allow it in this room," and she rose and drew up her portly figure in some pride, and no little expression of anger on her face, while she shook out the stiff folds of her black silk dress. "If the place doesn't suit you; you can leave and get a better if you can; but not one word shall you say in my hearing against any of Madam's friends."

"Good gracious, Mrs. Hopkins, you're enough to frighten anyone. I wasn't aware I'd said anything against anybody, and I'm sure and certain if I did, I didn't mean it. I have no fault to find with my place, I'm well enough satisfied with it, but I'm not partial to Miss Neville," yet at the same time Mason gathered up her work, and thrust it hastily into the box which she closed noisily, as if the spirit was ready to fly out, if she only dare let it.

But Mason knew well enough that Mrs. Hopkins was not to be trifled with, she could say a great deal, but beyond a certain point she dare not go; for as soon as the other chose she could silence her. All her airs and assumed grandeur were as nothing, and were regarded with cool disdain and contempt, but reign paramount the housekeeper would—and did; her quiet decided way at once checked and subdued the lady's maid, and all her pertness and boasting fell to the ground, but the sweep of her full ample skirts expanded with crinoline annoyed and vexed Mrs. Hopkins much more than her words; the one she could and did check; the other she had no power over, since Mrs. Linchmore tolerated them, and found no fault.

Mason partly guessed it was so, for she invariably swept over something that stood in her way when Mrs. Hopkins was present, either some coals from the coal box, or the fender-irons, the latter were the more often knocked down as Nurse so particularly disliked the noise. Mason had even ventured upon the tall basket of odds and ends from which Mrs. Hopkins always found something to work at, and which stood close by her side as she sat sewing. It would have stood small chance now of escape could Mason have found an excuse for going near it.

"Well Mary, has the work been found?" asked Mrs. Hopkins, as the girl came back.

"No Ma'am, it hasn't; Miss Neville says she supposes she must have mislaid it somewhere," while Mason curled her lip as much as to say, "I could have told you that."

"Well, you had better go and look over your young ladies' wardrobes; there's no telling sometimes where things get put to, at all events it's as well to search everywhere."

And Mary went, but of course with small chance of finding what she sought for, as it still lay snugly enough under the shelf in Charles' desk, while he appeared totally unmindful of it or indifferent as to its existence; but then the last two days he had been indifferent to almost every thing. He could not account for Miss Neville's coldness and stiffness; surely he had done nothing to offend her, yet why had she treated him so discourteously at the lake, and turned away with scarcely a word?

He had seen her walking with Vavasour; surely if she had done that, there could be no great harm in her remaining to say three words to him. He had also seen Mr. Hall one morning hasten after her with a glove she had dropped accidentally, and she had turned and thanked him civilly enough, even walked a few paces with him; then why was he to be the only one snubbed?

It irritated and annoyed him. He thought of the hundred-and-one girls that he knew all ready to be talked to and admired. There was even his proud cousin Frances unbent to him; yet he was only conscious of a feeling of weariness and unconcern at her condescension.

Amy's manner puzzled him, and at times he determined on meeting her coldly; at others that he would make her come round. What had he done to deserve such treatment? he could not accuse himself in one single instance. But then Charles knew nothing of his sister-in-law's interference. That one visit of hers to the school-room had determined Amy on the line of conduct she ought to adopt. There was no help for it, she must be cold to him; must show she did not want, would not have his attentions, they only troubled her and brought annoyance with them. She was every bit as proud as Charles. What if he thought as Mrs. Linchmore did? She would show him how little she valued his apparent kindness, or wished for his attentions.

Ah! Amy was little versed in men's hearts, or she would have known that her very coldness and indifference only urged the young man on; and made the gain of one loving smile from her, worth all the world beside.

Charles was sauntering quietly home through the grounds from the next day's skating on the lake, when the children's voices sounded in the distance; he unconsciously quickened his steps, and soon reached the spot where they were playing.

"Another holiday!" he exclaimed, as he saw at a glance that Miss Neville was not there.

"Oh! yes, Uncle, isn't it nice. We have enjoyed ourselves so much."

"I wish I had known it," he replied, "for I would just as soon have had a game of romps with you, as gone skating. You must let me know when you have a holiday again."

"That won't be for a long time," said Edith, "Fanny's birthday comes next, and it isn't for another six months."

"Whose birthday is it to-day then?"

"No one's. We have been having a regular turn-out of the school-room, all the books taken down and the cupboards emptied, because Miss Neville has lost her work."

"Lost her work, has she?" said Charles, not daring to look the two girls in the face, as he took a long pull at his cigar, and watched the smoke as it curled upwards.

"Yes, Uncle, lost her work; such a beautiful piece she was doing; we can't find it anywhere, and Miss Neville is so vexed about it."

Vexed, was she? He wished he had taken the thimble and scissors as well. He felt a strange satisfaction in learning something had roused her, and that she was not quite so invulnerable as he thought.

"Was she very angry?" he asked.

"Miss Neville is never very angry," replied Edith, "but she looked very much vexed about it. I think she thought some one had been playing her a trick, as she would not allow Fanny to say it had been stolen."

"I dare say she will find it again. It will turn up somewhere or other; you must have another search," and away he walked, knowing full well that unless he brought it to light it never would be found, and that all search would be fruitless.

Soon after, as the children walked towards the house, they met Robert Vavasour.

"Well young lady, and where are you going to?" asked he of Fanny, who, having Carlo attached to a chain, was some way behind her sister and cousin.

"We are going home, Sir," said Fanny, with some difficulty making the dog keep up, by occasionally scolding him, which he seemed not to mind one bit, but only walked the slower, and tugged the more obstinately at his chain.

"I have a little favour to ask of you," said he, "will you grant it?"

"What is it, Sir?" asked Fanny.

"Will you wait here a few minutes until my return?"

"Yes. But oh! please don't be long."

"Not three minutes," said he, as he disappeared.

"Fanny! Fanny! are you coming?" called Edith, returning; "we are late, it is nearly four o'clock."

"I cannot come," said Fanny, "I have promised to wait for him," with which unsatisfactory reply, Edith went on and left her.

And Fanny did wait, some—instead of three—ten minutes, until her little feet ached, and her hands were blue with the cold, and her patience, as well as Carlo's, was well-nigh exhausted, he evincing his annoyance by sundry sharp barks and jumping up with his fore paws on her dress. At last, her patience quite worn out, Fanny walked round to the front of the house, where, just as she reached the terrace, she met Mr. Vavasour.

"There," said he, placing a Camellia in her hand, "hold it as carefully as you can, for it is not fresh gathered, and may fall to pieces, and take it very gently to your governess."

"Yes Sir, I will; but oh! what a time you have been, and how she will scold me for being so late, because it rang out four o'clock ever such a time ago, and Edith and Alice are long gone in."

"Then do not stand talking, Fanny, but make haste in, and be careful of the flower."

"But you must please take Carlo round to the left wing door for me, as Mamma does not like his coming in this way. You see his paws are quite dirty."

"I suppose I must, but it's an intolerable nuisance."

But the dog had not the slightest idea of losing his young mistress, and being dragged off in that ignominious way, but resisted the chain with all his might.

"Suppose we undo his chain, and let him loose," suggested Robert. "I dare say Mamma will excuse his intrusion for this once."

Away went Fanny, faithfully following out the instructions she had received, and carrying the flower most carefully, when suddenly a hand grasped her shoulder rather roughly.

"Oh! cousin Frances, how you startled me!" said Fanny.

"Where are you going to with that flower?" and she pointed to the Camellia Fanny held so gently between her small fingers.

"It's for Miss Neville, cousin."

"For Miss Neville is it? I suspected as much. Give it to me; let me look at it."

"No, it will fall to pieces. He said so; and that I was to be very careful of it; so you musn't have it."

"Who gave it you? Speak, child; I will know."

But little Fanny inherited the Linchmore's spirit, and was nothing daunted at the other's stern, overbearing manner. In fact her little heart rose to fever heat; so tossing back her long, thick hair with one hand, while with the other she put the flower behind her, and looking her tall cousin steadily in the face, she replied defiantly—

"I shan't tell you."

"How dare you say that, how dare you speak to me in that rude way; I will know who gave it to you. Tell me directly."

"No I won't, cousin."

Frances raised her hand to strike, but Fanny quailed not; she still held the flower behind her back, away from the other, and made her small figure as tall as she could, planting her little foot firmly so as to resist the blow to her utmost when it did come.

But it came not. The hand fell, but not on Fanny.

With a strong effort Frances controlled herself, and determined on trying persuasion; for she would find out where she got the flower.

Now Frances had been dressing in her room, and had accidentally seen from her window Charles talking to the children; so when she, unfortunately for Fanny, met her in the passage, and saw the Camellia, she naturally enough concluded he had sent it. If not he, who had? but she was certain it was Charles; her new-born jealousy told her so.

Still the child must confess and satisfy her, must confirm her suspicions, and then—but though Frances shut her teeth firmly, as some sudden thought flashed through her, yet she could not quite tell what her vengeance was to be, or what measures she would take; she only felt, only knew she must annihilate and crush her rival, and remove her out of her path.

"I do not want the flower, Fanny," commenced she in a low voice, meant to propitiate and coax.

"You would not have it, if you did!" replied Fanny, not a bit conciliated or deceived at the change of tone and voice.

Frances could scarcely control her anger.

"You need not hold it so determinately behind you. I am not going to take it from you."

"No! I should not let you."

"Nonsense! I could take it if I liked, but I do not want it; and I know where you got it too, Fanny."

"No you don't, cousin. I am sure you don't."

"But I do; for I saw your uncle give it you, just now."

"If you saw him, why did you bother so? But I know you did not see him. You are telling me a fib, cousin Frances, and it's very wicked of you!" said Fanny, looking up reproachfully.

At this, as Frances thought, confirmation of her doubts, her rage burst forth.

"You little abominable, good-for-nothing creature! you have the face to accuse me of telling a falsehood; I will have you punished for it. Your Mamma shall know how shamefully you are being brought up by that would-be-saint, Miss Neville."

"If you say a word against my governess," retorted Fanny, "I will tell Mamma, too; all I know you've done."

"What have I done? you little bold thing, speak!" and she grasped the child's arm again, so sharply that Fanny's face flushed hotly with the pain; but she bore it firmly, and never uttered a cry, or said a word in reply.

"Say what have I done. I will know."

"You stole Miss Neville's work," replied Fanny fearlessly. "No one thinks it's you, but I know it, and could tell if I liked."

"Tell what?"

"That you took my governess's work," repeated Fanny. "I know it was you; because I saw her put it away in her basket before we went out, and when we came home again it was gone, and she has never found it since."

"What are you talking about? I think you are crazed."

"No, I am not. What did you go into the school-room for that day, while we were out? There's nothing of yours there; and why did you look so angry at Miss Neville, when we all came upstairs, if you had not taken away her piece of embroidery to vex and annoy her."

"Was it on that day Miss Neville lost a piece of work?"

"Yes, it was only half finished, too; and you took it, you know you did."

"And you say some one took it while you were out walking?"

"Yes."

Frances lifted away her hand from Fanny's arm, where it had been placed so roughly, and let it fall helplessly to her side.

Gradually she drooped her eyes, and slowly moved away.

"It is too much," she said, with a deep sigh, while the child stood mute with astonishment at the effect of her words, she being old and wise enough to see they had not only disarmed, but wounded and hurt Frances, and stung her to the quick.

And so they had.

Frances knew well enough she had not taken the work. Was it Charles? and was that the reason why he had looked so guilty when she unexpectedly entered? It was not the mere fact of being caught in the school-room. No; it was a cowardly fear lest she should have seen the theft that had made him start, and answer at random, and appear so confused. All was accounted for now.

Yes; he it was who had taken it, and for what? She paused and looked back. Fanny was following at a respectful distance. She waited until she came up.

"You know not what you have done, child," she said, sternly, with just a slight tremble of the lips and lower part of the face. "I will never forgive you for telling me."

She went on, and the now startled child went on too, knowing full well that her governess must be growing anxious.

And Amy had grown anxious at her prolonged absence, and after awaiting Mary's fruitless search for her in the shrubbery and garden, had gone herself in quest of her, first to Julia's room, thinking she might be there, or at the least they might be able to give her some information; but neither of the sisters had, of course, seen anything of her, so Amy retraced her steps, and had reached the end of the gallery, when Charles turned the corner.

They met face to face.

He held out his hand. Amy could not refuse to take it, indeed it was all so sudden, she never thought of refusing.

"Have you hurt your hand, Miss Neville?" he inquired, seeing she held out the left, while the right was in some measure supported by the thumb being thrust into the waist belt.

"Slightly," replied Amy, and would have passed on, but he was determined this time she should not evade him.

"What is the matter with it? How did you hurt it?"

"It was wrenched," she said, hesitatingly, and a little confusedly. "I do not think there is much the matter with it."

"Wrenched!" echoed he, in some surprise. Then, all at once, the thought seemed to strike him as to how it was done, and he added, decidedly, "It was yesterday, at the lake, holding my horse. Confound him!"

Amy did not deny his assertion, indeed she could not, as it was true.

"Are you much hurt?" he asked again, in a kind voice.

"I think not. It is bruised or sprained, that is all."

"All!" he repeated, reproachfully and tenderly.

But Amy would not raise her eyes, and replied, coldly, "Yes; I can scarcely tell you which."

"But I can, if you will allow me."

And in spite of her still averted face, he drew her towards the long window, near where they were standing, she having no power of resisting, not knowing well how to, so she held out her hand as well as she was able.

He held the small, soft fingers in his, and took off from her wrist the ribbon with which she had bound it.

It was much swollen and inflamed, and was decidedly sprained. He looked closer still, until his breath blew over those clear blue veins, and he could scarcely resist the temptation of pressing his lips on them—might, perhaps, have done so—when they were both startled.

A dark shadow floated towards them, and danced in the light reflected from the windows by the last red rays of the fast fading sun, right across them.

It was Frances, returning, full of anger and wounded feeling, after her meeting with Fanny.

Scornfully she stood and looked at both, while both quailed at her glance, and the proud, angry look in her eyes.

Charles was the first to recover himself. "Miss Neville has sprained her wrist badly, Frances. Come and see."

More scornfully still, she returned his gaze, and then saying, with cutting sarcasm, "Pray do not let me disturb you," she swept on, as though the ground was scarcely good enough for her to walk on, or that her pride would at all hazards o'er master any and every thing that came in her way.

So she passed out of their sight.

"It is too much," she repeated again, "and more than I can bear," but this time there was no rebellious sigh, nothing but pride and determination struggling in her heart.

She went into her own room, and locked the door, so that the loud click of the key, as she turned it in the lock, startled again those she had left in the gallery.

"My cousin is not blessed with a good temper," remarked Charles, "though what she has had to vex her I know not, and do not much care;" but at the same time, if Amy could have read his heart, she would have seen that he was inwardly uncomfortable at her having caught him.

"I am sorry," was all Amy said, but it expressed much, as taking the ribbon from his hand, and gently declining his proffered assistance of again binding it round the injured wrist, she left him.

And Amy was sorry. She could not think she had done wrong in allowing Charles Linchmore to look at the sprain, simply because she could not well have refused him without awkwardness; besides, he took her hand as a matter of course, and never asked her permission at all; but then might not Miss Strickland imagine thousands of other things, put a number of other constructions upon finding them in the embrasure of the window together alone.

It was very evident from her manner that she had done so, and Amy shrank within herself at the idea that perhaps she also would think she was leading him on, and endeavouring to gain his heart, and he, too, as Mrs. Hopkins had told her, the inheritor of the very house she lived in.

As a governess, perhaps she had done wrong, she ought not to have allowed him to evince so much sympathy; but what if she explained to Miss Strickland how it had all happened, there would then be an end to her suspicions; her woman's heart and feeling would at once see how little she had intended doing wrong, and feel for her and exonerate her from all blame or censure.

So Amy determined on seeking an interview with Frances. It was, as far as she could see, the right thing to do; and she went; when how Frances received her, and how far she helped her, must be seen in another chapter.

VOLUME II

CHAPTER I

NEWS FROM HOME

"The smith, a mighty man is he,
With large and sinewy hands;
And the muscles of his brawny arms
Are strong as iron bands.
His hair is crisp, and black, and long;
His face is like the tan;
His brow is wet with honest sweat;
He earns whate'er he can;
And looks the whole world in the face,
For he owes not any man."
LONGFELLOW

It was just sunset as Matthew the pikeman went out to receive toll from some one passing, or rather coming quickly up to the gate.

It was market day at Brampton, so Matthew had to keep his ears open, and his wits about him, for generally he had a lazy post, with scarcely half a dozen calls during the day.

A spare thin man was the occupier of the light cart now coming fast along the road; who as he drew near the gate threw the pence—without slackening his horse's pace—at least a foot from where the other was standing.

"There's manners for you!" said Matthew, stooping to look for the money, "chucks the ha'pence to me as though I was a thief. Hates parting with 'em, I 'spose."

"Or hates touching you with the ends of his fingers," said a voice at his side.

"Good evening to yer, Mrs. Grey," said he, civilly rising and looking up, "Well, I'm blessed if I can find that last penny," and he counted over again those he held in his hand, "I'll make him give me another, next time I sets eyes on him, I know."

"What's this?" said Goody Grey, turning something over with her stick.

"That's it, and no mistake. Why I'd back yer to see through a brick wall, Ma'am."

"There!" said she, not heeding his last remark, and pointing out the cart going slowly up a neighbouring hill, "he's too proud to shake hands with his betters, now. Pride, all pride, upstart pride, like the rest of the fools in this world. And he used to go gleaning in the very fields he now rides over so pompously."

"Can yer call that to mind, Mrs. Grey?" asked Matthew, eyeing her keenly and searchingly.

"Call it to mind! What's that to you? I never said I could, but I know it for a truth."

"Folks say there's few things yer don't know," replied Matthew, somewhat scared at her fierce tone.

"Folks are fools!"

"Some of 'em; not all. Most say yer knows everything, and can give philters and charms for sickness and heart-ache and the like."

"Folks are fools!" repeated she again.

"Well I know nothing, nor don't want to; but," said he, dropping his voice to a whisper, "if yer could only give me a charm to keep her tongue quiet," and he pointed with his thumb meaningly over his shoulder in the direction of the cottage, "I'd bless yer from the bottom of my heart as long as I live."

"What blessing will you give me?"

Matthew considered a moment, as the question somewhat puzzled him. Here was a woman who had apparently neither kith nor kin belonging to her, one who stood, as far as he could see, alone in the world. How was he to give her a blessing? She had neither children, nor husband to be kind or unkind to her; she might be a prosperous woman for aught he or the neighbours knew, or she might be the very reverse. She never seemed to crave for sympathy from anyone, but rather to shun it, and never allowed a question of herself on former days to be asked, without growing angry, and if it was repeated, or persisted in, violent.

Presently Matthew hit upon what he thought a safe expedient. "What blessing do yer most want?" he asked cunningly.

"None! I want none."

"I'll give yer one Ma'am all the same. Most of us wish for something, and I'll pray that the one wish of yer heart, whatever it is, yer may get."

"How dare you wish me that?" she said in a fierce tone, "how dare you know I've any wish at all?"

"'Cos I do. That's all," replied Matthew sullenly.

"Who told you? Speak! Answer!"

"Good Lord! Mrs. Grey, ma'am; how you scare a man. Who should tell me? I don't know nothing at all about yer; how should I? All I know is that most folks has wishes of some kind or another; nobody's satisfied in this world, and in course you ain't, and so I just wished yer might be, that's all; there's no great harm in that, is there?"

"I told you folks were fools; but I think you are the biggest fool of the lot."

"Come, come, don't let's have words. I didn't mean to vex yer, you're a lone woman with not a soul to stand by yer, and the Lord knows what you've got on yer mind."

Then seeing her eyes flashed again he hastened to change the subject.

"It's a fine evening, anyhow," said he.

"We shall have rain."

"Rain!" and Matthew looked up overhead, but not a vestige of a cloud or sign of a storm could he see.

"Yes, rain, heavy rain, like the weeping of a stricken, woeful heart."

And she was passing on; but Matthew could not let her go so; he must have the charm, even at the risk of offending her again. He had thought of it for days past, it was the one wish of his heart; he had longed and sought for this opportunity and it must not slip through his fingers thus, so he said meekly, but still rather doubtfully,

"Well it may be going to rain; yer know a deal better than I do, and I won't gainsay yer? we shall know fast enough afore night closes in. And now Mrs. Grey will yer give me the charm?"

"You don't need any charm."

"Can't be done without," said he decidedly. "I've tried everything else I know of, and it ain't no use," said he despairingly.

"Well," said Goody Grey, after a moment's consideration, "do you see this box?" and she took a small box out of her pocket and filled it with some of the fine gravel from his garden, whilst Matthew looked eagerly on as if his life depended on it. "When next you are on your road to the Brampton Arms, and are close to the yew tree which grows within a stone's throw of the door, turn back, and when you reach home again take the box out of your pocket and throw away one of the stones, and don't stir forth again, save to answer the 'pike, for the rest of the evening."

"And then?" questioned Matthew.

"Then there's nothing more to be done, except to sit quiet and silent and watch your wife's face."

"Where I shall see ten thousand furies, if I don't answer her."

"You are a man, what need you care? Do as I bid you every time you are tempted to go to the Public-house; never miss once until the box is empty. Then bring it back to me."

"And suppose I miss. What then?"

"How do you mean?"

"Why; what if when I finds myself so near the door of the Public—you see, ma'am, it's a great temptation—I turns in and gets a drop afore I comes home?"

"Then you must add another stone instead of taking one away, and don't attempt to deceive me, or the charm will work harm instead of good."

Deceive her; no. Matthew had far too much faith in the charm to do that; there was no occasion for her fears.

"And is this the only charm you know of?" he asked.

"The only one. When the box is empty the cure is certain; but remember the conditions, a silent tongue and not a drop of drink; the breaking of either one of these at the time when the charm is working, and a stone must be added."

"The box'll never be empty in this world," said he, with a deep sigh; "but I'll try. My thanks to yer all the same, ma'am."

"You can thank me when you bring back the box. How is Mrs. Marks?"

"Pretty tidy, thank yer," but he looked crestfallen, notwithstanding his assertion. "I never know'd her ill; she's like a horse, always ready for any amount of work, nothing knocks her up."

"Sometimes the trees we think the strongest, wither the soonest," said Goody Grey passing on, while Matthew leant against the gate and counted the stones in the box.

"There's eight of them," said he. "I wish it had been an uneven number, it's more lucky. Eight times! More than a week. It'll never be empty—never!" then he looked up and watched Goody Grey almost out of sight, and as he did so her last words came across him again.

What did she mean by them? Did she mean that his old woman was going to die? Then he considered if he should tell her, and whether if he did she would believe it, and take to her bed at once, and leave him in quiet possession of the cottage and his own will; somehow his heart leaped at the thought of the latter, although he shook his head sadly while the former flashed through him.

"There's mischief abroad somewhere, Mrs. Marks," said he, entering the cottage.

"Was when you was out," retorted she; "but it's at home now, and likely to remain so for to-night."

"Who was talking of going out? I'm sure I wasn't. I never thought onc't of it, even."

"Best not, for you won't as long as I know it. You were drunk enough when the young master passed through the 'pike to last for a precious sight to come; you're not going to make a beast of yourself to-night if I can help it."

Mrs. Marks was scrubbing the table down. She was one of those women who, if they have no work to do, make it. She was never idle. Her house, or rather cottage—there were only four rooms in it—was as clean as a new pin; not a speck of dirt to be seen, and as to dust, that was a thing unknown; but then she was always dusting, scrubbing, or sweeping. Matthew hated the very sight of a brush or pail, and would have grumbled if he dared; but he dared not; he was thoroughly henpecked. Had he been a sober man this would not have been the case; but he was not, and he knew it, and she knew it too; and knowing his weak points she had him at her mercy, and little enough she showed him. He answered her fast enough sometimes, but he dared not go in opposition to her will, even when he came reeling home from the Public-house. Appearances were too against him: he being small and thin, she a tall, stout, strong-looking woman. Certainly the scrubbing agreed wonderfully with her, and there seemed little prospect of Goody Grey's prophecy being verified.

"Who was it passed through the 'pike, just now?" asked she.

"White; as owns the Easdale Farm down yonder, with no more manners than old Jenny out there—the donkey,—she lets her heels fly, but I'm blessed if this chap don't let fly heels and hands both."

"Chap!" reiterated Mrs. Marks, "where's your manners? He's a deal above you in the world."

"May be. But Goody Grey don't say so. She says he was no better nor a gleaner time gone by."

"She!" replied Mrs. Marks, contemptuously. "What does she know about it? She's crazed!"

"Crazed! no more nor you and I. She's a wise woman, and knows a deal more than you think."

"I am glad of it," said Mrs. Marks sneeringly, "for it's a precious little I think of either her or her sayings."

"She went through the 'pike same time as 'other did, and told me all about him."

"Why don't you be minding your own business, instead of talking and gossiping with every tom-fool you meet."

"She's no woman to gossip with, or fool either; she made me tremble and shake again, even the fire don't warm me," said he, lighting his pipe and settling himself in the chimney corner.

"I'll take your word for her having scared you. There's few as couldn't do that easy enough."

Matthew's hand went instinctively into his pocket; he could scarcely refrain from trying the effect of the charm, but it was growing dusk, and he was afraid that for that night at least it was too late.

"Wait a bit," said he in a low voice, "Wait a bit;" but his wife heard him.

"Was that what she said?" asked she.

"No, she said—" and Matthew took the pipe out of his mouth so that he might be heard the plainer, "she said; 'all trees wither the first as looks fat and strong.' That's what she said."

"Trees fat and strong! Are you muddled again?"

"No, I'm not," replied he doggedly, "that's what she said, and no mistake; the very words, I'll take my oath of it; and if you don't see the drift of 'em I do."

"Let's hear it."

"Well," said Matthew solemnly, "she meant one or t'other of us was going to die," and he looked her full in the face to see how she would take it, expecting it would alarm her as it had done him.

Mrs. Marks put down the scrubbing brush, and resting her arms on the table returned his gaze.

"Oh! you poor frightened hare," she said, "So you think you are going to die, do you? Well I'd have more spirit in me than to list to the words of a mad woman."

His astonishment may be better guessed at than described. He had so entirely made up his mind that his wife was the one Goody Grey had so vaguely hinted at, that he never deemed it possible any one could think otherwise; least of all Mrs. Marks herself: he glanced downwards at his thin legs, then stretched out his arms one after the other and felt them, as if to satisfy himself that he had made no mistake, and that he really was the spare man he imagined.

"No, you're deceiving yourself," said he, "I'll declare it wasn't me she meant. She said fat, I call it to mind well; and I'm as thin as the sign post out yonder and no mistake."

Then he glanced at the stout, strong arms of his wife, now fully developed with her determined scrubbing. "If she meant anyone," said he decidedly, "she just meant you!"

"Me!" screamed Mrs. Marks, "Is it me you are worriting yourself about, you simpleton? There, rest easy; I'm not afraid of her evil tongue; not that I suppose I've longer to live than other folks: I'm ready to go when my time comes and the Lord pleases; but I'm not to be frightened into my bed by Mrs. Grey or any woman in the parish. No, she's come to the wrong box for that. I'll hold my own as long as I have the strength for it, and am not to be ousted by any one; not I!" and Mrs. Marks nearly upset the pail in her violence, as she swept the scrubbing brush off the table into it.

"Hulloa!" cried a voice, as the latch of the door was lifted, and a stout strong-looking man entered with a good-humoured, cheerful face. "Anybody at home? How are you Mrs. Marks? I'm glad to see you again, and you too," he said, grasping and shaking Matthew's hand heartily.

"It's William Hodge of Deane!" said she in surprise, "Who'd have thought of seeing you down here, and what brings you to these parts?"

"Business," replied the other laconically.

"Something to do with the Smithy, eh?" questioned Matthew.

"Just so."

"You still keep it on, of course."

"Of course."

"There don't stand there cross-examining in that way," called Mrs. Marks, as she opened a cupboard at the further end of the room, "but attend to your own business, and just go and draw some ale, while I get a bit of bread and cheese ready. Supper won't be served up yet," said she apologetically, returning and spreading a clean snow white cloth on the table; "but you must want a mouthful of something after your long journey."

"I can't wait supper, I'm in too great a hurry; thank yer all the same."

"Are you going further on?" asked Matthew, coming in with the ale.

"No. I'm to put up at the Brampton Arms for the night, or may be two—or perhaps three," he replied.

"I'm sorry for that," said Mrs. Marks. "I hate the very name of the place. They're a bad set, the whole lot of 'em."

"That don't signify a rap to me. I shan't have nothing to do with any of 'em so long as they let's me alone, that's all I care about. I shan't trouble 'em much 'cept for my bed."

"And now for a bit of news about home," said Mrs. Marks, as her visitor began his supper, or rather the bread and cheese she had set before him. "How are they all down at Deane? And how's mother?"

"I'm sorry to say I've no good news of her; she've been ailing some time, and the doctor's stuff don't do her no good; he says she'll go off like the snuff of a candle. But there, she's precious old now, and well nigh worn out. I've a letter from your sister Martha—Mrs. Brooks—telling yer all about it;" and he searched and dived into his deep pockets for it, and then handed it to her.

"Is Jane as queer as ever?" asked Matthew, in a low voice, as his wife was perusing the letter.

"Yes, worse nor ever, I think; scarce ever opens her lips, and stares at yer awful, as though she had the evil eye."

"I always thought she had; she wor as strange a woman as ever I set eyes on."

"Well!" said Mrs. Marks, looking up from her letter, "I suppose I must say yes. Perhaps you'll just look in, Mr. Hodge, when the time comes for you to go back to Deane, and I'll give you the answer."

"I won't fail," replied he.

"What are yer going to say yes to?" asked Matthew.

"Martha says mother's dying, and she wants to know what's to become of Jane, and if she can't come here."

"Here!" exclaimed Matthew. "The Lord save us."

"Save you from what?" asked Mrs. Marks angrily.

"From having a crazed creature in the house. Who knows but what she might burn the house down about us; Mr. Hodge says she ain't no better in the head than she used to be."

"If she was ten times as bad as she is, she should come. It's a sin and a shame to hear you talk so of your own wife's sister and she nowhere to go to, and the cottage big enough to hold her."

"Why can't your sister Martha take her?"

"Just hear him talk," said she, derisively, "and Martha with more children than she knows what to do with; and a husband as is always ailing. Why you've no more charity in you than a miser; there, go and draw some more ale, and have done with your folly. Least said is soonest mended."

Mrs. Marks had two sisters and a mother living at Deane, some forty, or it might be more miles, from Brampton. Martha, the youngest, was married, and blessed—as is too often the case with the poor, or those least able to afford it—with nine children, and a sick husband; the latter worked hard enough when his health permitted, but then there was no certainty about his being able to earn wages. A cold caught and neglected had given him a fever and ague, and the least chill brought on a return of it. His wife, almost as energetic a woman as her sister, Mrs. Marks, but with a more mild and even temper, earned a living by washing, and did the best she could to keep them all; and her management certainly did her credit, her house being as clean as Mrs. Marks', although not so constantly scrubbed or washed.

The other sister, Jane, lived with her mother, an old woman of seventy-five, who, until now, had borne her age well, and looked certainly some ten years younger, but then she had always enjoyed the best of health; was up betimes in the morning, summer and winter, and about her small farm and dairy, which she managed better than most did with half-a-dozen hands to help them.

Ever busy, and uncommonly active, her illness was totally unlooked for, and least expected by Mrs. Marks, who read and re-read her sister's letter several times, to assure herself there was no mistake; that she really was struck with paralysis and not expected to survive many days, and then what was to become of Jane? Jane, who was so totally dependent on others, who lived as it were on sufferance, rarely doing work, or helping her mother in any way, or interesting herself in any one single thing. If she willed it she worked, if not, she remained idle; her mother never grumbling or finding fault, while the girl who helped her was severely rated as an idle good-for-nothing if any one portion of her daily work was neglected.

There were days when Jane would milk the cows, churn the butter, even scour out the dairy itself, and work willingly and well—she had been out to service in her youth—but these days were few and far between; she usually roamed about at her will, sometimes half over the parish, or else sat at home perfectly quiet and silent knitting, she never did any other kind of needlework; or if unemployed she would clasp her hands together over her knees, her eyes either fixed on vacancy, or restlessly wandering to and fro, to all appearance, as the neighbours said, not exactly a daft woman, but one whose mind was afflicted, or had been visited with some heavy calamity, the weight of which bore her to the ground, and was at times more than she had strength to bear or battle against.

Such was the sister Mrs. Marks had determined on befriending, there being little doubt she would carry out her intention, notwithstanding Matthew's decided aversion to it; and that Jane would ere long be in quiet possession of the one spare room in the cottage.

William Hodge, her present visitor, also came from Deane, and kept the small blacksmith's shop, or parish smithy. He had two sons, one a good-for-nothing, ne'er-do-weel. Also, well probably a sorrow and constant anxiety to his parents, who had been absent from home now for several months, and at his wife's earnest solicitations Hodge had come down to Brampton to seek him, they having heard accidentally of his being there or somewhere in the neighbourhood.

"How's Mrs. Hodge, and your sons?" asked Mrs. Marks, as Matthew went off once more for the ale.

"Sons!" he repeated. "Ah! there's the rub, you've hit the right nail on the head now. Richard, as works the smithy is as good a lad as ever breathed; but Tom's turned out bad, and between you and I, 'tis he I've come all this way to look after. I'd turn my back upon him and have nothing more to do with him; but there, one can't always do as one wishes."

"Is Tom down here?"

"I've heerd so."

"What's he doing?"

"No good, that you may be sure," replied he, "since he's here on the sly. I'm afeard he's got into bad company, and gone along with a terrible bad lot. The old woman thinks he's turned poacher, and most worrits and frets herself to death about it; so I've come to try and find him, and get him back home again, that is if I can. It'll most break his mother's heart if I don't."

"God grant he isn't with them as murdered poor Susan's husband?"

"Amen," replied he solemnly.

"One of 'em got hanged for that, God rest his soul, though he deserved it; but there's lots of 'em about; they say the gang is more desperate like since then, and have vowed to have their vengeance on Mr. Grant, the Squire's head keeper, but there, it don't do to tell yer all this; bad news comes fast enough of itself; we'll trust and hope Tom isn't with none of these."

"Well, we've all got our troubles," said Mrs. Marks again, seeing he made no reply. "I begin to think those as has no children is better off than those as has 'em."

"Ye've less trouble, no doubt of it."

"Less trouble! oh, I've mine to bear as well as the rest of yer; why there's Matthew, with no more spirit in him than a flea, and all through drink. He'll go off to the public, though 'tis half a mile and more away, whenever my eyes isn't on him."

"That's bad."

"Bad! It's worse than bad. Here's mother dying, Jane not to be trusted to come here alone, and Matthew not able to take care of himself no more than a baby! How I'm to manage to get to Deane I don't know, nor can't see neither how it's to be done."

"If I was you, I'd go somehow. They'll think badly of you if you don't, and as for Marks, leave him to get drunk as oft as he likes, for a treat; I'll wager my life on it, he'll be sober when he sees your face again, my word on it."

This, to Hodge's mind, was satisfactory reasoning enough; but not so to Mrs. Marks. She would like to know who was to take care of the 'pike, during her absence, if Matthew was unable to do so? This was a question Hodge had not foreseen, and when asked, could not reply to. However, after a little more talking, they came to the friendly arrangement that Mrs. Marks should start on the morrow for Deane; Hodge, in the meanwhile, keeping house with Marks, while she was absent; her stay, not under any circumstances whatever, to extend beyond a week.

It was an arrangement that satisfied both parties, as on considering the matter over, Hodge thought it was just as well he did not put up at the inn for any length of time, his being there might be noised abroad, and, although he intended passing under a feigned name, still Tom might easily recognise a description of him, be on the alert, and keep aloof until all was quiet again.

Mrs. Marks gave him sundry pieces of advice as to how he was to manage while she was at Deane, and among other things, cautioned him to beware of trusting Marks too much about Tom.

"If you take my advice," said she, "you won't tell him a word about him, that's if you want it kept quiet, I never trust him with a secret. He's the man for you if you want a bit of news spread, why it would be all over the parish in—well, I'd give him an hour's start, then I'd walk after him, and hear it all over again from everybody's mouth I met. It's ten times worse when he's got a drop of drink in him, then he'll talk for ever, and you'll may-be hear more than you care to, so mind, I caution you to be wary."

"I shan't wag my tongue, if you don't," replied Hodge.

"I!" exclaimed Mrs. Marks, indignantly. "I mind my own business, which I've plenty of, I can tell you, and don't trouble my head about other people's; let everybody take care of their own, which it's my belief they don't, or there wouldn't be so many squabbles going on in the village at times."

"You're a wise woman, Mrs. Marks."

"True for you," said Matthew, returning, "I'll back her agin a dozen women, twice her size."

"Hold your tongue, you simpleton," said his wife, "and give me the ale here; you've been a precious time drawing it. What have you been about?" added she, eyeing him suspiciously.

"Been about? Why just tilting the barrel, there ain't enough left to drown a rat in."

"Why don't you say a mouse, or som'ut smaller still. If I'd had my senses about me, I'd never have trusted you within a mile of it," said she, handing the mug to Hodge.

"I'll swear I arn't tasted a drop. I'd scorn to drink on the sly," replied Marks, attempting to look indignant, and glancing at his visitor.

"There, don't straiten your body that way, and try to look big, you meek saint, you! as scorns to drink on the sly, but don't mind telling a lie straight out; there ain't anybody here as believes you, leastways I don't. Why Mr. Hodge," said she, taking the empty mug from his hand, "you'd think I was blessed with the best husband as ever breathed, instead of the greatest rogue. Why you'd be a villain, Marks, if it warn't for knowing your wife's eye's always on you. You're afeard of it, you know you are."

"I'm a devilish deal more afeard of som'ut else; a 'ooman's eye only strikes skin deep, but her tongue do rattle a man's bones and make his flesh creep," muttered Matthew, turning away.

"There don't settle yourself in the chimney corner again, but come and help Mr. Hodge on with his great-coat. Hear to the wind how it's rising; 'tis a raw cold night outside, I take it."

"It's drenching with rain," said Hodge, as he stepped over the threshold and pulled up the collar of his coat preparatory to facing the rain, which was coming down in torrents.

"Rain!" exclaimed Matthew, as his wife closed the door on her visitor. "Who'd have thought it? But there, she said it would rain. Oh! she's a true prophet, is Goody Grey, and no mistake. I said she was a fearful 'ooman, and know'd most everything. The Lord save and deliver us, and have mercy upon us! for we none of us know," and he glanced at Mrs. Marks, "what's going to happen. Good Lord deliver us from harm."

"There go and put the pot on to boil for supper," said Mrs. Marks, turning on him sharply, "and don't stand there a chaunting of the psalms'es."

And with deep sighs and many inward groans, Matthew went and did his wife's bidding, but the psalms seemed uppermost in his mind that night; he seemed to have them at his fingers' ends.

CHAPTER II

A FRIENDLY INTERFERENCE

"No tears, Celia, now shall win
My resolv'd heart to return;
I have searched thy soul within,
And find nought but pride and scorn;
I have learn'd thy arts, and now
Can disdain as much as thou."
CAREW

Men fall in love every day, yet few of them like to be caught talking or acting sentimentally towards the object of their affections.

Charles was inwardly vexed at Frances' sudden appearance, and still more so at the sarcastic way in which she had spoken and acted. What business was it of hers to take either himself or Miss Neville to task? Was it not partly his fault the wrist was sprained, and would he not have been wanting in common politeness had he, when he accidentally discovered it, not tried in some measure to remedy it?

It was a bad sprain, there was no doubt about that, although she made light of it.

It ought to be looked to; but how to procure proper surgical attention puzzled him. Somehow he did not quite like being the bearer of the tidings to his brother's wife; he could fancy how proudly and contemptuously she would raise her head, and look him through with her dark flashing eyes; and how quietly—very differently from Frances—hint her displeasure at his interference, and turn his fears and sympathy into ridicule. He could not stand that; no, he was ready to face any open danger, but the covert, sarcastic glance and mocking smile of his sister-in-law was a little beyond even his courage. Yet it was necessary she should be informed of it if Amy was to be helped, which he had made up his mind she must be. How then was it to be managed?

Ideas and plans crowded into his brain one after another, but all more or less impracticable; as he stood at the window, where Amy had left him, hopelessly entangled in a web of perplexing thoughts.

There was, as I said, no restraining Anne's curiosity, she always gratified it, or tried to do so, whatever the risk. Certainly, if curiosity is, as we are told, a woman's failing, and men take every opportunity of reminding them of the fact, or rather laying it at their door, whether they will or not, Anne claimed a large portion of it. Why women should be thought to have a larger share of curiosity than men remains to be proved; surely if it be a sin, it is a very small one in comparison to the long list of sins of greater magnitude not laid to their charge, and if not to woman; then to whom do they belong?

Anne had heard voices in the gallery, and had opened her door just sufficiently wide to allow of her obtaining a sight of those who were talking, and notwithstanding sundry hints from Julia as to the disgraceful way in which she was acting, she determined to see the end, let the cost be what it might. She could not hear what was said, but there could be no harm in just peeping and seeing what was going on.

It was with no little astonishment that she watched Charles and Amy apparently on such intimate terms of acquaintance, when the latter had only assured her the night before that she scarcely knew her cousin to speak to. Subsequently, Frances' arrival on the scene, and evident anger and scorn, astonished her still more.

That Miss Neville was a flirt had crossed her mind ever since the day she had caught her coming home with Mr. Vavasour; but here she was apparently hand and glove with Charles. She did not see cause for any such display of temper as Frances had made; still, she thought it a shame Miss Neville should take all the men to herself, when there were lots of other girls in the house ready to be made love to, now, of necessity, left to their own devices, and dull enough in consequence.

Anne began to think Miss Neville was not acting fairly, and certainly not openly. Why should she have two strings to her bow, while Anne could not conjure up one, for she counted Mr. Hall as nobody, and disdainfully thrust the thought of him aside, as his image presented itself in full force; even as she had gazed at him but last night, over the balusters drenched to the skin, looking the true personification of a country parson, but totally dissimilar to the beau ideal of Anne's imagination, which she had snugly enshrined somewhere in a small corner of her heart. It seemed ridiculous to imagine him falling in love, and least of all with her, who had determined on marrying a man with fierce moustaches and whiskers, and these Mr. Hall could never have. No, he should not fall in love with her; she would not have it.

Why should such an uncouth being be always dangling after her, while Miss Neville, with no trouble at all, came in for all the loaves and fishes, and she obliged to content herself with the fragments? If all the beaux in the house were to be monopolised in this style, it was time Mrs. Linchmore invited others who would be able to look at Miss Neville without immediately falling down and worshipping her, as though she were an angel. She had no intention of losing her temper, as Frances had done, but she did not see why she should not let Charles know she had seen him, so out of her room she marched at once, and went up straight to where he still stood by the window.

"What on earth have you done to offend Frances?" asked she, beating about the bush, "she looks as surly as a bear."

"I might ask you that question, seeing she had evidently been put out before I saw her."

"I was peeping through a crack in the door, and could not help laughing to see the rage she was in."

"She may remain in it, and welcome, for aught I care," replied Charles, trying to appear indifferent, but at the same time showing some slight symptom of temper.

"So may somebody else," said Anne; "but you know very well she was mortified at seeing you hold Miss Neville's hand, and—and—I don't think it was right of you, Charles."

He looked up as if he could have annihilated her. "I am the best judge of my own affairs," said he, slowly, "and as for Miss Neville, it is impossible she could do wrong."

"I do not accuse Miss Neville of doing wrong; but I think my cousin, Mr. Charles Linchmore, is playing a double game."

Charles bit his lip, but made no reply.

"You may take refuge in a sneer," continued Anne, somewhat hotly, "and play with Frances' feelings as much as you like, and as much as you have done, and few will trouble their heads about it; but it's a shame to carry on the same game with a governess, who cannot help herself, and is obliged, nay expected, to put up with slights from everybody."

"Not from me, Anne."

"Yes, from you, who are making love to two girls at the same time."

"How dare you accuse me of so dishonourable an action?" exclaimed Charles.

"Dare? Oh, I dare a great deal more than that," replied Anne, tossing her head.

"Any way, you could not accuse one of much worse."

"It is the truth, nevertheless, and I cannot see that there is anything daring about it. The daring is not in my speaking, but in your own act."

"I never made love to Frances, or if I did, her own cold pride annihilated any partiality I might have had for her."

"Partiality!" uttered Anne, sarcastically, "Defend me from such partiality from any man. I wonder you did not say flirtation; but even your assurance could not summon courage to tell such a fib as that."

"A truce to this folly, Anne, or I shall get angry, and you can't convince me I ever—" he hesitated a moment—"loved Frances. Allowing that I did show her a little attention, I don't see she is any the worse for it."

"You have succeeded in making her miserable, although you have not broken her heart, and now want to play Miss Neville the same trick; but I won't stand by and see it, I declare I won't; my woman's heart won't let me; so, if you begin that game, we wage war to the knife. I cannot help pitying Frances, whom I dislike, and will not, if I can help it, have to pity Miss Neville also."

"There is no reason why you should. Miss Neville is superior to a dozen like Frances." Anne opened her eyes at this, but wisely held her tongue. He went on,

"I swear, Anne, I'll never give you reason to pity Miss Neville; but she has sprained her wrist, I think very severely. That confounded brute was the cause of it."

"Man or beast?" she asked. "'Tis difficult to know which you mean."

"My horse," replied he, determined not to be laughed into a good temper. "She would hold him at the lake when I asked her not to; but women are so obstinate, they will have their own way; there is no reasoning with them. I would not have allowed her if I could have foreseen what was going to happen, but how could I? and now the mischief is done, and she is pretty considerably hurt."

"All her own fault, according to your account, so why should you vex yourself about it? Men generally send us to 'Old Harry' under such circumstances."

"But I consider it to have been partly my fault; I was a fool to allow her to hold the horse, and a still greater one, inasmuch as now the mischief is done, I am unable to help her."

"In what?"

Charles made no reply; he was thinking could Anne help him in his difficulty? She might if she liked, but would she? Could he trust her? as in evincing so much sympathy for Miss Neville would she not partly guess at his secret liking for her—if she had not guessed it already?

Anne was good-natured and truthful enough; had she not just plainly told him he had done wrong? but that he would not allow of for a moment. It was the natural thing to do, and would have been done by any one under similar circumstances. How could he help being sorry? how could he help feeling for her? Dr. Bernard must be sent for, the sprain might get worse. Charles, like most men when their minds are set on attaining any one object, determined on carrying his point. The more difficult the accomplishment the more resolute was he in attaining it, and clearing all obstacles that stood in his way.

"I'm going to Standale," said he, suddenly looking up.

"To Standale! You have just three hours to do it in; we do not dine before eight, so I dare say you will manage it."

"Yes. Have you any commissions?"

"None, thank you. It will be too dark for you to match some wool for my sister. I know she wants some. Men invariably choose such unseasonable hours for their jaunts, when they know it is impossible for women to load them with commissions."

"Do you not think it would be as well to mention to my brother's wife that I am going to Standale? She might like Dr. Bernard to call to-morrow and see Miss Neville, and prescribe for that injured wrist."

"Nonsense, Charles! It cannot be so bad as that; and besides, you said it was caused entirely through her own obstinacy, so let her bear it as best she may, as a just punishment for her sins."

Then seeing he looked serious and a little annoyed, she added, "Of course you can do as you like about it."

"I shall be ready to start in less than ten minutes," replied he. "You can meet me in the hall, and let me know the result of your communication with Mrs. Linchmore."

"That is what I call cool," said Anne, as Charles vanished; "he does not like to tell Isabella herself, so makes me the bearer of the unpleasant news, and I dare say thinks I am blind and do not see through it. Well, the cunning of some men beats everything. I believe the wretch is fast falling in love with Miss Neville, if he is not so already. At all events, it strikes me, cousin Frances stands a very good chance of being cut out; so she had better control her temper instead of allowing it to get the better of her as it did to-day."

Then, as if a sudden thought struck her, she turned and darted away after Charles.

"I tell you what it is," said she, breathlessly, coming up with him, "I do not mind doing this little act of mercy for you; but at the same time I must first go and see Miss Neville. It would never do to have Isabella asking me how she looked? What was the matter with her? and lots of other questions, that I could not answer; so you must have patience and give me half-an-hour's start."

"Half-an hour!" cried he, looking at his watch. "Why it is nearly five o'clock now."

"I must have half-an-hour, I ought to have said an hour. Why, if it is so late, not put off your journey to Standale until to-morrow. Is your business there so very pressing?" asked she, slyly.

"Yes. I must go this evening," replied he, evading her look.

"Men are so obstinate, there is no reasoning with them. Is not that what you said of Miss Neville?"

"This is quite a different thing."

"Oh! of course, quite different, when it suits your convenience; but I am not convinced."

"Women never are," muttered Charles, turning on his heel.

In the meanwhile Fanny had carried the flower in safety to her governess, her little mind full of wonderment as to what her cousin Frances could have meant; why she had looked so strangely and spoken still more so?

Children are great observers, and often think and see more clearly than their elders give them credit for. So it was in the present instance. Fanny felt certain her cousin did not like Miss Neville should have the flower, that she was jealous of her, and disliked her; and the child settled very much to her own satisfaction that it was all because her governess was so pretty, and had such lovely hair; even more golden than Edith's, while Frances' was as nearly approaching black as it well could be.

Amy was a little indignant on seeing the flower, and hearing from Fanny that "he had sent it to her." She recognised the Camellia at a glance. It was the one Robert Vavasour had gathered for her in the greenhouse; she knew it again, because in arranging the bouquet for Mrs. Linchmore its stem had been too short, and she had added a longer one, and secured it by winding a piece of thread round; it was there still, while some of the pure white leaves of the flower were becoming tinged with brown; evidences of the length of time it had been gathered.

"He said it was not quite fresh," said Fanny watching her governess, as she thought noticing its faded beauty, "but I thought you would like it just as well, because you are so fond of flowers."

"Who desired you to give it me?"

"That tall dark gentleman who walked home with us one day, the day you lost your embroidery." Fanny could not get the latter out of her mind, it was uppermost there.

It was Mr. Vavasour, then who sent it; and why?

Amy remembered his having asked for the flower she had gathered for Mrs. Linchmore, and her refusal to give it. Had he now sent it to show her that another, even Mrs. Linchmore, had been more willing to oblige him than she had; as also how little value he placed on the gift? Or probably their meeting in the greenhouse had escaped his memory, and perhaps he merely wished to please her, seeing how fond she was of flowers, and thought any flower, however faded, was good enough for a governess.

As she stood by the fire her hand unconsciously wandered towards the bars; in another moment the poor flower would have been withered, the heat would have scorched it.

"Oh! don't burn it, Miss Neville, please don't," exclaimed Fanny. "It isn't half dead yet; and I have had such trouble in bringing it you safely, because cousin Frances wanted it."

"Miss Strickland?"

"Yes. She got in such a rage, you never saw anything like it; but I would not let her have it. I was determined she should not. She knew it was for you too, and it was that made her so angry. She told a fib as well, for she said she saw Uncle Charles give it me, and you know it was Mr. Vavasour."

"Did you tell her so?"

"No" replied Fanny, triumphantly, little thinking how every word was grieving her governess. "No, I didn't; she tried very hard to make me say, but I wouldn't; see," said she, baring her arm, "I'll show you what she did. There! see that; only look, Miss Neville," and she pointed to some deep blue marks, plainly the impression of four lines like fingers, "wasn't it spiteful and naughty of her?"

Amy looked up in surprise and compassion. Was it possible Miss Strickland, usually so calm could have so far lost her temper, as to hurt her so severely. Spiteful? yes it was worse than spiteful, it was wicked. If she had shown so little mercy to a child who could not have intentionally harmed her what would be the result of the appeal she meditated making to her womanly feelings? would she feel for her and help? she who had shown none for a helpless child? Amy's heart sank within her, and she began to fear she was in a sea of troubles, that would take a wiser head than hers, and a stronger hand and heart to extricate her from.

And all this time the little girl stood with bared arm before her governess, waiting for and claiming her pity, while the four blue marks seemed more plainly visible each time Amy looked at them.

Would Miss Strickland ever wound her as deeply? Words she did not care for, they were often lightly spoken, and soon perhaps regretted or forgotten; but acts were different things, they caused injuries, and heart-aches to last a life-time. They might like words be regretted, but could never be recalled, causing irreparable mischief.

Fanny's arm gave Amy a disagreeable insight into Frances' character, one that was altogether new and unexpected. Julia Bennet had often spoken of her, and always from the first as a proud, cold girl, wrapped up in self, with no interest in the every day cares of life, or affection for home ties or duties; but fond of society, and caring for little beyond it, living in the world and only for its approval and worship; a being neither exacting nor demanding homage, but taking it to herself as a matter-of-course and right, yet it was evident to Amy, that though she assumed the appearance of a goddess, she, like many a Homeric deity, was affected with a mortal's worse passion—revenge, and Amy shivered slightly as she thought of the coming interview, fearing an explanation might be more difficult than she had imagined, and that instead of a few quiet words, it might be a stormy warfare.

"You must have your arm bathed, Fanny," she said, putting the sleeve down in its place again, and hiding from sight the ugly marks. "I am sadly afraid you must have been very naughty for Miss Strickland to have punished you so severely. Why was she angry with you? What did you do to annoy her?"

"Nothing, Miss Neville. She tried to make me tell her who sent you the flower; and because I would not she got angry, and wanted to snatch it from me. It was cousin Frances began it all; she caught hold of me as I was coming along quite quietly, and never thinking of her at all."

"But you must have vexed her, Fanny. It is impossible she could have injured you so severely without."

"Well, perhaps I did, a little—only just a little. I found out," said Fanny, looking down, "something she thought was a secret, and only known to herself, and she could not bear to think I knew it."

"You found out a secret?"

"Yes," replied Fanny, hesitatingly; "but I must not tell you what it is, Miss Neville. Please don't ask me."

"I will not, Fanny; but at the same time I hope it is nothing wrong that will not bear the telling. I am sadly afraid that appearances are against you. I fear now more than ever that you must have seriously offended or wounded Miss Strickland. Are you sure, quite sure, Fanny, that you cannot trust me with the secret?"

"Oh, I must not tell you, indeed I mustn't. You are wrong, too, in what you think. I have done nothing bad, Miss Neville; do believe me, and please don't think badly of me."

"I will try not to, Fanny."

"Oh, how I wish I had come in with Edith when she asked me, and never waited for anyone, then I should never have seen cousin Frances," and fairly overcome with all her little heart had been suffering during the past hour, Fanny burst into tears.

"I have made my appearance at a most unfortunate moment," said Anne, opening the door. "Good gracious, child! don't cry like that; you are roaring like a mad bull, and will make a perfect fright of yourself into the bargain. There, do stop. I promise you, you shall be forgiven whatever your sin, and receive the kiss of forgiveness on the spot, if you will only have done and be quiet."

"Go, Fanny," said Amy, "we will talk over this quietly by-and-by, go and desire Mary to see to your arm."

"Thank goodness she is gone," said Anne, "now I can begin to breathe again. If there is anything in this world I hate, it is the cry of children and cats; I class them both together, as I don't know which is the worst of the two, all I do know is, that when children once begin, they never know when to leave off."

Then suddenly she caught sight of the Camellia, and took it up, while Amy most sincerely wished she had burnt it.

"Where did you get this Camellia?" asked she.

"Fanny brought it me a few minutes ago," replied Amy, blushing slightly, feeling she was in a manner evading the question.

But Anne was far too point blank to be put off, and had Amy but considered for a moment, she would have remembered how hopeless it was to check or elude Anne's curiosity. She returned to the charge at once, without one moment's thought or hesitation.

"Who gave it her?" she asked shortly.

"I believe Mr. Vavasour did."

"Of course I expected as much. Here are you like some saintly nun, shut up in a cloister, no one supposed to get even a glimpse of you, and yet for all that, you receive more attention than all us poor girls put together, who are dressing and walking, laughing and talking, and doing I do not know what else besides to please the men. You may smile, but I can tell you I think it no laughing matter. Upon my word, it is a great deal too bad."

"The flower is not worth having," replied Amy, constrained to say something. "It is faded."

"Not worth having! now I do call that ungrateful, when I dare say the poor man has done his best to please you. I know I should be thankful enough at having such a graceful compliment paid me; but there, I never have the chance of showing my gratitude to anybody, seeing no one ever pays me the compliment of even sending me a dead flower!"

"I am sure Mr. Hall would."

"Oh! the monster, don't name him, pray. Thank goodness he has not found out my penchant for flowers, or I believe I should find him waiting every morning at the bottom of the staircase, with a bouquet as big as his head, composed of ivy berries and Christmas holly; he decorates his church with them, and I have no doubt thinks them preferable to the most lovely hot-house flowers; here, take your Camellia," and she held it out at arm's length.

This was a ruse on Anne's part to induce Amy to hold out her arm, so that she might, as it were by accident, discover the sprain, having determined in her own mind, after leaving Charles, not to let Miss Neville know a word about his solicitude; he had appealed to Anne's good nature, and she was willing enough to help him to get a dozen doctors—if he wished it—to see her, but then Miss Neville must not know anything about it; there was no reason why she should, but every reason why she should not.

Anne would not, by the slightest word or hint, soften Miss Neville's heart towards her cousin; people must manage their own love affairs themselves, and if they got into scrapes, not get others into a mess as well; besides, Anne knew well enough, or rather guessed it, that neither Mr. or Mrs. Linchmore would exactly approve of it, while as for Charles, she hoped Miss Neville would pay him out in the same coin as he had paid Frances. If her cousin was foolish enough to fall in love with the governess, it was his fault, Anne was not going to take the blame, or have anything to do with it.

Then it was evident to Anne's quick sight that Mr. Vavasour was getting up a flirtation too, and if Miss Neville was wise she would improve upon that, there being no one in the world to say a word against his falling desperately in love with her, if he liked; he was a rich man, and his own master entirely, and ought to have a wife to help him spend his money, whereas Charles's fortune was all built upon expectations; it was true he had some four or five hundred a year, but that might, in the end, starve a wife, or turn her into a household drudge.

There was not a shadow of doubt in Anne's mind which of the two ought to be the object of Miss Neville's choice; but true love never did run smooth, and she supposed she would choose Charles, simply on account of the difficulties that stood in her way. She only wished, with a sigh, she was the chosen one, instead of Miss Neville—and then—what a dance she would lead the two!

"What is the matter with your wrist?" asked she, as Amy of necessity stretched out the left hand for the flower.

"I have sprained it."

Anne never asked the why or wherefore,—which might have surprised Amy had she thought at all about it; knowing, as she did, her inquisitiveness,—but examined it at once.

"Yes, it is a bad sprain, and how swollen the fingers are! and how funny it looks," said she laughing. "Why you might as well be afflicted with gout. How it burns! I should be quite frightened if it was mine."

"I am not in the least so," replied Amy. "I am going to bathe it in cold water presently. I think that will do it good."

"How can you possibly know what will do it good; you ought to have old Dr. Bernard to see it."

"Oh, no!" exclaimed Amy hastily, "there is not the slightest necessity for any such thing. I cannot bear the idea of it; pray do not think of it for one moment, I would rather not see him."

"Well, it is horrid, the idea of having a medical man, and knowing that for the time being, you are bound to follow wherever he leads; I hate it too. But old Dr. Bernard is so mild and meek, so fatherly-looking, with his grey hair or hairs—he has only got about twenty round his shining bald pate—so different to our young doctor at home, who comes blustering in, cracking his okes; and then sends medicine enough to kill the whole household. Of course Isabella knows about your arm?"

"No, not a word, and I hope she will not."

"Hope no such thing, please, as I shall tell her of it the very first opportunity I have."

"Pray do not, Miss Bennet. It will be quite well to-morrow."

"It will not be well for days; and as for not telling Mrs. Linchmore, I always do what I say, and if you were to talk until Doomsday you would not reason me out of it. Only think if it were to bring on fever; you might get seriously ill and die, imagine what a mischance, obliged to have a funeral and all kinds of horrors; and then, how do you suppose us poor visitors would feel. I am sure we are dull enough as it is; at least, I am; so in compassion to our poor nerves, you must see that dear old Dr. Bernard. It is no use whatever fighting against your destiny," and without waiting for a reply Anne went away, thinking she had managed admirably well, seeing she had carried her point, without in the least compromising Charles.

She looked into the morning-room on her way down: there was no one there but Alfred Strickland having a quiet nap to while away the time before dinner, and Mr. Hall; the latter with his legs as usual, tucked away out of sight, a book in his hand; but fortunately for Anne his face turned away from its pages, towards the fire; so she crept softly away without disturbing either.

In the hall, to her astonishment, she met Charles, impatiently awaiting her, cloaked and booted for his cold ride.

"Well, what success?" asked he.

"How ridiculous!" exclaimed Anne angrily. "There is such a thing as being too punctual. If I am to do as you wish, I will not be hurried; I am a woman as well as Miss Neville, and look for as much consideration. Besides, I said half an hour, and half an hour I will have;" and without waiting for a reply she passed on into the drawing-room, while Charles, throwing off his great coat, followed.

But he was doomed to be terribly tried, for there sat Mrs. Linchmore, the object of Anne's search, deep in the mysteries of a game of chess with Mr. Vavasour.

Anne sat down and took up a book. "It will never do for me to disturb them," said she, quietly, rather enjoying the joke of Charles' discomfiture, now visibly expressed on his face.

A muttered exclamation of impatience, which sounded very much like an oath, passed his lips.

Anne slightly winced at this. She thought the case getting desperate.

Why should Charles be in such a tremendous hurry?

It was not a case of life and death. She really thought, considering she was doing him a favour, he might have a chat, and make the time pass pleasantly and agreeably, instead of letting her see how entirely his heart was wrapped up in another girl. Only that her word was passed, from which Anne never deviated, she would have thrown up the office she had undertaken, and have nothing more to do with it.

Time passed on, not as it generally does, with swift fleet wings; but even to Anne, who did not care how it went, heavily and slowly, very much in the same way as the game of chess was progressing. Charles evinced his impatience by crossing his legs, uncrossing them, taking up a book and tossing over the pages; for not one word did he read or desire to; and finally, as the small French clock on the mantel-piece chimed six, he threw down the book and exclaimed impatiently—

"When the devil will that game be over?" Then catching Anne's astonished look, he laughed aloud, and said, "You do not often see me out of temper, cousin?"

"True, but then I never recollect having seen it tried."

"Or tried so severely as it is now."

"Men have no patience, see how quietly I take it."

"You! you have no interest in the matter."

"Have I not? And pray may I ask do you suppose it is very pleasant for me to be sitting here doing nothing. There are Alfred and Mr. Hall, both in the morning room, alone, waiting to be talked to, and I might have them all to myself, for the next half hour, and certainly all the time I have been wasting on you and your affairs. Have a little more gratitude Sir, or you may get some one else to manage for you."

"You are a good girl, Anne, but a shocking flirt."

"Oh yes! abuse me as much as you like, it will do you good, and perhaps make you in a better temper; as I said before, men have no patience. As long as things go smoothly and quietly they are all right; but when things happen contrary or not exactly as they wish, they get into a rage, and do not know how to bear it like us poor women, who are taught it every hour of our lives."

"I never remember to have heard such a piece of moral wisdom from your lips before Anne."

They were here, much to the intense delight of Charles, interrupted by the voices of the chess players.

"That was a very pretty checkmate," said Robert Vavasour, "so totally unexpected and unperceived."

"Who has beaten?" asked Anne, going towards them, as Charles went out of the room, leaving her to do as best she could for him.

"Mr. Vavasour," replied Mrs. Linchmore, "he always does."

"Not always; you won two games of me last evening."

"Or rather you allowed me to; but I do not mind being beaten sometimes, it is tiresome never to win."

While the chess-men were being put away, Anne considered how she should begin her story, which, now it had come to the point, seemed more difficult than she had imagined. At length a bright idea struck her.

"I hate chess," she said, "and cannot think what pleasure there can be in poring over such a dull game. I would a thousand times rather play the children's Race game; there is something exciting in that, but poor Miss Neville is too ill to play now."

"Ill!" exclaimed Mrs. Linchmore. "Miss Neville ill?" while one of the chess-men slipped from Robert Vavasour's fingers, and rolled over on to the soft hearth rug, instead of into the box as he had intended.

"Yes, she has sprained her wrist," continued Anne, giving the chess-man a gentle kick with her foot as it lay close beside her.

"Is that all? I thought at least it was the small pox, or scarlet fever," said Mrs. Linchmore.

"Although it is neither one nor the other," said Anne, "still it is very bad, and ought to be seen to."

"Do you speak from your own personal observation?"

"Yes. I have been sitting with her for some time, and certainly think she looks ill and feverish; her hand is swollen an awful size. I should be quite frightened if it were mine, and told her so. I dare say old Dr. Bernard though would soon put it all right."

"He shall be sent for to-morrow," replied Mrs. Linchmore, "should she be no better, but perhaps a night's rest, and a little of Mrs. Hopkin's doctoring, may make her quite well again. Do you know how she sprained it?"

"I never asked her," replied Anne, evading a direct reply, "all I know is, it is very bad."

"If no better to-morrow, I will send for Dr. Bernard in the afternoon," said Mrs. Linchmore, quietly.

"To-morrow afternoon," repeated Mr. Vavasour quite as quietly, and before Anne had time to shape any answer in reply, "But perhaps Miss Neville is in a great deal of pain; a sprain is an ugly thing sometimes, and at all times painful."

"It is quite impossible to send to-night," replied Mrs. Linchmore, decidedly. "Mr. Linchmore will not return from Standale himself much before ten, and I never send any of the servants so far without his sanction. It strikes me there is a little unnecessary haste and compassion displayed for my governess."

Robert Vavasour was silenced; but not so Anne, she came to the rescue at once, rather nettled.

"I am sure, Isabella, I don't care a bit about it; only I thought as Charles was going into Standale,—I suppose to ride home with your husband at night,—he might as well call on Dr. Bernard as not; or leave a message to say he was wanted."

As there was no good reason why he should not, Mrs. Linchmore was obliged to acquiesce, though apparently,—and she did not care to conceal it—with a very bad grace, and without the slightest solicitude expressed for her governess.

"I have managed it for you," said Anne, going out into the hall, where she found Charles striding up and down, impatiently; "such a fight as I have had."

"Never mind about the fight, Anne. Am I to call on Dr. Bernard?"

"Yes."

The word was scarcely spoken, ere to Anne's astonishment, he had caught her in his arms, and kissed her.

"You're a dear good girl, Anne," he said, "I swear there's nothing I wouldn't do for you!"

"How rough you are, cousin!" exclaimed Anne, struggling from his hasty embrace. "I'll do nothing for you, if this is the style I am to be rewarded with. It may be all very well for you, but I don't like it."

"Here's another then," laughed Charles, "and now for Dr. Bernard, I suppose he's the best medical man in the place?"

"Oh! for goodness sake," said Anne, aghast at the bare idea of facing Mrs. Linchmore, if any other were called in. "Do not go to any one but old Dr. Bernard, whatever you do; Isabella will never forgive me; she is in a tremendous gale as it is. Do you hear, Charley?" said she, catching his arm as he was going off.

"All right," said he, laughing at her fright, and leaving her only half convinced as to what he intended doing. "I'll tell him to call the first thing in the morning."

Anne held back the hall door as he passed out.

It was pouring with rain, but he was on his horse and away in a second.

"Why he must be desperately in love with that Miss Neville," said Anne, "to go off in such torrents of rain; he'll be drenched to the skin before he gets to the park gates. Well, I wish I could be ill, and somebody—not that Hall—go mad for me in the same way."

And Anne sighed, and smoothed the hair Charles had slightly disarranged.

CHAPTER III

THE LETTER

"They sin who tell us love can die!
With life all other passions fly—
All others are but vanity.
In heaven ambition cannot dwell,
Nor avarice in the vaults of hell.
Earthly these passions, as of earth—
They perish where they draw their birth.
But love is indestructible!
Its holy flame for ever burneth—
From heaven it came, to heaven returneth."
SOUTHEY

Against the mantle-piece in the morning-room leant Mrs. Linchmore; one hand supported her head, the other hung listlessly by her side, while in the long taper fingers she clasped an open letter. A tiny foot peeped from under the folds of her dress, and rested on the edge of the fender; the fire burnt clear and bright, and lent a slight glow to her cheeks, which were generally pale.

She looked very beautiful as she stood there; her graceful figure showed itself to the best advantage, and her long dark lashes swept her cheek, as she looked thoughtfully on the ground.

Mrs. Linchmore was not a happy woman; she had, as I have said, married for money, and when too late, found out her mistake, and that money without love is nothing worth.

When scarcely seventeen, she had loved with all the fervour and truth of a young heart's first love; her love was returned, but her lover was poor, they must wait for better times; so he went abroad to India, full of hope, and firm in the faith of her to whom he was betrothed; to win honour, fame, glory, and promotion; and with the latter, money wherewith to win as his wife her whom he so dearly loved.

Scarcely three years had passed slowly away, when Mr. Linchmore wooed the beautiful Isabella for his bride; he was young and handsome, and unlike her former lover, rich. Did she forget him to whom her young love was pledged? No, she still thought of him, love for him still filled her heart, yet she smothered it, and became the wife of the wealthy Mr. Linchmore, with scarcely a thought as to the suffering she was causing another, or remorse at her broken faith and perjured vows.

Shortly after her marriage, she heard of her young lover's hasty return, and what a return! Not the return he had so often pictured to her in the days gone by, never to be lived over again; but he came as a sorrowful, broken-hearted man, mourning the loss of one who was no longer worthy of his love, one for whom he had been willing to sacrifice so much, even the wishes of those nearest and dearest to him—his father and mother, whose only child he was.

His death soon after nearly broke his mother's heart; some said it was occasioned from the effects of a fever, caught in an unhealthy climate, but Mrs. Linchmore, his early love, dared not question her own heart when she heard of it, but gazed around, and shuddered at the magnificence of the home for which he had been sacrificed. Then remorse and anguish, bitter anguish, must have been busy within her, but she showed it not; outwardly, she was the same, or it might be a little prouder, or more stately in her walk, more over-bearing to her servants, with all of the proud woman, and none of the girl about her.

The envy of many. Ah! could they but have seen the wretchedness of her heart, the hollowness of her smiles, would they have envied her? Would they not rather have been thankful and contented with their lot, and changed their envy into pity?

This was what she dreaded. Their pity! No, anything but that. To be hated, feared, disliked, dreaded, all—all anything but pitied. To none would she be other than the rich, the happy Mrs. Linchmore; and so she appeared to some, nay, to all. Henceforth her heart was dead and cold, no love must,—could enter there again.

She became a flirt, and a selfish woman, without one particle of sympathy, and scarcely any love for her husband. How dissimilar they were—in ideas, thoughts, feelings, tastes—in everything. She took no trouble to conceal from him how little she cared for him; he who loved her so intensely—so truthfully.

In the first early days of their married life he strove to win her affection by every little act of kindness, or devotion that his love prompted; but all in vain;—he failed. All his deeds of kindness all his love elicited no answering token of regard, no look of love from her; she was ever the same—cold, silent, distant; no sweet smile on her face to welcome him home, no brightening of the eye at his approach, no fond pressure of the hand: truly she loved him not, yet no word of unkindness or reproach ever crossed his lips, even when she turned away from his encircling arm as he stooped to kiss his first-born, no word escaped him—but his look,—she remembered that long after; it haunted her dreams for many a long night.

How she had betrayed and deceived, him who fondly thought before their marriage that she loved with all a girl's first love; yet he forgave her for the sake of his children, and blamed himself for the change; he had perhaps been too harsh, too stern to her. Kind, unselfish man! poor short-seeing mortal! It was not you, it was her unfeeling, cruel heart.

Lately, instead of flirting and laughing with all and every one as she had formerly done, she singled out one to whom for the time being all her smiles were directed. At balls, at parties, riding, or walking, it mattered not, the favoured one was ever at her side; she danced with only him, rode with him, talked alone to him, or leant on his arm when tired.

Human nature could not stand this; she had gone too far. At length Mr. Linchmore's spirit was roused, at length her conduct had maddened him; he had borne uncomplainingly her coldness, but his honour she might not touch; none should lift a finger against the wife of his bosom, the mother of his little ones. She might receive homage from all; but his spirit roused, his pride rebelled at the marked attentions of one. High words ensued between husband and wife, which might almost be said to be their first quarrel, so silently had he endured her want of love; but now he stood firm, and she was defeated.

This event caused a considerable alteration in both parties. Mrs. Linchmore saw that however quietly her husband might brook the knowledge of her coldness, or the wrong she had done in marrying him without love; yet there was a boundary beyond which even she dared not step. He might appear easy and weak, but deep in his heart lay a strong firm will she could not thwart, a barrier not to be broken through, nor even touched with ever so gentle a hand. She might be heartless, might be a flirt; but beyond that she might not go. She felt also that her husband no longer trusted her, even searched her conduct, so she took refuge in pride, and open cruel indifference to his words or wishes, more galling than her former thinly veiled coldness. He had found out she loved him not; what need for further deceit?

And Mr. Linchmore? Had his wife judged him rightly? Yes, even so. The sad truth that she loved him not had crept slowly yet surely into his heart, vainly as he had striven to crush it; her indifference he had borne without resentment, hoping that in time she might be brought to love him; for he still loved her passionately, as also sternly, almost harshly, if I might so say. His was not a nature to change, and then his love for her had been the one deep, intense feeling of his manhood, a love that nothing short of death could change; but with his knowledge of her deceit had gone his trust; and latterly almost his respect. He now lived hoping that time might change her heart, or draw it towards him—a hopeless wish, since the very presence of him she had wronged, and who had innocently wrought his and her own life-long misery, was a reproach and bitterness to her. No wonder he was severe and stern! Yet there were times when his old impetuous nature would have sway, and shut up in his room alone with nothing but despairing thoughts, he would pace it in utter anguish of spirit, hoping, looking for what never could be, namely, the love of his wife. And so they lived on. She fearing his love. He mourning hers.

What did she care for the dark Frenchman of whom her husband had grown jealous? and who had singled her out from among a multitude it might be for her haughty beauty, or it might be for the éclat of being thought the favoured one of her who was the centre of admiration around which so many flocked at Paris the winter before Amy's arrival at Brampton? He had no intention, that man of the world, of falling in love with her; it was a flirtation, nothing more, and cost neither a pang. That she encouraged his attentions was without a doubt; that she despised him was without a doubt, too, seeing his absence—for Mr. Linchmore had positively forbidden him the house—did not cost her a sigh, not even a thought. What mattered it if he went? there were others to pay her the self-same attentions, others as gay and fascinating. So she went on her way in no degree wiser or better for the obstacle she had stumbled upon in her path, the provocation of her husband's wrath.

Flirt she must. How otherwise divert her thoughts? those thoughts that crowded so relentlessly into her brain, threatening to overwhelm her with the memory of the one loved and lost; him whom she had thought to forget, or of whom she had hoped to crush out the remembrance.

Ah! her heart was not all coldness. Did she not love her children passionately; and were not her very faults, bad as they were, caused by the one false step—the forsaking her early love?

The storm between husband and wife blew over; it was not outwardly of long duration, and again Mrs. Linchmore singled out another—it mattered not to her whom she flirted with. "La belle Anglaise"—as she was called—cared not; life to her was a blank—a dreary waste.

Alas! how much misery it is in woman's power to make, how much to avert or remove. Man's comforter, sharer of his joys, partaker of his sorrows, ever ready to pour into his ear the kind word of comfort, consolation, and hope; whose soft, gentle hand smooths his pillow in the hour of sickness; and whose low, sweet voice assuages his pain, and bears without complaint his sometimes irritable temper. What would he do without her? How much good can she do, and alas! how much evil. Few, very few women there are without some one redeeming quality. Few, very few, we hope, like Mrs. Linchmore.

But to return to our story.

Ere long, with a deep drawn sigh, Mrs. Linchmore raised her eyes, and recalled the thoughts—which had been wandering away into the past,—to the present time, and to the letter she held in her hand, and began to peruse its contents, a troubled unquiet look resting on her face, as she did so.

It was the answer to the letter she had written at her husband's earnest solicitations, to Mrs. Elrington.

"ISABELLA MARY—(so it began)—

"Your heart deceived you not when it warned you I should not accept Mr. Linchmore's invitation. God forbid I should ever see your face again; it would be pain and grief to me, and recall to life recollections, now long hidden and buried in my heart. I never wish to look on you again, though God knows I have long since forgiven you, and that my ever constant prayer is, that I may think of you without bitterness, and ever with charity.

"It was an evil dark day when first I saw you, and will be a still darker one for me if ever I see you again. I could not trust myself even now—though long years have passed away since we met last—to meet you face to face. It would bring the image of one too forcibly and vividly to my mind; even now my hand shakes and trembles with emotion; and my eyes swim with tears, bitter, blinding tears, as I write.

"Do not mistake me, do not think I write this letter to reproach you, I do not. I have never reproached you; or, at least, I have striven to stifle all ill-feeling. I promised him, on his death-bed, to forgive you and learn to think of you with, if possible, kindly feeling and pity; and I trust I have been enabled to fulfil that promise. No, I do not reproach you, but I leave your own heart to do so; long, long ago, if I mistake not, it must.

"Miss Neville has told me you are cold, stern, and seldom smiled; you are changed indeed. Changed more than I, if I were your bitterest enemy, could have wished. Alas! that one wrong, wilful, wicked act could have entailed so much misery and sorrow.

"I will not lay down my pen without thanking you for your kindness to my young friend, Amy; she says you are very kind. And here again I would repeat what I said in a former letter to Mrs. Murchison, that she has been tenderly nurtured, and I would not that her young spirit should be broken. Forget not your promise to treat her more as a companion and friend, than as a governess, or as the latter class are sometimes treated. I am inclined to doubt any promise of yours being kept, but I have Mr. Linchmore's word, and I am content.

"And now farewell. May God forgive you, as I do. When your hour of death draws near—for in this changing and transitory life, we know not what a day may bring forth, or how soon we may be summoned away, and perhaps I shall never write to you again—may it smooth your dying hour, and give peace to your then troubled, remorseful heart, to know, that she whom you so deeply injured and so cruelly deceived and whose life you helped to render desolate, has forgiven you.

"ELLEN ELRINGTON."

There was an expression of pain on Mrs. Linchmore's face as she read, but not a sigh not a tear escaped her; perhaps those had all been shed long ago, or surely those sad, earnest words, from a sorrowful heart would have moved her; but ere she closed the letter and looked up, the painful look passed away, and a sarcastic curl had settled on her lip, and shone brightly in her full dark eye. She crushed the letter in her hand as she would perhaps have crushed the writer, if she could, and laughed aloud; a laugh so hollow, so forced, its very echo would have made one's blood run cold; but there was no fear of its being heard, she was still alone, as she felt with satisfaction as she glanced hurriedly around.

Again she laughed. But this time the tones were more subdued, the echo was scarcely heard.

She crushed the letter more tightly in her hand, until the clear blue veins were almost swelled to bursting, while she murmured, "so much for Mrs. Elrington's letter. Did she think to frighten and make a coward of me. Pshaw! she was mistaken; I am altered and changed, for it amused me."

But though she gave vent to these words, such were not her feelings. She was in reality deeply moved; past scenes had risen up vividly before her, with all the hopes and fears, joys and sorrows, of her girlish days. As she read word after word, line after line, of the letter, those days became more vivid still; and the old loving, gentle feelings crowded together at her heart; she was again the loving and beloved of him of her early choice; again, in fancy, sitting by his side, weeping bitter, passionate, despairing tears, as on the morning they had parted, then with the hope of meeting again; but it had been for the last time—for ever—and as the last word, with all its dreadful import came steadily into her heart, she could in very desolation have thrown herself into the large arm chair and wept more despairingly, more passionately still; but no, she was Mrs. Linchmore, cold and stern; Miss Neville had said so,—she must be herself again. So she crushed the old regretful feelings, and stifled their dying moan with that bitter, ghastly laugh.

On the table was a beautiful small bouquet of hot-house flowers; she drew out a bright scarlet one, and arranged it in her hair at the glass over the chimney piece.

"I may be cold and stern—I may be changed—but—I am still beautiful." Such were her thoughts as she stood gazing at herself long after the flower had been arranged to her satisfaction.

But now a step sounded on the stairs; it echoed in the lofty hall; it approached the door. Suddenly she remembered the letter, and hastily snatching it from the ground where it had lain forgotten, she hurriedly threw it into the fire.

There was a bright light for a moment, then it was gone, and a thin black substance floated lightly on the coals, showing where the letter had been; this she buried at once, deep—deep beneath the burning coals, until not a vestige remained, and turned to greet her visitor.

It was her husband.

He entered, drew a chair near the fire, and sat down, while his wife, with no visible trace of the emotion she had but lately felt, busied herself with some fancy work, so that her eyes might not meet his, or they must have revealed a little of the passions that had been struggling within; at all events she dared not raise them, but kept them obstinately fixed on the canvas in her lap, and worked on in silence, expecting her husband to be the first to speak: but he did not, he took up his newspaper and read it as perseveringly as she worked.

Ere long the silence grew oppressive; the crumpling of the paper as Mr. Linchmore turned it in his hand annoyed and irritated her; her thoughts were still half struggling with the past; she must bury that, and bring them forcibly back to the present time, so she spoke; but try as she would she could not do so without showing a little irritation of manner.

"The paper appears to engross your attention entirely, Mr Linchmore. Have you found anything so very interesting in it?"

He looked up in surprise, then quietly laid it on the table, as he replied, "Perhaps I did not speak, as I have rather unfortunate news for you, 'Lady Emily'—Mrs. Linchmore's riding horse—has gone dead lame."

"Lame!" exclaimed Mrs. Linchmore in a vexatious tone of voice. "It must be something very sudden then; she was perfectly well the last time I rode her, there was not the slightest symptom of lameness about her then."

"That was some time ago," rejoined her husband.

"Only a few days, or a week at the utmost. What is the matter with her? or what has caused the lameness?"

"A nail has been accidentally run into her foot in shoeing. There has been great carelessness no doubt."

"It is always the case that whenever I wish to ride or drive something happens to prevent me, for the last two or three months I have noticed it. What is the use of having servants if one cannot trust them, or horses either, when they are never fit to be ridden?"

"There are other horses in the stable, Isabella, would carry you just as well as Lady Emily, but you never will ride them."

Mrs. Linchmore was not exactly a timid horsewoman, but she was not courageous enough to ride a strange horse, whose temper and habits she was unacquainted with. She had ridden the mare constantly for the last five years, and knew her temper well, and after the first canter was over all nervousness was gone, and she could talk and laugh and ride without fear, or the slight timidity she might have felt at first starting.

"I promised to ride into Standale with Mr. Vavasour," said she.

"Shall I order the bay to be brought round for you, Isabella? You will find him even quieter than Lady Emily."

"You know I hate strange horses, Mr. Linchmore. I wonder at your proposing such a thing. After being accustomed to one horse for so long, I should be nervous."

"I will ride with you with pleasure," was the reply, "and give you confidence if I can, and see no accident happens."

But no, her husband's escort was very different to the promised pleasure she had looked forward to with Mr. Vavasour.

"Thank you," replied she coldly, "but I shall stay at home, and give up all idea of riding until my horse gets well."

"Very well, Vavasour can ride into Standale with me if he chooses, I am starting for it in half an hour. By-the-by, what report did Bernard give of Miss Neville this morning?"

"Nothing very much the matter, I believe," said she carelessly, "simply a sprain caused by some folly or another."

"I am glad it is nothing more serious; she looks a delicate girl."

"Some people always look so. I believe she is strong enough; we were always from the first led to expect a rather fragile person."

This was an unwise speech of Mrs. Linchmore's, as it recalled Mrs. Elrington at once to her husband's mind, and he asked—

"Have you received any reply to the letter you wrote to Mrs. Elrington, Isabella?"

"Yes. Miss Neville gave me a message to the effect that she did not intend," said she sarcastically, "honouring our poor house with a visit."

"Did she write to Miss Neville?"

"I fancy not. I think it was mentioned by Mrs. Neville, in a letter she wrote from Ashleigh."

"And Mrs. Elrington has never answered your letter?"

"No. I suppose she thought the message good enough for us."

There was no quivering of the lip, no tell-tale blood in her cheeks, nothing to betray the falsehood she was telling, save her eyes, and those she still bent down. She could not have met her husband's gaze.

"Strange," murmured he, "that she should so long keep aloof from us. I should have thought she would have wished to heal up old quarrels."

"You know her not," was the reply. "I told you she would not come, and implored you, almost, not to ask me to write to her."

"It was my fault you wrote, and I cannot help feeling sorry at her discourtsey; it is so different from what I should have thought she would have done. I liked the little I saw of Mrs. Elrington, she was a true Englishwoman. I wonder what she disliked me for. I suppose she did dislike me?" asked he.

"Yes, thoroughly. You supplanted her son."

"But you never cared for him, Isabella?" and this time he waited for the eyes to be raised to his.

But they were not. Mrs. Linchmore bent lower still over her work, so that not only the eyes, but the face was almost hidden. She seemed to have made some mistake, for, with a slight hasty exclamation, she took the scissors and cut out, hurriedly, what a few moments before she had been so busy with.

Again he repeated the question, but not sternly, only sorrowfully and slowly, as if he almost feared the answer, or guessed what it would be.

"You never cared for him, Isabella?"

But the emotion or embarrassment had passed away, and although Mrs. Linchmore did not look up to meet his gaze, now so searchingly bent on her, she laid down her work and patted the head of the lap-dog lying at her feet.

"I liked him as I do Fido," replied she, perhaps a little mockingly. "He was a pretty plaything."

But the answer did not satisfy Mr. Linchmore. He withdrew his eyes from her face and sighed. Did he doubt her? Alas! a strange, sad thought had long filled his mind, and would not be chased away.

"I am glad you did not love him, Isabella," was all he said.

And then he sat silent for some time. At length he spoke again, somewhat suddenly. "To revert to Miss Neville," he said. "I feared her illness might be caused from dulness or ennui. She is so much alone—too much for one so young. Miss Tremlow, even, hinted at it to me the very first day she came downstairs; but I do not see what else is to be done, with these young men in the house."

"I invited her down the other day, but she would not come."

"I am glad she did not. Why did you ask her?"

"You told me to yourself, Mr. Linchmore. You surely cannot have forgotten it; and besides, we promised to treat her more as a young friend than as a governess."

"True," he replied. "I now regret we ever gave such a promise. It would be far better for Miss Neville, for although we treat her as a friend, who amongst our numerous acquaintances will? They do not know her as we do, and will simply treat her as a governess, nothing more. I neither like Miss Strickland's apparent haughtiness, which amounts to rudeness, or Vavasour's attentions, which almost amount to a flirtation with her."

"The first is unaccountable to me; but the latter—what harm can there be in that?" replied Mrs. Linchmore.

"To Miss Neville there might be harm. She might lose her heart to him, for she is no flirt; he is," said he, decidedly, and his wife could not attempt to contradict him, "and would as soon break her heart as not; perhaps be a little proud of it, and certainly think less about it than he would at breaking his horse's neck in leaping a fence."

"You are very uncharitable."

"Not at all. My opinion is, Vavasour intends getting up a flirtation with Miss Neville, just to pass the time away; perhaps you had better see to it, Isabella, and try and give her a hint. You could easily do it, without appearing to have noticed his attentions to her."

"The very way to make her fall desperately in love with him; women always do with those they hear abused—our hearts are so pitiful. Much better let her do as she likes, she has plenty of sense."

"As you will, Isabella; but I must not see her feelings trifled with; there is nothing half so sad as to love without return—hopelessly."

And again he turned his face, and looked sorrowfully at his wife, as if expecting or longing for some slight mark of affection; but she gave none, and rising slowly, he went out.

Mrs. Linchmore was once more alone.

The preceding conversation, at least the latter part of it, had been entirely to her satisfaction. It must not be supposed she had been a blind spectator to Vavasour's attentions to Amy. She had heard of the first walk from Frances, she had seen the second, and imagined that, perhaps, having remarked the looks with which, once or twice, Mr. Linchmore had watched his attentions to herself, he had had recourse to a ruse-de-guerre, and now flirted with the governess, as the most harmless girl he could pick out, whilst all his looks, all his petits soins, were directed and given to her.

She laughed at the idea of outwitting her husband; not that she cared for Vavasour, but the flirting spirit was strong and powerful within. Old memories and associations, instead of softening had only hardened her present life, and made her look back more regretfully to the past, more hopelessly and bitterly to the future.

"Miss Neville is certainly very beautiful," mused she, "but so quiet, so meek; no animation about her, nothing to charm such a man as Mr. Vavasour with." Then she wondered if she herself possessed that power.

She rose up, and again stood before the glass, which reflected back her proud, beautiful face, with the conscious haughty look, that if beauty had the power to charm it was hers, she need fear no rival.

Then she re-arranged the flower which she had previously pinned in her hair, and a smile, sparkling with pleasure, showed that she was satisfied.

Mr. Linchmore judged Robert Vavasour's character more justly than his wife, although neither quite understood it. The mystery of his birth was the shadow continually haunting Vavasour's path, and making him thoughtless and trifling towards women. If his mother, as he believed, still lived, where was her gentle, tender love? Why had he never felt it? Why had she so cruelly deserted him, and left him to fight his own way in the world, with no name but a false one? His heart hardened against womankind. If a mother could be false to her child, what woman could be true? What woman worth living or caring for? They were triflers all, and to be trifled with; so he held no reverence in his heart for them, but flirted with his hostess thoughtlessly, and admired her as he would have admired any other beautiful woman; as he admired Amy, and would have flirted with her also if she would have let him.

Would his heart ever be touched by love? ever see reason to regret or recall the rash vow he had made that no woman should ever hold a place in his heart, seeing that in loving her he would have to plead, not only his love, but his nameless birth.

CHAPTER IV

THE INTERVIEW

—"Earthly things
Are but the transient pageants of an hour;
And earthly pride is like the passing flower,
That springs to fall, and blossoms but to die."
HENRY KIRKE WHITE

*"Whoever looks on life will see
How strangely mortals disagree."*
CAWTHORNE

It was almost dusk as Frances Strickland, who had been sitting for the last hour before the glass trying the effect of a wreath of fuschias she intended wearing at some forthcoming party, laid the flowers on the dressing table with a dissatisfied sigh as her maid entered the room with candles.

"At last!" exclaimed she, impatiently, "what have you been about, Jane? I thought you would never come; make haste and dress me for dinner, as I wish to try the effect of these flowers in my hair."

Proud and haughty as Frances was to her equals, she seldom or ever showed much pride to her maid, or if it did occasionally peep out, it was instantly checked and controlled.

Jane was useful to her young mistress in more ways than the mere dressing her, and brushing her hair. She was an incessant talker, and found a willing listener in Frances, who silently encouraged her in repeating all the gossip and tittle-tattle of the servants' hall: as in this way Frances flattered herself she found out with little trouble the character as well as the sayings and doings of those around her.

Jane was perfectly well aware of Frances' failing, consequently indulged her propensity of talking to the utmost, and when she had nothing to relate, drew somehow from her own fertile brain and lively imagination, or added many wonderful improvements to the story already at her fingers' ends. Sometimes Jane was cross, or as she expressed it—"had a bad head-ache," and then it required all Frances' tact and ingenuity to get her to utter a syllable; and cunningly as she thought she cross-questioned her on these occasions, Jane's cunning equalled if not surpassed her mistress's, as she generally contrived to guess at what she was aiming, and either added fuel to the fire already kindled there, or quenched it altogether.

On the present occasion, Jane was especially communicative, and as she smoothed the raven tresses of her hair, talked away to her heart's content, now of this thing, now of that, until at length she approached the subject nearest her own heart and that of her mistress', namely, Miss Neville.

The loss of the piece of embroidery, and the search that had been made for it, had annoyed and irritated many of the servants, and especially Mason, who had long had a dislike of the governess, though she had not openly expressed it; then, Mr. Linchmore's apparent partiality for her? Why should Miss Neville come into the room just as she pleased when Madam was dressing, and give her opinion as to how she looked, and what she wore, even sometimes to the very ornaments themselves, throwing the lady's maid completely into the shade, where before she had reigned paramount, with no one's opinion or taste asked but her own. So Mason grew jealous, and took in the end a dislike to her, as servants often foolishly do to governesses; and only waited her time to manifest it.

Mrs. Hopkins' decided tone and speech in Miss Neville's favour, and the 'setdown' she gave Mason, only rooted her dislike the more firmly; if it had not been for the governess she would not have had that; and as birds of a feather flock together, so she had impressed upon Jane, during their many friendly chats, her opinion of Miss Neville: that she was a nobody, who gave herself airs, and interfered where she had no business to, and as to the lost piece of work, there was no doubt whatever that she suspected some of the servants, and most likely meanly accused them of taking it; otherwise, why was such a fuss made, and why had they been questioned as to whether they had seen it?

Jane readily believed all that was told her, and determined on shewing Miss Neville on the very first opportunity she had, that she thought her in no way better than herself, so meeting her one day accidentally in the corridor coming upstairs, she tossed her head and pushed rudely past her, allowing the baize door to slam to, without so much as offering to hold it open for her to pass through.

Amy gently and indignantly remonstrated with her on her rudeness, which she saw at once was intended, and silenced the second impertinent action, namely the answer hovering on Jane's lips; but though silenced, Jane went away more firmly impressed and convinced that Mason was right, and that Miss Neville was an upstart and a nobody.

"The idea," said she, as she recounted the adventure to Mason. "The idea of Miss Neville's teaching me manners, and ordering me to bridle my tongue; I'd like to see her as could make me do it, that's all; I'll teach my lady to bridle her tongue, and keep her sauce to herself."

Mason's temper was not a passionate one; Jane's was, and vindictive too; she felt convinced, judging from what she should do were she in Miss Neville's place, that the latter would immediately repeat all that had taken place to her young mistress, so she determined to be beforehand with her, and have, as she called it, the first say; whereas Amy had almost forgotten the circumstance, and certainly had no wish to recall it.

"Did you give my message to Mrs. Linchmore?" asked Frances, "I almost hope you did not, as I am so much better. I intend after all going down to dinner."

There had been a long silence, uninterrupted save by the noise the brush made as it passed through the soft dark hair.

"Yes Miss, I did, and they all said they were sorry to hear you had such a bad head-ache."

"All!" exclaimed Frances, "I desired you to give the message to Mrs. Linchmore. Why did you disobey me?"

"Well, Miss, I'm sure it was no fault of mine that Miss Neville happened to be in the room."

"Miss Neville!" exclaimed Frances.

"Yes, Miss Frances, I thought it would surprise you, but I know it was her, because I saw her through a chink of the door as Mason held it open; besides Mason says she is always there, trying to butter her bread, as the saying is; and after I'd given the message, which I should not have given if I'd known she had been there, I heard her and Mrs. Linchmore say they thought you was a very perverse and disagreeable girl; of course they didn't know I was so near, or they wouldn't have spoke so loud."

"And how dare Miss Neville have a word to say in the matter concerning any affairs of mine!" said Frances, thrown off her guard by the suddenness of Jane's announcement, and drawing her head up proudly, so as to almost drag her hair through Jane's fingers, and totally disarrange the long silken plait she had just completed.

"Law! Miss! I'm sure I can't say," replied Jane somewhat surprised in her turn at the extraordinary emotion she witnessed, and delighted that so far she had succeeded beyond her hopes.

"Then you ought to know; I don't believe one word of it."

"It's true all the same, Miss, whether you believe it or no, and I'm sure there's some people as is always picking other people to pieces, and more especially those as is much above them in station; and if I don't mistake Miss Neville thinks herself a mighty fine lady, and as Mason says tries—though she doesn't say she manages it—to turn Mrs. Linchmore round her thumb."

A gentle tap at the door here interrupted Jane, and she hastened to open it, but before she could do so the imperious "come in," of Frances was answered by the door softly opening and shutting; a light footstep crossed the room, and Amy Neville herself stood by the table.

Frances looked surprised.

"This is a most extraordinary intrusion, Miss Neville," said she rising. Then added sarcastically, "to what fortunate circumstance am I to ascribe the pleasure of your company?"

"No fortunate circumstance," replied Amy, almost as proudly, "has induced me to come here."

"Perhaps unfortunate, then," suggested Frances, in the same tone, still standing, and never asking her visitor to sit down.

"You are right," said Amy, quietly.

But this quietness enraged Frances, predisposed as she was to quarrel with her, and inwardly hating her, as she did; so she answered, angrily—

"And do you suppose I have nothing better to do than to listen to unfortunate circumstances, related by unfortunate people; for I suppose you are come with some absurd story. I care nothing for you or yours, and have no wish to listen to anything you have to say," and turning away, as rudely as she had spoken, Frances once more seated herself at the table, and desired Jane, who had been looking on in astonishment, to go on with her hair.

"But you must listen," replied Amy firmly, her eyes flashing at Frances' insulting tones and speech. "I have something to tell you,—an explanation to give,—a circumstance to explain; indeed you must listen."

Frances mused.

"Must listen," she repeated presently. "If that is all, pray talk on; as to whether I answer or no remains to be seen. No one ever yet compelled me to do aught against my will; therefore I advise Miss Neville,— determined as she seems,—to think twice before she puts me to the test. I must also state I am rather hurried, the dressing bell having rung long since."

And Frances carelessly wound the two long plaits Jane had plaited round her head.

"I have little to say; I shall not detain you long."

"Pray begin," said Frances. "Jane be more careful, that hair-pin hurts me. Well, Miss Neville?"

But Amy answered—

"What I have to say is for your ear alone; Jane cannot be present."

"I have no secrets from Jane; you need have no fear of her repeating anything she hears."

"Still, what I have to say, Miss Strickland, cannot be said before her."

"Really, Miss Neville, your conduct is most extraordinary, not to say presuming and impertinent. Jane is necessary to me, I cannot dress without her assistance. I am late as it is, and cannot send her away."

"If you will allow me, I will assist you."

"Well, I'm sure!" exclaimed Jane, who had been listening in secret wonderment to the fore-going conversation, and anticipating the dismissal she was now about to receive. "Well, I'm sure! I'm the last woman in the world to wish to pry into other people's secrets. Thank God, I've none of my own to trouble me, and don't care who hears what I say; and thank you, Miss Neville, for your good opinion of me," said she, with a slight bend, and, throwing the dress she held in her hand across the back of a chair, she marched indignantly from the room, taking care not to close the door behind her.

But Amy followed, and shut it, a proceeding that still more incensed her, as she had fully intended hearing something, if not all, of what passed, and learning, if possible, what secret enmity there was, or ill feeling between the two; as, with all her cunning and quickness, for once Jane was at fault. "Never mind," thought she, as she proceeded in search of Mason, to whom to unburden her ill-treatment. "I've been beforehand with you, with all your caution, Miss Neville, and I'm much mistaken if Miss Frances likes you one whit better than I do, and that's a precious deal, I can tell you," and Jane laughed; "though I'm puzzled to know why she got on her proud horse so soon. Yes, I'm fairly puzzled; but I'll find out yet. All those airs and graces didn't come from what I told her. No, no; I must be awake, and keep my eyes open. I'm not so easily deceived. Shut the door as tight and close as you will—say your say, whisper your secret, yet, for all that, Jane will be up to it, and fathom it out."

Amy and Frances were alone.

How different were the thoughts and feelings of both!

Declining her companion's assistance in dressing, Frances seated herself in an easy chair by the fire, her feet in their rich worked slippers resting on a footstool; her small jewelled fingers playing impatiently with a small gold heart attached to a bracelet she wore round her smooth white arm, her eyes emitting from under their dark lashes looks of defiance and scorn—for Frances, as I have said, cared not to hide her feelings, or had not yet learnt the habit of doing so;—a determined expression about the corners of her mouth, as if she had fully made up her mind what course to pursue, and that neither argument nor persuasion should induce her to abandon it.

She sat looking like some empress, awaiting the victim about to be sacrificed or made to bend to her haughty will.

A faint idea as to what Amy's explanation would be arose in her mind, how should she take it? should she remain silent, or answer it, and so lead her on until her whole heart should be probed,—laid bare before her? yes, she would do the latter, would penetrate into the very secret recesses of her heart; find out what her thoughts were, and how much she cared or did not care for her cousin, and then gradually retreat when she had her at her mercy. "We," so she reasoned, "cannot both triumph—one must be defeated—one must fall—and that one must be Miss Neville."

Amy stood a little apart.

She, too, had a determined expression playing round the corners of her mouth, and her tall, graceful figure was drawn up proudly to its full height; yet there was softness, gentleness in the very way she stood, one small fair hand tightly clasped round the injured wrist, as it rested delicately on the back of the chair, as if to keep down some strong inward emotion with its tight grasp; there was pride—there might be a touch of haughtiness, too—for she was but a poor weak mortal, but there was no anger, no defiance, no doggedness about Amy's looks. Her clear dark grey eye quailed not beneath her companion's hard cold gaze, it flashed as brightly, but there was neither malice, nor hatred, nor revenge in it; all was soft and womanly, though had opportunity offered or occasion required it, it might have returned scorn for scorn.

The two young girls were alone.

Yet both remained silent; perhaps both feared to be the first to speak, or wished her companion might break the silence becoming every moment more painful and embarrassing.

Twice Frances turned her head impatiently, but meeting Amy's steady gaze, her eyelids dropped and again she leant back in the soft cushioned chair, and played with the locket as though she could not rest quiet: if her lips were silent her hands must be employed—she must appear careless and unconcerned, and uninterested in what was to follow.

Amy never attempted to move or speak. There she stood gazing at Frances, but seemingly engrossed by other thoughts, for a close observer might have detected a slight, almost imperceptible trembling of the under lip, and a nervous twitching of the fair fingers of the left hand as it rested softly on the other.

At length, stooping as though to brush something off her wrapper, Frances spoke.

"Well, Miss Neville, how long is this farce to last, this silence continue? I have already intimated my wish to be alone, and that I do not care to be troubled with anything you may have to say; yet, hurried as I am, you seem to take little heed as to the length of time you detain me. Have the kindness to begin and end quickly."

Amy started. Her thoughts had been far away. Once again she had gone over in thought all those pleasant, joyous days, when the world seemed all so fair and bright, and the days had flown too quickly by; and at night, she had slept the sleep of happiness and peace, without a thought for the morrow, save to find or try and make it as happy as the one that had gone before.

Ah! how many days had fled since then; how many sorrows and trials had she seen and experienced. Each day now was but a sad counterpart of the yesterday that had been, no bright looking forward, no trembling certainty of happiness; all seemed drear, and the future a blank to her troubled mind.

Again Frances spoke.

This time her voice was firm, though she still steadily avoided meeting Amy's gaze.

"When is this wonderful explanation to take place, Miss Neville? If you have changed your mind about it, pray say so at once, that I may call Jane, and continue my dressing."

"Miss Strickland," began Amy, falteringly, for Frances' cruel manner had made her even more nervous than when she entered the room; "you must have guessed, you must be aware that—that—"

But instead of helping her, Frances laughed, and that gave Amy the courage she lacked, for her cheek glowed, and her eye flashed, and calmly and without hesitation, she went on at once.

"Have patience, Miss Strickland. I will go on quickly. You saw me yesterday talking to your cousin in the corridor, and I was led to infer from your manner, that you imagined I had done wrong in staying to speak with him, and I thought if I could only explain to you how accidentally it all occurred, you would exonerate both him and me from blame and unkind suspicion."

Frances raised her head haughtily. "I have so many cousins, that I must trouble Miss Neville to explain herself more fully, as I am unable either to recall the circumstance, or to remember which cousin was honoured by Miss Neville on the occasion referred to."

"Which cousin? I know but one—Mr. Charles Linchmore."

"I understood Miss Neville to be a lover of truth. If you know that Charles Linchmore is my cousin, may I ask what relation his brother can be?"

Amy was silent. Neither shame, fear, nor anger kept her so, for presently, a torrent of words burst from her lips, and she hurried on as if nothing could stop her; no, not even Frances' mocking gaze, or the seemingly indifferent manner with which she listened.

"Miss Strickland, why torture me thus? Think you that the change in my position has changed my feelings, my heart, my very nature? Think you I am a stone, or my heart dead within me, that I can stand calmly by, and hear such cutting cruel words from you, and not feel them bitterly? How could I look into your face the other day, or listen to your words, and not feel that you were judging me harshly; it was not possible, neither is it possible I can go on in my daily path of duty, until at least I have attempted to clear myself of the wrong I see you think me capable of. I have lived to see my fairest dreams vanish, and have bowed with submission to the will of One who is wiser then I,—have neither murmured nor fought against the burden God has seen fit to cast upon me, though it has been, nay, is, heavy and severe; and though my spirit has been sad and weary, cast down almost to the dust, yet I have had strength given me to fight against all repining, unthankful thoughts, and although not perhaps exactly satisfied with my lot in life, still I know it might be much worse; that many others suffer more than I do." And Amy's voice sank almost to a whisper, still and low.

But Frances was in no way moved by it, and replied as hardly and tauntingly as before—

"Go on, pray, Miss Neville, or is this all you have to say?"

"All? Ah, no! I could talk for ever. My feelings have been pent up—kept back for days, weeks, months past. You have loosened them, and they must have sway. I cannot restrain them now. Oh, if you had ever felt as I have felt, you could never sit there so indifferently, and not feel some pity for me; have I not been as tenderly and delicately nurtured? as much love lavished on me? and yet it is all past and gone, and I am alone in the world. There is comfort in once again being able to talk—to tell of all that is binding my heart so tightly—burning my brain. I have shed tears, but they have brought no relief. I have pictured to myself happier days, such days of love and peace, but they have vanished from before me. I have dreamt pleasant dreams, but with the morning sun they too have disappeared, and all is cold, stern reality. Oh, I could talk for ever if I thought it would move you to think better of me."

"You have my free permission to do so if this is what you come to ask; only you must excuse my being a careless or inattentive listener, as really your conversation interests me so little."

"And are you so strangely devoid of pity, then, or is it because you do not think me worth any? Alas! alas! when rich I was courted, flattered, and even loved; now, as the poor governess, I am despised and deserted," and again Amy's voice was low and plaintive.

"I never had the pleasure of knowing you in those palmy days you speak of; as a governess of course you must not expect to find much pity; it would be just as well to leave the history of your reverses—I hate everything sorrowful—and return to the starting point of your conversation, my cousin."

"I will," replied Amy. "I met Mr. Charles Linchmore yesterday accidentally in the corridor, as I was returning from a fruitless search for Fanny; he saw that I had injured my hand, and simply asked to look at it, that was all; you came by just then; your manner—your words, Miss Strickland, gave me the impression that you had misjudged me, and I shrank from the feeling, and could not rest until I had explained how it all happened, thinking,—but it seems I was wrong,—that your kind, womanly feeling and pity would at once feel for me, seeing the delicate position I occupy in this house."

But Amy's words only kindled the fire already smouldering in Frances' heart. Did they not recall to her remembrance the flower Charles had sent her? The embroidery he had taken? The hurt she had received from his horse? The interest he had afterwards taken in her welfare?

"I know you misjudged me, Miss Strickland; do not be afraid to say so."

"Afraid!" repeated Frances, scornfully, "No, you are mistaken; do you suppose I should consult your feelings?"

"No," replied Amy, sorrowfully, "I am sure you would not; I might have thought otherwise a few minutes ago, but now—"

"Now, I hope you are convinced that whatever I thought on the occasion referred to, I think still."

"I am sorry," replied Amy, much in the same tone she had said it to Charles the day before, "because you are wrong."

"I am not. Do you suppose I am blind, and do not see the interest he takes in your welfare?"

"Scarcely more so than he would show to a stranger whose wrist had been injured partly from his own fault in saying his horse was a quiet one, when the accident proved it to have been otherwise. Your manner, Miss Strickland, placed me in a very awkward position. Mr. Charles Linchmore noticed it as well as myself, and I think it irritated and annoyed him, but I, of course, had no right to feel hurt; I will try and act differently for the future."

But Frances answered not. Slowly her brow contracted—slowly her passion seemed to rise.

Suddenly she stood up and confronted her fancied rival, hatred, revenge, anger, by turns burning in her eyes, while at each sentence she uttered she stamped her foot impatiently, as if to give emphasis to what she said.

"How dare you tell me what he thought of me? I don't believe a word of it! Do you suppose I am a simpleton? a fool? and cannot see that you care for him, perhaps love him; and would prejudice me against him, cause disunion if you could, but it is useless—utterly useless—for I love him, Miss Neville;—loved him long before you knew him—long before you ever saw him,—yes, you may stare; I am not ashamed to repeat it—loved him—worshipped him if you will. What is your love, compared to mine, but a paltry, insignificant, nameless thing? What is your love that it should be preferred before mine? You whom he has known only so short a time. There is nothing in the world I would not give up for him; home, everything: for what are they all in comparison to his love? There is nothing I would not do to win him; nothing too great a sacrifice,—his love would compensate for all, and more than all."

Amy stood as if thunderstruck, while Frances, who had paused for a moment, went madly on. The ice was broken,—Amy knew of her love, she was glad of it, and cared not what she said.

"You talk of pity for your feelings: what are they in comparison to mine? You have never seen him you love, deserting, forsaking you for another. You have never seen his love grow colder and colder, his eye less bright when it met yours, and his smile less kind; you have never felt the cold touch of the hand that once warmly pressed yours, or found that your words have been spoken to careless ears, your conversation listened to heedlessly—indifferently; when before, every word that fell from your lips was waited for with impatient eagerness; you have never known the bitterness of estranged love; you have never known what it is to feel that all your deep strong love is unsought, unvalued, uncared for, that nothing, not even all your tenderness can recall the heart that once loved, once beat for you alone. You talk of sorrows. What are your sorrows compared to mine? You talk of trials; have you ever been tried like this?"

Frances stopped, overcome by her emotion, and wept violently and passionately; but her tears were caused more by the angry vehemence of her manner than from sorrow.

Who could have believed that the pale proud girl that nothing seemed to animate, nothing seemed to rouse, had such deep strong feelings within her? that beneath that cold, proud demeanour, fiery, unruly passions lay sleeping, requiring but a touch to call them forth with angry violence.

"Miss Strickland," said Amy, gently and pityingly placing her hand on her arm, "believe me, I never suspected, never guessed all this, or I should have made some excuse, some allowance for the manner in which you spoke to us on that day."

"To us," exclaimed Francis, as she dashed away the soft hand, "already you talk of him so; perhaps he has already told you he loves you, and when next you meet it will be to triumph over me, and talk with pity of her you have supplanted."

"No, never! Miss Strickland," replied Amy quickly; "you wrong me, I never could do so; pity you I certainly should; but triumph in your sorrow! Never! your suspicion is unjust, you wrong me, you do indeed!"

"And what if I do wrong you? there is no great harm in that. But I do not judge you harshly; I know you well enough; I know you will glory in being able to say you have supplanted proud Frances Strickland."

"Again let me assure you such will never be the case; from my heart I pity, will keep with you, if you will let me, and if he cares not for you, strive to lead your thoughts from him, and help you to conquer your love and learn if possible that there are other things to strive for besides his love, things that ought never to be lost sight of."

"And pray what may these wonderful things be?" asked she sarcastically.

"Your own self-respect, and the esteem of those around you."

"Self-respect! Esteem! Am I a child that you pretend to teach me? Did I think myself deficient in morals I should not come to Miss Neville to learn them."

"I do not pretend to teach you, Miss Strickland, neither do I wish to intrude my advice where I see it is not wanted."

"You do well. I want neither advice nor assistance from any one. My mind is fully made up how to act, I will enter heart and soul into it, and it will be strange if I do not succeed; so you had best, of all my friends," and Frances dwelt contemptuously on the last word, "wish me success."

"I am in total ignorance as to what your plans are; and therefore am not able to give any opinion on the subject."

"I shall be delighted to unravel them: it is but fair we should start together in the race we are to run."

"You are mistaken, Miss Strickland. There is no race to run. I shall never strive to win the love of one who cares not for me; besides I want it not. Mr. Charles Linchmore is,—can never be, anything to me; we are friends; nothing more; you have deceived yourself in imagining otherwise. I will never wilfully or deliberately deviate from the path of duty my conscience points out as the right and safe one to follow."

"Neither do I intend to; my conscience tells me Charles once cared for me; he cannot have forgotten me, have ceased to love me altogether; his love is only estranged for a time, not alienated for ever."

"I trust it may be so, and that if he ever cared for you—"

"Ever cared for me?" exclaimed Frances, "I tell you he loved me. Yes," added she passionately, "and his love shall return. Oh! I will enter heart and soul into it, he must—nay shall love me again. That you, meek and passionless as you are, love him, I wonder not; but that he should return your love? it must not! shall not! cannot be! I will move heaven and earth to aid me; I will humble my pride, sacrifice my ambition, all! all! I will suffer degradation, poverty, such as you complain of, all for him; and when at last he finds out, as he must, how I have loved him, knows all my heart's devotion, all its deep tenderness; I feel and know he will love me again as of old, as I know he once did. It cannot be that I should be doomed to a life of misery, without one bright ray to cheer the darkness of my lot, one bright spot to lighten my days."

"It is a sad life," replied Amy, "the one you have pictured, and the only one I have to look forward to."

"You!" cried Frances in the same passionate tone, "you! what matters it? Your love is but a child's love, your love is but a name. Oh, would," and she clasped her hands eagerly together, "would I could tell him—would he could know the value of the heart he rejects—what deep earnest love burns there for him. And he will know it, he shall know that the heart of proud Frances Strickland is all his own; then he will, he must, despise the love of such a weak, simple girl."

"I love him not," replied Amy, while her face and even neck crimsoned with the words.

"Talk not to me!" replied Frances, wildly. "I tell you it shall be so; the day shall come when he shall spurn you from him, cast away your love—scorn it—trample upon it. I tell you his love shall be mine, wholly, entirely mine, and none other's. You shall never be his. You think, perhaps, that the means to attain this end will be difficult and impossible. I tell you if there be means on earth to accomplish it—it shall be done. I will thwart all your fine plans; when you think yourself most secure, I will step in like a dark cloud, and hang about your path, hurling all your fond schemes to the ground. If he is not mine, he shall be no other's. Go! leave me."

"No, Frances Strickland, I will not, cannot leave you with such hot, revengeful feelings warring in your heart. I would have you think otherwise than what you do before I go. You are speaking in haste and passion and are scarcely aware of what you are saying. When the present feelings which now agitate you pass away, cooler moments will succeed; you will then be sorry I am gone, and that you cannot recall what you have said."

"Never! never!" cried Frances angrily and vehemently. "I will do as I have said, I will enter heart and soul into it, and since you have dared to love him, so I will ruin you if I can in his eyes."

"Shame on you, Miss Strickland, for so far forgetting your womanly feelings as to seek to injure one who has never intentionally done you harm. Shame on you for encouraging such revengeful feelings and badness of heart; for striving to render another as unhappy as you are yourself. All womankind, if they knew it, would think ill of you, and hold you in utter contempt. As for me, I scorn your words—your acts—and care little for the premeditated evil you threaten me with. Yes, I the poor dependant, separated from home,—mother,—friends, with none to help and befriend me, save One who has said He will be a father to the fatherless. Strong in his strength, and confident in my own purity of heart, I reject your words—your threats—with scorn, and pity you!"

How beautiful Amy looked, as for a moment she stood confronting Frances with all the strong emotions she felt flashing in her soft eyes, and chasing one another by turns over her face.

If a look could have turned Frances Strickland from her purpose, surely she would there and then have repented; but there was no sign of wavering, no pitying expression in her eyes, and turning away without another word, Amy left the room.

As the door closed upon her, the revengeful, unpitying expression died away from Frances' face, and burying her face in the soft crimson cushions of the chair, she wept, as only women can weep, passionately—convulsively.

After a while, she slowly raised herself and while sobs shook her frame, murmured with difficulty.

"Is it possible that I can have lost his love? Has he indeed taken it from me and given it to that girl? My God! that I should have lived to see it. Was ever anguish equal to mine? A drowning man catching at a straw is an enviable fate compared to mine; for I have not a straw even to lay hold of. To think that I should live to see myself deserted—cast aside without a thought. Oh! if I could only cast him off as easily, and revenge myself by weaning her love—for I know she must love him—poor and pitiful as it is, from him; so that he might feel some of the woe I suffer. If I could only do that. But no, I cannot—I cannot; I must love him."

Again she wept bitter, passionate tears, then went on despairingly.

"I cannot have been deceived; surely he did love me? I cannot have fancied it; oh! no, no; I am sure he loved me until he saw her. Oh! why did he ever see her? Why did they ever meet? And why was I so angry and proud with him when I found them talking together?"

She stopped again. Then went on bitterly and gloomily, while she clasped her hands tightly together over her bosom as if to check the tumult within, and stifle the sobs that shook her.

"I was proud—too proud. Yes it must be so,—he often said I was proud, but he shall say so no longer; to him at least, I will be a different being. Even if he never loved me, I will make him love me now—I will be all softness, gentleness, without a sign of the burning passions I feel. But should he speak of her?" and Frances tossed back her hair from her forehead impatiently, "yes, even then I will smother all pride, all angry feeling. I will win him yet, if he is to be won; no obstacle shall stop me. He shall learn to think me warm-hearted and generous, though to others I still seem cold and proud. Yes, I will rouse myself; I will no longer despond. I will cast aside all doubts and dismal forebodings. I will triumph over her yet, and trample her under foot; I wonder I could be so foolish as to weep," and, hurriedly rising, she bathed her eyes, so as to efface all trace of the emotion she had undergone, and then once more summoned Jane to her presence.

And Amy?

She went at once to her own room, sad and heavy at heart, and pondered long and deeply on all that Frances had said, and dreaded to think what might be the end of her plots and machinations. She foresaw she would leave no stone unturned to gain her end; and what might she not urge, what stories invent? Her hope,—all hope of softening Frances' heart and exonerating herself from blame, had failed utterly. The interview from which she had hoped so much had done harm, and evidently roused angry, jealous feelings, which Amy would believe and persuade herself there was no foundation for. She would not allow, for a moment, that Charles Linchmore had a thought for her, and as to loving her, that could not be. Amy even felt vexed and angry, and indignant with Frances, for so insisting upon it. She wondered what Frances would tell him, when next they met; and could not help feeling an undefinable dread—a sensation of coming evil. Suppose she should tell him that, though unsought, Amy's love was his, the bare supposition of what he would think brought tears into her eyes, but she hastily brushed them away, for Amy was not one to give way to needless sorrow, and tried to smile and think how foolish it was to weep, when there was yet no cause for it.

Yet, as she arrived at this conclusion, Frances' evident dislike to her, combined with her passionate, revengeful temper rose up before her; and what might they not lead her to do; "and he," murmured Amy mournfully, "does not know half she is capable of, and will believe anything she says of me. How I wish we had never met! How I wish she had never loved him!"

Poor Amy! she scarce knew what she wished, or what to think. One moment she was confident, at another she doubted, and trembled she scarce knew why.

CHAPTER V

DOUBTS AND FEARS

"Why so pale and wan, fond lover?
Prithee, why so pale?
Will, when looking well can't move her,
Looking ill prevail?
Prithee, why so pale?

Why so dull and mute, young sinner?
Prithee, why so mute?
Will, when speaking well can't win her,
Saying nothing do 't?
Prithee, why so mute?"
SUCKLING

"The wrist is better," was Dr. Bernard's next report of Amy; "but Miss Neville is ill and feverish, and must be kept perfectly quiet."

So there were no more lessons for some days; while Julia installed herself by Amy's bedside as head nurse, aided by Mary; and sometimes Mrs. Hopkins came, bringing a jelly or some nicety she had prepared with her own hands to please the invalid; Amy, therefore, was not dull, with so many friends to cheer and take care of her.

During these days Charles was restless and unhappy; was it not partly his fault she was ill? How he accused himself of being the author of all the mischief that had accrued from the simple fact of having allowed her to have her own way, when he might have so easily prevented it; nor was he in any way consoled when Julia said to him, "Well, you must confess, Miss Neville has nerve now, and is not afraid of her own shadow; for I have never heard her once complain of pain; she bears it like a martyr."

How he envied Dr. Bernard his privilege of seeing and speaking to Amy, and would have waylaid him at every visit if he had only dared. To ask news of his patient would betray too evident an interest in her welfare; so although Charles saw him come and go every day, yet he was obliged to wait patiently, sometimes for hours, until he could catch sight of Anne. Anne, who kept out of his way as much as she could, who had determined on having nothing to do in the matter, now found herself dragged into his confidence, whether she would or no. How she regretted the curiosity that had induced her to join him that day in the corridor; if it had not been for that she would had been free now, and not troubled with the knowledge of the fact that he had certainly fallen in love irretrievably with his sister-in-law's governess; but then he looked so miserable and unhappy, Anne could not help pitying him, she was too kind-hearted not to do that. So every day she gave him news of Amy, and consoled herself with thinking things had gone too far for any interference of hers to do any good; but, at the same time, she would be the bearer of no kind messages, no books, no flowers; and Charles often flew into a rage, and they parted bad friends in consequence, only to find him awaiting her the next day as anxiously as before.

Anne wondered sometimes how it would all end, and whether Amy loved him or no, and whether Frances guessed how things were going on. Anne did not like Frances, and had often felt sorry at Charles's seeming partiality for her, and thought how unsuited they were to make each other happy; and yet only last year everyone had looked forward to an engagement between them as almost a settled thing. How devoted he had been; but then perhaps he had found out what a temper Frances had, so proud and jealous—so imperious a will. Men did not like that, so she concluded that during the few months that had intervened, he had thought better of it and changed his mind. Besides, they were cousins, so there was an excuse for his paying her more attention than he would have done had there been no relationship between them.

Amy's illness was more of mind than body; she heard old kind Dr. Bernard say so, and knew it well herself, and tried hard and earnestly to rouse and be herself again, but all to no purpose; it would not do. She had worried and fretted, and thought, and allowed her mind to dwell too much on the eventful interview she had had with Frances, to shake off so easily the weight that was pressing on her mind, and sinking her spirits. Julia was kindness itself, and did all she could to comfort and cheer her, but then she knew nothing of Frances' unkind suspicions and unjust opinions, or of the fear Amy felt lest she should tell Charles what she so erroneously and determinately adhered to, namely, that her love was his, although unsought, unasked, and unwished for.

It was this fear kept Amy ill. If she could only have unburthened her mind to Julia and told her that! But she could not, and so she lay quiet, very quiet, and did all they wished her to do, those kind nurses; but still she did not get well, and it was nearly a fortnight before Dr. Bernard pronounced her better, and in a fair way of recovery.

Then, as she grew convalescent, she dreaded the idea of meeting Charles Linchmore again, lest he should have heard and believed Frances. How she wished his leave had expired and he were gone, so that she might never see him again, never hear of him, and she blushed painfully one day when Anne happened to mention his name, to the no small astonishment of the sharp-sighted Anne, who noted it at once, and drew her own conclusions therefrom.

In the meantime Frances had not been idle. Determined on gaining her end, she went cunningly and cautiously to work, and while Amy was ill the field was all her own.

First, she must find out how much of Charles's heart had been given to Amy; so, controlling her feelings by a strong effort of will, which made her appear a little colder than she really was, and was worthy of a better cause, she led him to talk of Amy, and wept afresh at each new proof he gave of how much he thought of and cared for her. Still she did not, would not despair. Like all the Linchmores, Charles was proud. If she could only touch that; only rouse a jealous feeling within him, the battle would be won.

How well she remembered his hasty exit from the school-room and the angry, jealous expression of his face. Was it not that that had first led her to think he cared for another, and that his love was lost to her, or nearly so?

All the fears Amy was suffering and tormenting herself with were groundless. Not for worlds would Frances have allowed Charles to think Amy cared for him, or returned his love. No, that would take him from her for ever, and oh! the anguish that thought cost her. So while Amy was fidgeting and worrying herself, Frances was trying all in her power to lead Charles to think that Amy's heart was Mr. Vavasour's, and as Amy grew better, and able to resume studies again, so Charles became more depressed and irritable, and more unlike his former self than ever.

Amy no longer passed her evenings upstairs alone, but came down into the drawing-room. Mr. Linchmore would have it so. Dr. Bernard had said her illness was principally caused by anxiety of mind, and Miss Tremlow had hinted her fears that the governess was too much alone for one so young, so he mildly but gently insisted upon it, overruling Amy's scruples and his own.

This great change in her life at Brampton was viewed very differently by those most interested in her. Frances hated it, as bringing her and Charles on more intimate terms of friendship, and he himself hated it, as giving Vavasour an opportunity of paying her more attention than before.

Robert Vavasour was the only one pleased with the arrangement. Knowing nothing, suspecting nothing, of what was passing around him, he was glad to see her, and sat down by her and told her so the very first evening she came down, much to Charles's intense disgust, who kept sullenly aloof, in a wretchedly bad temper, which not even his cigar or Bob could dissipate or soothe, although he angrily left the room and had recourse to both; but neither had any good effect, his mind was too thoroughly engrossed with the governess.

Another consequence of Amy's evenings being spent downstairs was that she had little time for writing home. Often instead of the four closely-written crossed sheets of paper, only one found its way into the envelope, and that one sometimes scarcely filled, and hastily written. But Mrs. Neville never complained; she fully believed that as Amy said, so it was; not the will but the time was wanting.

Sometimes there was dancing of an evening, and then Amy was expected to contribute her share to the evening's amusement by playing the piano for the dancers, who never seemed to tire. Sometimes her head ached sadly, and her fingers grew quite stiff, and she stumbled dreadfully over the notes, but no one heeded it, or seemed to mind it, and she played on until relieved by Julia or Anne, who soon learned to guess the true reason of the false notes.

The tight fitting black dress and little plain collar, that had often annoyed Anne, were now laid aside in the evening for a plain white muslin, made high, without ornament or ribbon of any kind, confined at the waist by a broad band. It was simple, but suited her well; and many a proud beauty, conscious of her own loveliness, would have fallen into the shade beside the governess in her plain white muslin.

There was a dignity as well as beauty in Amy: the one attracted, the other commanded the respect of everyone. There was something truly feminine about her—grace in every movement, sweetness in every smile, sad as her smiles were now; and her manner was so devoid of affectation, yet so soft and winning, what wonder that she was loved by some, and hated as a dangerous rival by others.

Amy sat at a small table writing home, her head bent gracefully forward, and her fair fingers guiding the pen rapidly over the paper, as she added a few lines to the hastily-written note begun that morning. Her hair—it looked almost golden by the fire-light—was plainly braided, though the brush had scarcely been able to smooth the waving luxuriant masses—and wound simply round a comb at the back of her small head—'Madonna-wise,' as Charles had once said.

Her naturally fair complexion—so fair, that it almost rivalled the clear white muslin dress—was set off by a slight colour which tinged her cheeks, caused, perhaps, by the eagerness with which she wrote; for Amy knew full well, that the dinner over, she would have to go below, with no chance of finishing her letter that night, for the morrow's early post.

But now her task is done; a pleasant task for her, so filled as her heart is with love for her fond and anxious mother. A few tears glistened in her eyes, as she sealed and directed the letter, and, "I wish dear Mamma would write to me," fell scarcely audible from her lips.

It was nearly a month since Mrs. Neville had written; not once during all the time of Amy's illness; but then she knew nothing of that, Amy never mentioned it; it would have made her mother too anxious and unhappy.

How slowly the days crept by! and how anxiously every morning Amy looked forward to the afternoon, when the postman made his appearance at the park; yet each day she was disappointed, Mrs. Neville did not write.

Mrs. Elrington wrote constantly, at her friend's earnest request and wish, so she said. But did this satisfy Amy? No; she longed once again to see her dear parent's handwriting; she felt an aching void at the heart; and was most anxious and nervous, fearing she knew not what, whilst a thousand wild suggestions filled her brain, and sad thoughts trembled in her heart.

Amy's desk was scarcely shut ere Mrs. Hopkins came in. She hesitated half-way between the door and the table, uncertain whether to advance or not, but Amy's voice soon assured her.

"Come in, Nurse," said she, "and sit down. I am not busy; I have been writing, but my letter is finished, so I am quite ready to talk to you, which will be far pleasanter to me than sitting alone."

"Thank you, Miss; it is so long since I had a talk with you—not since your illness; I hope you are feeling well and strong again?"

"Quite, thank you; I am entirely out of the doctor's hands now, and hope I shall not want him again for a long time. How are you and Mason getting on? more amicably, I hope?"

"No, I can't say we are; her head is filled with French nonsense. It was a thousand pities Madam ever took her to France, she has never been the same woman since—such airs and graces; such bends and courtesies! such twistings of her body! and as for her waist, why it's just half the size it was; I wonder she doesn't burst sometimes—I'm sure her face looks red enough, and all through being squeezed so tight; but there, it's no business of mine, I only wonder Madam puts up with it.

"Then as to master," continued Mrs. Hopkins, "I never did see a gentleman so altered as he is. I thought the staying at Brampton, and having company here, would have enlivened him; but Lord bless you, Miss, he is worse a great deal. He always was grave, like; but then he'd a pleasant smile and good word for everybody in the house; but now—" Nurse sighed, stroked and doubled up the corner of her apron, and looked thoughtful.

"And now?" asked Amy, enquiringly.

"Now, Miss, he's quite altered, quite changed—melancholy, like. 'Tis true he says, 'Good morning, Mrs. Hopkins;' but that's all. The butler tells me he seldom smiles with the company; but sits and talks like a gentleman absent in his mind."

"You surely must be mistaken, Nurse," said Amy, thoughtfully, "I see no difference."

"Very likely not, Miss; but we servants see it. There's scarce anything ever goes on amiss in a house that servants don't notice it. I don't pretend to know why master's changed; but certain as I am sitting here, he is changed. May-be he has something on his mind. How different his father was. God rest his soul, poor old gentleman."

"Was his father much liked? was he popular at Brampton? for all seem to respect and love the present Mr. Linchmore."

"He never lived long enough down here for people to know enough about him to like him. He wasn't over and above fond of his lady, nor of her doings neither—so I've heard my mother say. He was, by all accounts, a very wild gentleman in his youth."

"And old Mrs. Linchmore, his wife. Why was he not fond of her?"

"She was a fearful woman!" replied Mrs. Hopkins, drawing her chair nearer Amy's; "very handsome in her youth. Mr. Linchmore married her for her beauty, and sorry enough he was for it afterwards. That's her picture hangs over the chimney-piece in the dining room, and a beautiful face it has; only too proud and stormy, like, to my mind."

"Did you ever see her?"

"Yes, Miss. I mind her just before she died. Six months before that happened, the housekeeper, who was a friend of my mother's, got me the under housemaid's place here. I seem to see the lady now, tall and straight as a needle, with such a stately step and proud look; her eyes bright, black, and piercing as a hawk's, although she was gone forty and more. I used to tremble whenever she looked at me, and many's the time I've run for the life of me down the long gallery to get out of her way. Oh! she was a fearful lady!"

"How so?" inquired Amy, hoping to gain some intelligence as to why her room was so pertinaciously kept closed.

"They say, Miss," replied Nurse, glancing uneasily about her, "that the house was haunted when she was alive. I can't say as ever I saw anything; but I believe it all the same, and so did my fellow-servants, though it was never whispered between us; certainly she was no good christian any more than Tabitha, her maid, who had lived with her ever since she was a girl, and knew all her secrets; and would be muttering to herself all day long. This was a strange house then, and I don't wonder the villagers were 'frighted to come near it."

"Why so? surely a woman could do them no harm?"

"Well, Miss, they said she could, and did do a deal of harm to them she didn't like; and then there was that bad story they had about her husband's cousin."

"What was that, Nurse?"

"I can't scarce tell you all the rights of it, Miss, only what I've heard people say, as you see it happened afore my time; but 'twas all about a cousin of her husband's, who had been adopted by his mother. My old mistress was fearful jealous of her, as well she might be if all accounts was true about her gentle, loving ways. But there, they didn't save her from being suspected by Mrs. Linchmore of carrying on at a shameful, scandalous rate with her husband, Mr. Linchmore. Poor young lady! She disappeared one night, and 'twas given out that she had fled from the Park to hide her shame. But there, people ain't blind; and then she never came back again, and so the villagers whispered 'twas a darker deed than that took her away so sudden."

"But what did Mrs. Linchmore's husband say?"

"He and his wife had fine words about it, Miss, and he went off soon after and left her for good. But there worse than that happened; for his poor mother, her as adopted Miss Mary—that was the poor young lady's name, Miss—broke her heart about it all, and died. She was a nice, good old lady, and very fond of Miss Mary, and on her death-bed she told my mother she died believing the young lady innocent; and no one was ever to believe anything else until they saw Miss Mary again, and then all wou'd come right, and everybody hear the truth. But there, we never did hear the truth, for we never saw Miss Mary again; so it was just as well the old lady was took when she was, and went so happy and peaceful."

"But her daughter-in-law, your old mistress, what became of her? I think she died suddenly, did she not?"

"Very, Miss Neville. She would have no one but Tabitha to wait on her when she was ill; but none of us cared much about that; and they used to abuse one another terrible sometimes. It was a long time before she'd see the doctor, and then she wouldn't take his medicine; we found all the bottles ranged like a regiment of soldiers in the cupboard after she died—not even the corks out of them, or a drop of medicine taken. When she got worse she wouldn't lay in the bed, but had the mattress moved off on to the floor. She died that very night quite sudden, for none of us thought her so bad as that, not even the doctor; but there, he was quite a young man, and I mind well his coming in the morning. She hadn't been so well the evening before, so he came quite early, as I was cleaning down the hall. I went upstairs with him, and knocked twice at my mistress's door, but nobody answered; so the doctor opened it, and went in, and I followed, terribly frightened, but so curious like, I couldn't keep back anyhow."

Nurse paused, and then sunk her voice almost to a whisper as she went on,

"Oh! what a terrible sight we saw. My mistress was quite dead; one of her hands clutching the bed clothes, the other thrown above her head, and closed so tight, it looked as though the nails were buried in the flesh. Her eyes were wide open, and a frightful look her face had, as though she had died in torments.—She was an awful corpse;" and Nurse shuddered, and her hands trembled as she stirred up the fire.

"But where was Tabitha? How was it she had not called for anyone?"

"She was lying by the side of the bed on the floor, and at first I thought she was dead, too; but she came to life again when we carried her into the open air, and a scared look she had when she opened her eyes; but it was weeks before she got well again, and then she left, and none of us felt sorry, I can tell you."

"Did she give you no account of the lady's death?"

"The doctors said she died in a fit, but we all knew her end was something awful, for one of the maids who had been put to sleep in a room near, in case she might be wanted, told us she heard in the dead of the night an awful noise in Mrs. Linchmore's room—it woke her; and then a loud talking; as if my mistress was angry about something, and presently a loud scream and laughter; and then she was so frightened she dropped off insensible, like, and didn't come to herself until she heard us all astir with Tabitha in the morning."

"Where was Mr. Linchmore?"

"He was away abroad somewhere with his two little boys; and didn't get here till three or four days after her death. We all thought he would shut up the house and go abroad to foreign parts again, as he had done for years past; but no, he had it all fresh painted and papered; all except his wife's two rooms,—there's a dressing-room adjoining, but only the one door for the two—he never went near them again I believe, but can't say for certain, as I married and left the place. My mistress was buried in great state, ever so many carriages and grand folks,—some of them from London,—and a mighty lot of beautiful feathers nodding and bobbing over the hearse; but for all that we wern't sorry to lose her, we all feared her, and though a crowd assembled in the churchyard, 'twas out of curiosity, many of the villagers never having seen such a grand funeral before; there wasn't, so I heard my old man say, a wet eye amongst them, not even the master's, and as for the company of mourners, Lor' bless you, Miss, they laughed and joked over their luncheon afterwards as though they had been to a wedding."

"Has Mrs. Linchmore's room never been occupied since her death?"

"Never, Miss, that I know of. I don't think my old master ever went into it again; my present master don't seem to love it neither, and as for Madam, she says it's the worst room in the house; all old fashioned and gloomy."

"I should like to see the room some day, Nurse, will you show it to me?"

"I, Miss? I wouldn't go into it for any money. John at the lodge says he's seen a queer sort of light there lately; bright and blue, like. Half the maids in the house are talking about it; and go about in couples to turn the beds down. But he only saw it once, and then for only half a minute, so perhaps it was his fancy."

"Is the door kept locked?"

"I shouldn't like to go to sleep if it wasn't. Yes, Miss, the key's kept down in my room below. I couldn't bide comfortable in bed with it in my room above stairs, at night. No, I was mortal afraid of the old lady when she was alive, and couldn't face her dead anyhow, and she such an awful corpse too."

Just at this moment Anne, who had entered the room unperceived, clapped her hands. Nurse nearly dropped off her chair with fright; even Amy was startled.

"Now, that serves you right!" exclaimed the intruder, "for talking about such horrible things. Mrs. Hopkins, let me put your cap straight; now don't tremble so, and shake your head, or I shall put it on awry,—there that will do; and now come away, Miss Neville; who would have believed you were so superstitious? Imagine Miss Tremlow's astonishment when she hears it. 'Miss Bennet,' said she, just now, 'if you are going upstairs do let Miss Neville come down with you; and open the door ve—ry—gent—ly, as I dare say she is busy writing home.' Instead of which my gentleness nearly frightened you into fits, and instead of writing you are listening to all kinds of horrors."

"What a mad young lady she is," soliloquised Mrs. Hopkins, as the two girls left the room together, "I declare for the moment I thought it was my old mistress herself; she used to clap her hands just that way when she was vexed. I'll go below, it's lonely here now Miss Neville's gone. She's a sweet young lady and deserves a better husband than that Mr. Vavasour, who John says is hankering after her, and makes eyes when Madam isn't looking. There's no good in a man as keeps company with two young women at once, and one of them married too, he ought to be ashamed of himself; but there, I suppose it's only what the gentry call flirting. Ah! well, for my part I don't like it; and how Miss Neville's mother would vex if she knew it. I musn't forget her letter neither, but'll put it with the rest for the post; and that reminds me I never gave her the one that came for her this afternoon, but I'll lay it on her dressing table, she'll be sure to see it when she goes to bed. Poor dear! I suppose she'll be kept up pianning it till her fingers are most ready to drop off."

CHAPTER VI

THE WARNING

"Oh! life is like the summer rill, where weary daylight dies;
We long for morn to rise again, and blush along the skies;

For dull and dark that stream appears, whose waters in the day,
All glad, in conscious sunniness, went dancing on their way.
But when the glorious sun hath 'woke, and looked upon the earth,
And over hill and dale there float the sounds of human mirth;
We sigh to see day hath not brought its perfect light to all,
For with the sunshine on those waves, the silent shadows fall."
CAROLINE NORTON

Frances Strickland was seated at the piano, singing, when Anne and Amy entered the drawing-room.

"I wonder who asked or persuaded her to sing, for she always requires an immense amount of pressing. However, so much the better for you, as she will, I doubt not, remain perched on the music-stool half the night," said Anne.

Amy sat down in her usual place, near the window, so as to be almost hidden by the heavy drapery of the curtain, and mechanically her eyes wandered in search of Mr. Linchmore, as her thoughts dwelt on Mrs. Hopkin's words, "Master has something on his mind."

Was it so? Was it possible? and if so, why was he unhappy? Young and inexperienced in the ways of the world, Amy had no suspicion of the real cause of Mr. Linchmore's sadness; in fact, as she told Mrs. Hopkins, she had not remarked it. Why should he be changed? What should he be sad about?

Often, in after days, Amy wished she had never found out the dreadful cause of this alteration.

Mr. Linchmore held a book in his hand, but his eyes had wandered from its pages. Amy followed their direction.

At the farthest end of the room sat Mrs. Linchmore, and by her side Mr. Strickland. Listlessly she sat, and listlessly she appeared to be listening to her companion's words, although he seemed to be exerting himself in an unusual manner to please her, not a yawn, or symptom of fatigue about him. They seemed to have changed places, the weariness all on her part; she was evidently inattentive and absent.

Robert Vavasour leant against the back of the sofa on which she sat; like Mr. Linchmore, he held a book in his hand. Was he reading it? No. Impossible! the leaves were turned over carelessly, and at random, two or three together, not one by one.

A little farther off sat Anne, laughing and chatting merrily with Mr. Hall, while he was bending low, and speaking, in a soft, subdued voice, such things as only those who love know how to speak—Anne looking pert, and trying to appear indifferent to his words.

"He loves her!" thought Amy, as she watched them, "and she? yes, I think she does, or will love him too. How happy she looks, not a cloud to darken her bright path; everything is smooth for her, and appears in gay, golden colours. Happy Anne! May the light that sparkles in your eyes never be quenched, nor your merry laugh be chased away by the sad, sorrowful look that tells of the heart's best hopes faded away, and bright days gone never to return."

Again Amy looked towards Mrs. Linchmore. Robert Vavasour had taken the vacant seat by her side. Alfred Strickland was gone.

How different she appeared! No longer listless or inattentive, her face was brightened by smiles. She was all animation, talking and laughing almost as merrily as Anne.

How sad it is to see those we love smiling on others as they never smile on us, or whilst our hearts are overcharged with sorrow and heaviness, theirs are careless and unconcerned, insensible to our misery, if not even mocking our anguish. Then it is that in bitterness of heart we could lie down and die, or at least weep drops of agony, to think that our love could be so lightly valued, or we ourselves so neglected and forsaken.

Mrs. Linchmore knew her husband's eyes were watching her, knew, too, partly the agony of his heart, yet she trifled on, caring little for the feelings of him whose slightest wish she should have studied to please, and striven to obey.

Mr. Linchmore closed his book. It accidentally fell to the ground. His wife,—whose attention had been seemingly engrossed by Robert Vavasour, nevertheless watched her husband uneasily. When would his patience be exhausted? When would his pride take the alarm? Now! thought she, as she started at the slight noise the book made as it reached the ground. Calling to remembrance her husband's previous suspicions, she asked Mr. Vavasour to beg Miss Neville to play for a dance.

He was at Amy's side as Mr. Linchmore rose from his chair. Very stiffly she received him.

"Does Miss Neville intend retiring from observation all night? It was with some difficulty I found her out in this out of the way corner."

"This is my usual seat when I am not required to play. I should have thought Mr. Vavasour had seen me here too often to have searched for me elsewhere."

"You are right, I did not look for you elsewhere. What I meant to say was, that I wished you would take a seat somewhere, where one might catch a glimpse of you, instead of beneath the shade of this detestable window curtain. Have I got into a scrape by so wishing?"

"Certainly not," replied Amy.

"You think too little of self, Miss Neville. Look at Miss Strickland, who always plants herself in the most prominent position, so that no one can fail remarking her the moment they set foot into a room."

"Do you not think it is rather her beauty strikes the eye of a stranger?"

"It may be so. I do not admire her."

"Not admire her?" exclaimed Amy, "I must condemn your bad taste, surely everyone must think her beautiful."

"Because everyone thinks so, is that a reason why I should?"

"No, but most men admire beauty. It seems so strange you should not."

"I have the bad taste not to care about mere beauty such as Miss Strickland's; she is too proud, and, if I mistake not, her temper is none of the sweetest; no, I shall not choose my wife for her pretty face."

"Perhaps you seek a miracle of perfection, mind and face both."

"No miracle, Miss Neville, for I have seen both."

He looked at her so earnestly, that Amy felt confused, while Charles, who savagely watched them at a distance, felt as surly as a bear, and as miserable as he well could be. He could stand it no longer.

"Miss Neville," said he approaching them, "Has Vavasour given you Mrs. Linchmore's message?"

"No. I quite forgot it," replied he, "It was something about dancing wasn't it? but I for one don't care a rush about it."

"Because you do not, is no reason why others should not," retorted Charles, turning on his heel.

"The next time a message is entrusted to Mr. Vavasour," said Amy rising, "I hope he will not forget to deliver it. I will ask Mrs. Linchmore if it is her wish I should play."

"Stay, Miss Neville, I can answer the question She does—but—"

"Thank you, I need no further commands," replied Amy proudly.

As they left the recess, Alfred Strickland,—who sitting close by had overheard almost every word,—turned lazily round on the sofa.

"Well done for the schoolmistress!" muttered he, "by Jove! how she snubbed Vavasour. That last was a settler!"

Robert Vavasour leant over Amy as she arranged the music and commenced playing.

"You misjudge me, Miss Neville; but I hope a time will come when you will think better of me."

"I do not think badly of you," replied Amy as he turned away.

"Thoroughly snubbed! old fellow, eh?" said Alfred Strickland, as Vavasour passed the sofa where he still sat, "never mind, cheer up! and better luck next time!"

"Did you speak, sir?" exclaimed Vavasour fiercely.

"No, no, nothing of any consequence. It's chilly, don't you find it so?"

"Very," replied Robert, as he passed on.

Had Mr. Linchmore, as Mrs. Hopkins said, anything on his mind, or was he blind to all that was passing around him? Partly so; he had seen Vavasour's flirtation with his wife with uneasiness and displeasure, determined in his own mind to put a stop to it; but the scene suddenly changed. Miss Neville appeared, and he immediately transferred his attentions to her, or certainly a great part of them.

For a short time Mr. Linchmore was puzzled, but ere long he set him down as that most selfish of human beings, one who systematically storms a woman's heart until it succumbs to him, and is all his own, when gradually and quietly he releases himself from his victim, and leaves her heart to break or recover as best it can.

A female flirt is bad enough, but there are oftentimes excuses to be made for her. She becomes so from the force of circumstances, from undue admiration or a natural love of it; from some secret sorrow, or unhappy home, made so by a husband's desertion, something there must be to urge her on.

But how many men glory in and boast of their conquests, and tell of the many hearts they have broken. How sad is the idea of some young girl, just entering life, made the sport of one of these. She surrenders her truthful, guileless heart, in all its first strong love, to him who she truly believes is all her young fancy ever pictured in her brightest dreams—all that is good and noble.

Too late she finds out her mistake, too late knows she has been deceived, and her heart trifled with. She becomes in her turn a flirt, and her heart hard and callous. The world is no longer in her eyes the bright world it was, but a hollow, heartless pageant.

Mr. Linchmore liked Amy. Should such be her fate? Should he sit quietly by and see her heart thus sacrificed, her peace of mind so destroyed? God forbid! If he had the power to prevent it; it should never be. So he watched her and Mr. Vavasour narrowly, determined to warn her himself.

The grand piano Amy played on was so placed as to command a view of the dancers, as they flitted past her. Robert Vavasour, although he said he cared not a rush for it, was flying along in a waltz with Mrs. Linchmore. Somehow Amy did not like seeing him so soon with her again, she felt sorry; and her eyes involuntarily sought Mr. Linchmore, but she had not far to look, he was close beside her; and placed a chair as she finished playing.

"You must be tired, Miss Neville," he said kindly.

"No; I am so accustomed to play, that I think the dancers would get tired before I should."

"My wife never tires."

"How beautiful she looks to-night!" said Amy.

Mrs. Linchmore was always well dressed; this evening, perhaps, more simply than usual. A rich white silk dress, fitting her to perfection, with a few scarlet roses in her hair and bosom.

"She grows more beautiful every day," replied he, sorrowfully. "Are you fond of gaiety, Miss Neville?"

"Yes, I think so, or fancy I should be. I have seen little of it; but it must be so pleasant to thoroughly enjoy oneself."

"I doubt if very many feel it to be thorough enjoyment; even balls and parties have their cares; but you would hardly think so to listen to the talking and merriment around."

Anne, at this moment, played a galop, and again Robert Vavasour whirled past with his hostess.

"Mr. Vavasour dances well," was all the remark Mr. Linchmore made. "You appear well acquainted with him, Miss Neville. Is he an old acquaintance?"

"No. Oh, no!" replied Amy, hurriedly and confusedly.

"He is a man who soon ingratiates himself with the fair sex. Of a proud, reserved nature, a word from his lips is of more weight with them than half the good deeds of a better man. He is a man who could humbug the wisest, and flirt with the silliest; and without the slightest intention of losing his own heart, or becoming entangled himself. He is not a marrying man; and for that simple reason every girl will try to win his heart; or will fall into the snare he sets, believing that she is the chosen one, and that his iron will and heart has succumbed to her; and be naturally proud of her supposed conquest, until she finds out her mistake, as most assuredly she will."

"I have warned her," thought Mr. Linchmore, as he left her, nor stayed to see the effect of his words.

While Amy inwardly murmured, "I shall never fall into the snare."

CHAPTER VII

MISGIVINGS

"Coquets, leave off affected arts,
Gay fowlers at a flock of hearts;
Woodcocks to shun your snares have skill,
You show so plain, you strive to kill.
In love the heartless catch the game,
And they scarce miss, who never aim."
GREEN

How often it happens that in realising our fondest hopes, we experience not the happiness we expected.

Each and all of us, at some unhappy period of our lives, have been led to exclaim, "Ah! if this state of uncertainty were but at an end, this suspense over. Let the worst come, we are prepared for it: it cannot make us more miserable than we are." Yet fortified as we deem ourselves against the worst, braced up as it were, and prepared for aught that may happen; how feeble we are, at the very best, when the ruin, sickness, death of those we love, or whatever sorrow it may be, overtakes us; how often—always—unequal to bear the blow. Then we sigh for our former state of uncertainty; it was bliss compared to our present grief, when, fancying ourselves prepared for the worst, gentle hope filled our hearts, and bade us look trustfully onwards for bright smiles, wreathed with roses; where, alas! we found only tears beneath a crown of thorns.

"Such is life; The distant prospect always seems more fair; And when attained, another still succeeds, Far fairer than before,—yet compassed round With the same dangers and the same dismay; And we poor pilgrims in this dreary maze, Still discontented, chase the fairy form Of unsubstantial happiness, to find, When life itself is sinking in the strife, 'Tis but an airy bubble and a cheat."

Thus it was with Amy Neville. She had been uneasy and unhappy at not hearing from her mother; evil forebodings had filled her heart, and all kinds of imaginary fancies her brain. She had sighed again and again but for one short letter of explanation, clearing away her mother's mysterious silence, and lifting the veil that seemed to hang so gloomily and heavily between her and her home.

It came. It had arrived the evening before. It was the letter Mrs. Hopkins had forgotten to give her, and had placed on her dressing table, and there Amy found it on retiring for the night.

How eagerly she seized and perused its contents, read and re-read every word of it, till her eyes ached and swam with tears, and she could no longer trace the handwriting on the sheet of paper. Then wearily she crept to bed, and placing the letter beneath her pillow, so as to be able to read it again the first thing in the morning, fell into a troubled sleep, with but one thought at her heart, and that one, that her beloved parent had been ill,—very ill.

The letter was from Mrs. Elrington, assuring her that although Mrs. Neville had been seriously ill, all danger was over now, and the invalid in a fair way of recovery; yet Amy, whose eyes were heavy with recent tears and unrefreshing rest, could scarcely reconcile to herself that it was so, and how her heart beat as she read an account of her mother's sufferings. How gladly would she have watched by the sick bed, and ministered to her relief. How gladly have shared with Mrs. Elrington in the kind attentions and unremitting care she knew she had bestowed on her good and gentle parent.

Mrs. Elrington's letter was kindly and thoughtfully worded, well calculated to soothe and tranquillise an anxious daughter's heart.

Mrs. Neville, she said, had certainly been very ill, though not in any immediate danger. It had been her express wish throughout that Amy should not be told of her illness, as there was no necessity for her incurring an expensive journey at such an inclement season of the year; "and," continued Mrs. Elrington, "your mother rightly judged that had you known she was ill, your anxiety would have been great if not allowed to share in nursing her. Thank God, she is able to leave her room, and now reclines on a sofa in the little parlour, and is gradually regaining her usual strength, though we must not expect her to become well all at once; but I hope in a few weeks she will be able to occupy her usual seat as of old, in the easy chair by the fire-side, which said chair Sarah is very busy making a new chintz cover for, in readiness for the invalid, and in honour of the day when she first sits up. So dear Amy," concluded Mrs. Elrington, "you must keep up your spirits and your roses, or your mother will outvie you in both when you see her again, and be sure that I will send for you at once, should she not go on as well as we could wish."

And with this letter Amy was obliged to rest satisfied, though for many days after that she grew nervous and restless as the hour for the post drew near; and could scarcely control the impatient desire she felt to walk half way down the road to Standale to meet the postman. Once she did walk down.

Though now approaching the end of January, it was quite like a November day—foggy, with a thick drizzling rain falling, yet Amy heeded it not, but walked quickly on, wrapped in a thick seal-skin cloak.

She passed through the village and reached the turnpike gate. Here at the cottage door stood William Hodge.

"A nasty damp day, Miss," said he, touching his hat civilly.

"Yes," replied Amy, "quite a change from the cold, frosty, snowy weather we have had."

"We shall have more rain yet, I'm thinking."

"I hope not. How are Mrs. Marks and her husband?"

"Well. Very well, thank'ee, Miss."

"Are they from home, that you have charge of the Gate?" asked Amy, surprised at seeing a stranger.

"Mrs. Marks is, Miss, and that's why I'm here. I'm keeping house with her husband while she's away. Her mother's took very bad."

"I am sorry to hear that; but I hope it is nothing serious?"

"Well I don't expect anyhow she'll get over it, Miss, she ought to be dead by this time, and if she isn't I can't bide here no longer, I must be turning about home. Mrs. Marks promised fairly enough to bide only a week, and it's near upon three by my calculations. She's going to bring back a sister along with her, one that's dazed," and he tapped his forehead with a knowing look.

"A sad charge," replied Amy, "and one rather unsuited to Mrs. Marks."

"I don't know that, Miss. Yer see neighbours think Jane wouldn't be so bad if she worn't humoured, and she ain't likely to get much of that down here. To my thinking Mrs. Marks is just the right sort to cure her; she'd racket any poor body to their senses, if 'twas possible."

"Has Mrs. Marks' sister always been in such a sad state?"

"All as I can tell yer, Miss, is, she worn't born so, it's comed on her since, and when I've said that I've said all I do know about it. Her mother comed down years ago now to Deane,—that's my home, Miss,—with three daughters. Mrs. Marks was one of 'em, she married off, and came down here with her husband. Then t'other one she married too, but as for Jane, she never had no chance of a husband, for who'd marry a 'dafty,' Miss? They was pretty close people, and never wagged their tongues with nobody, so nobody knew nothing at all about them nor where they comed from; only folks make a guess at things somehow; and down at Deane they thinks they comed from Stasson, a place none so far from this neither; and more than that Miss, that Jane was the reason why they comed so sudden and secret, like; but there, if they thought the sight of a new place 'ould cure Jane they was mighty mistaken, for from that day to this she've never been no good at all to them, and to my thinking never will be."

"It's a sad story, indeed," replied Amy.

"You may depend upon it, Miss, if we knew the rights of it, it's a bad, as well as a sad story, but there, I've no call to say so. For certain, Miss, there's a something very strange and mysterious 'bout Jane.

Perhaps the Brampton folks'll turn out more cute than the Deane ones, and find out what 'tis. It's on my mind, and has been scores of times, that Jane's mortal afeard of summut or other."

Amy smiled at Hodge's suspicions, and passed on.

Marks did not make his appearance, fond of a gossip as he was, and of saying good-morrow to everyone who passed through the 'pike. Probably the "Brampton Arms" was too strong a temptation, and,—as Hodge had predicted it would be,—he was taking his swing there while he could, though three weeks was rather a long time to be intoxicated; but then there was the better chance of his being sober when Mrs. Marks did return, and he should begin to try the effect of the "charm."

On Amy went. The road seemed quite deserted, not a soul to be seen, even the donkeys which usually grazed along the hedges were nowhere.

As Amy walked on her thoughts unconsciously wandered towards Jane and the strange account Hodge had given of her, and anxious as she was about her mother's letter, her mind was almost as much occupied now with Mrs. Marks' sister. She and the letter seemed irretrievably mixed up together in hopeless confusion. The fact was, Hodge had excited Amy's curiosity without being able to satisfy it in the smallest degree, so she was making innumerable conjectures at the truth, all more or less improbable when they came to be analysed. Would the Brampton people be more clever than the Deane ones, and find out what seemed such a puzzle, and, as Hodge said, mystery to everyone? There was Mrs. Taylor, the village chatterbox, she surely would ferret it out, and what a wonderful tale she would make of it. Amy thought she would call at her cottage some day and broach the subject, and hear what she had to say about it. It could do no harm to hear what the village gossip said of poor crazy Jane and her sorrowful story.

As she arrived at this conclusion, a horseman came in sight. It was Charles Linchmore. He was almost close by ere he recognised her. Then he drew rein.

"Miss Neville!" he exclaimed, in surprise, "surely after your illness it is hardly prudent for you to be out on so damp a day."

"It will not harm me," replied Amy.

"Are you going much further? You will find it very dirty walking. Would it not be wiser to return home?"

"No, I think not, as least not just yet; I am too anxious to remain at home. The walk will do me good."

"I doubt that last assertion very much. It can do no one good being out in such weather," and dismounting, he walked by her side.

"Why did you venture?" she asked.

"I? Oh, nothing brings me to grief. I am a soldier, and ought to rough it."

"Are ladies in your opinion so fragile that a slight shower will wash them away?"

"This is not a slight shower, Miss Neville, but a nasty, misty rain, that does a deal more damage than a heavy down-pour."

"I do not agree with you. The one is certainly disagreeable, but the other thoroughly drenches, and is more than disagreeable—it makes one out of temper."

"I have thought more than once that that latter assertion of yours is with you an impossibility."

"Ah! you were never more deceived. I am feeling vexed now," replied Amy.

"Now?" returned Charles.

"Yes. I have been terribly anxious all day, and it vexes me to hear anyone say I should return home, when I have come out purposely to get rid of my weariful thoughts. I know such a damp mist as this will never harm me half as much as they would."

Charles waited, hoping she would say more, but she did not, so he broke the silence.

"I have been to see Grant," he said.

"I trust there has been no more fuss with the poachers?"

"No," replied he carelessly, "but it seems they expect an attack to-night, that is, they are going out in expectation of something of the kind."

"Of a fight with the poachers?"

"Yes; they had scent of them last night, but did not come up with any. To-night they hope for better luck, and Grant and a lot of the game watchers are going in quest."

"It seems to me such a sad way of risking one's life," said Amy.

"Property must be protected, Miss Neville. None of these fellows going out to-night go with the idea of losing their lives."

"Perhaps not; but look at the fate of poor Susan's husband."

"You mean the man who was shot? That is a bad spoke to put in the wheel of your argument, as his sad end has only urged on those who are left to annihilate such a set of ruffians. I have half made up my mind to join in the night expedition."

"You!" exclaimed Amy hastily, "pray do not think of such a thing," and then fearing she had said too much—betrayed too deep an interest in his welfare, added, "every one would think it foolish!"

"Would you?" he asked.

"I? oh yes! of course I should, and besides, every one would be so anxious. What would Mrs. Linchmore say?"

"My brother's wife's opinion is naught to me. Would you be anxious, Miss Neville?"

"I shall be anxious for all those who put their lives in jeopardy to-night," replied Amy, coldly, "And now as I see nothing of the postman, I think I will turn back."

"Are you expecting a very important letter?" asked he, harshly, his jealousy creeping to the very tops of his fingers. Surely it must be some one she cared very much about, to induce a walk in such weather.

"My mother is ill," replied Amy.

The words were simple enough, but he fancied they were spoken in a reproachful tone; or otherwise his suspicions at an end, he was ready to accuse himself. Disarmed at once, he was too generous not to make the one atonement in his power. Springing on his horse, he exclaimed,—

"I will fetch the letter for you, Miss Neville," and was out of sight in a moment.

Amy turned, and retraced her steps homewards, thinking he would soon overtake her, as it was past four o'clock, and the postman always reached the Park by half-past; so that he must of necessity be some way on his road when Charles would come up with him. But no, she walked on, reached the turnpike, and next the village; and then she loitered, went on slowly, and at length stopped and looked back. Still no signs of him.

She went on more slowly still, through the village, and at last, delay as she would, reached the park gates; then an anxious, restless expression came over her face, she began to feel nervous, as she always did now when the chance of meeting or seeing Frances Strickland presented itself, with ever that one fear at her heart, that she should know or find out Charles Linchmore was doing her any act of kindness, however simple, and in revenge, tell him what she suspected and accused her of.

Amy hesitated ere she entered the park. Should she retrace her steps? She turned as if to do so, then the thought came across her, what if he should think she wished him to walk home with her? Hurriedly she went through the gate, and tried to shake off the fear she felt of being seen with him, but the very speed she walked at now, showed she could not, while, instead of walking up the long avenue, she struck across the park.

But all to no purpose, for just as she emerged again into the drive, close to the house, a horse's hoofs rang out over the ground, and Charles Linchmore came up with her, his horse bespattered with mud, as though he had ridden hard and fast.

"Here is your letter, Miss Neville," said he, "I almost feared I should miss you, and that you would have reached home," and again he dismounted, so that there was no chance of escape, or of hurrying on.

"I am sorry you should have had so much trouble on my account, Mr. Linchmore, thank you very much for my letter," and her eyes brightened, as at length she recognized her mother's hand writing on the envelope.

"I am fully repaid by seeing the pleasure the sight of the letter gives you."

"Yes, it is my mother's writing, so she must be better."

"You would have had it sooner, but there had been some accident or delay with the train, I did not stop to hear what. It had not arrived long before I got there."

"Had you to go all the way to Standale? How very kind of you!"

"Not at all. It was just as well you turned back," and he pointed smilingly at the muddy state of his boots.

"I think it very kind indeed of you," replied Amy again, and then wished she had never said it, because he looked so more than pleased.

They were close to the house now; to the windows of which Amy dared not raise her eyes, but hurriedly wished him "good-bye."

"I will get your letters for you every day, Miss Neville," he said, as he pressed her hand rather warmly in his.

"No, no. Do not think of it for a moment," she said, and passed on.

That evening, when Amy took her pupils down stairs, she found on entering the drawing-room, all the ladies clustered around Mrs. Linchmore.

"Such a piece of work, Miss Neville," said Anne, advancing from the circle, and going over to her, "here are all the men wild to go on a poaching expedition—so fool-hardy, isn't it?"

"What does Mr. Linchmore say to it?"

"He's going too, I believe. It is all that abominable Charles's doing; he came home with some fine story or another Grant had told him, and sent all the rest mad. I call it downright folly."

"I met Mr. Charles Linchmore this afternoon," replied Amy, "and he mentioned his intention of going with Grant, but I thought little of it then, as I fancied it would most likely fall to the ground when the time for action came."

"You were wrong, then. For the plan was seized on with avidity as soon as proposed, but I am surprised at Mr. Linchmore, I did not for one moment think he would have seconded it. As for Charles, any hairbreadth danger pleases him. I do not believe he has ever been in a real fight, so he thinks to try a mock one."

"I hope it may simply prove such," replied Amy, "but the last was anything but a mock fight; I do not think you were here at the time, but I dare say you may have heard of it."

"Yes, and it is just that that makes us all fearful; as to Frances, she is just wild about it, I know, but to look in her face you would think her a piece of adamant, for aught you can find written there. I wish Charles would give it up; I think if we could only get him to throw cold water on it, the rest would soon follow his example. Do you mind helping me to try, Miss Neville?" asked Anne, knowing full well in her own heart that Amy's voice would have its full weight with one of the gentlemen at least.

But Amy declined. She felt she dared not so brave Frances; and Anne, after expressing her belief in her unkindness, left her.

Frances' face did look like adamant, so still and set; and yet she was feeling at her heart, more perhaps than any one there present in that large room. Would her voice have any weight with Charles? Would he stay behind if she asked him? While a chill fear crept over her as the thought flew through her of what might happen if he went; might not his fate be that of the man they had spoken of so recently? might he not be brought home even as he was—lifeless—and she never see him more? and then what would life be worth to her? As she watched him in the circle round Mrs. Linchmore, laughing and joking, and turning the fears of those near him into ridicule, she felt that now he was so near danger he was nearer and dearer to her heart than he had ever been before. He should not, must not go, if she could prevent it.

Presently he moved away from the rest. She went and joined him.

"Charles," she began, "are you really in earnest?"

"About what, Frances?"

"Determined on this expedition in spite of all opposition?"

"Of course I am. What made you think otherwise?"

"I thought you might have been persuaded to stay."

"Then you thought wrong, cousin," said he, laughingly.

"It is surely no laughing matter, when we are all so anxious."

"It is that very circumstance makes me laugh. We must not show craven hearts just because women cry and sob."

"But we are not doing anything of the kind."

"At heart some of you are."

"I am not for one," replied she, indignantly annoyed that he should suspect her.

"Then why ask me to stay?"

"Because you were the one who started the expedition; and if you say nay, all the rest will."

"And think me a fool for my pains. No, Frances, what needs—must. I shall not draw back now, it is not my way, as you know; I am sorry for you, if any one is going you particularly care about. I'd have my eye on him if I knew who he was, but I don't."

This to her? Frances could have wept with vexation. Was it possible he did not see it was for himself she was anxious? Perhaps she did look a little reproachfully as she replied, somewhat sorrowfully,

"No one is going I care about. Only take care of yourself, Charles."

At another moment the words might have struck him, and perhaps sent conviction into his heart; but now?—

"Then do as I told my brother's wife just now," he replied; "have supper ready for us by the time we come back; I'll answer for our doing justice to it."

"Can you think of nothing but eating and drinking?" she asked, bitterly and yet could have thrown herself on her knees, and implored and besought him to stay. Ah! if only in days gone by she could have allowed her warmer nature to have had play, have crushed out her pride and stubbornness, things might have been different between them, and she have been dearer to him; now she was his cousin, nothing more, and with no thought of what she was suffering, he turned away without any reply, rather annoyed at her words than otherwise.

A few moments later he joined Amy.

"I trust you do not give me credit for being such a sinner as the rest of your sex do? or throw all the onus of this expedition on me, Miss Neville?"

"Every one seems to think it originated with you."

"Perhaps it did; but then every one need not follow in my footsteps. Surely I am not answerable for any one but myself?"

"It seems," replied Amy, evading his question, "to have thrown a damp on every one's spirits. I suppose it must be undertaken now?"

"If you had said the last words to me to-day, Miss Neville, it might have been different."

Then, as she made no reply, he added, "You do not ask me to stay."

"I would do so, if I thought you could retreat honourably."

"And you do not think so? You do not blame me for going?"

"Certainly not. Things have proceeded too far. You must go. I am only sorry to see so many sad faces."

"Thank you, Miss Neville, those are my own feelings entirely. I am in no way to blame for the actions of others, and should have gone myself, whether or no. Good-bye.—God bless you!" he added, softly, as he held her hand in his.

It was only for a moment; even Frances could not have found fault with the length of time he held it, and Amy scarcely felt the pressure of his fingers; yet she felt and saw the mark his ring had made as his hand clasped hers so tightly; felt and thought of it for many days after that.

Nearly all the gentlemen passed out after Charles. Robert Vavasour hesitated as he drew near the spot where Amy sat; but she did not look up from the book she held in her hand; and, after a moment's delay, he, too, went out, and most of the ladies followed.

"Are you not going Alfred?" asked his sister, advancing towards an easy chair, near the fire where he had made himself especially snug.

"What's all the row about?" said he.

"You know as well as I do. What is the use of pretending ignorance? Are you going or no?"

"Have they all been such fools as to go?"

"Most of them have."

"What a confounded shame not to let a man enjoy a quiet evening. I suppose I must go with the rest, but it is a deuced bore all the same."

"You think everything a bore that entails a little trouble."

"Yes, I do. That fellow Charles ought to know better than to drag us out against a rascally set of low ruffians."

"Don't work yourself into a rage," said his sister, "it is not worth while."

"No, of course not," replied he, yawning and closing his book. "Well I suppose I must be off, so here goes."

"I ought to have been born the man, not you," said Frances, contemptuously.

"With all my heart," said he, "and what an easy life I would have had of it."

"I do not find my life such a very easy one. You had better make haste if you are going. There, they have opened the hall door."

"I'll owe Charles a grudge for this," said he, rising slowly, and seemingly in no hurry to be off, "turning us all out on such a damp, dirty night. As black as pitch too," said he, as he reached the hall, and glanced through the half-opened door.

His sister helped him on with his great coat, he grumbling all the while, and vowing they ought to go to bed, instead of going out on such a fool's errand, risking their lives for sheer humbug, as far as he could see.

His sister listened in silence, and then said suddenly,—

"Take care of Charles, Alfred, will you?"

"Oh, yes," he replied; "and who will take care of me, I should like to know? I may get a sly dig in the ribs, while looking after my neighbours."

"No, no, you will be safe, but he is so rash and foolhardy. Do take care of him Alfred, promise me you will?" and she laid her hand entreatingly on his arm as she spoke.

He looked surprised as he heard her words and noticed the action, and turning round, caught a glimpse of her pale face.

"Well, don't look like that, Frances; I'll make no promises, but I'll try and do the best I can for you. Good-bye."

And he, too, was gone. They were all gone, and Frances turned again into the drawing-room, where Amy still sat apparently so quiet and still, but inwardly listening intently to the last foot-fall; the last faint echo of one voice. Now she lost it,—again it reached her ear—was gone!

CHAPTER VIII

A DARK NIGHT

"The moon had risen, and she sometimes shone
Through thick white clouds, that flew tumultuous on,
Passing beneath her with an eagle's speed,
That her soft light imprison'd and then freed:
The fitful glimmering through the hedgerow green
Gave a strange beauty to the changing scene;
And roaring winds and rushing waters lent
Their mingled voice that to the spirit went.
To these she listen'd; but new sounds were heard,
And sight more startling to her soul appear'd;
And near at hand, but nothing yet was seen."
CRABBE

Amy felt oppressed in spirit as the last sound of Charles' voice reached her ear, nor dared she question her heart wherefore she had listened for it, why she had strained every nerve to catch its sound. Was she allowing a warmer feeling to enter her heart than she had hitherto entertained? Was she beginning to care more for him than she ought? No; she would not allow it. She merely felt grateful for his kindness, that was all, for he was kind to her, there was no doubt of that, and her heart could not but be touched by it, so lonely and so uncared for as she felt; so utterly alone in that large house.

Had he not on that very day ridden several miles for her pleasure? and had he not offered, nay promised, to fetch her letter every day? and she had been obliged to give him but cold thanks for his kindness, and still colder looks, when her heart was all the while longing to tell him how more than grateful she felt. Even but a few moments ago, she knew she had been cold to him; but it could not be helped. It could not be otherwise, it must ever be so between them. And yet as she recalled his last words, and the fervent "God bless you," she thought that had she not been a governess, he might have loved her. Now, it could never be.

She grew restless; the quiet stillness around her became oppressive, most of those who were left having retired into the drawing-room; so when the children had said good night she took them up to bed herself, and as each little one knelt down, she joined earnestly in the simple prayer that "God would bless dear Papa and Mamma, and all their relations and friends."

Mary did not put them to bed, one of the other servants did the office for her. Amy enquired where she was, and whether she was ill?

"No, Miss, not ill," replied the girl, "only worrying herself."

"About what? I trust she is in no trouble."

"Well, you see her father's gone out against the poachers to-night."

"True," replied Amy. "Poor girl! I quite forgot her interest in the matter."

"She's most worrying and fretting herself to death about it, and all to no good, as we all tell her, but she won't listen to none of us."

"Words are poor comfort in such cases."

"Yes, Miss; and what's worse, I believe they've threatened to do for him, her father—I mean."

"That may be mere idle report; there is no authority for the rumour."

"Except the words of the man that was hung, Miss."

"Poor wretched criminal! Do not let us talk or dwell on such scenes. I will go and see Mary, if you will show me the way."

"Indeed I will, Miss, and I'm sure it will do her good. She's in her own room."

And, guided by the other, Amy went.

Mrs. Hopkins sat by the side of the bed on which Mary lay, worrying and fretting herself to death, as her fellow-servant had said, and refusing to be comforted or calmed.

"Ever ready to do any one an act of kindness, Miss Neville," said Mrs. Hopkins, as she rose on Amy's entrance. "This is sad work."

"Yes; it is an anxious time for all of us, but it is surely not wise to give way to imaginary evils, which after all may only exist in our own brains and foolish fancies."

"No one knows," sobbed Mary, "how I love my father."

"We all believe it, Mary. Do you know that your mistress's husband is also gone with the rest?"

"No one has threatened his life, like they have my father's."

"But will your crying remedy that? Will it not make things a thousand times worse, by making you too ill to see him when he does return?"

"He may never return, Miss, never!" sobbed Mary afresh.

"It's of little use talking, Miss," said Mrs. Hopkins, "she will cry and worry; and nothing will stop her that I can see. She will be sorry and ashamed enough to-morrow when she thinks of it."

"I think she should hope the best, and not so readily look forward to the very worst that can happen. Try and think that there is a good and kind Providence watching over us all, Mary."

"I do. But it's no use Miss—no use."

"Here drink this, Mary," said Mrs. Hopkins, handing her some salvolatile, "It's no use talking, Miss, we must dose her."

"I believe it is the best plan," replied Amy, half smiling; then as the girl sat up to drink it she added, "If you must cry, Mary, why not go down below? you can cry just as well there, and watch for the men's return."

"Oh! I daren't, I daren't—" she said.

"Her father will be quite frightened when he does see her face," said Mrs. Hopkins, as she bathed her forehead with cold water, "and as for her, she won't be able to open her eyes to look at him they're that swelled."

Amy seeing her presence could do no good, left, and went to the school-room, intending to spend the rest of the evening in writing home, but she found the attempt useless, so she closed her desk and put away her pen in despair. Reading was better than writing, she would fetch a book. She glanced at the bookshelves Charles had made and put up for her but a few short months ago. He was nothing to her then; simply Mr. Linchmore's brother, but now?—Again she grew restless. Why would her thoughts so often wander towards him? He could never be more than a friend, never! She would go below. The gloom and solitariness of the room struck her more forcibly than it had ever done before, and she grew nervous and timid and stole away to the drawing-room.

When she entered it, she was surprised to find how soon things had resumed their usual course. Mrs. Linchmore was at the piano singing, Anne at a game of drafts, every one chatting and laughing as though nothing had occurred to disturb their hearts, Amy could hear the rattle of the bagatelle balls quite plainly in the inner room from where she sat, and the sound jarred upon her nerves. Surely Frances could not be one of the players, for Amy well knew how anxious she must be; and she crossed the room to where Julia had taken up her position by the fire, and looked in as she passed the arch which divided the two rooms. No, Frances was not playing—was not even there.

"I feel entitled to roam about at will," said Amy, seating herself by Julia, "as so few of the gentlemen are here, and I think you look lonely. Are you anxious, Miss Bennet?"

"Very."

"I wonder what time they will be home?"

"It may be early, it may be late. Can you imagine how my cousin is able to sit there and sing to those boobies?" and she pointed to where Mrs. Linchmore sat, with one or two young men as listeners.

"Some people are able to control their feelings better than others," replied Amy.

"You are always ready to think kindly of everyone, Miss Neville; but there is no excuse for her; she is in no way put out; her voice is as clear as a bell, and to hear the way in which she is singing that mournful, pathetic song, you would imagine her to be a woman of deep feeling, when in reality she has none, not even for her good, kind husband."

"Mary, the children's maid, is fretting herself to death upstairs," replied Amy, anxious to change the subject.

"What is the matter with her?"

"Her father is the gamekeeper, Grant."

"And her lover one of the game watchers, I dare say."

"No, I think not, at least I heard no whisper of it."

"Perhaps not; but girls don't fret to death for their fathers; they must die in the course of nature, but a lover is not easily replaced."

"I never heard you speak so unkindly," replied Amy.

"No, you must not mind it; I am not myself to-night. I feel out of spirits, and could have a good cry, like that foolish old Miss Tremlow did just now; I marshalled her off to bed, for if anything was to happen she would send us all crazy."

"I see Mr. Hall has not gone with the rest."

"No. And much as Anne talks about men being brave and fearless in danger, I am certain she is glad of it."

"Perhaps she has not found out that she cares for him?"

"Many women, when it is too late, find out they care for a man. Look at Frances, for instance."

"What of her?" asked Amy nervously.

"Nothing, only I fancy she is au désespoir," said Julia carelessly.

"I do not see her anywhere."

"No, you would not, when her feelings are such that she can no longer hide them. Then she hides herself."

It was even so. Frances had hidden herself away in the library; she could no longer sit in the glare of the many lamps, and listen to the laughing and talking going on around; and not only listen, but be obliged to talk herself. It was too much, she could not do it. Instead of trying, like Amy, to shake off the gloom that oppressed her, she nursed it, and sat alone, sullen and miserable.

Had not her voice failed to persuade Charles to stay; failed to win one kind word from him? Had he not, the rather, heartlessly mocked at her anguish? Had he not left her and gone over to Miss Neville, and given her his last parting words, the last clasp of his hand? When, if he had cared for her, every moment would have been precious to him, even as it was to her. How she wished she could hate him? But still the cry of her heart was "He shall not love her."

It was true she was advancing slowly, very slowly; but still, to advance at all, was better than making no progress, to feel that Amy was having it all her own way, and she without the power of preventing her, doomed to sit quietly and look on at the wreck of all her hopes of happiness. But that last should never be, and her eye flashed more brightly as she thought that not one single opportunity had she lost of loosening the hold Amy seemed to have over Charles's actions, the interest she had created in his breast.

Ever on the watch, and restless when Charles was absent, lest he should meet with her rival, and she not be there to prevent his joining and walking with her, her life was one perpetual state of disquietude and excitement.

He should never find out Amy loved him. Never! never! So Frances sat on in the gloom of the one small lamp, and thought such thoughts as these; and bitter enough they were to her. How she hated to see Amy enter the drawing-room each night, and more especially this last evening, when instead of sullenly standing aloof, as he had once or twice done, Charles had joined her. Had they met without her knowledge, and had she won him over to her again, sent all the jealous suspicions which Frances had instilled into his mind, to the winds? Oh! if it should be so? She sprung from the chair, and walked up and down the room, in utter desolation of heart.

And so we must leave her, and return to Amy.

The evening had worn on. It was growing late. Twice the butler had himself come in and replenished the fire. Was he also anxious? Amy thought so, as she watched his face, and noted how he loitered about the room, and was in no hurry to be gone; but glanced round gravely, as he went slowly out, and again, a few moments after, entered it once more, looked to the lamps, and a number of other things there was no occasion for.

Still the hours crept slowly on; again her thoughts were with the absent, again they wandered into the park. There, far away, was one coppice she knew right well; so thick the bushes, so close the shade, she could almost fancy she was there, so vividly did it come before her. Surely it would be there the poachers would be, there the affray would take place, there they would watch and meet with them.

Each hour now seemed to drag more slowly than the last, the minutes were hours to her impatient fancy; while the noise of the company, the noise of the piano grew intolerable. Oh! if she could go out into the park, and learn what was doing; even if not near, she could still hear if a shot were fired, and that would be something gained; but then she might be missed—might be enquired for? No. It would never do to be found out alone in the grounds, on such a night. Was all the game in the world worth the misery of such thoughts as these? Oh! the agony of waiting—and waiting for what?

Amy trembled, and a slight shudder passed through her; her anxiety was growing past control.

The music was still playing, surely she would not be missed; and rising softly she passed into the hall. Should she go into the library, where Frances still moodily paced up and down? No, she would hear nothing there. On into the billiard-room she went.

There was no lamp alight, she was glad of it; all was darkness, save for the flickering of the fire in the grate. She drew near, and tried to be patient and hope for the best; but it would not do, her thoughts would turn to one.

As she grew accustomed to the gloom, each object became dimly visible. There was the table; it was but yesterday all those who were now absent had played on it. Would they ever meet there again? How well she remembered seeing Charles Linchmore; it was not so long ago, she could almost fancy she was passing by the door now—waiting for Fanny, who had rushed to Papa on some fruitless errand—and that she saw his form as he leant across the table; but no, he might never play there again, nor ever live to return home.

She could bear it no longer, but went over to one of the windows, passed behind the curtain, drew back the shutter, opened the window softly, and looked out. The rain had passed away, and the moon shone brightly enough when the thick clouds that were hurrying across it would allow. It was not a very cold night, at least Amy did not feel the cold even in the thin light dress she wore; her eyes were fixed on the one part of the Park where she guessed they must be; her ears straining to catch every sound. But none came. All was silent and still.

How long she stood she never knew, she was aroused from her thoughts by a dull, distant sound. She listened intently.

It came from the other side of the park. Her fears had deceived her. They were coming at last. It must be them. Relieved at last, she drew back from the window, then returned again, but stood further in the shade. They must pass by. She would stay and see them.

The sound she had heard became more distinct, then faded away with the wind which blew in gusts through the leafless trees, then grew nearer still. Strange no voices reached her ear,—now—yes, it was near enough for her to distinguish the heavy tread of men's footsteps.

Nearer and nearer they came.

It was no tread of many feet, but the dull heavy tramp of footsteps treading in unison together. It could not be they; they would not walk like that; so silently, so strangely.

Still Amy waited and watched—a heavy fear slowly creeping over her heart, and almost staying its beatings.

They came nearer still; yes, onwards they came round the turn of the drive as it swept up to the house; they passed it, and now their dark forms came slowly but surely on in the varying moonlight, with still that one dreadful tread. They were close by; passed under the window where she stood. What was that dark object they carried so fearfully, so carefully?

Amy moved away from the window, reached the door of the room, and stood in its deep shade like a statue of stone, every nerve strained, every pulse beating almost to bursting.

The servants had heard it then, or had they like Amy been watching? There stood the grey-headed butler; how ominous was his face, how grave the faces of those men near him, all waiting, all dreading—what?

Mr. Linchmore was the first to enter; a painful, anxious expression on his face.

"Thank God!" exclaimed the old butler, as he saw him; he had been anxious for his master, whom he had known as a boy. Were his fears then at rest? No; he was again about to speak, when,—

"Hush!" Mr. Linchmore said. Then to those behind, "tread softly," and again, "where is your mistress?"

He passed quickly on, almost brushing Amy's dress, as she stood so white and still in the shade, looking on, watching, noting everything.

The other half of the hall door opened; on they came, those dark forms, and others with them, steadying them, clearing the way for them as they went.

They bore a litter, but the form that rested so motionless on it could not be seen, a cloak covered it.

One man stood quite close to Amy as he held open the door for the rest to pass through. She touched his arm gently. She tried to speak, but her tongue refused to utter those anxious words. But there was no need; he looked in her face and understood the mute anguish, the agonised look of her eyes.

"It's only one of the young gents, Miss. Mr. Vavser I think they calls 'im."

It was not Charles Linchmore, then. The reaction was too great. As they bore the litter on past her up the staircase, she uttered no cry, but her slight form trembled for an instant—wavered—and the next fell heavily almost at Charles' feet, as he hastily entered the hall.

CHAPTER IX

GOING AWAY

"Our faults are at the bottom of our pains;
Error in acts, or judgment, is the source
Of endless sighs; we sin, or we mistake."
YOUNG

"It is not granted to man to love and to be wise."
BACON

For a moment Charles stood mute with amazement, the next he bent over the poor prostrate form, and lifted it tenderly in his arms.

"Bring her in here," said a voice, while a hand was laid on his arm, and he was impelled with gentle force into the library. There he laid Amy on the sofa, and kneeling by her side, took the small lifeless hand in his, and pressed it to his lips and forehead; then gently pushed the soft fair hair off her face, and as he did so felt the marble coldness of her cheek. Then a strange fear crept over him: he rose, and bent his ear close to her mouth; but no gentle breathing struck his ear. All was still and silent, even his loving words and the endearing names he called her, failed to bring back life, or restore warmth to that still and apparently lifeless form.

He turned his face, now blanched almost as white as the one he was bending over, to Frances, for it was she who had asked him to bring Amy there, and now stood by the door so despairingly, watching his every action, listening to his words; those loving, cruel words which told how completely, how entirely his heart was another's. If he could but have seen into her heart, how averse he would have been to ask her assistance for Amy! How much misery might have been spared him.

"Is she dead?" he asked, fearfully.

"Dead!" exclaimed Frances. "No, she has only fainted."

"I never saw any one look so like death," he said softly, as he again took her hands and chafed them in his.

"Perhaps not. I dare say your experience is not very great?"

"Can nothing be done for her? must she die like this?"

"A great deal might be done for her," replied Frances, advancing, "but nothing while you bend over her in that way. I will soon bring her to, if you will only let me come near."

"Then why in the name of fortune don't you begin to try something? For God's sake, Frances, do rouse yourself a little from that cold marble nature of yours, and throw a little warmth and feeling into your actions."

She took no notice of his hasty, almost angry words.

"Could you fetch me some Eau-de-Cologne?" she asked. "Go quietly," for he was rushing off in desperate haste, "it is as well no one suspects or knows of this, and bring a glass of water also."

"Dead!" thought Frances, as she gazed at the pale inanimate form, "I wish she was; how I hate her; but for her none of these dreadful thoughts would enter my head. Am I not a murderess, wishing her dead? and it is all her fault, all; she has taken his love from me, and in taking that, has made me wicked, and put all these cruel revengeful feelings in my heart."

She bathed her with the Eau-de-Cologne Charles brought, even dashed some of the cold water into her face; but all to no purpose; not a sign; not a movement of returning life gave Amy; the shock had been too great; she lay as dead.

As Charles stood and watched all the efforts Frances made, as he thought, so indifferently, he grew impatient.

"Where is Anne? or Mrs. Hopkins?" exclaimed he, "confound that woman! she's never in the way when she's wanted," and he was for darting off again, only Frances restrained him.

"Do not call either of them," said she, "even you must not remain here when Miss Neville returns to consciousness."

"I shall stay, whatever happens," he replied, decidedly.

Had he made up his mind to tell Amy he loved her?

"She would not like it," she replied, "would any woman like to think such a secret was found out?"

"What secret?"

"That of her love for him."

"For him! For who?"

"I thought you knew," replied Frances, quietly.

Too quietly, for her apathy maddened him, and he exclaimed angrily.

"For God's sake, Frances, speak out, you'll drive me mad with your cold replies and words!"

"Hush! Go away, she is coming to."

"I will not stir!" he replied, "until you tell me why she fainted."

"She saw them bring Mr. Vavasour into the hall, and—"

"How could she tell it was him?" he asked, suspiciously, with a half-doubt on his mind.

"I do not ask you to believe me," replied Frances haughtily, "you asked me to answer you, and I have done so."

"Not my last question."

"I should have thought a lady's word would have been sufficient; but as it is not so, you had better ask Joe, that man that comes here sometimes with Grant. I heard him tell Miss Neville it was Mr. Vavasour that had been killed, and then—"

"Then?" he asked.

"She fainted."

Whatever Charles thought, he said not a word; a determined, despairing expression stole over his face; he looked hard at Frances as if he would read her very soul, but she returned his look, and flinched not. Presently a faint colour returned into Amy's face; he moved away, placed the glass he still held on the table, and said slowly, for even the tone of his voice had altered, and was unsteady and husky,

"Tell her he is not dead,—not much hurt, even—"

And without a look, or even a glance at Amy, he went with a slow, uncertain step across the room. As he reached the door, Amy moved slightly and sighed, but ere she opened her eyes, the door had closed on his retreating form, and he was gone.

"Are you better now?" asked Frances kindly. She could afford to be kind now she thought the field was won, and Charles' heart turned from her, she hoped for ever.

"Thank you, yes," said Amy, confusedly, and striving to collect her thoughts. "How came I here? Who brought me?"

"Do not talk just yet, you are scarcely equal to it. One of the men carried you in here."

"One of the men? No one else saw me, then?"

"No one."

Then it could not have been Charles Linchmore's voice she had heard, as she lay only half-restored to consciousness? Nor his form she had dimly seen retreating through the half open door, as she opened her eyes? She must have fancied it.

"I was so shocked, Miss Strickland," began Amy, trying to make some apology for her fainting, "and you know I am not very strong yet, and—"

"Do not make any excuses, Miss Neville; the sight was enough to frighten anyone. I felt sick myself, but there was not much occasion for it, as I have ascertained Mr. Vavasour is not much hurt; but I thought, as you did, he was dead."

Amy made no reply, she was too truthful to do so. It was best Miss Strickland thought that the reason and cause of her faintness.

"Had you not better remain a little longer?" continued Frances. "There is little chance of any one coming in here; and they will be all at supper presently."

But no—Amy felt well enough to go; longed to get away to the quiet of her own room, and went.

Dr. Bernard, hastily aroused from his sleep, came and stayed all night at the Park. He corroborated Charles's opinion: Mr. Vavasour's was but a slight wound. The faintness and insensibility that had alarmed them so, proceeded more from the effects of a severe blow on the head, which had stunned him for the time being. In a few days, with a little quiet nursing, he would be all right again; so the excitement and fears of everyone tamed down, and the supper prepared at Charles's suggestion was partaken of heartily by everyone but himself, and he was nowhere.

Two of the poachers had been overpowered, after a desperate resistance, and taken; but the rest, all armed with sticks, or some other weapon of defence, had succeeded in getting clear away, though not without injuring, not only Robert Vavasour, but two of the night watchers also. One man kept his bed for weeks afterwards, and was unable even to appear and give evidence against the two men who had been taken; one supposed to be the man who had fired the shot, either purposely or accidentally, that had wounded Robert, while at the same moment a severe blow from some murderous weapon felled him to the earth, and in the confusion which this occasioned the rest got clear away, though not without a suspicion that some of them had been disabled by the shower of blows with which they were assailed; they proved themselves, as Charles and others had hinted they were, a desperate set of ruffians, whom the recent violent death of one of their band had in no wise alarmed, but the rather made them thirst to revenge it.

Charles Linchmore was up betimes the next morning, and away across the park long before any of its inmates save the servants were stirring. He had passed a sleepless night. At one time Amy's love for Vavasour appeared as clear as day; the next he doubted, and could not make up his mind that it was indeed so. Morning found him still unreconciled to the thought, still undecided. Frances might have been mistaken; he would seek Joe, and find out what had been told Amy. It was impossible the man could have any interest in telling him a lie.

He had not far to walk, Joe met him at the lodge gate, where he was evidently detailing to the man and his wife who kept it, an exaggerated account of the last night's affray.

"Good morning, Joe," began Charles, "how are you and the rest after last night's work? and where are you off to now?" as Joe touched his cap, and was proceeding onwards.

"Up to the house, Sir. The Master bade me bring news this morning of the two men who got hurt, Sir."

"Well, how are they?"

"There ain't much the matter with one, Sir; but Jem's awful bad, his head swelled most as big's two, Sir. Mr. Blane—the village doctor—wouldn't give much for his life, I reckon."

"Your Master will be sorry to hear it. And now, Joe, I want a word with you. How came you to tell one of the ladies last night that Mr. Vavasour was dead?"

"Please, Sir, I couldn't help it; the lady did look so kind of beseeching at me, and tried to speak; but, poor lady, she was that bad at heart she couldn't say a word. I could no more refuse nor tell her, Sir, I should have been afeard to; unless I'd had a heart as hard as a haythen's, and I hadn't, Sir, so just out with the news, and—"

"That will do; be more cautious in future."

And away went Charles with still faster strides than before; half over the park and then home again, and up to his room, where he thrust his things hastily into his portmanteau; it was but a few minutes' work, and then he was off downstairs again. Here he met Anne.

"Why Charles," said she, "where have you been all the morning? We have finished breakfast. What a lazy creature you are!"

"I am going to make a start of it," replied he. "I am off to join again."

"Going back to your regiment!" exclaimed Anne in amazement at the sudden announcement. "When?"

"Now, this moment."

"What will Isabella think? How surprised she will be!"

"No, not a bit of it, she is too accustomed to my sudden movements, and scarcely volunteered a remark when I told her."

"But your leave is only half expired?"

"Isn't it?" he replied, as if he had never thought at all about it. "Well, so much the better, I can knock about abroad for a short time. Good-bye."

Anne looked in utter bewilderment, until she suddenly caught sight of the sorrowful, despairing expression of his face. What had happened?

"Don't say good-bye like that, Charley," said she, her kind heart roused at once at the sight. "Something has vexed you. Can I help you in any way? I am ready and willing, if you will only tell me how."

"No. I am past help, Anne," and he dashed away a tear which had started at the sound of her kind voice, and then added bitterly—"I am a fool to care so much about it!"

"About what, Charles? Do tell me, I am certain I could help you."

She pitied him entirely, and would have braved a dozen Mrs. Linchmores to have seen the old happy, merry expression on his face again.

"You have always been kind, Anne, and so I do not mind telling you, what I dare say you have seen all along, although I've been such a blind fool to it! It's no fault of hers, Anne,—but—but she loves another."

"Impossible! I don't believe it!" said Anne, hastily, forgetting all her wise resolutions of never helping him to find out Amy cared for him.

"Nor I, for a long time," and he thought of the long sleepless hours he had passed in pacing up and down his room. "But it is so."

"How did you find it out? Did she tell you?"

"No; but some one else did, little suspecting the interest I had in the matter. I could not believe, at first, that all my hopes were to be dashed aside at once in that way. I could have sworn she took an interest in me, but there I have convinced myself and—and—I am a miserable wretch, that's all, with my eyes wide open to my dreadful fate. Bid her good-bye for me, Anne. I could not trust myself to do so without showing her I love her. Thank you for all your kindness." And he wrung her hand. "Where is Frances?"

Frances! What had she to do in the matter? Anne's curiosity was roused, and for once rightly, and in a just cause. She had long thought Frances bore no good feeling towards Miss Neville; perhaps she was jealous of her, for it was certain Amy had supplanted her in Charles's affection;—if he ever had any for her. Ah! that was it. It was all as clear as day to Anne now. But if it was as she suspected, Charles was, indeed, a fool to believe it; she was certain if she were in his place she would not, but then men were so easily convinced of a woman's falseness; but how could he look in Amy's eyes and believe it? Miss Neville a flirt? Impossible! But then Anne suddenly recollected how she had thought so herself, simply because she and Robert Vavasour had walked home together. No, after all she could not blame Charles so much, perhaps she should have thought the same. At all events, she determined to watch Frances closely when she gave her his message.

"Charles wants to speak to you, Frances; he is in the dining-room." And Anne fixed her eyes full on her face as she spoke.

But Frances was gaining experience every day; learning to attain a self-possession and control equal to any emergency.

Only a faint—very faint, colour tinged her cheeks as she replied,

"Charles must wait until I have finished reading this chapter; I am too interested to leave off in the middle of it."

"Oh! very well. I will tell him so; but you will miss shaking hands with him, as he is going away."

This time Anne succeeded. Frances' face expressed the utmost astonishment, while her cheeks paled to an almost marble whiteness.

"Going away!" she gasped. "How? When?"

"How? By the train I suppose. When? Now this moment. You had better come at once if you wish to see him."

She followed Frances to the dining-room, and stood at the window while she went up to the fire where Charles stood. Anne watched them.

He turned his face, still with the same gloomy, despairing expression, towards Frances and said a few words. What were they to cause her pale face to flush so hotly, while a proud, triumphant look shone brightly in her eyes? Anne would have given worlds to have heard them, certain as she was they contained some clue to the mystery shrouding his hasty departure.

They were said, those few words, and he moved towards the door. Frances followed him after an instant's thought, and arrested his footsteps, slow and uncertain as they were. Anne could hear quite plainly now.

"One moment, Charles. I am so sorry you are going," said Frances.

"Never mind," he replied, "it is best I should go."

"I suppose so. I suppose you must go?"

"You know I must. You best of all others," he replied, sternly.

"Alas! yes," was the reply.

The next moment he was whirling rapidly past the window in a dog cart; with Bob seated on the cushion at his side, instead of running at the horse's heels as he usually did. "The only living creature who cared for him," as Charles had once said to Miss Neville; become doubly dear now she had proved faithless. Bob nevertheless seemed uncomfortable in his exalted post, and did not approve seemingly of his new position in society; for while his Master cast not a glance behind him, saw not Anne's sympathising face at the window or Frances' tearful one; he seemed to give a wistful side-look—as well as the jolting of the cart on the hard gravel would allow—at the comfortable home he was leaving for the Barrack yard, and his old surly companions of the canine species he had so often fought and won many a hard earned battle with, for Bob, though not a savage dog, never allowed a liberty to be taken with him without resenting it.

CHAPTER X

JANE

"Oh, memory, creature of the past!
Why dost thou haunt me still?
Why thy dark shadow o'er me cast,
My better thoughts to chill?

I spread my fingers to the sun,
No stain of blood is there;
Yet oh! that age might see undone,
The deeds that youth would dare!"
ANON

Mrs. Marks had returned home. Her mother was dead, and she had brought back Jane as she had threatened, much to Matthew's intense disgust. He was afraid of his wife's tongue, but had been so long accustomed to hear it going, that he could not understand a woman who could keep hers quiet, and sit the whole day long by the fire-side, scarcely saying a word, in his own favourite corner too,—seldom lifting her eyes from her knitting. As he watched the progress of the socks she was making, he vowed in his own mind never to wear them when they were finished, believing as many of the ignorant in his class of life do, that they would be bewitched, and cause him to meet with some harm, perhaps fulfil Goody Grey's prophecy that some one in the cottage was going to die.

He found it more difficult than ever to resist the temptation of going to the "Brampton Arms," now that his home was even more uncomfortable than it used to be. How could he seat himself at the other corner of the fire-side, and smoke his pipe, with his sister-in-law's eyes so constantly and intently fixed on him? Matthew longed to see Goody Grey to ask for a new charm to spirit away Jane and her unholy presence, which was a constant irritation to him. Meanwhile he had twice tried the effect of the charm and each time apparently without the slightest success; as not only had Mrs. Marks eyes, but her tongue also, flashed ten thousand furies at his extraordinary silence, while Jane, to whom during the storm he looked for sympathy, sat perfectly heedless, and mindful only of her dreadful knitting.

William Hodge was still with the Marks', when he heard of the poaching affray and its consequences. His mind was at once filled with alarm, and he determined on going into Standale. What if his son should be one of the men taken, and now lodged in the jail there?

Hodge kept very quiet at first, and talked it over with Mrs. Marks,—who had returned a few days after,—and at length made up his mind to go to the town and gain a sight of the two men; but this was easier said than done, he had to wait quietly until they were brought up before the magistrates; when he returned to the cottage with the satisfactory intelligence that neither bore the slightest resemblance to his son Tom. Still he was more certain than ever that Tom was down there, for on mentioning his name casually to the landlord of the inn where he had put up, a man seated in the bar had turned round suddenly, eyed him keenly, and asked him to join him 'in a glass.' This, Hodge, who had his wits about him, was not slow to do, and both played at cross questions with the other, and tried to find out where each came from, and where bound to; but each proved a match for his fellow in cunning and sharp-sightedness, and they parted mutually dissatisfied, certain in their own minds that each could have revealed something of interest in which they both took part, had he so willed it.

A few days after Hodge's return, as he was going across the fields, he again met with his acquaintance of the inn, who passed him close by without renewing their former intimacy, indeed, without a word or greeting of any kind, as though they were strangers, and now met for the first time. Hodge thought he must have been mistaken in his man; but no—a second and yet a third time, he met him on different days; and now Hodge was convinced he was right—they had met before; but why this apparent forgetfulness on his part? Why this perpetual crossing of his path? Hodge grew uneasy, perhaps the man was employed as a spy to watch him? If it was so, there was nothing for it but to return home; but the thought of his wife's sorrowful face, as he should tell her of his fruitless search, deterred him, and he waited yet another day, hoping that a few hours might disclose his son's whereabouts, and unravel the mystery of his absence; but no, the days crept on, and still found him as far from the clue as ever, while he never stirred from the cottage without seeing his mysterious friend, or it might be enemy, either close by or in the distance, too far off to distinguish his features; but there was the unmistakable slouching walk, awkward gait, and broad-brimmed hat.

"Mrs. Marks, Ma'am," said Hodge one day, when they were alone, with only Jane in the chimney-corner for company, and she was supposed to be just nobody, "I've come across that man again, and I don't like the look things are taking—I think they look sort of queer. I never done no harm to nobody, why should this chap follow me about like a dog? I'm beginning to think he's a kind of spying to find out what my business is down here, leastways, I can't see what else brings him so often in my road."

"Why not up and ask him, like a man?" exclaimed Mrs. Marks.

"Well, Ma'am, you see, that's just what I would like to do. Many's the time I've had it in my heart; but somehow I'm afeard to."

"Afraid! Well, Mr. Hodge, I thought you'd more pluck. I know there's few men would frighten me, if I was in your place. Good Lord! what's the world coming to when all the men's so chicken-hearted!" said she, indignantly.

"And the women so uppish!" retorted Hodge, somewhat angrily. "I wouldn't be afraid to knock him down with one blow of my fist," and he stretched out his strong muscular arms, and clenched his knuckles, "if he came to me openly and insulted me; but it's this underhand way of going to work that bothers me. I'd like to pick a quarrel with him, Ma'am, that I would, and bad luck to his walks for the future, if I did; that's all!"

"If those are your opinions, William Hodge, I'm sorry I spoke. I've never set eyes on the man myself; but I think you're over-suspicious, maybe."

"Not a bit too much so. What for should he come across me wherever I go. I saw him the other night as Matthew and I came home. It was broad moonlight, and he was hidden away under the shade of the trees, just before you come to the mile-stone; but I saw him for all that, and so I do most every time I set foot outside the cottage. What the devil can he want with me? and why was I such a born fool as to tell my real name?"

"That's it," said Jane, from the chimney-corner, as if talking to herself. "It's the devil puts all the badness into our hearts."

"Don't mind her," said Mrs. Marks, seeing Hodge looked startled. "She understands nothing, and is only talking to herself. And now what do you mean to do?"

"I must go home agin, as wise as I was when I came."

"And without a word of Tom? Why Mrs. Hodge will nigh break her heart."

"It can't be helped. I've done all I can. You see, I've been thinking this man may be a kind of spy of the Squire's, and on the look-out for Tom, and if so, I may do him more harm than good by staying here. Who knows? perhaps he's guessed I'm Tom's father, and so thinks, by dodging me, to catch him, so, you see, I'd best be on the road home; he won't learn nothing there, save a cracked crown, if he comes that way meddling."

"I tell you what it is," said Mrs. Marks, "you go along home, and leave me to ferret it all out. I've never said nothing all this time you've been racking your brains, and walking about most over the whole country, till I should think you knew every stone and stick in it. I warrant a few weeks don't go over my head before I get at the bottom of it all. You men think yourselves mighty clever; but, after all, there's nothing like getting a woman to help you over the stile."

"Well, Mrs. Marks, I believe you're most right. It's certain I couldn't leave the business in better hands. I know you'll do the best you can for me."

"Of course I will, there's my hand on it. And now just point out this chap in the wide-awake, and I'll be bound to say I'll find out every secret concerning him. And if he knows anything about Tom, why I'll find that out, too; so just rest easy in your own mind, and keep quiet, and bid Mrs. Hodge do the same; and take my advice, and be off home to-morrow—you won't do no good down here, only harm."

And home Hodge went.

A few days after his departure, as Matthew was lounging at the turnpike gate, who should pass through but Goody Grey. As she came in sight at the turn of the hill, Matthew began to prepare his thoughts as to what he should say to her. She would be sure to ask about the success of the charm; he felt proud at the idea of being able to tell he had not added to the number of stones in the box, but on the contrary two had been thrown away. What a fortunate thing for him Mrs. Marks was out, he could talk to Mrs. Grey without a chance of her shrill voice calling him and bidding him attend to his business, and not be gossiping out there.

"Good morning, Mrs. Grey," began he, taking up a position so as to command a view of the whole road by which the enemy, in the shape of his wife, should first come in sight on her way home.

"The same to you," replied she civilly, and was passing on, when—

"I've tried the charm, Ma'am," said Matthew, mysteriously.

"The what?" asked she sharply.

"The charm, Mrs. Grey. The box with the gravel in it, that you give me."

"True, I had forgotten. What was the result?"

"If you mean what good did it do, why then it just did no good at all," said Matthew, sorrowfully.

"How often have you tried it?"

"Twice, Ma'am, I'm proud to say; and a hard matter I found it, going so nigh the Public, that I could most smell the baccy, and hear the drawing of the beer; but there I stuck to the 'structions yer give me, and turned back home agin, but only to hear my wife's tongue going faster and sharper than ever."

"I dare say, at first, it may be so; but persevere, and in the end your wife will be silenced."

"I wish I could think so," he replied; "but I'm afraid, Ma'am, her tongue have been going so long now, that nothing 'cept a miracle won't stop it."

"Is Mrs. Marks at home?"

"No, Ma'am, she's out. And that's another thing bothers me, she's taken to going out all hours now, no matter what kind of weather 'tis. It's a puzzle to me where she goes to, tramping about in the mud."

"Well, I cannot help you there," replied Goody Grey, "her tongue I might stop, but not her actions, you must look to those yourself."

"And so I mean to, Mrs. Grey, so I will," said Matthew, determinately. "I only thought so this very day, as I was leaning on this very gate, just before I saw you."

"It is a wise resolution, but fools see wisdom or learn it sometimes."

"Don't you begin that old story agin, Ma'am, nor say one word about the trees that's going to fall; for I can't abide it, and don't want to know nothing about what's going to happen. Death's near enough for us all, but we don't want to be knowing when he's going to knock us up."

"Where there's a storm there's sure to be a wreck," said she.

"Stop there, Ma'am," replied Matthew, "and don't be after looking that way at the cottage. What do yer see?"

"I saw the face of a woman at the window."

"No, that yer couldn't," replied he, "Mrs. Marks is out!"

"Are you sure she is out?"

"Lord save yer, Mrs. Grey, in coorse I am. Didn't I watch her out? and wouldn't I have heard her voice calling out after me, long afore this," and Matthew grinned at the very idea.

"Who was it then?"

"Yer couldn't have seen no one. There's only crazed Jane in the place, and she don't never move out of the chimbly corner for no one. She's no curiosity, like Mrs. Marks says I have."

"Who is crazed Jane? Where does she come from? and what does she in your cottage?"

"Just nothing save to be knitting all day long, and follering me about with her big eyes. She's my wife's sister, yer see, and is living with us, she don't need no charm to keep her tongue quiet. She's just the only woman I ever met as could, saving yer presence, Ma'am; and is every bit as knowing as yerself, and could tell yer a deal if yer liked."

"About what?"

"About whatever yer liked to ask her. It's my belief she could tell the weather just every bit as well as yerself. If yer'd lost anything she'd know where to clap eyes on it again, just as yer did the bit of copper t'other day, and a deal of other things as don't cross my mind now."

"I don't believe it! I don't believe it!" exclaimed Goody Grey fiercely. "If I did—I'd tear her very heart out, if she didn't tell me."

And she passed on, leaving Matthew horrified at her words. He watched her all the way down the road, which she traversed with a quick, hasty step, striking her staff defiantly into the ground as she went, until the turn of the road took her out of his sight.

"What a fearful body she is!" thought he, as he turned into the cottage.

But there his horror and astonishment was still further increased at finding crazed Jane lying in a heap on the floor.

At first he was for rushing to her aid; but on second thoughts, he reached his hat off the peg, and darted out of the cottage. There taking to his heels he ran as fast as his legs could carry him along the road Goody Grey had taken.

"For the love of Heaven!" said he overtaking her, "come back!"

"Come back!" exclaimed she, "and what for should I come back?"

"To take away the curse and witcheries yer've put upon Jane; or she'll die."

"What are you raving about? What have I to do with Jane and her curses?"

"Yer know well what I mean, Ma'am; yer've most killed her with yer evil eye. I know yer're a fearful 'ooman, and a wise 'un too, but for the love of Heaven don't leave her like that, but come back."

"You're a fool!" replied Mrs. Grey, "I've no more power over her than a fly," and she passed on, bidding him seek his wife's help.

And again Matthew started off faster than before to find Mrs. Marks, with an inward malediction on Goody Grey.

He was scarcely out of sight ere she halted;—hesitated—then turned back with rapid steps towards the cottage.

Jane had fallen near the window from which Goody Grey had seen her gazing, and lay almost under it, so as to be entirely concealed from the broad glare of its light. She lay on her side with one arm across her face. Her visitor gently moved away the arm, and looked at her. It was but a momentary glance, and the fainting woman rested, as I have said, away from the light. Was it this made Goody Grey fail in recognizing her? or was it the sharp, pinched features, and worn haggard face, with those deep furrows ploughing it so roughly in every direction.

Filling a jug with water, Goody Grey lifted Jane, and tried to force some down her throat, then dashed the rest over her face and forehead, but her efforts at restoring life were useless, and after a few more ineffectual attempts she left her, and went and seated herself by the fire, thinking perhaps it would be but neighbourly to remain and await Mrs. Marks's return.

Not many minutes elapsed ere Jane opened her eyes, and the first object they rested on was the old woman's face and figure, as she sat looking at the fire, her profile fully marked out, and apparent to Jane's gaze, whose face assumed a terrified, horror-stricken look, as she almost glared at her, seemingly too fascinated or frightened to look away.

Evidently Jane's memory served her better than Goody Grey's did, for she recognized her, although the old woman did not, and after a minute or two she sat up on the floor, and clasping arms round her knees, buried her face in them and groaned aloud.

Goody Grey started and turned at the sound, then rose and went over to her.

"Are you better?" she asked kindly, "you've had a long faint."

Jane made no answer, only moaned and shivered from head to foot.

"You are too cold to drink this water. Is there no brandy anywhere that I can get you? Try and get up, and I will help you over to the fire."

It was astonishing to hear the gentle, almost soft, sweet voice with which she spoke, so different from her usual harsh, sharp manner. But the more gentle she was, the less Jane seemed to like it, never raising her head or answering a word, but moaning and rocking herself backwards and forwards as she sat; and Goody Grey, seeing words or deeds, however well meant, were alike wasted upon her, rose to go; saying as she did so,—

"I'm sorry to see you so sullen, woman. Have you never a word of thanks to give me?"

But Jane continued silent as before.

"Well, well," she muttered, in something of her old, impatient, sharp voice, as she stepped across the threshold of the door. "That fool said she was a 'dafty.'" Then in a milder, almost sorrowful tone, she added "it is better to be crazed than broken-hearted."

Jane raised her head as she caught the last sound of Goody Grey's voice; then, as the last foot-fall died away, she got up stealthily, and closed and bolted the cottage door.

CHAPTER XI

THE CONSERVATORY

"All other ills, though sharp they prove,
Serve to refine and perfect love:
In absence, or unkind disdaine,
Sweet hope relieves the lovers' paine:
But, oh, no cure but death we find
To sett us free

From jealousie,
Thou tyrant, tyrant of the mind.

False in thy glass all objects are
Some sett too near, and some too far;
Thou art the fire of endless night
The fire that burns, and gives no light.
All torments of the damn'd we find
In only thee,
O jealousie!
Thou tyrant, tyrant of the mind."
DRYDEN

January had drawn to an end, and with Charles Linchmore had gone all the visitors from Brampton, save the Stricklands and Bennets, and they being cousins remained on, as Mrs. Linchmore said it would be wretchedly dull to be entirely deserted when Robert Vavasour was too weak to be moved, and kept her and Mr. Linchmore tied to Brampton. This plan appeared to please everybody but Frances, who seemed to require a great deal of persuasion before she would consent to remain, though at heart she was only too glad to stay; but Julia and Anne acquiesced at once.

Robert Vavasour's illness was of longer duration than was at first expected; even when the pain from the severe blow on the head abated, there was still the wound in his leg with the inflammation attending it, so that he could not leave his room for some few weeks after Charles's departure, and then only to come down of an evening and recline on a sofa in the dining-room, where all in turn tried, or did their best endeavours to amuse him, save one—Miss Neville.

As he lay there, evening after evening, with nothing better to do than watch those around him, he soon became aware that his eyes and thoughts were ever constantly with the governess, He watched her with no common interest. He who had vowed his heart should never soften towards any woman now found himself listening eagerly to catch the faintest sound of her voice, or the outline of her figure reflected in the glass as she moved across the room. As he noted her quiet ways, so different from the haughty Frances, or the bustling Anne, or the numbers of other girls he had known, he grew more in love with her than he liked to acknowledge to himself, and determined she should be his if she was to be won. If she loved him what to her would be the shade and mystery of his birth; for he would make no secret of it, but tell her all he knew, all that made him so reserved, and at times impatient.

Mr. Linchmore was wrong in the opinion he had given Amy of his character, for, although Robert Vavasour was ready to flirt with every girl or woman in the room, his hostess included, yet he had long felt Miss Neville was not to be so trifled with; she was superior to them all. A being to be reverenced and loved with all a man's heart. She must be his wife—if she so willed it—and if she did not, none other ever should. How he chafed with impatience at being obliged to lie so utterly useless and idle, when he would have given worlds to be at Amy's side pouring soft nothings—as men only know how to—into her ear and striving to win her love and make her his own.

Meanwhile Anne watched Frances as the spider watches the fly, but as yet had found out nothing likely to unravel the mystery shrouding Charles's hasty departure. She had sought out Amy almost immediately, and delivered the message and hurried adieux entrusted to her; had noted the agitation vainly attempted to be suppressed, the quick flushing of the face and trembling of the lips before the studied words came slowly forth expressing her thanks at his kindness in remembering her. Anne's heart opened to her, even as it had done but a short half-hour earlier to her cousin; and she pitied Miss Neville, and was more than half tempted to tell her all she knew—all he had said—but there was a something in Amy's manner that day which forbade Anne's communication; and she remained silent, yet waiting and watching ready to seize the very first opportunity of discovering and unravelling the plot, which seemed so persistently to baffle her; and then not only could she make two people happy, but what pleasure in being able to defeat Frances! What a triumph it would be!

Frances went on silently and secretly. Her wishes were only half fulfilled. The end was yet to be worked out.

She felt Anne suspected her the moment Charles drove away from the door; but what signified that? What could the simple Anne Bennet do? She was a mere worm in her path. A nobody. Still Frances was more cautious than ever and more wary. Anne was to be avoided, not openly, but secretly, while others of far more consequence were to be gained over, so as to drag Amy more completely into the snare, from which there was to be no escape.

There was no need to urge Robert Vavasour on now. Frances saw plainly enough that he was ready to sacrifice everything and anything to gain Amy's love; and she must be his wife; even if it broke her heart.

He was better now, able to walk about again, and generally devoted part of the evenings to Amy. Poor Amy! who saw not his love—wanted it not—yet felt grateful at his kindness in talking to her when nobody else did; besides, did it not keep him away from Mrs. Linchmore, with whom she could not bear to see him, fancying Mr. Linchmore always looked sad and dejected while he was at her side. Little did Amy think that while there was no fear of her losing her heart, Mr. Vavasour was fast becoming enslaved to herself for ever.

It was true Mr. Linchmore did not like Vavasour's attentions to his wife, but he liked his attentions and devotion to his governess far less. He felt his warning had been of no use, and that Miss Neville was falling into the snare he had essayed to lead her from. As he sat one evening resolving it all over in his mind for the twentieth time, Frances joined him.

There was no knowing how soon they might be interrupted, so she went to the point at once without hesitation.

"Mr. Vavasour has quite recovered from his recent illness, and appears to be making up for lost time in Miss Neville's good favour."

"He will hardly make good his footing there," replied Mr. Linchmore. "Miss Neville is too sensible a girl to be won over by a little fulsome flattery, however adroitly administered."

"But there seems more than flattery here; at least, I hope so."

"Why should you hope it?"

"For Miss Neville's sake, as I think—nay, am sure he is winning her heart."

"Impossible!"

"He does not think it so impossible, otherwise he would not be so devoted; men never are when the one object is proved to be unattainable."

"I trust you are mistaken, Frances. For if she loves him he will break her heart," replied Mr. Linchmore, sorrowfully.

"It is you who are mistaken. That she loves him I am certain, or she would never have fainted like dead when she heard he was wounded; and as for him, I believe he loves her with all his heart, only he is afraid to tell her so. At all events, her fate rests in your hands, to make or mar as you please." And having said all she wished, Frances left him to dwell and ponder on it as much as he liked.

Was it so? Did Miss Neville's fate, indeed, rest in his hands? If so, then, he must no longer remain inactive, but must bestir himself. He looked around, but during his conversation with Frances, short as it was, Miss Neville had disappeared. As Frances and the rest adjourned into the billiard-room for a game he again sought Amy; surely she had not gone with the rest? No; there she sat alone in the inner drawing-room.

"You are almost in total darkness, Miss Neville," said he, drawing a chair near her, as she sat within the shade of the alcove or arch dividing the two rooms.

The fire burnt low in the grate, while the lamps were all out save one, which threw a strange, fitful light every now and then across the room.

"Mrs. Linchmore likes this room kept dark; she says it is sometimes pleasant to come into, and a relief to the eyes after the brilliant glare of the other rooms," replied Amy.

"Perhaps she is right; it certainly is a pleasant rest for the eyes after the intense glare of the many lamps out there."

"Yes; and then one is almost sure of being quiet and alone late in the evening, as no one cares for this dull room then; the lamps are never trimmed after being once lit, but are allowed to die out as they like."

"Slowly, like the hopes of our hearts."

Amy looked up surprised.

"It is best to have no hopes," she said.

"That would be contrary to human nature. We all hope, even the most satisfied mortal, and sometimes our hopes last a life time, and only fade with our lives."

"It is true; but perhaps our hopes, if realised, would only render us miserable. It is best after all to go hoping on."

"It is best," he replied, quietly.

Amy thought what a strange mood Mr. Linchmore was in. Why did he speak and talk so gloomily? Had Mr. Vavasour vexed him again by devoting himself too much to his wife? or she been flirting more than usual?

This inner room they now sat in was not so large as the drawing-room, part of it being taken off for the conservatory, which ran its entire length, and then adjoined the drawing-room at the point where the arch which separated the two rooms terminated. In the day time the smaller room was the prettiest and most cheerful, as the windows at the end commanded a fine view of the magnificent woods and country beyond, with the lawn sloping down in front almost to the banks of the lake, whereas the view from the drawing-room on that side was entirely concealed by the conservatory.

As Mr. Linchmore silently revolved in his mind how he should begin about Mr. Vavasour; how broach the subject so as to find out how far her heart had been won—or as he thought, lost—thrown away on so unworthy an object; given to one who neither cared for or valued the rich treasure he had won, and Amy sat in silent wonderment as to what he would say next; the rustle of a silk dress was heard, and in another moment two forms were indistinctly seen through the flowering shrubs and exotics of the conservatory.

Amy's breath was hushed, her very pulse was stilled, as she distinguished Robert Vavasour and Mrs. Linchmore.

Yet why should they not have separated from the rest? There was nothing so very strange in it. But Amy felt as if some impending calamity hung over her, or was near, and she without the power of averting it; and would have given worlds to have turned and fled. Brave as she was, she felt a very coward now, and would have warned them how near they were to others if she could; but it could not be, the windows were closed, no sound might reach them.

And now Mr. Linchmore's eyes were fixed in the same direction. He had seen them, too.

Amy rose as if to go. She would leave him and join them, come what would, but—

"Sit still, Miss Neville," he said, sternly, and in a tone that compelled obedience, and Amy sank down again without a word; in dread and fear; feeling more utterly helpless than ever to avert the coming storm her heart suggested.

Once more she looked through the evergreens and tall dark plants. They were still there, close to one of the doors now, and almost opposite. He gathered and offered a flower.

That she received it with a flush of pleasure, could be surmised by the gentle bend of the proud head, and the soft smile which could almost be distinguished flitting across her features.

They came nearer still. Oh! when would they go away? What could interest them so deeply, and why did he look so earnestly in her now averted face? What could he be pleading that she would not—did not wish to grant?

She has turned her head towards him now, and is looking down on the ground as though loath to meet his gaze—is speaking—has granted his request, whatever it is, and he has seized her hand and is kissing it again and again.

A hasty, passionate exclamation from Mr. Linchmore, as he suddenly sprang to his feet, and in another moment would have dashed into the conservatory, shivering the slight glass door into a thousand fragments, but Amy threw herself in his path.

"Oh, stay, stay!" she said. "Don't go, please don't!"

"Away!" he said. "Out of my way! He shall rue this deeply!" and he tried to shake her off, but in vain; she clung more firmly to him than before, beseeching him to stay.

"Don't, don't go," she continued, imploringly. "I must not let you go! Pray, pray, listen to me; you will be sorry if you don't. Oh! Mr. Linchmore, be advised. You cannot tell why he has taken her hand."

"Villain!" he muttered, between his clenched teeth. "Scoundrel!"

"No, no! you are mistaken," said Amy, hurriedly, "indeed you are. How can you guess at anything? He may be entreating her good will, may be telling her of his love for another. Oh! Mr. Linchmore, be yourself again; don't give way to this sudden anger until you are certain you are right, and you may be wrong. Believe me, you are wrong. Oh, don't harm him, pray don't!" and Amy's eyes filled with tears, as she felt she could urge nothing more; was powerless if he would go.

But as her voice grew hushed, and she relaxed her hold, he turned and said,

"Miss Neville, you love this man?"

"Oh, no, no, no!" replied Amy, now fairly sobbing.

"Then why this interest in him? Why seek to palliate his conduct, base as I believe it to be?"

"I would not, if I thought it base, but—but I do not. I am but a poor ignorant girl, but I implore you, for your wife's sake—your own sake, do nothing rashly."

"I will not. I am calm again—as calm as you wish; but this must be sifted to the very core, must be explained till all is as clear as the moon, which shines so brightly through that half-darkened window. No half measures will satisfy me. I must not only be convinced, but feel so. You say he is pleading his love for another—entreating her good will in his behalf. Be it so. Then who is this other?"

He was quiet now, very quiet; with a firm, gloomy determination from which there could be no escape, no loophole to creep out of. All must be as clear as day. He had stood his wife's heartless conduct too long, he would stand it no longer. No half measures, as before, would now satisfy that angry husband, with the demon jealousy roused in his heart—that stern yet loving heart.

Alas! this jealousy, what mischief it causes. What hearts it sunders and wounds with its fierce stabs; and how powerless are most to rise above it or shake off its strong iron grasp. If once allowed to enter our hearts it is an enemy difficult to contend with; still more difficult to get rid of, for although only a small corner may be taken possession of or unwillingly granted it at first, yet in time what a much larger portion becomes its share.

"Who is this other?" again asked Mr. Linchmore, more gently.

"I cannot tell," replied Amy.

"I am willing to believe, Miss Neville, it is as you say; but there must be no more trifling or prevarication, matters have become too serious for that. This other you speak of. Who is she? I must know; and if this man's heart is capable of love, and she loves him," and he looked fixedly at Amy, and spoke more slowly as if wishing her to weigh well every word, "then let her be his wife; if she wills it so; but—it will be to her sorrow."

"You cannot tell that," replied Amy, seeing he waited for her to speak. "He may love her with all his heart."

"He may. But what is all his heart when he is so ready to trifle with others? Miss Neville," and his voice was still more gentle, and very pitying in its tone; "you are alone, perhaps feel alone in this house, and are young, very young to be so thrown upon the world, which you find a cold and desolate one, I have no doubt. He has been ever kind and courteous. I fear too much so, and I do not wonder he has created an interest in your heart, and at last won it. But he must not be allowed to trifle with it while I stand by. No. It shall never be!"

"Oh! Mr. Linchmore!" exclaimed Amy, now indeed feeling utterly desolate at this continued accusation, and belief in her love for Robert Vavasour.

"Hush!" he rejoined, gently placing his hand on her soft hair, as she sat with her face bowed in her hands. "Poor girl; poor desolate young creature; your happiness shall be my first care, you shall no longer feel alone; there is no need to tell me anything. I know all that your heart cannot speak, even to your fainting when you saw him brought home the other evening."

Amy's sobs burst out afresh; she felt totally unable to stay them or convince Mr. Linchmore he was mistaken.

"Well, well," he continued with a sigh, "it cannot be helped now, things must take their course; but with him I will have a reckoning," and the old stern look once more flitted across his face. "But fear not, Miss Neville; for the sake of your love for him, I will be calm and control my anger."

"You will not tell him I care for him—love him, Mr. Linchmore? Oh! no, no, you could not do so!" said Amy, with fear.

"I will not; that must rest with you alone, with that I can have nothing to do, your future happiness must be made or marred by yourself alone. You need have no fear, but trust; only trust in me, Miss Neville."

"And I shall see him, shall speak to him myself—alone?"

"You shall do so. He shall hear no word of your love from me."

"You promise it, Mr. Linchmore," said Amy, now for the first time raising her eyes to his.

"I promise it, Miss Neville, most faithfully."

"Thank you! thank you; then all will be right."

"I wish, oh! how I wish it could be otherwise," sobbed Amy, as he left her; "but I must not murmur, I must be thankful,—thank God it is no worse than it is; but how can he think that I love him?"

Amy felt utterly miserable. Did she deny Vavasour's being the cause of her fainting, would not Mr. Linchmore naturally enough wonder what had been the occasion of it? or perhaps in the end guess of her love for his brother, even as he had supposed it to be for Mr. Vavasour? No, rather let him think anything than that! a thousand times rather.

Mr. Linchmore had promised she should see Mr. Vavasour—there was some comfort in that; she could appeal to him, he would be reasoned with, would listen and believe her even if he loved her—if?—Amy began to think there was no need of a doubt, and that it was true he loved her. Why should Mr. Linchmore be deceived? All the latter's warnings, and Mr. Vavasour's kindness were accounted for now; but love her as he would, she could not be his wife. No—even if she had never had a thought for another, it could not have been, and now?—now she would never be any man's wife.

Alone? Yes, hopelessly alone. Alone with that one secret love in her heart, that no one must know or guess at, not even her mother. Yes, it was hard, very hard. Was she not striving hard to forget him? Perhaps she would die in the struggle, she felt so hopelessly unequal to face the storm; perhaps it was best she should die. But then her mother? Yes, she must live for her, and forget him. It would not be so difficult, seeing he loved her not, would perhaps never see her again. She was glad he had not known of her fainting. And who could have told Mr. Linchmore? Was it Frances?

CHAPTER XII

LOOKING FOR THE "BRADSHAW"

"Yet though my griefe finde noe redress,
But still encrease before myne eyes,
Though my reward be cruelnesse,
With all the harme, happs can devyse,
Yet I profess it willingly
To serve and suffer patiently.

There is no griefe, no smert, no woe,
That yet I feel, or after shall,
That from this minde may make me goe,
And whatsoever me befall,
I do profess it willingly,
To serve and suffer patiently."
WYAT

"I am two fools, I know,
For loving and for saying so."

DONNE

Amy was not the only one who wept that night; Frances also did so at heart, for very anger and vexation.

She had missed Mr. Linchmore almost immediately after she had sought Miss Neville; had suspected why he had done so, and managed to overhear almost every word of the latter part of their conversation, and when Amy went so sorrowfully out of the inner drawing-room Frances walked straight over to the fire, and seated herself in the easy chair where Amy had only a few minutes before sobbed out her very heart, almost.

Frances had good cause for tears and anger, feeling she was being foiled and defeated when the end was almost won. Her conversation with Mr. Linchmore had been a false move, she had urged him on too quickly; but for that, he never would have seen his wife and Mr. Vavasour, and all would yet have been well; now all was going on wrong—utterly wrong.

That Robert Vavasour would propose for Miss Neville was certain. That Miss Neville meant to refuse him was certain, too. The first she had fully calculated upon, but not the latter. She had intended the first to take place only when Amy had been so hopelessly entangled that she could not escape, could not say no, and now to be defeated at the very moment of victory, was almost more than her proud spirit could brook.

Was all her plotting to be of no use? all to be lost? and to be lost now? Now that the end was all but attained, and it wanted but one final stroke for Amy to be lost to Charles for ever!

A dull, heavy despair was fast creeping over her spirits; what could be done now? Oh! for some one to aid her! What if she spoke to Robert Vavasour, and urged him on to make Amy his at all hazards; she felt certain he loved her with all his heart. Suppose she told him of Amy's secret, and apparently hopeless love for her cousin, as the true reason why she would refuse to listen to his suit. But then again, he might be too proud to marry a woman whose heart was another's, on the mere dangerous chance of being able to win it in the end, and if he should think so and give her up? might not Charles hear of it and return, and then all her hopes be dashed to the ground, just as they seemed on the point of being accomplished?

Frances sat moodily by the smouldering fire, tapping her foot impatiently on the ground in utter vexation of spirit, her heart aching and her temples throbbing with the anguish of her thoughts. She had a strong ruthless will; but how to make others bend to it? How bring them under the influence of it? She chafed with angry vexation; no rest had she that night; but lay restlessly tossing about the bed, when at last, utterly worn out, she threw herself impatiently on it. It was the first drawback she had had in the task she had set herself to accomplish. If Robert Vavasour would only defer his proposal to Miss Neville for one day? Give her time to think of some fresh stratagem! But no. Mr. Linchmore had willed it otherwise. Had she not heard him tell Miss Neville he would have an explanation from Mr. Vavasour of what he had seen in the conservatory; and that Frances knew right well could lead but to one result: a repetition of his conversation with Mrs. Linchmore, disclosing his love for her governess.

As Frances drew up her blind in the morning, almost hating the winter's sun as it streamed in at the window, she knew a few short hours would decide Amy's fate and hers. A reprieve she could not hope for: it was simply impossible. Still she did not give up all hope; a trifle might yet turn the tide of events in her favour; so she went downstairs to breakfast, her head filled as much as ever with schemes and plots. How it beat with renovated hope as she heard that Mr. Linchmore had been suddenly called away on business early that morning. How she wished it might last for days!

The studies did not progress very happily that morning, although Amy set herself resolutely to work, and strove to drive away the troubled thoughts that crowded into her brain. But they would come back do what she would. How many false notes were played by Fanny, without being noticed, at her morning's practising; and mistakes made by Edith at her French reading without correction. Every moment Amy expected and awaited a summons from Mr. Linchmore; but none came; and as the morning wore on, she grew restless and impatient.

The afternoon drew on, and Amy grew still more anxious; could settle herself to nothing; but sat and watched the sun as it sunk lower and lower, and wondered at the reason of the delay. Mary entered with a letter. It must be later than she thought, almost half-past four, and still no summons.

She drew near the fire-light, and opened her letter. It was from Ashleigh, and as if to verify the old adage that troubles never come alone, her mother was worse, and Mrs. Elrington asked Amy to return home for a week, as she thought the sight of her daughter might rouse and cheer the invalid. It was the apathy and apparent want of energy the medical man feared, nothing else; and it was thought Amy's presence might dissipate it.

All minor troubles were now swallowed up in this; with tearful eyes Amy sought Mrs. Linchmore and obtained the wished-for leave. This time there was no regretful tardiness in granting it, no unwillingness expressed.

"Pray go as soon as you like, Miss Neville," she said, "and do not hurry back on the children's account, a week or so will make no difference to either them or me."

Amy felt grateful for her kindness in so readily granting her request, although the words themselves were somewhat stiffly spoken; but her thoughts were so entirely engrossed by her mother's illness and the feeling of being so soon at home again, they could not long dwell on anything else; all were trifles compared to that.

"I will not say good-bye," added Mrs. Linchmore, "as we shall meet again in the drawing-room this evening."

But Amy excused herself. She had so much to do, and to think of. There was her packing not begun even.

"Then I will make my adieux now. I trust you will find Mrs. Neville better, or at all events mending. I fear you will not see Mr. Linchmore; he was called away early this morning to attend the death bed of a very old friend of his, and had to start at a minute's notice; but I will desire the carriage to be ready for you at any hour you like to name, or you can send word by Mary."

Mr. Linchmore was away then; hence the reason of his not having fulfilled his promise. Amy was glad of the reprieve, perhaps before her return, things might wear a different aspect; at all events, her heart felt lighter, and she went to her room with a less weight on her spirits.

"Where is your governess?" asked Frances, entering the school-room soon after Amy had left it to seek Mrs. Linchmore.

Fanny was nursing her doll, and scarcely deigned to look up as she replied, "She is busy packing."

"Packing!" exclaimed Frances in bewilderment. "Packing! and for what?"

"To go away," was the curt answer.

Go away. Another step backwards in the wheel of fortune.

"She is not going for good?" she asked.

"Oh! no. Only for a week. Are you not sorry, cousin? I am," said Fanny, in somewhat of a saucy tone. The child still remembered the "Holy Work:" thought of her hurt arm.

"Very sorry," replied Frances sincerely enough. What could she be going away for? but anxious as Frances was, she disdained to ask the children, but sat down and awaited quietly Miss Neville's coming.

Amy went on steadily with her packing, which, with Mary's help, was soon finished, and then went down to the library to look at the "Bradshaw," and find out which was the very earliest train by which she could start on the morrow. But it was not on the table. She turned over the books one by one, removed the inkstand and papers, but her search was fruitless. It was gone.

As she stood undecided what to do next, Robert Vavasour came forward; she had not noticed him in the dim uncertain twilight.

"Can I assist you, Miss Neville?" he asked. "What is it you look for?"

"I was looking for the 'Bradshaw,' which is usually kept on this table; but it is gone."

"It is here," he replied, taking it off a chair, where it had been hastily left by Mr. Linchmore in the morning. "Allow me to find out what you wish, this book is a puzzle to most people."

Amy explained her wishes. "You are going away?" he asked.

"Yes; but only for a short time, a fortnight at the furthest."

"It is a long time—to me," he said, gently; then lit the taper, and busied himself with pen, ink, and paper, and the 'Bradshaw;' while Amy stood by, wishing she had not come down, but had sent Mary, or one of the children instead.

After dotting down the times of the trains as they arrived and left the different stations, he closed the book; still he did not look up, or give her the memorandum.

"Thank you," said Amy, "that will do very nicely."

"You cannot leave the Standale station before the 9.10 train," he said presently, "that is express, and will take you with less delays on the road than any other, and will only detain you some twenty minutes or so, when you join the ordinary train. I will write this time table out better and more clearly for you, and let you have it before you start."

"Do not take that trouble. What you have written will be quite guide enough for me. Good-bye, Mr. Vavasour," and she held out her hand.

He hesitated a moment, then took it in both his, and held it fast.

"I cannot say good-bye, Miss Neville." All the love he felt for her was welling up into his heart, and striving to be heard. He must speak. "I cannot let you go thus," he said, "had you remained it would have been otherwise, and I would not have opened my heart to you yet; but, as it is, I cannot help myself. Miss Neville, I never loved any woman till I saw you—never thought I could do so. I had but a poor opinion of your sex. Had not my mother deserted me, and was not that enough to fill my heart with hatred and bitterness? There is a mystery shadowing my birth, which seems to me to be growing darker and darker every day. I have no claim even to the very name I bear, and cannot tell you who my parents are; perhaps this silence is better than the knowledge that they live, and are ashamed to own me. I thought I was too proud to ask any woman to overlook that, and vowed I never would; but then I trifled with them all, even with you. Do you remember the flower I sent by Fanny? how many a sleepless night has the remembrance of that folly cost me? But, knowing all I have now told you, all that at times drives me to the solitude of my lonely home, and distracting thoughts, will you come and comfort me,—pity me—love me? Amy, I love you with all my heart. Will you be my wife?"

He could not see her face, the light was too uncertain, and she stood in the shade; but he felt that she trembled as she withdrew her hand from his.

Yes, it was even so. Amy was quite prepared when he began, to say she did not love him; but he claimed her pity, and her woman's heart felt for him at once.

"Will you let me love you, care for you, Amy, as never woman was loved or cared for before? Speak to me, Amy, say one word—one word of hope."

But Amy could give none. "I am sorry," she replied, falteringly, "believe me, deeply sorry; but hope? Alas, Mr. Vavasour, I can give you none."

"You do not love me?" he asked, sorrowfully.

"I like you, have always liked you. You have been so kind to me, the only one almost who has; and I have felt grateful for that—it would be strange if I were not; but I do not love you," she said softly, fearing the pain she was causing.

"I have been premature in asking your love, I know. I have had so little opportunity of winning it, how could I expect you would love me with scarcely any wooing at all. May I ask you one question, Miss Neville? I feel I have no right to ask it, and it may be a death-blow to my hopes?"

"Yes," replied Amy. How could she refuse, and he so sad and heart-broken.

"Forgive me; but has another claimed your love?"

"No. No other has ever spoken to me of love, or loved me," she said sadly.

"Thank you, Miss Neville. Then I will—must hope. Why should I not win your love, when I love you so very dearly; how dearly you know not? I will wait patiently; but strive to win you I must. In my dreary, sad life it is the one bright star to lead me on to better things. I have trifled away life—hated it at times; but now I will begin to live. You are going home, Miss Neville, let this tale of my love be as if it had never been. I will be content to take my chance with others; let us be friends again, as hitherto. I promise no word of love shall ever pass my lips. When you know me better, and, perhaps, judge me better than you do now, then once again I will ask you to be my wife; and then, if you reject me—well. Then we must never meet again; but while your heart is free I must hope. Shall it be so?" he asked.

Alas! what could she say? She could not tell him her love was another's unasked and unsought for, when she was striving to shut it out of her heart for ever. She could only murmur that she did not love him, and could give no hope. While he, thinking her love yet unwon, believed it might be his in the end, and that he had told her of his love too soon.

"You will not refuse my request, Miss Neville, will you?" he asked, sorrowfully.

"I do not like to refuse," she replied, "and yet I doubt if I ought to grant it. It will only make both you and me unhappy, because it can lead but to the same result as now."

"I dare not think so," he said. "Surely God will be more merciful than to leave my life an utter blank. No mother's love have I ever known; mine has been, and is a dreary, unloved lot. Is it a wonder my heart clings to you, loves you so madly? and yet you will not even let me try and win you; but would shut out all hope. If you loved another; then—then indeed I would not plead; but, as it is—it is scarcely kind, Miss Neville; forgive me for saying so."

"Believe me, I do not wish to be unkind," faltered Amy. "I think my decision would have been the kindest in the end. But enough; it shall be as you wish, only you must not blame me hereafter."

"Neither now nor ever!"

And so they parted, both sorrowful at heart, both feeling the future which seemed to loom so gloomily for each; neither daring to look beyond the shadow even now flitting across their path.

Little did Frances Strickland think while loitering in the school-room awaiting Amy, that the very meeting she had come to prevent had taken place.

Just as she was growing impatient, and wondering at the unwonted delay, Miss Neville entered.

"I have been waiting to make my adieux," she said, "having heard you were going away, and I did not like you should go without a word of farewell."

Amy was quite unprepared for this, and looked her surprise.

"Do we part friends, Miss Neville?"

"I can scarcely say yes," replied Amy, "our acquaintance has been but short, and—and—you have never liked me, Miss Strickland; if you recollect you almost told me so once."

"Ah, you have not forgotten that stormy interview. But I was angry and passionate. I have regretted what I said then ever since. Even you must know I never carried out my threats."

"I cannot tell," replied Amy. "I know I feared them, and the thought of what you had threatened—the shame—made me ill. No, Miss Strickland, we can never be friends."

"And why not?"

There was a slight touch of hauteur in her tone, do what she would to hide it. Amy saw it, and felt more than ever convinced Miss Strickland did not like her; never would like her. Why should she so persistently wish to be friendly now, after all her anger and rudeness Amy could not divine, but she suspected Frances, and thought some motive lay hidden deep in her heart. She answered coldly,

"Our paths in life lie so very wide apart, that being friends is simply impossible."

"Not so," replied Frances. "Our lives may be nearer knit together than you think; you will not be always teaching."

"As yet I see no reason to think otherwise, and as I think I told you once before, I am reconciled to it, or I trust nearly so." And Amy felt she was growing more ungracious every moment.

Perhaps Frances saw it too, for she held out her hand as she said, "Do we, or rather are we to part friends, Miss Neville?"

"I do not wish we should part as enemies. Good-bye, Miss Strickland." She wished she could thank her for coming, but she could not.

"Well, good-bye, I think you will be sorry some day for refusing my friendship. I suppose you will not come down this evening; so this is a final leave-taking."

She turned as if to go, then stopped. Her anger at Amy's refusal got the mastery over her wise resolutions, and her eyes flashed fire as she said,

"There can be no middle course, Miss Neville; if you will not have me as a friend, I can be a bitter enemy."

"I know it," replied Amy, "and cannot help it."

"Very well, then, I bid you beware! We shall see which is defeated. You or I. I will be relentless."

And she passed out.

"Why do you look so sad, Miss Neville?" said little Fanny, creeping up close to her, "I am glad you don't like her, because I know she can't bear you."

"I don't know, Fanny. She says she does, or rather did."

"But that's a story. Only see her eyes when she went away!"

"Yes, Fanny; but that was my fault. I fear I was not wise to brave her; but then it could scarcely have been otherwise. I could not like her."

"I know I don't!" replied the child, "and am glad no one does. She nearly pinched Edith's arm a minute ago like she did mine, because she told her Uncle Charles put up those book shelves for you; and oh! she looked so angry. She's just like the dog in the manger. Isn't she?"

Ah! Had there been no such person as Uncle Charles in the world, these two young girls might have been friends. But as it was; that was the sore point which kept their hearts, the one so distant; the other so revengefully inclined. Frances, who nursed and encouraged her love, knew it was so: while Amy, who dared not think of or allow her love, tried to imagine a hundred other reasons as the true cause of her dislike.

The children were up betimes in the morning to take a tearful farewell of their governess; Fanny crying heartily and aloud, until severely rated by Anne Bennet, who, with her sister Julia, was also there bidding good-bye while Amy's boxes were being stowed away in the carriage.

"I can't help crying," said Fanny, when rebuked, "indeed I can't! so it's of no use, Cousin Anne."

"Then cry to yourself, child; or stay, here is my hankerchief to stuff into your mouth; your noise is enough to scare an inmate of Bedlam, and nearly drives us all crazy. Good-bye, Miss Neville; you will write to me, won't you? A long letter, mind, when you are settled at home."

"I have promised your sister a letter," was the reply.

"Just like my luck. I ought to have asked you sooner. But I shall write to you all the same. I dare say I shall have lots of news that Julia will know nothing about."

Then the carriage drove away, and Amy wondered why Mr. Vavasour had never given her the time-table as he had promised, and felt a little disappointed at his forgetfulness; either he did not care for her so much as she had imagined, or he felt her going away too deeply; at all events his non appearance made her feel sad. She had learned to like though not to love him.

But when she reached the Standale Station, and the carriage steps were being let down; the first person she saw was Mr. Vavasour, awaiting her at the door.

"Mr. Vavasour! you here?" she exclaimed, involuntarily, and perhaps with a slight welcome of gladness in the tone.

"Yes; why not? Did you suppose I would let you go alone, and uncared for? The train will be here in another moment; I almost feared you would be late."

Then he went away for her ticket, and presently she was leaning on his arm as they walked along the platform. It seemed like a dream.

"Here is the time-table, Miss Neville," he said, as soon as she was seated in the carriage, "I think you will be able to understand it, and you must allow me to lend you this railway rug, it will be of use to you, both going and returning, and I shall not require it," and he drew it over her feet as she sat, "I wish you a safe journey, though I fear it will scarcely be a pleasant one; I trust you will find Mrs. Neville better. God bless you."

There was a banging of doors, the whistle sounded, and she was carried away out of his sight, feeling she had been more cared for and thought of during those few minutes than she had ever been before in all her life; yet his last three words stirred her heart strangely, bringing as they did that last sad evening of Charles Linchmore's stay at Brampton vividly before her, when he had held her hand, and softly said the same words.

VOLUME III

CHAPTER I

IS THERE A FATE IN IT?

"The grief of slighted love, suppress'd,
Scarce dull'd her eye, scarce heav'd her breast;
Or if a tear, she strove to check,
A truant tear stole down her neck,
It seem'd a drop that, from his bill,
The linnet casts, beside a rill,
Flirting his sweet and tiny shower
Upon a milk-white April flower:—
Or if a sigh, breathed soft and low,
Escaped her fragrant lips; e'en so
The zephyr will, in heat of day,
Between two rose leaves fan its way."
COLMAN

Amy had been some three weeks at home, and as yet there had been no improvement in Mrs. Neville's health to justify her daughter's return to Brampton. There was the same lassitude, the same weariness. She would lie on the sofa day after day, with no bodily ailment save that of weakness, and an utter inability to get better, and apparently with no wish to do so. She never complained, but was ever grateful and content. It was as if life were waning away imperceptibly, and her spirits, which had always bravely struggled through all her trials and sorrows, had at last sunk never to rise again.

Amy seldom left her, but generally sat by her side, on a low footstool, reading or working. Sometimes Mrs. Neville would lay her hand gently on the fair masses of hair, and Amy, whose heart was very sorrowful, would hold her head lower still so that her tears might fall unseen.

There was something peculiarly tender and very pitying in the way the hand was placed on her head; at least Amy thought so, and strove more than ever to be cheerful, lest her mother, who lay so silently watching her, should guess at the secret grief in her heart which she was striving so hard, and she trusted successfully, to overcome; while, as yet, no word of it had passed between them. If Mrs. Neville thought her daughter's spirits less joyous, or her manner more quiet, while her eyes no longer flashed with their old bright expression, but at times drooped sadly under their long lashes, she said nothing; and Amy, while obliged sometimes to talk of her life at Brampton, never mentioned Charles's name; yet in the solitude of her own room she sometimes thought of him, and how as she had sat at one of the cross-stations, on her road from Standale, awaiting the arrival of the train that was to take her on to Ashleigh, she had seen Charles amongst the crowd hurrying into the one bound for Brampton; while she, soon afterwards, was speeding along over a part of the very way he had so recently travelled. Both had been waiting some twenty minutes at the same station, and yet neither had been near enough to speak, but had been as effectually separated as though miles had divided them, instead of so many yards. Strange fatality! which might have altered the future lives of both.

Yes, he had gone to Brampton the very morning she had left it: one half hour later on her part, and they would have met. She was glad she had not missed the train, and that they had not met. Glad that she was absent from the park, and not obliged to see him day after day, or hear the children talk, as they sometimes did, of their uncle.

Julia often wrote to Amy all the chit-chat of the park. How Charles Linchmore had returned, and was often at Frances' side; and how the latter's airs had become more intolerable in consequence. How Anne snubbed Mr. Hall as much as ever; but was, in Julia's opinion, more pleased with him, and more contented to put up with his grave reproofs than she used to be; and how Julia thought it would be a match in the end, and wondered what kind of a clergyman's wife she would make. And lastly, that Mr. Vavasour had left the park.

Anne also wrote, but only once, and her letter was short; yet Amy read it over and over again, until she knew the last few lines by heart, and wondered what they meant; or whether they were hastily written, and had no point or hidden meaning, but were simply penned and then forgotten, as many things often were, that were said by Anne Bennet, in her quick impulsiveness. "Come back, Miss Neville," she wrote, "we all want you sadly. As for Charles, he is not himself, and will be lost!"

These were the words that troubled Amy, were ever at her heart all day, and chased away sleep from her pillow, until her tired overwrought brain relieved itself in silent, secret tears—tears far more painful than passionate sobs. Those are at the surface, and soon over, they cure grief by their very bitterness, and by the self-abandonment of the sufferer; the others lie deeper and break the heart.

These words of Anne's, whether incautiously written or not, determined Amy on not returning to Brampton, until Charles Linchmore's leave had expired; and that, she knew, must be in another week or so. If Miss Bennet meant he was fast losing his heart to Frances, and that Amy must go back to wean him away, how little she knew of the pride of her woman's nature. What! seek, or throw herself in the way of a man's love? Scarcely wooed, be won? Amy shrank at the very idea. No, if her love was worth having it was worth winning; and that,—not with the sternness of man's nature, not by the force of his strong will, not by exciting her jealousy with another, but by gentleness and kindness; and then her heart reverted to Robert Vavasour, and she wished she could love him, for had he not ever been kind to her? and gentle, very, even when she had pained him most.

He had been very kind to her, there was no doubt about that, not only to her, but for her sake to those most dear to her. At one time came some beautiful hot-house grapes, at another some delicate game. Little Sarah called them the gifts of the "good unknown."

The rail was open all the way to quiet Ashleigh now, and although the place did not boast of a railway van or even porter, still the station master always found some willing lad ready to take the basket to the cottage, and great was the excitement it caused to Sarah and even quiet old Hannah, but then the latter always knew her darling Miss Amy would marry an Earl at the very least.

Mrs. Neville never questioned, but looked more searchingly in Amy's face, laid her hand more caressingly those days on her head, and spoke more softly and lovingly, while Amy never said a word.

Once, when Sarah came dancing into the room, in her wild spirits, with another beautiful bunch of grapes, Mrs. Neville laid her thin, wasted hand on Amy's, and said gently,—

"Is it all right, Amy?"

"All," was the reply, and Mrs. Neville leant back again, apparently satisfied.

But things could not go on thus for ever. Robert Vavasour, in his lonely home, thought more and more of Amy, and the days he was idly wasting away from her, when he ought to be striving for her love. At length, his solitude became unbearable, he could stand it no longer; whether wise or no, he must leave Somerton, the place was growing unbearable to him, and go to Ashleigh. But could he go without an intimation of some kind to her he loved? Yes, he must; for how send a note to Amy? Would she not look upon his letter as an impertinence, seeing she had given him no permission to write? So he made up his mind to go to Ashleigh without warning, for come what might, he must go.

Robert Vavasour was not of an impulsive character, apt like Charles to be led away on the sudden spur of the moment, but he felt that remaining at Somerton would never advance his interest with her in whom all his dearest hopes of life were centred; he should simply lose the kindly feeling he had already gained in her heart, or what was worse still, be forgotten altogether.

The craving wish to see her, grew stronger and stronger within him each day, until he could no longer refuse to gratify it, and ere another week passed over his head, he was speeding along the road to Ashleigh, arriving there by the one o'clock train.

It was a stormy day, heavy showers of rain, with occasional sunshine, but Robert Vavasour, who saw everything couleur de rose, was charmed with the lovely scenery and quaintness of the cottages; in one of which,—perhaps the prettiest in the place,—he secured some, pleasant rooms for the time of his stay and then walked out in the hope of meeting her he loved. Vain hope! as Mrs. Neville seemed so much weaker, Amy did not leave her side. Hannah and little Sarah passed him on their way down the lane, and on their return, gave rather a high-flown account of the tall, handsome gentleman they had seen. Amy never guessed, or even thought of Robert Vavasour, but her heart fluttered strangely as it quickly passed through her mind that it might be Charles Linchmore. But alas! she failed in recognising the description so eagerly given and descanted on by Sarah.

The morning of the next day was hopelessly wet, and Robert Vavasour's courage rose—with his anxiety to see Amy,—to fever heat; and, determined to see her at all hazards, he bent his steps towards the cottage.

Sarah, tired of the dulness within doors, was gazing idly from the window, little thinking that her curiosity concerning the stranger she had seen only the day before was so soon to be gratified. But there he was coming along the road, and very eagerly the little girl watched him.

"Oh! sister Amy," cried she, "here's the gentleman I saw yesterday, do come and look at him before he goes out of sight; he'll turn down the elm tree walk in another moment."

But before Amy could have reached the window, had she been so inclined, he had opened the little gate, and was coming up the gravel walk.

Sarah shrank away from the window, and clapped her hands with delight. "Why he's coming here, only think of that, Mamma. Oh! I guess it must be the 'good unknown' himself."

In another moment all doubt was at an end, and Robert Vavasour in the little sitting-room, welcomed and thanked by Mrs. Neville at least, and Sarah also, if he might judge by her glistening eyes, although she was too shy to say a word, while Amy, if she did not say she was glad to see him, did not rebuke him for coming, nor appear to look on his visit as an intrusion; and soon he was quite at home with them all, and when Amy, who had been out to Hannah, to try and make some addition to their homely dinner, returned, she was surprised to see on what friendly terms he was.

"I am afraid, dear mamma," she said, "you are exerting yourself too much. You are so unaccustomed to see a stranger."

"Scarcely a stranger, Amy. Mr. Vavasour claims our friendship for his kindness; and besides, he tells me he has known you for some time."

"Some two months, is it not?" replied Amy.

"Hardly so long, I think, Miss Neville. It seems but yesterday since I first saw you."

"Are you only here for the day?" asked Amy.

"I am here for a week," he replied; "some good lady in the village has allowed me to take up my abode with her for that time, or it may be longer, as any one would be tempted to remain in the clean pretty room she showed me."

"It must be Mrs. Turner, Mamma; her cottage is so very nice."

"If it is," replied Mrs. Neville, "you will have no cause to complain, Mr. Vavasour; we stayed with her for a day or two on our first arrival, and were much pleased with her attention, and the cleanliness of the house."

"Is this place often visited by strangers? It must in summer be a lovely spot. It is prettier than Brampton, Miss Neville."

"Prettier, but not so grand; and the views are not so extensive."

"You prefer Brampton?"

"Oh, no! Ashleigh is my home, and then I like it for its very quietness."

"It will no longer be quiet," replied Mrs. Neville. "Stray visitors have often reached it since I have been here; and now the easy access to it by rail will, of necessity, bring more, and Ashleigh will, perhaps, become immortalized by the lovers of pic-nics. But here is Hannah to announce dinner. You must excuse my joining you, Mr. Vavasour, as I am unable to leave the sofa."

After dinner the weather changed; the heavy clouds cleared away, and a faint gleam of sunshine shone out.

Amy proposed a walk, as she thought her mother would be glad of a little rest and quiet after her exertion, so with her sister she went with Robert Vavasour down into the village.

So dreary as the lane looked now, with its tall leafless trees! But their visitor was charmed with everything, and would not allow its desolation. They inspected his new abode, which turned out to be Mrs. Turner's; then through the village, and home by road, and found Mrs. Elrington had come to spend the evening—and what a pleasant one it was! Even Amy allowed that, although she did not feel quite at rest within herself, or satisfied at Robert Vavasour's having come to Ashleigh; still she found herself later on in the evening laughing and chatting, in something of the old spirit, at seeing her mother take an interest in the conversation, and not nearly so weary and tired as she usually was.

"You are so very good," said Amy, as she went out to open the cottage door for Robert, as he went away.

"Good! Miss Neville. How? In what way?"

"In being content with our dull life here."

"It is anything but dull to me. My life lately has been a simply existing one—the slow passing of each day, or counting the hours for the night to arrive, and bring a short respite from the monotony of a dreary life. Being here is—is heaven to me! in comparison to my late existence at Somerton Park."

There was no mistaking the impassioned tone in which this was said. Amy hastened to change the subject.

"I am sure your visit has given Mamma pleasure."

"Mrs. Neville seems a great invalid, I do not wonder at your anxiety for her while absent." As a stranger he had remarked the exhaustion and weariness, although to Amy her mother had seemed so much better.

"Do you think she looks so very ill?" she asked, anxiously.

"I think there is great weakness," he replied, evading a direct answer. "Have you a clever medical attendant here?"

"Yes, I think so. Dr. Sellon, is at least, very kind and attentive, no one could be more so; he says Mamma merely wants rousing, and we must not allow this apathy and weariness to increase, but strive to divert her mind, even as it was this evening, and all through your kindness."

"Ashleigh is a lovely spot, but rather too quiet for an invalid whose mind requires rousing, and whose vital energies seem so prostrated. I should suggest a total change of scene. A new and novel life, in fact, in a place perfectly strange to her, would, I should think, conduce more towards her recovery than all the doctors and medicine in the world."

"Dr. Sellon has never said so; never even hinted at such a thing," replied Amy, thoughtfully. Alas! how could it be managed, even with the sacrifice of all her salary.

"Have you had any further advice?" he asked.

"No. I wrote the other day to Dr. Ashley, our old doctor, who attended us all for so many years. I thought perhaps he might be coming this way and would call; but, although he wrote me a very kind reply, he does not even hint at such a stray chance happening."

"Does he offer any opinion or advice on Mrs. Neville's case?"

"Yes. You can read it if you like," and she took it from her pocket and gave it to him; "only do not mention anything about it to Mamma, she might not like my having written; or it might make her nervous in supposing herself worse than she is. It is not exactly a secret," she added, blushing slightly, "as Mrs. Elrington knows of it, and approved of my letter."

"Do not wrong me by supposing I should think so, Miss Neville. I will take it home, and read it at my leisure, if you will allow me. Good night."

The door closed, and he was gone before Amy could reply; but as she turned to re-enter the sitting-room, she sighed and murmured,

"There is a fate in some things. Is there in my life?"

CHAPTER II

FOR BETTER, FOR WORSE

"My life went darkling like the earth, nor knew it shone a star,
To that dear Heaven on which it hung in worship from afar.
O, many bared their beauty, like brave flowers to the bee;
He might have ranged through sunny fields, but nestled down to me;
And daintier dames would proudly have smiled him to their side,
But with a lowly majesty he sought me for his Bride;

And grandly gave his love to me, the dearest thing on Earth,
Like one who gives a jewel, unweeting of its worth."
MASSEY

A fortnight passed away, and still Robert Vavasour lingered at Ashleigh, although he seemed no nearer winning Amy's love than when he first came; yet he could not tear himself away. Sometimes he was gloomy and desponding; and on these days he never came near the cottage. At others his hopes rose when only a smile or glance kinder than usual came from her he loved, and then he was the life of the little party. But when he fancied Amy was beginning to care for him a little more, she would suddenly shrink within herself again, and become as cold and reserved as ever, but then he never thought that it was his almost tender manner that chilled and frightened her, lest he should think she was encouraging his suit. Still he hoped on, would not despair. What lover ever does? and he loved her so dearly.

One morning, finding Mrs. Neville alone, he told her of his love for Amy, of the compact between them, and of his hopes. The widow did not discourage them, she liked Mr. Vavasour, and would have rejoiced at seeing Amy his wife; still she would not influence Amy in any way, but leave her free to choose for herself; but since she loved no other,—and Mrs. Neville half sighed as if she almost doubted it,—she thought in time the young girl's heart might be won.

And with this Robert Vavasour was obliged to be content. Content? he was anything but that; he was impatient, and fretted at the delay and slow progress he was making, he would have been more than human if he had not; but with Amy he was ever kind and gentle; she knew nothing, saw nothing of his anxious heart and sometimes despairing hopes.

And so the days flew on, Mrs. Neville neither better nor worse; some days more languid, at others less so and able to sit up; but with no certainty about it, so as to lead those most anxious to believe she was in anyway advancing towards recovery.

One morning they were surprised by a visit from Dr. Ashley. He had taken a holiday, he said, and thought he could not do better than run down to see his old friends, and was putting up, strange to say, at Mrs. Turner's, whose cottage had been pointed out to him as the prettiest in the village; and had certainly stretched like india rubber for the occasion, but then the gentleman already lodging there had kindly consented to share the parlour with him; and they were to dine together during his stay.

If Amy suspected Robert Vavasour of being concerned in this sudden move, she said nothing; but then she had grown very silent of late; perhaps she pondered these things more deeply in her heart; certain it was she ceased to be so distant and reserved to Robert, and he in consequence became more gentle and loving. Perhaps if Amy's thoughts could have shaped themselves into words, they would have been, "He does not love me or he would be here; and I? what can I do?"

But Charles Linchmore's staying away was no proof that he did not love Amy, believing as he did that her heart was another's; had he not thought so, not even his sister-in-law's frowns and sarcasms would have kept him from her side. As it was, he knew not even of Robert Vavasour's presence at Ashleigh, as Amy, when she wrote to Julia and Anne, never mentioned it, feeling sure of a bantering letter in return; as of course they would guess of his love for her, and imagine it was going to be a match, whether she denied it or no; certainly they would never think of the true reason that had brought him—namely, her refusal.

It was the second and last day of Dr. Ashley's stay; one of Mrs. Neville's worst days, and she had not as yet made her appearance downstairs when Mrs. Elrington entered the room where the two sisters sat.

"Mamma has not come down yet," said Amy, "she was very wakeful all night, and I persuaded her to rest a little longer this morning, although she was very loath to do so, on Dr. Ashley's account."

"Has he been to see her yet?"

"No, but I am expecting him every moment. Mamma was so much better yesterday that perhaps she is now suffering from the over-excitement of seeing him."

"Very possibly. Old times must have come before her so forcibly, and they are but sad ones for your mother to look back to. It is perhaps just as well Dr. Ashley should see her at her worst. What is his opinion of Mrs. Neville?"

"I did not ask him, and he never volunteered to tell me; but I must ascertain to-day. Do you not think I ought to?"

"Certainly I do, Amy; you would be wrong if you did not. I think if I were you I would ask his true," and Mrs. Elrington laid a stress on the word, "opinion on your mother's case."

"Do you think her very ill?" asked Amy.

"Yes, Amy, I do," replied Mrs. Elrington, gently. "That is to say, I think her very weak, weaker than she was when I wrote to you after her recovery from the severe illness she had."

Amy sighed. "I sometimes fancy," she said, "that Ashleigh, lovely as it is, does not suit Mamma; you know her quiet life here is so very different from what she has been accustomed to; but I do not see how a change is to be effected."

"It would be a great expense, certainly."

"It would, and the means to effect it with will be smaller; as I fear, Mrs. Elrington, I shall have to resign my situation at Brampton; I cannot leave Mamma so lonely, neither can I be happy away from her while she is so ill."

"I have been thinking the same thing, Amy; your mother certainly does require all your care and attention. It would not be right to leave her."

"Do you think Mrs. Linchmore will be annoyed at my leaving in the middle of my quarter without any hint or warning whatever?"

"Not under the circumstances, Amy. You were happy there?"

"Yes, as happy as I shall ever be away from home; I was very fond of my pupils, of Edith especially."

"Was she the youngest?"

"No, the eldest. An orphan niece of Mr. Linchmore's, and adopted by him at her mother's and his sister's death. I shall regret leaving Brampton. I think change must be one of the worst trials of a governess's life."

"It is a sad one, no doubt, when, as in your case, a governess happens to be attached to those she is leaving. Perhaps," continued Mrs. Elrington, as she rose, "I had better not wait to see your mother now. As soon as you have made up your mind, Amy, I would advise your writing at once to Mrs. Linchmore without delay."

Amy leant back in her chair very sorrowfully after Mrs. Elrington had gone. If she had had any doubt about the propriety of leaving Brampton, her mother's old friend—she, whose advice she so valued— had cleared it away; it was evident the step must be taken, however slow her heart might be to break asunder the one tie that yet seemed to bind her to Charles Linchmore.

"What are you thinking of, Amy?" asked Sarah, who had been watching her sister for some time. "You look so sad."

"Do I? I was thinking of Mamma, and whether we could do anything to make her better; and about my leaving Brampton, Sarah."

"But that will be so nice to have you always here; you can't be sorry about that, sister."

"But then I shall lose a great deal of money; and Mamma will have to go without a great many things she really wants. Port wine cannot be bought for nothing, Sarah."

"Ah! what a pity it is we are not rich, then we might take her back to our dear old home. I am sure she would get well there. Don't you think so?"

"She might, Sarah. But I think if change is to do her good, she will require a greater change than that."

"Further off still?" asked the child. "Where to, Amy?"

"I cannot tell; but Dr. Ashley can."

"But can't you guess at all? Not even the name?" persisted her sister.

"No. But I think somewhere abroad; a long way off. And that would cost money. Yes, more money than we have, a great deal," sighed Amy.

"Ah!" said the child, "when I'm grown up I'll marry a man with lots of money, just like Mr. Vavasour. Hannah says he's awfully rich; and then he should take us away to a lovely place by the sea-side where Mamma and all of us could live like princesses. I am sure she would get well then."

This innocent remark of Sarah's was a home-thrust to Amy; a death blow to her hopes, and roused her at once. Should she sit so quietly and passively when her mother's life was at stake? Nurse and hoard up a love in her heart that she was ashamed had ever entered there from its very hopelessness and selfishness? There was Dr. Ashley coming up the walk, she would first ask his opinion as to the necessity of a change; and if he thought it necessary? Then—then. Once again Amy sighed, and said, "It is my fate; it must be so," and then went out into the other room, and quietly awaited the doctor's coming.

Some ten minutes elapsed, during which Amy was restless and anxious; still she would not pause to think now, lest her heart should give way; so she walked about even as Frances Strickland often did in her impatient moods, took up the books one by one off the table and looked at their titles—read them she could not—and then the doctor's heavy tread sounded on the staircase, and she went out and met him.

"Will you come in here, Dr. Ashley?" she said. "I want to thank you for so kindly coming to see Mamma. It is so very kind of you." Amy knew nothing of the ten pound note so carefully stowed away in his waistcoat pocket for the expenses of his homeward journey.

"Pray say no more, my dear Miss Neville," he said. "It pains me."

And Amy did not. Perhaps she thought it was painful to be thanked for what in her innermost heart she half suspected he was paid for.

"How did you find Mamma, Dr. Ashley?" she asked.

"Well, not quite so bright as yesterday, but still no material change for the worse. Dr Sellon tells me she often has these ups and downs."

"Any unusual excitement appears to weaken her for the time. Dr. Sellon does not attend regularly. I only call him in when I think Mamma really requires it."

"Quite right. Your mother's case is one requiring care and—and everything good and strengthening you can give her."

"Do you think Mamma very ill?" Amy could not bring herself to ask if he thought she would recover, although that thought had been at her heart for days, and she had driven it away and would not give it utterance.

"There is weakness,—great weakness," he replied. "I cannot see that Mrs. Neville has any other disease."

"But—but I fear you are evading my question, Dr. Ashley. I wish to know exactly what your opinion is of Mamma."

"My dear young lady," he said, kindly, "the opinion I have given is a true one, though perhaps not all the truth, and—well, she requires great care. There is a prostration of the vital powers—great want of energy. She wants rousing. Every means should be tried to accomplish that; otherwise, I need not say, this weakness and debility will increase, and of necessity do mischief."

"Every means," replied Amy, "but what means? what must I do?"

"Whatever lies in your power: whatever the patient, which I know she is in both senses of the word, expresses a wish for. She should be humoured in everything, but I need not tell you that, Miss Neville."

"And can nothing else be done?—no change of air tried?"

"Decidedly, if possible. It is the one remedy needful; the only remedy, in fact, and I should have named it at first, only I deemed it impracticable of accomplishment."

"You think Mamma might recover if she went away?" asked Amy.

"With God's help, I do; but the step should be taken at once. If delayed it might be too late. And now, keep up your spirits and hope for the best. Remember there is nothing so bad as a tearful face and aching heart for your mother to see."

"Too late!" Those words rang in Amy's ears all day. It should not be too late. And yet how nearly had her mother been sacrificed to her blind infatuation for one who she now felt had never loved her, but only carelessly flirted to trifle away the hours that perhaps hung heavy on his hands. Alas! what would Mr. Linchmore say, did he know that the very fate he had warned her would be hers if she allowed her heart to become enslaved by Mr. Vavasour, had even overtaken her at the hand of his brother.

Not many days after Dr. Ashley had gone, a letter arrived from Anne Bennet. It ran thus:—

"Brampton Park,
"February 25th.

"MY DEAR MISS NEVILLE,

"I have almost made up my mind to torment you with a letter every day, this place being so dull and dreary that the mere fact of writing is quite a delightful episode in my long day. I should be happy enough if Frances were away; but you know how I always disliked that girl. Just imagine my disgust, then, at her remaining here, for, of course, Julia has told you she herself and every one else is gone, excepting Frances and Charles; the latter, I suppose, remains in the hope of soon seeing you. Why don't you come back? I declare it is shameful of you to remain away so long, when you must know how wretched you are making him, and how devotedly he loves you. I should not tell you this, only Frances drives me to it, and I am just at the root of a grand secret. Julia behaved shamefully—would not help me in the least, as she would persist in declaring it was curiosity—how I hate the word!—so I had nothing for it but to take Mr. Hall into my confidence, the result of which has been that I have promised, some long time hence, to become Mrs. Hall; and for the time being, we are turned into a pair of turtle-doves, only instead of billing and cooing, we are snapping and snarling all day. Adieu. Answer every word of this letter, especially that relating to Charles, who is, I am certain, as devotedly yours as

"Your loving friend,
"ANNE BENNET."

This letter, with its mention of Charles Linchmore, pained Amy, and roused her slumbering pride. She would answer it at once, every word of it, and for ever put an end to Anne's mention of his name. She should see that Amy was as proud in some things as the haughty Mrs. Linchmore herself, or the defiant Frances. No woman should think she would stoop one iota for any man's love; while as for Charles, Anne was deceived in her belief of his love for her, even as she had been; but it was not well her heart should be reminded of the one image still slumbering there. Was she not as much bound to Robert Vavasour as if she were already engaged to him? or did she ever prevent his coming to the cottage by being ungracious?

No; Amy had made up her mind to love him, and was ever ready to listen to his words, or walk with him. No fits of dread despair assailed him now. His whole life seemed a bright sunshine; even the dull, desolate walk up from the village was pleasant, because every step brought him nearer to the cottage.

That evening—the evening of the day that brought Anne's letter—Amy, while old Hannah cleared away the tea things, went to her room and answered it. The doing so cost her many bitter thoughts, and perhaps a few tears were hastily dashed away. When it was done, her head ached sadly. She went to the window and threw it open. It was a lovely moonlight night. She crept softly downstairs and out into the garden, and leant over the little green gate at the end.

Some ten minutes passed sadly away, and then a step sounded on the crisp gravel. Amy knew well it was Robert Vavasour's, still she did not move or turn her head. Was he going home without saying good night to her? or had he missed her and guessed where she was?

"It is a cold night, Miss Neville," he said as he drew near. "Is it wise for you to be out without a shawl or wrap of any kind?"

"The lovely night tempted me," she replied, "I thought it might cool my head, for it aches sadly."

He did not reply. Amy too was silent; perhaps she guessed what he would say next.

Presently he laid his hand on hers as it rested on the woodwork of the gate. She did not withdraw it, and then he boldly took the small fair hand in his.

"Amy," he said, softly, while she trembled exceedingly, "do you remember I said I would ask you once again? The time has come. Amy, will you be my wife? I love you more dearly than when I first asked you in the old library at Brampton."

She did not shrink from him or his encircling arm as she replied, "I think I love you now; I am sure I like you better, and will try to love you with all my heart. If this will satisfy you, then I will be your wife."

And it did satisfy him, and he pressed his lips on her clear high, forehead, as, like a weary child, she laid her head on his shoulder as he gently drew her towards him.

"I am very timid," she said, "and you must be patient, and not expect too much from me at first."

These words, spoken so entreatingly and dependently, claiming, as they seemed to him, all his care and kindness, calmed him at once; he must be patient, and not frighten away by his too tender words the love only just dawning for him.

"My darling," he whispered, "you will never find me other than kind and gentle with you. You have made me very happy, Amy."

"Have I ever caused you unhappiness?" she asked, seeing he waited for a reply.

"Only twice, Amy. Once when you tried to shut out all hope from my heart, and again when I fancied you cared for Charley Linchmore."

That name! How it jarred through the chords of Amy's heart! Only a few moments ago she had determined on tearing it out, and never allowing another thought of him to enter there again. Was he dear to her still; now that she was the affianced bride of another? and that other, ought he not to know of her foolishness and folly? ought not every thought of her heart to be open to him now? Yes, now; from this time, this hour; but not the past; that could only bring sorrow to him, shame to her. No! no! She could not lower herself in the eyes of Robert Vavasour, he who loved her so dearly, and whom she had just promised to try in time to love with all her heart. All her heart! Was this trembling at the mere mention of another's name the beginning of her promise? Would she ever forget Charles Linchmore? Ever love another as she could have loved him?

Amy shivered slightly; but Robert Vavasour, who loved her more than his life, felt it.

"You are cold, little one," he said, "and must go in. You know, Amy, I have the right to protect you from all ill now," and he led her back gently towards the cottage.

CHAPTER III

LISTENING AT THE DOOR

If thou hast crushed a flower,
The root may not be blighted;
If thou hast quenched a lamp,
Once more it may be lighted;
But on thy harp or on thy lute,
The string which thou hast broken
Shall never in sweet sound again
Give to thy touch a token!

If thou hast bruised a vine,
The summer's breath is healing,
And its clusters yet may glow
Thro' the leaves, their bloom revealing;
But if thou hast a cup o'erthrown
With a bright draught filled—oh! never
Shall earth give back the lavished wealth
To cool thy parched lips' fever.

Thy heart is like that cup,
If thou waste the love it bore thee;
And like that jewel gone,
Which the deep will not restore thee;
And like that string of heart or lute
Whence the sweet sound is scattered,—

Gently, oh! gently touch the chords,
So soon for ever shattered!
MRS HEMANS

Anne had scarcely exaggerated when she told Amy that Brampton Park had become dull and stupid. It certainly had subsided into its old dullness, while the days themselves were even more dreary-looking than the house. Spring had commenced, the trees were beginning to put forth their blossoms, and the cold frosty weather had passed away; still the days were misty, and sometimes even foggy, with drizzling rain. Riding parties were scarcely ever attempted, and a walk was almost out of the question; while dancing and music were things unknown—the first impracticable, the latter no one seemed to have the spirits for. Mrs. Hopkins no longer walked about the corridors in stately importance; even Mason's crinoline seemed to have shrunk somewhat, as she flaunted less saucily about than when certain of meeting some one to whom to show off her last new cap.

The two young girls still staying at Brampton did not get on very well together, although there was little show of outward unfriendliness on either part. Frances had long since found out that Anne Bennet disliked and suspected, even watched her; but no fear had she of being detected—her plans, so she flattered herself, had been too secretly and deeply laid for Anne's simple mind to fathom them; such a worm in her path she could tread upon whenever she liked, and utterly crush when it pleased her. So secure was she that often Anne was attacked with one of her sarcastic speeches. But Anne was too wary to be betrayed into an open quarrel, which would, most likely, have resulted in her being obliged to leave Brampton; so she contented herself by either treating her words with silent contempt or retorting in the same style, with the secret determination of some day having her revenge, much to poor Mr. Hall's dismay, as he was, of course, faut de mieux, as Anne said, taken into her confidence.

Some twenty minutes Anne had been standing at one of the windows of the morning-room, which being just above the library, commanded a pretty good view down a part of the long avenue, through the branches of the still almost leafless trees.

It was about a month since the eventful evening on which Amy had penned her reply to Anne.

Charles, who had been reading, suddenly rose, and threw his book, with a gesture of weariness, on the table.

"Are you going out?" asked Frances, laying her embroidery in her lap, as he rose.

"Yes; it's close upon half-past four, and I shall just get a stroll before dinner; the book has made me stupid."

"So has my embroidery. I think I will go with you, if you will let me."

"You!" exclaimed Anne, from her distant post, ever ready to knock on the head any chance that drew the two together; "why your feet in their dainty boots would get soaked through and through, and you catch your death of cold. Do not encourage such self-immolation, Charles."

"Yes," laughed Charles, "your town-made boots, Frances, were never made or intended for country wear. Anne's are, at least, an inch thick, and wade through any amount of mud or dirt: so if either of you come, it must be Anne."

"I should say Anne would be a lively companion," retorted Frances, savagely. "I suppose by this time she could tell us how many drops of rain fall in a minute, and how many rooks have perched on the trees during the last half-hour."

"I wish one of the rooks would fly and bring me the letter from Miss Neville that I have been expecting, and have been looking out for all the afternoon."

This reply, with its allusion to the governess, Anne knew was the severest thing she could say; so, with a self-satisfied look at Frances' flushed face, she went away to put on her things.

But her water-proof cloak could not be found—was nowhere. Anne was a great deal too independent to summon servants to her aid, so she must needs go down stairs to look for it, remembering, as she went, that she had hung it on the stand in the hall to dry. She was returning upstairs with it on her arm, when Charles's voice sounded in the morning-room. Anne hesitated a moment; but Frances's low mysterious tone was too great a temptation to be resisted, and with a half-frightened guilty look, she drew near the door and listened, thinking, perhaps, the end to be attained justified the means she was employing in attaining it.

"My heart misgives me sometimes as to whether I did right in leaving her so precipitately, without a word," Charles was saying.

"What would have been the use of speaking?" was the rejoinder, "when she so evidently cared, or rather showed her love for Mr. Vavasour."

Anne could not hear the reply, and again Frances spoke.

"I thought I never should recover her from that death-like faint."

"If any woman deceived me, she did. I could have sworn she cared for me, on that very evening. How she trembled when I took her hand," said Charles.

Again Anne was at fault with the answer; but whatever it was Charles's reply rang loud and clear—

"I hate that fellow Vavasour!" he said.

"Hush! hush!" said Frances; and Anne could imagine she was entreating him to talk lower; then the rustle of her dress was heard, and swift as thought Anne flew lightly and softly up the thickly-carpeted stairs. As she paused at the top, breathless and panting, she heard the door below gently closed.

"Too late!" said she, with a smile of pleasure; and then went with something of a triumphant march to her room; where, shutting the door, she gave vent to one of her ringing laughs, which quickly subsided into a repentant, regretful look. "How shameful of me to laugh at such wickedness," said she, aloud; and then, settling herself in an old arm-chair, began to think over what she had heard, and draw her own conclusions therefrom.

This to Anne's quick mind was not very difficult; she guessed it all, or almost all, at once, and never for a moment doubted they were talking of Miss Neville. Had she not given them the clue when she mentioned her name, before going up to dress?

So Miss Neville had fainted. But where, and when? and how had Frances managed to persuade or convince Charles that the faint was caused by love for Mr. Vavasour? Charles had said, "That very evening." What evening? Was it the night before he went off so suddenly from Brampton? the night Mr. Vavasour had been brought home wounded and insensible? Was it possible Amy had fainted at seeing him? Yes, she might have done so; it was most probable she had; and yet that, as far as Anne could see, was no proof of her love for him. The sight might have grieved and shocked her, as it might have done any woman so timid as she was, and nervous and weak from the effects of recent illness.

Anne had indeed arrived at the root of the mystery, and that in a manner she had little dreamed of. What a deep-laid plot it seemed, and how artfully and successfully concealed from her! She felt half inclined to rush boldly down, confront Frances, and tax her with her falsehood and injustice to Miss Neville; but on second thoughts she restrained herself and determined for once on assuming a new character. She would take a leaf out of Frances' book, and act as secretly and silently.

As Anne sat ruminating a knock sounded at her door. What if it should be Frances? She sprung from her chair and busied herself in putting away her things ere she answered, "Come in;" but it was only a servant with letters, and at last Miss Neville's reply that she had been expecting for so many weeks.

"Tell Mr. Charles," said Anne, "that it looks so very wet I have changed my mind and shall not go out. He need not wait for me."

"Let Frances go out with him, if she likes," thought Anne; "hers will be but a short-lived pleasure. I will defeat her to-morrow," and then she once more sat down, and opened Amy's letter.

"Saturday.

"MY DEAR MISS BENNET,

"I feel much pleasure in congratulating you on your engagement to Mr. Hall, and trust the day is not so far distant as you seem to imagine when you will settle down into a pattern clergyman's wife. I fear there is little chance of our meeting again as you so kindly wish, as the very delicate state of my mother's health precludes all possibility of my leaving home at present. It is therefore imperative I should resign my situation with Mrs. Linchmore, much as I shall regret leaving her and my pupils. Your allusion to Mr. Charles Linchmore pains me. May I ask you to be silent on that subject for the future; as, even in joke, I do not like any man being thought to be desperately in love with me, and in this instance Mr. Charles Linchmore barely treated me as a friend at parting. With every wish for your future happiness in the new path which you have chosen,

"I am,
"Yours very sincerely,
"AMY NEVILLE."

This was the letter Amy had written, and which ought to have reached Anne a month ago, but Amy had entrusted the posting of it to a boy named Joe, who always came up every Sunday afternoon after church to have his dinner at the cottage. Unfortunately Joe forgot all about the letter, and before the next Sunday came round he was laid up with a fever, then prevalent at Ashleigh; and when able to get about again the letter never occurred to him until the first Sunday of his going to church; when again he donned his best suit, and on kneeling down, the letter rustled in his pocket. Joe's conscience smote him at once, and as soon as service was ended away he flew to the village post-office, spelling out as he went the address on the envelope; which, when he found was no sweetheart, but only a young lady, he concluded could be a letter of no consequence, and determined on saying nothing about its lying so long neglected in his pocket of his Sunday's best. Joe was not wise enough to know that trifles sometimes make or mar a life's happiness.

Before Anne left her room she made up her mind how to act; not a word would she say that night to Charles, because nothing could be done, but on the morrow she would open his eyes, show him the snare into which he had fallen; the folly he had been guilty of through the cunning and duplicity of Frances.

Anne sang all the way downstairs to the drawing-room as she went to dinner. The idea of having detected the proud Frances had perhaps more to do with this exuberance of spirits, than pleasure at Miss Neville's being done justice to, and Charles made happy; as for Mrs. Linchmore's frowns, Anne never gave them a thought.

Charles spirits were, if anything, more forced than usual; Frances more reserved and silent, so that Anne's vivacity and evident good humour showed in their brightest colours.

"What spirits you are in, Anne," remarked Mrs. Linchmore.

"Perhaps friend Hall is on the wing," laughed Charles.

"Or perhaps," replied Anne slowly, "my rooks have given me a lesson in—in—"

"Cawing," suggested Frances, impertinently.

"Why not in keeping a silent tongue?" Anne replied, with a scarcely perceptible touch of temper in the tone of her voice. "There is more wisdom in that, or perhaps my birds are wise birds, and have given me a hint where to find the golden link to my chain that has been missing so long."

"When did you lose it, Anne?" asked Mrs. Linchmore, "this is the first I have heard about it."

"Some two months ago, the morning after that poaching business," and Anne looked steadily at Frances; "but it is of no consequence now. I find my chain can be joined again without it."

Frances quailed before that steady, searching look; then rose and crossed the room, passing close by Anne as she went. "Miss Bennet," said she, with one of her coldest and most sarcastic smiles, "Miss Bennet has recourse to enigmas at times,—enigmas not very difficult of solution, although I for one cannot see the point they aim at," and she passed on.

Anne watched her opportunity all the evening, but to no purpose. Frances' suspicions were roused; it was impossible to get speech of Charles, and Anne was obliged to go up to bed with the rest, without having given one sign, or being able to say one word to him.

But Anne was not to be thus foiled; as soon as she gained her room she sat down and penned a note to Charles. She had something of great importance to tell him; would he meet her in the library before breakfast, at eight o'clock? and then away she flew in fear and trepidation down the long, dark corridors, and knocked at Charles's door.

"It is I, Anne Bennet," she said. "Open the door, quick! Make haste, I am frightened to death!"

In another moment the door opened.

"What is it?" said he, with a look of surprise.

She thrust the note into his hand, and was hurrying away.

"Stay, let me light you," he said.

"Oh! no, not for worlds!" she replied, then fled hastily, and gained her room without being seen.

Anne was too restless to sleep much that night, and was up and away downstairs the next morning before the hour she had named, and grew quite impatient at the slow movement of the minute hand of the clock on the chimney-piece, as she walked up and down awaiting Charles's coming.

Suppose he should not come? But, no, he must think it was something important to drag her out of bed at that unearthly hour, full two hours before her usual time. But there was a step coming along the hall now; then the door opened and Charles entered.

"You are sure Frances did not see you?" asked Anne.

"Yes," replied he, in some amazement, "but her maid did."

"Then I have not a moment to lose," said Annie, "come here and listen to me. Do you remember meeting me on the stairs, the morning you left Brampton so hurriedly? and your refusal to tell me why you had determined on doing so? or rather that you left because you had heard that Miss Neville no longer loved you?"

"No, Anne, no, you are wrong," replied Charles, decidedly, "I told you I had found out that Miss Neville had never cared for me, that her heart was entirely another's."

"It is all one and the same thing. I told you then that I did not believe it, and asked you to tell me how you had found it out, did I not?"

"You did. But why rake up old feelings which only tend to wound and bruise the heart afresh?"

"I am glad they do; if they did not I would not say one word in Miss Neville's defence."

"Defence! You talk strangely, Anne. Don't whisper hope to my heart, which can only end in misery and despair. I dare not hope."

"You will hope when you have heard all."

"What have you to tell?" he asked, almost sternly.

"Only this: that you left Brampton because Miss Neville had fainted on seeing Mr. Vavasour brought home wounded."

"What surer proof could I have of her love for him?" he asked, sadly.

"Proof! Do you call this proof?" said Anne, angrily, "do you forget how ill Miss Neville had been? how nervous and weak she yet was when this occurred? Was it a wonder she fainted? or a wonder that Frances, who hated and disliked her, should seize upon that accident to betray you both? And why? Only because had you told Miss Neville of your love, or divulged what you had seen to me, you would never have fallen into this snare so artfully laid for you, so cunningly worked out by Frances."

"Who told you it was Frances?"

"She herself," replied Anne, boldly facing the danger. "I have never left a stone unturned since that morning I met you on the stairs almost heart-broken. I was determined to find out why it was so. I suspected Frances, and have watched her all these long weeks, but she was too deep for me, too artful; and I never should have detected her, had I not over-heard her conversation with you yesterday. Then I found it all out; and I tell you Charles she has deceived you."

"Go on," he said, "convince me it is so, and I will thank you from my heart, Anne; and—no, I am a fool to hope!" and he strode away towards the window.

"You are a fool to despair! I tell you Charles, if any woman ever loved you, Miss Neville did. Were not the tears ready to start from her eyes when I gave her your message, and told her you were gone? You allowed her to think for weeks that you loved her, and then, for a mere trifle, left her without explanation or word of any kind. You behaved shamefully; while she never gave you an unkind word. The severest thing she ever said of you, was said in a letter I received from her yesterday. I told her you loved her, because I knew she was miserable thinking you did not; and read what she says."

He took the letter from her hand, his face flushing while he read it. "If Frances has deceived me? If she has dared to do it?" he said. "By Heaven! she shall rue it deeply!"

"And she has done so," pursued Anne, "and you are more to blame than she in allowing yourself to be deceived. How could you doubt Miss Neville? How believe that she, of all women in the world, would give away her heart unsought. You have condemned her unheard, and without the slightest foundation, and have behaved cruelly to her, and deserve to lose her."

"Not if she loves me," he cried, starting up, "not if any words of mine have power to move her. God knows whether I shall be successful or no; but she shall hear how madly I love her."

"Are you going to see her? and when?"

"Now, this instant! your words have roused me to action!"

He was gone. Anne went into the drawing-room and stood by the window. Some minutes slipped by, and then Frances entered.

"Come here!" said Anne. "Come and look at Charles."

Frances advanced and looked eagerly around.

"I do not see him," she said.

"Hark!" said Anne, "What is that?"

It was the hasty canter of a horse's feet. In another moment Charles dashed past.

Anne remembered the last time he had gone away. How she and Frances had stood together at the same window, even as they did now; only with this difference, that then, Frances' face was the triumphant one. Now they had changed places.

Anne could not—did not pity her, as she drew near and took hold of her arm.

"He has gone to tell Miss Neville he loves her," said she cruelly, as Frances looked enquiringly in her face.

Frances paled to an almost death-like whiteness as she grasped, "God forgive you if he has. I never will!"

CHAPTER IV

TOO LATE

"So mournfully she gaz'd on him,
As if her heart would break;
Her silence more upbraided him,
Than all her tongue might speak!

She could do nought but gaze on him,
For answer she had none,
But tears that could not be repress'd,
Fell slowly, one by one.

Alas! that life should be so short—
So short and yet so sad;
Alas! that we so late are taught
To prize the time we had!"
CHARLES SWAIN

It was the evening after Amy had pledged herself to Robert Vavasour. The sun had slowly faded away, and twilight threw but a faint light into the room where she sat close to her mother's feet.

Amy had been reading to Mrs. Neville and the book still open; lay in her lap, but it was too dark to read now, too dark for her mother to see her face, so Amy drew closer still ere she broached the subject nearest her heart. There was no shrinking or timidity, as there might have been had her love been wholly his, whose wife she had promised to become.

"Mamma, did Mr. Vavasour ever speak to you of his love for me?" The words were spoken firmly, though almost in a whisper.

"He did, Amy; and he also said you had refused his love."

"I knew so little of him then, that when he named his love it seemed like a dream, so sudden and unexpected. I had never given it a thought, or believed such a thing possible. I know him better now; he is so good, so kind."

She paused, perhaps hoping her mother would speak, but Mrs. Neville said not a word, and Amy went on somewhat falteringly, although she tried hard to speak steadily.

"Mamma, I promised last evening I would be his wife—"

"Have you done wisely, Amy? Are you sure you love him as his promised wife should?"

"Yes," replied Amy, dreamily. "I like him, I am sure I like him very much indeed,—and—and then he is so gentle and loving with me; surely no one could help liking him."

Mrs. Neville half raised herself on the sofa. "Amy! Amy! liking will not do. Do you love him, child?"

"Yes, Mamma. Yes, I think so."

"Only think, child? Nay you must be sure of it. Ask your heart if the time passes slowly when he is absent from the cottage. Do you watch and wait, and listen for his returning footsteps? Do you feel that without him life is not worth having, the world a blank? Is your whole heart with him when he is at your side? Do you tremble when his hand touches yours; and your voice grow softer as you speak to him? Do you feel that you dare not look up lest he should see the deep love in your eyes? if so Amy, then gladly will I consent to give you to him. But if not, I would rather, far rather see you in your grave than wedded to him."

Amy was silent; not from any wish to draw back from her word or plighted troth; no, she had made up her mind to be Robert Vavasour's wife, her mother's thin wasted hand as it rested on hers only strengthened that resolution; the very feebleness with which she raised herself on the couch showed Amy how very weak and ill she was, and this one act might restore her to health. She did not hesitate, she would not draw back; had Charles loved her, it might have been different, but convinced of his falseness and trifling, no regret for him, now struggled at her heart, only shame that she could ever have allowed it to be drawn towards him, unsought.

"You hesitate. You do not answer, Amy?" said Mrs. Neville, sadly, "and have deceived yourself and him."

"No, Mamma, you are wrong. Although I do not love Mr. Vavasour like that; still I do love him, and in time, when I am his wife, I shall very dearly."

Mrs. Neville sighed. "In this one important step of your life, Amy, when your whole future well-being depends upon it, there should be no secrets between us, recollect this one act may entail much misery; you cannot tell how much. Think of being bound for life to a man you do not love, think of the remorse you will feel at not being able to give him the love of your whole heart in return for his. Amy, my child, his very presence would be painful to you, his very love and kindness your greatest punishment and sorrow."

"Yes Mamma, if I did not love him; but it will not be so. I shall love him."

"And yet Amy, your very words almost forbid it, and fill my heart with fear and trembling," and again Mrs. Neville clasped her daughter's hand, while Amy, fairly overcome, bent down and laying her forehead on the soft pitying hand, burst into tears.

"Hush, Amy! hush! You have done foolishly, but there is yet time; better give him sorrow and pain now than later."

"No, Mamma, no; there is no need to give him pain," said Amy, presently.

"Alas!" replied Mrs. Neville, "then why these tears?"

"I weep," answered Amy, flinging—dashing back the tears as they crowded into her eyes, "I weep to think I have allowed my heart to think of another; one, too all unworthy of a woman's love; one who flirted and pretended to care for me; I weep for very shame, mother, to think how foolish I was, and how unworthy I am to be Robert Vavasour's wife."

"You have been unhappy, my child, so unhappy; but I almost guessed it when I looked in your face months ago."

"Yes, but not unhappy now, Mamma. I was very miserable, for I thought he loved me until he left me— went away without a word. Oh! mother, that was a bitter trial to me, and instead of trying to rouse myself and cast his image out of my heart, knowing I had done wrong in ever loving him, and doubly so now I had found out his cruel unworthiness, I nursed my love; bemoaned my fate; and steadily shut my heart against Mr. Vavasour. But it could not be; he was too noble hearted, so patient under my waywardness; sorrowful, but never reproachful; and—and so Mamma I have promised to become his wife; and am happy, not grieved or sad, at the idea; no, I will be his faithful, loving wife, and in his true heart forget this early foolish love that caused me so much unhappiness, and nearly lost me the heart of him who is now to be my husband."

"You are right, Amy, to forget him, right to tear his image from your heart; a man to treat you so is unworthy of any woman's love; and yet—yet I am scarcely satisfied. I fear this engagement. Is it not hasty, too hasty? Do not rush into a marriage hoping to escape from a love, however unworthy, still struggling at your heart; such a mistake might make the one regret of your whole life."

"I do not. I will not," replied Amy firmly, as she rose, and stooping over her mother, kissed her fondly; "If this is the only reason you have, dear Mamma, for fear, then rest content: my engagement with Mr.

Vavasour is for my—all our happiness; will you try and think so? I should feel very unhappy indeed if you refused your consent; or that my marriage grieved you."

"It does not grieve me, Amy. Only," sighed Mrs. Neville, "I wish he had been your first love."

"Nay, that is foolish, Mamma. Now often have I heard you say that few girls marry their first love."

Again Mrs. Neville was silent. "Have you told Mr. Vavasour of this old love, Amy?" asked she presently.

"Oh! no, no, Mamma. What good could it do? It would only grieve him; I,—I told him this much, that I—I hoped to love him better in time."

"And he was satisfied?"

"Quite," answered Amy, "and will you not say you are too, dearest Mamma?" and she laid her head lovingly on her mother's shoulder, and looked entreatingly in her face.

"God bless and protect you, my child," said Mrs. Neville fervently, drawing her closer still, and kissing her fondly. "May He guide and strengthen us both, for indeed I am very sorrowful, and scarcely know whether this marriage is for my child's happiness or no; but I pray it may be with all my heart. You have your mother's best, holiest wishes, Amy."

So Amy Neville became, with her mother's sanction, Robert Vavasour's affianced wife.

Yet for days after that Mrs. Neville's heart seemed troubled and ill at ease, and she lay on the sofa watching, noting Amy's every look or action, until, by degrees, the troubled anxious look wore away; Amy seemed so contented and happy that her mother, who, in her secret heart, wished the marriage might be, gradually lost her fears, and each hour gained renewed confidence and hope. She grew better and stronger, and this alone in itself was sufficient to bring back the smiles into Amy's face, while each day disclosed some fresh trait of Robert Vavasour's goodness and kindness of heart. It was his voice read of an evening to her mother and never seemed to weary. It was his hand raised the invalid, or lifted her, as her strength increased, from the sofa to the easy chair.

Amy rejoiced in the change, and while she never allowed her thoughts to wander to the past, with all its cruel hopes and fears, so she never halted or looked onward to the future; her life was of to-day, neither more nor less. Her mother was better; it was her act, her will, that had done it all. She was contented that it should be so, and fancied herself happy; perhaps was at this time really so, and might have been for ever, had she never seen Charles Linchmore again, never known how he, not she, had been deceived, but that was to be the one thorn in her onward path.

In less than a month Amy was to be married. Mrs. Neville's objections as to haste were overruled, even old Mrs. Elrington had sided with the rest; but then Mrs. Neville knew nothing of Dr. Ashley's opinion, or that Amy had confided to her old friend the necessity there was for an immediate change.

They were to go to Italy. Amy, her husband, and mother, with little Sarah, and even old Hannah accompanying them. What a pleasant party it would be! Already Amy began to picture to herself the delight she would experience in watching her mother's restoration to health and strength in that warm sunny clime, and how happy she would be by-and-by in bringing her back when quite well, to live in her own and Vavasour's home, that home he had so often talked to her of, and where, in a few weeks, she would be roaming about at will as its mistress.

The days crept on steadily and surely slowly to all but Mrs. Neville, and with her the time seemed to fly; she was anxious and restless, while her doubts and fears only shaped themselves in words in old Hannah's presence; to the rest, even to Amy, she was passive and quiet, apparently resigned, only at heart sad.

But old Hannah was a remorseless tyrant, who, feeling deeply and sorrowfully her darling's departure from home, sighing and even dropping a tear or two in secret, yet she never allowed Mrs. Neville to bewail it, but, on the contrary, seemed to look upon her doing so as a weakness and sin, requiring a steady though somewhat underhand reproof. Perhaps the very strength of mind Hannah displayed encouraged and strengthened her mistress.

"We are to lose Miss Amy to-morrow, Hannah," said Mrs. Neville, in a sad tone of voice. "I wish the wedding had not been so sudden."

"There, Ma'am, I don't call it sudden at all in the light wind," then silently and steadily went upstairs to change her bridal attire for a travelling dress.

It would be quite half-an-hour before Vavasour could return; so she sat quietly awaiting him in the little sitting-room, perhaps for the first time that day feeling sad, just realising her position as a wife, and looking onwards into the future.

She sat lost in a dreamy reverie, and heard not the swift opening and shutting of the little garden gate, or the sound of the still swifter step across the gravel walk, until it sounded quick and strong in the passage; then she started and arose quickly. Her husband had returned! and sooner than she expected. With a smile she turned to greet him, but it was Charles Linchmore who stood in the doorway, flushed and heated with the haste and impatience of his hurried ride from the station, and still more hasty journey.

Amy's heart stood still. Why had he come? Then, woman-like, almost guessed before he spoke what he had come to say. But ere she could recover from the sudden shock of his presence he, with all the old impetuosity of his nature, was at her feet, pouring forth his long pent-up love, with all its wild jealousy and anguish. How he had been deceived by Frances, and driven well-nigh distracted. How through Anne's agency he had found out her deceit, and had started at once to explain all and be forgiven; how he believed now she had loved him, and still loved, or would love him again; all—all he told, while his words came fast and strong. Amy never attempted to stay them, neither could she, if she would. So he went on to the end; then looked up into her face, that white, wan, pale face, bending so sadly over him, with an agonised stony look spread over each feature, striking dismay into his heart and soul.

"Speak to me!" he cried passionately. "Only say you forgive me my hasty belief in your falseness, only say that you love me still, and that I am not too late to make amends. Amy! my own Amy, speak to me!" and again he looked up beseechingly, with all his deep, earnest love written on his face, and speaking in his eyes.

But she was silent and still, very still.

Then the hand he held so tightly drew away from his hot, burning ones, and turning slowly, showed the wife's symbol, the plain gold band encircling the one small finger, while the pale, sad lips parted, and words came mournfully at last, but slowly and distinctly, settling like ice about his heart.

"It is too late—I am married."

Again that hasty, hurried step sounded, ringing out fiercely in the passage and along the quiet gravel walk. Once again the gate swung harshly and roughly on its frail hinges; then the sudden rush of a horse's quick hoofs rung out startlingly in the still, soft air, and in another moment died away in the far-off distance.

"Where is your mistress? is she ready?" asked Vavasour of Amy's new maid, as ten minutes later he hastily entered the cottage.

"My mistress is not ready, Sir," was the reply, with a pert toss of the head, while a peculiar expression played round the corners of her lips. "She is in the parlour, Sir. Mrs. Elrington thinks it's the heat of the day and the worry that has caused her to faint away."

Yes; Amy lay on the sofa, quiet and motionless with scarcely any sign of life on her pale, sad face, while onward, onward, faster and faster still, rode Charles Linchmore.

Would they ever meet again; and how?

CHAPTER V

DEFEAT

"Art thou then desolate
Of friends, of hopes forsaken?
Come to me! I am thine own.
Have trusted hearts proved false?

Why didst thou ever leave me? Know'st thou all
I would have borne, and called it joy to bear,
For thy sake? Know'st thou that thy voice hath power
To shake me with a thrill of happiness
By one kind tone?—to fill mine eyes with tears
Of yearning love? And thou—Oh! thou didst throw
That crushed affection back upon my heart.
Yet come to me!"
"'Tis he—what doth he here!"

LARA

The great bell rang out at the lodge gate, and Charles Linchmore dashed up to the Hall almost as hastily as he had left it, and with scarce a word of greeting to the old butler, whom he passed on his way to the drawing-room, and never staying to change his dress, he strode on, all flushed and heated as he was, with his hurried journey and desperate thoughts, until he stood face to face with Mrs. Linchmore.

"Why Charles!" exclaimed she, "what on earth has happened? What is the matter?"

"Nothing," he replied. "Where's Frances?"

"Nothing," she rejoined, indignantly, "to come into the room in such a plight as this! Look at the splashed state of your boots; and then your face. No one can look at that and not suspect something dreadful having happened. I never saw anything so changed and altered as it is."

"I dare say. I don't much care."

"Are you mad? Where have you been?"

"Nowhere. Where's Frances?" he asked again.

"I do not know. But I advise you to make yourself a little more presentable before you seek her. These freaks—mad freaks of riding half over the country, no one knows where, are not agreeable to those you come in contact with afterwards," and Mrs. Linchmore pushed her chair further away from him, and smoothed the rich folds of her dress, as though the act of doing that would soothe her ruffled temper.

"It was a mad freak," replied he, and without waiting for another word, or tendering an apology for his disordered dress, he strode away again, with the full determination of finding Frances.

Every room below stairs he searched, but in vain; she was nowhere, and driven reckless by the agony of his thoughts he went straight up to her own room, and opened the door.

She was lying on the sofa, her eyes red and swollen with weeping, passionate, hopeless tears at the thought that long before now he and Amy had met, and he consequently lost to herself for ever.

"Charles!" she exclaimed, springing off the sofa, her cheeks flushing hotly with surprise and pleasure.

But another glance at his face, and her heart sank within her, for its expression almost terrified her.

He closed the door and came and stood opposite to where she was, looking as though he would have struck her.

She quailed visibly before his menacing glance. Then resolutely regained the mastery over herself, and drawing up her figure proudly, she said,

"Do you know this is my room? I wonder how you dare come here."

"Your room? Well, what if it is, I care not," he replied. "I am reckless of everything."

"But I am not; and—and," she hesitated, and tried again to steady her beating heart, "what—what has happened, Charles, that you look so strangely?"

"Happened? Can you ask me what has happened, you who have wrecked the hopes of my whole life."

"I, Charles? You talk in riddles; I do not understand you."

"You dare not say that!" exclaimed he, hoarsely. "You know well that I loved her with all my heart and soul, and you—you schemed to draw her from me. I would have laid down my life for her; and you guessed it, and told me she loved another, and, like a fool, I believed you. You have driven me to despair; her to a life-long living death; and this, all this, I have dared to come and tell you."

"It was no lie. She never loved you!"

"She did!" he cried, hotly; "I swear she did. I saw it; knew it but a few hours since."

"You have seen her?" asked Frances.

"Seen her! Yes; and I wish to God I had died before seeing her," and he clasped his hands over his damp brow in an agony of grief.

"See," he said, presently, "are you not satisfied with my sufferings? Look here;" and he drew his hand across his forehead and temples, and showed the large drops that fell from them. "I loved her as my life. My life, do I say? She was more than life to me, and I have lost her; and this—this is your devil's work."

"Lost her!" echoed Frances, inquiringly.

He heeded her not; but walked the room with rapid strides, then gradually calmed again, and then again burst forth with the hopeless agony of his thoughts, as he recalled Amy's last words:

"It is too late, I am married."

"Aye," he said, despairingly, "too late to save us both; too late, indeed."

Frances could not listen calmly, or see unmoved the strong man's agony; but she never once repented the evil she had wrought, but rather gloried at heart in having so successfully separated him and Amy; and the more so now, because she saw how madly he loved her. She waited quietly, almost afraid to speak, until the paroxysm of grief had exhausted itself. Then she said, timidly,

"Too late, Charles. Did you say too late?"

But her words roused him to fury again.

"I did," he cried; "I said too late; God knows I was too late. A day, only a day earlier, and I should have been in time to save her!"

"To save Miss Neville? And from what?"

"From what?" he cried; "you are not satisfied with my sufferings, then? but would drain the last bitter drop of agony in my cup—the telling; the naming—Oh, God! She is married!"

Married! Frances was not prepared for this. A mist swam before her eyes; a sudden faintness seized her, and she clung to the back of the sofa for support.

"Yes, married!" he cried, fiercely seizing her arm. "You would have me tell you, and you shall hear it too, and remember it to your dying day; and I—I saw her only an hour after she was lost to me for ever."

But Frances' tongue was stayed, and she never answered one word.

"You have driven me mad," he continued savagely, "and it is a mercy you have not a murder on your soul, for, by Heaven, I was tempted more than once to take my life on my road down here? Do you hear?" he cried.

"Oh, Charles! don't, don't talk so wildly: you will kill me!"

"Kill you! No, I don't wish to do that; I'll only wish you half the misery you have caused me, and that shall be your punishment and my revenge."

And then he turned to leave her; but Frances sprang forward and stopped him.

"Do not go away like that, Charles. Do not go, leaving almost a curse behind you. I have not been guilty of half the wickedness you accuse me of. I did say Miss Neville did not love you; but—but I believed it."

"You did not," he cried. "You hated and then you slandered her."

"And if I did, it was your fault; yours, for you taught me to love you."

"You love me! It is like the rest false, and a flimsy attempt to palliate your wickedness."

"No, no; it is true. I have loved you for years past," exclaimed Frances, sinking on her knees, and hiding her face, "and—and I thought you loved me, too, until she came and took your love away; and then I hated her—yes, words cannot tell how much I hated her. What had I in life worth living for when your love was gone? and I thought if I could only take her away from you, your heart would come back to me again. If you have suffered, what have not I? and she never could have loved you to have married another. Oh! forgive me, Charles, forgive me! and don't—don't hate me."

"Forgive you!" he replied. "No; years hence, when we meet again, I may, but not now."

"Years hence? Are you going away, then? Oh! you cannot be so cruel!"

"In another month I shall leave England, perhaps for ever,—a broken-hearted wretch, with an aimless, hopeless existence. All this you have driven me to, and yet you ask me to forgive you. For her sake— hers, of whom I dare not trust myself to speak—I will not, cannot forgive you!"

The bitterness of his grief was over; the first burst was past; and he spoke calmer now, although his every word, the tone even of his voice, sank like ice into Frances' soul, convincing her how hopelessly she loved.

"Oh! say not so, Charles," she cried, "or you will crush me utterly. See,—see how I must love you to kneel here, and to humble my pride so entirely as to tell you I—I love you."

"Love! Does love break the heart of the loved one as you have broken mine? Call you such a deadly feeling as this, love? Say, rather, that you hate me."

"No, no; never! Whatever you do, whatever you say, I shall love you still,—love you for ever!"

"Give me your hate," he replied, "I would rather have that."

But Frances only answered by sobs and wringing her hands.

"If," he continued, "you have wrecked my happiness and hers through love of me, I wish to God you had hated me!"

"I could not," sobbed Frances, utterly overcome. "You—you won my love two years ago. Yes! you loved me then."

"Never!" he cried vehemently, almost savagely. "Never! I swear it!"

"Cruel!" murmured Frances.

"Cruel? Yes; what else do you deserve? Had you never told me that falsehood—never deceived me I—I might; but it is too late—all too late. And yet how I love her, love her to madness, and she the—the wife of another!" and he groaned and clenched his hands together, until the nails seemed buried in the very flesh, in utter anguish at the thought.

"Don't talk of her so, Charles, you will break my heart. Have some pity."

"Pity! I have none. What had you for either her or me. I tell you I have no mercy, no pity, only scorn and—and—" he would have said hate, but somehow the word would not come to his lips, as he looked at the bent, bowed figure kneeling so humbly before him.

"Oh! don't go! don't go, Charles. Say one, only one kind word," cried Frances, imploringly, as he turned again to leave her.

"Don't ask me," he replied, "for I have none to give. Don't ask me, lest I say more than I have done. Pray God that he will change your revengeful, cruel heart. I pray that we may never meet again."

"Oh, my God, he's gone!" moaned Frances, as the door closed upon him, "and not one kind word, not one. Oh! I have not deserved it! indeed I haven't," and burying her face in the sofa cushion, she burst into a fresh passion of hopeless, despairing tears.

After a few moments she raised her head again and sobbed and moaned afresh, as she cried.

"He was cruel to the last, and all through her. Oh! I will hate her tenfold for this, and work her more misery if I can. I will never repent what I have done. Never! but will make her suffer more frightfully, if—if possible, than this!"

She tossed back her hair, and almost for the moment regained her former proud bearing; for, strange and unnatural as it may seem, this desperate resolve of making Amy, if she could, more wretched than she had already, soothed and calmed for a time the hopeless nature of her thoughts, and was the one hope that supported her through the long, terrible hours of the night that followed.

CHAPTER VI

AMY'S COURAGE FAILS HER

"New joys, new virtues with that happy birth
Are born, and with the growing infant grow.
Source of our purest happiness below
Is that benignant law, which hath entwined
Dearest delight with strongest duty, so
That in the healthy heart and righteous mind
Even they co-exist, inseparably combined.

Oh! bliss for them when in that infant face
They now the unfolding faculties descry,
And fondly gazing, trace—or think they trace
The first faint speculation in that eye,
Which hitherto hath rolled in vacancy;
Oh! bliss in that soft countenance to seek
Some mark of recognition, and espy
The quiet smile which in the innocent cheek
Of kindness and of kind its consciousness doth speak!"
SOUTHEY

Time passed rapidly onwards; heedless, in its flight, of bruised hearts or desolate homes, but ruthlessly brushing past, hurrying on far away with careless front and iron tread; perhaps ere he came round again those hearts would be healed and those homes joyous again. Such things happen every day, and well for us that it is so.

The first year of Amy's married life passed quietly by; just as the second dawned her son was born, but ere the third came to its close, her mother faded with the dying year.

Mrs. Neville had been so much better during the first year of their sojourn abroad, so almost well again, that, as her last illness drew on, Amy, who had seen her almost as weak at Ashleigh, could not believe that she would not recover, and wilfully shut her eyes to what to others was so apparent, that this was a weakness even unto death. And so it was. Mrs. Neville died, and for a time Amy was inconsolable; even her baby's caresses failed to cheer and rouse her heart.

Her husband returned with her to England. Amy wept bitterly as she stood in that home, where so often she had so fondly hoped to have welcomed her mother.

Many changes had occurred during Amy's absence.

Anne Bennet had married and was now living steadily enough—so she said—with her husband at his old curacy, not many miles distant from Brampton.

Charles Linchmore, after his sad meeting with Amy, had returned for one night to the Park, and after his stormy interview with Frances, had, much to the astonishment of his brother and every one else but Anne, exchanged and gone abroad.

Frances was still unmarried, perhaps still plotting on and waiting for one whose heart could now only be filled with anger and hatred towards her. But what woman does not hope? Perhaps she hoped still.

A new governess reigned at Brampton in Amy's stead; the third since she had left. Surely there was some mismanagement somewhere? or Mrs. Linchmore had grown more exacting and overbearing; more dissatisfied with the means taken to please her?

Little Sarah was away in London at school; while old Hannah reigned supreme as head nurse to the youthful heir.

Amy was happy, notwithstanding the remembrance that like a dim, indistinct shadow flitted across her of that first sad love. Was he happy? and what had become of him? these were questions sometimes in her thoughts, although her heart was with her husband, who loved his fair young wife with all his heart, even more dearly than when first they married; while as yet nothing had occurred to check that love.

Robert Vavasour had been absent from his home a fortnight. It was the evening of his return to Somerton.

Amy drew a low chair close to her husband by the fireside as she said, "How glad I am to have you back again; I have missed you so much, and felt quite lonely, even with little Bertie."

Robert looked down fondly in his wife's face. It was pleasant to know that his coming had given pleasure to her he loved.

"And how was dear Sarah," she asked. "Did she look quite well and happy? Quite contented with school? Pray give me all the news you have, to tell."

"And that will be little enough," he replied. "As to Sarah she looked the picture of health, and gave me no end of messages for you; but I am afraid I have forgotten them all; my memory fails me completely now I have you at my side."

"Well I hope you have not forgotten the present for Bertie: his little tongue has talked of nothing else all day."

"I know I did not forget my little wife," he said, as taking a ring from his pocket he placed it on her finger.

"You are always good and kind," she replied, "always thinking of me."

"Always, Amy."

"And now do tell me all you have been doing this long time, and where you went, and whom you saw. Surely you must have some adventures worth relating?"

"No, none. I went simply nowhere; London is chill enough in November, and even had it been otherwise the charm was wanting to induce me to go out. I saw few people I knew; but I met some old friends of yours, yesterday."

"Yes?" said Amy, inquiringly.

"Can you not guess who?"

Amy's heart whispered the Linchmore's; but refused to say so.

"Have you no curiosity?" he asked, "I thought you were all anxiety a moment ago."

"No, I shall not guess," replied his wife. "You must tell me."

"Must!" he laughed. "And suppose I refuse. What then?"

"You will not," she said.

"You are a tyrant, Amy. It was the Linchmores. I met him accidentally at the door of the club."

"Ah! you went to the Club. You never told me that," was all she said.

"Neither have you told me how many times you have been into the nursery to see Bertie since I have been away."

"The cases are totally dissimilar," laughed Amy. "But what did Mr. Linchmore say? Was he glad to see you?"

"Yes: and took me home to dine with his wife."

"Mrs. Linchmore! How is she."

"Much the same as ever; just as haughty and hard-looking."

"Hard-looking? I never thought her that."

"My wife always has a pleasant thought for everybody," returned Vavasour proudly; "but beautiful as Mrs. Linchmore undoubtedly is, there is a great want of softness in the expression of her face."

"She treated me well, and I had no reason to—to find fault with her." There was a little hesitation, as if the heart did not quite keep pace with the words. Perhaps her husband noticed it, for he looked away ere he spoke again, as if not quite sure that what he had to say next would please her.

"I am glad it was so, as Linchmore asked us to go and stay at Brampton for a time."

Amy started visibly.

"But you refused," she said hastily.

"I did at first, but he would take no refusal."

"You did not promise to go, Robert? Oh, I hope you did not!"

"I could not well refuse. Nay, do not look so sad, Amy; rather than that, you shall write a refusal at once. We will not go, dearest."

And Amy would have given worlds not to; but did not like giving an untruthful reason as the motive for staying away; still, how else could she shape her refusal, or excuse herself to her husband. She dared not tell him that revisiting old scenes, the old familiar walk and rooms, would recall by-gone memories afresh in her heart—another's words! another's looks! No, she could not tell him that; yet as she sat with her hand in his and looked into his face how she longed to open her heart and tell him all! all of that bitter, never-to-be-forgotten past. And yet she reasoned again as she had reasoned once before, against the whisper of her heart, and her mother's better judgment, that it could do no good, but only pain and grieve her husband to think that she, his wife, had ever cared for, or even thought of another; and she sighed as these sad recollections one by one came into her heart.

"Why do you sigh Amy?" asked her husband.

Alas! the question came too late; her resolve had been made and taken. She sat silent, though she would have given worlds to have been able to throw her arms round his neck and tell him all.

Robert drew her fondly and tenderly towards him. "As my wife, Amy," he said, "none shall ever dare whisper a word or even breathe a thought that can reflect upon your former life at Brampton. Have no fear, little one, but trust in me."

He had misinterpreted her silence, and thought the repugnance she felt at going back to Brampton was caused by pride. Well, perhaps it was best so.

"We will go, Robert," she whispered tremblingly, while the words she ought to have spoken remained unsaid, and with her husband and little Bertie she went to Brampton, simply because she saw no help for it.

It was one of those things that must be, and she nerved her heart to brave it.

CHAPTER VII

THE FIRST DOUBT

"And the strange inborn sense of coming ill
That ofttimes whispers to the haunted breast,
In a low tone which naught can drown or still;
Midst feasts and melodies a secret guest:
Whence doth that murmur wake, that shadow fall?
Why shakes the spirit thus?"
MRS HEMANS

With a faint shadow of some coming evil, a dull foreboding at her heart, Amy once again found herself driving up the long avenue of Brampton Park.

How things had changed since first as a timid, shrinking girl, she had entered its gates! How her heart had throbbed and beaten since then! been tried and strained to its very utmost. How much she had suffered; how much rebelled and murmured at. Involuntarily she drew closer to her husband, as she felt how near and dear she was to his heart: surely, with his strong hand to protect and guide, his loving heart to shield her, what had she to fear?

Amy half expected to see the children as of old on the terrace impatiently waiting to embrace her as she stepped from the carriage; but no, only the old butler bowed, and seemed glad to see her, as she exchanged a few words with him, ere he ushered her with becoming ceremony into the drawing-room, where Mrs. Linchmore at once advanced to greet her, and for the first time in her life, much to Amy's astonishment, kissed her; but then she was no longer Miss Neville, but Mrs. Vavasour. Ah! things had changed indeed.

Mr. Linchmore was as friendly and courteous as ever, with the same honest welcome as of old; yet Amy thought him changed, but could not quite see wherein the change lay. His hair was becoming slightly tinged with grey, but that could not make the alteration she fancied she had discovered; then he was surely graver and quieter as he handed her into dinner, more silent and reserved; while Mrs. Linchmore, if any thing, was more animated, more beautiful than ever; and she watched for the hard look Robert Vavasour had spoken of, but in vain; it was not there, could not be; while her face was so filled with smiles and good humour.

Again Amy glanced at Mr. Linchmore. Surely her husband had made a mistake; for there the hard look was gravely stamped on each feature, and Amy sighed as she saw it, and wondered how the change had been wrought.

Amy saw nothing of the children all that evening; the next morning she went to the school-room to see them.

Away down the long corridor, past the very window where she had stood long ago with Charles Linchmore. Did she think of that now? or of the events that followed quick and fast upon it; or recall to mind the dark form of Frances Strickland, halting on the very ground she now stood on, then fading away, not softly and slowly but fiercely and hurriedly, in the distance—leaving a strange fear at her heart, only too well realised in the past events of her life. If Amy remembered all this, she never stayed her footsteps, but passed quickly on through the baize door, and in another moment the children's arms were about her neck, their kisses on her face; while Miss Barker, the new governess, rose in stately horror at this infringement of her rules.

"Really young ladies, your reception of Mrs. Vavasour is boisterous in the extreme. Allow me, Madam, to apologise for my pupils."

"Oh! but this is Miss Neville, our dear Miss Neville!" cried Fanny, then catching Miss Barker's still more frigid look, hung her head and dropped her hands she was in the act of clapping with delight, to her side.

"We are old friends," said Amy, smiling: "very old friends, pray do not check them, I am so glad to see they have not forgotten me; and allow me to apologise in my turn for the interruption in their studies my sudden entrance has occasioned."

Miss Barker smiled complacently. "Will you not be seated?" she said.

"Thank you. I have come to ask, with Mrs. Linchmore's sanction, for a holiday."

Miss Barker's brow clouded again.

"I scarcely know what to say to this request, which has come on rather an unfortunate day. Fanny has not, as yet, been able to darn her torn dress in a satisfactory manner; Alice cannot make her sum prove; and Edith has mislaid her thimble—carelessness and untidiness combined."

Each child looked down guiltily, as her shortcoming was being told in a grave voice; while Amy felt inclined to smile at the frigid tone, evidently freezing each little warm heart; but Miss Barker's look forbade even a smile or word, and a dead silence followed.

"In the hope," continued she, presently, "that you will all try and do better to-morrow, I will accede to your Mamma's request. Put away your books, young ladies."

They all rose slowly, very differently from their quick, joyous manner in Amy's time, cleared the table, then returned; and, notwithstanding Miss Barker's frowns, stationed themselves close to their old friend.

"Here is a chair for you, Edith; pray recollect that stoop in your shoulders I am so frequently reminding you of; Alice, my love, try and sit still without that perpetual fidget; Fanny, I am sure Mrs. Vavasour would rather you came a little further away; there is no need for you to stand; here are plenty of chairs in the room."

Amy grew wearied with her slow, methodical manner, and finding-fault tone, never raised or lowered in the slightest. It was a relief when she went away, and left Amy to talk to the children as she would, without feeling that a pair of small grey eyes were disagreeably fixed on her face.

As soon as she was gone, Alice climbed off the stiff high-backed chair, where she had been perched, and settled herself quietly on Amy's lap; Edith with a great sigh of relief from the depths of her heart, knelt, regardless of the poor shoulders, on one side; while Fanny flew to the other, exclaiming, "Oh! isn't she disagreeable, Miss Neville?"

Amy could not conscientiously answer no, so evaded a direct reply, and merely said, "I am no longer Miss Neville, Fanny, you must try and call me Mrs. Vavasour."

"Yes, so we have, all the time you've been away; but now you've come again it's so natural to say Miss Neville."

"And," said Edith, "we think of you so often, and always wish you back again."

Then they talked away of old times, until Amy's heart grew sad. "Let us go and see Bertie," she said.

Away went the children, with something of the spirit of by-gone days. It was well for them they did not stumble upon Miss Barker, as they danced along the passage; or sad indeed would have been the result of the expedition.

Bertie was astonished at seeing so many new faces, and hid himself shyly beneath Hannah's apron, from whence at first, he refused to be coaxed or tormented; but by-and-by a small curly head and bright eyes peeped forth, and at length he surrendered at discretion to little Alice, as being the least formidable of the invaders.

How he prattled away! while his tiny feet seemed never weary of running to and fro to fetch toys for his new friends' inspection. Amy was soon quite overlooked, and Hannah's existence forgotten altogether, until suddenly reminded it was time for his morning's nap; when, notwithstanding a determined resistance on his part, he was eventually overpowered and carried off to bed, with a promise of having a romp with the children some other day.

Hannah had suddenly become within the last few days wonderfully dignified. The moment she entered the house where her young mistress had lived as a dependant, she thought in her heart that most likely the servants would be looking down upon them, or setting themselves up in consequence; so she determined upon giving herself airs, if nobody else did, and assumed at once a reserve and stateliness quite foreign to her nature; but which, nevertheless, fitted admirably to the tall, portly figure; gaining Mrs. Hopkins' confidence, and setting Mason's airs at defiance, while it won for her the respect of the other servants, who never ventured upon a word in her presence, even of disparagement against Miss Barker, whom they all cordially disliked.

It was strange what bad odour the latter stood in, trying as she did her utmost to make herself agreeable to all parties. Her appearance was certainly against her, her face at first sight being anything but a prepossessing one. One felt a strange dislike at making her acquaintance, which dislike was scarcely lessened upon a more intimate knowledge of her. Then her tall, freezing looking form was as little ingratiating to the eye, as the fawning, wiry voice was to the heart and Mason had been heard to say, that of the two, Miss Neville, even with all her "stuck up" airs, was twice the lady; but the lady's maid distrusted the tongue that flattered her mistress more boldly and cunningly than she did; while Mrs. Linchmore, although she smiled blandly enough, and took little or no notice of the flattery, was sensible of a feeling of relief when the stiff, starched form was no longer present.

Hannah made her acquaintance one morning on the lawn, and was no little astonished at the tight corkscrew curls tucked under the bonnet, and the prim, patronising tone with which the governess addressed her; but nurse did not belong to the house; there was no occasion to conciliate her. Evidently

Miss Barker was no admirer of young children, for as little Bertie ran up to Alice, she exclaimed, "Dear me, what a fat child!"

Hannah looked at her for a moment with indignation, and replied, "fat, yes, Ma'am, Master Bertie, thank God, is fat," and then added, in an under tone, loud enough to be heard, "It's just as well if some others were as fat!" and viewed, as she turned away, the lady's thin, spare form with utter disgust.

Amy and her husband were the only visitors at Brampton, yet no one seemed dull. Amy could never be dull with her child, and Mrs. Linchmore appeared ever happy and contented.

They were good musicians, both Mrs. Linchmore and her guest; the former excelled in playing, the latter in singing. Amy's voice was sweet and musical, not wanting in power—one of those voices so charming to the senses, claiming the attention of every hearer, thrilling through the heart with wonderful pathos, leaving pleasing memories behind, or else the eyes filled with tears, as some mournful notes stir the soul with long forgotten memories.

Mrs. Linchmore's voice was at times too powerful, grating harshly on the ear; she dashed at the notes in the quick parts, and handled them too roughly and rapidly; there was a want of feeling pervading the whole, which made one feel glad when the voice ceased, and the fingers alone glided softly over the keys. It was marvellous how fast they flew; while the notes sounded clearly and distinctly, like the tinkling of bells. Now the tune swelled loud and strong; then appeared to die faintly away under the light touch of those wonderful fingers. Mrs. Linchmore knew she played well, however much Amy excelled her in singing, and would sit down after one of the latter's songs, and enchant her listeners with some soft, beautiful air, played to perfection; then would come a song, and after that another piece, short, but more silvery sounding than the first, while Amy's voice was well-nigh forgotten, and Mrs. Linchmore, with her beautiful smiling face and pleasant words, was considered the musician of the evening, and had all due homage awarded her. As it was in music, so it was in everything else, Mrs. Linchmore took by right of "tact" what Amy ought to have laid claim to, but then, one was a woman of the world, the other only just entering it. Amy wanted confidence; Mrs. Linchmore none.

As the days grew shorter still, Robert Vavasour whiled away the long evenings by again, as of old, playing at chess with his hostess, while Amy, who did not understand the game, sat and talked or sang to Mr. Linchmore; at other times she grew weary of those long games, so entirely engrossing her husband's attention, and brought her work or a book, and drawing a chair close by, watched the progress of the play.

By degrees the players themselves claimed her attention; how deeply interested they seemed! how intent on the pieces! Amy, as she plied her needle diligently at the work in her lap, was constantly looking at Mrs. Linchmore. How often her dark eyes flashed across the board in her adversary's face, and when the game was at an end how she laughed and talked, and how the rings sparkled on her white hands, as she re-arranged the pieces again in their places. Amy thought she wore too many rings: they certainly danced and flashed in the lamp light, and dazzled her so that she felt quite fascinated, and wondered what Robert thought, and whether he admired her, or saw still the hard look. Amy half wished he did, or that she possessed only a quarter of the power Mrs. Linchmore seemed to have of pleasing him. Perhaps he had found his evenings dull with only his wife to talk or read to. Why had he not told her he was so fond of chess? she might have learnt it; yes, she would learn it; and again Amy glanced at the board to watch the pieces and try and make out how they moved; then tired of looking, her attention would be once more riveted on Mrs. Linchmore, and with a dissatisfied sigh she wished herself back at Somerton.

Thus came the first doubt to the young wife's heart; yet scarcely known to her, save for a strange cold feeling stirring sometimes within.

Anne rode over one day to Brampton, and the flying visit of her old friend did Amy good: marriage seemed in no way to have altered her, she was just as merry-laughing and joking in much the same style as ever. Her husband was as proud of her as he well could be, rebuking her at times, not with words, but a look, when he thought her spirits were carrying her a little too far, while Anne appeared to look up and reverence him in all things, being checked in a moment by his grave face.

The morning passed pleasantly. As Anne rose to go she said, "Tell Isabella I am sorry to have missed seeing her, although I should have been more sorry had you been absent, as my visit, strictly speaking, was to you, in fact for you alone."

"I will give the first part of the message," replied Amy laughing, "and bury the other half in my heart, as it would be but a poor compliment repeated. Why not remain to luncheon; I expect Mrs. Linchmore home very shortly, she has driven into Standale."

"Standale! I thought she hated the place."

"The place, yes; but not the station."

"What on earth has taken her there?"

"To meet a friend."

"Man or woman?" laughed Anne.

"Indeed I never asked," replied Amy. "It was quite by accident I heard her say that unless Mr. Linchmore made haste she would not arrive in time to meet the train."

"Oh! then he has gone too. Depend upon it, it's some old 'fogy' or another; Miss Tremlow, perhaps, with her carpet bag stuffed full of yellow pocket handkerchiefs; you know," continued she, mimicking that lady's tone and manner, "this is such a damp place, and the rheumatics are worse than ever."

As Anne rode away Amy remained at the window with little Bertie, who had been brought down for inspection and approval, and duly admired and caressed.

"I wish Anne had been going to remain, Robert," said Amy, "she is so pleasant."

"She is all very well for a short time," he replied, "but really her tongue, to use rather a worn out simile, is like the clapper of a bell; always ringing."

"Do you think she talks too much?"

"Most decidedly I do."

"But you do not admire a silent woman," said Amy drawing near the fire, and placing Bertie on the hearth rug.

"More so than a very talkative one; but there is such a thing as a happy medium."

Amy sighed. "I wish we were back at Somerton," she said.

"Is my wife home-sick already? Would she not find it dull after Brampton?"

"I could not find it dull. Should I not have you—" she would have said all to myself, but checked herself and added—"you and Bertie."

"Why not have left out, Bertie?" he replied, "I shall grow jealous of that boy, Amy, if you always class us together. Can you not forget him sometimes?"

"Forget him? Oh! no, never!" said Amy, catching up the child, who immediately climbed from his mother's arms on to Robert's knee and remained there; while his father, notwithstanding his jealousy, glanced proudly at his boy, and caressed both him and his mother.

"Ah! you are just as fond of Bertie as I am," she said, as her husband drew her to his side.

But even as she spoke she became conscious of a shadow between her and the light which streamed in through the large bay window of the dining-room; while Vavasour rose and held out his hand saying apologetically, "We did not hear the carriage drive up."

"No, I could hardly expect you would, with so much to interest you within doors."

Amy arose quickly as the voice struck her ear.

"Frances! Miss Strickland!" she said.

"Yes, the same. You look surprised. Did you not expect me?"

"No," replied Amy, shortly.

"It is quite an unexpected pleasure, and has surprised us both," returned Robert, as he noticed his wife's unusual manner.

"It is my fault. I told Isabella not to mention I was coming," returned she. "Perhaps I wanted to see if you would be pleased, or recognise me; every one says I am so very much altered."

"I see no difference," replied Amy, as Frances glanced straight at her.

"There is none," she answered, and the tone went to Amy's heart with a nervous thrill. "And so this is your boy. What is he called?"

"Robert," answered Amy, feeling for the first time a strange dislike at saying his pet name. But her husband was not so scrupulous.

"We call him Bertie," he said.

"And so will I. Come and make friends, Bertie. What lovely hair he has, so soft and curly. I suppose,—indeed I can see,—you are quite proud of the boy, Mr. Vavasour."

"Mrs. Vavasour is, if I am not."

"Of course. All mothers are of their first-born. Do not go so near the fire, Bertie. You make me tremble lest anything should befall you."

What could happen to the child? Amy drew him further away still, then took him in her arms as if only there he was safe and shielded from all harm.

When Frances left the room Amy sighed more deeply than before, yet scarcely knew why she felt so low and sad, or why Frances' appearance should have brought with it a nervous dread; save that in that long-ago time, which she had tried to bury and forget, Frances had been her bitterest enemy, and she could not but feel that her coming now was disagreeable to her, nay more, caused a sudden, nameless fear to arise in her heart; and now although Frances' words were friendly, yet Amy detected, or fancied she did—a lurking sarcasm in their tone.

"I wish we were back at Somerton, Robert," she said.

"Again!" exclaimed Robert, "now Amy, you deserve to be scolded for this. What an impatient little woman you are! Shall we not be home in a month?"

"Ah! in a month;" sighed Amy again, as she drew her child nearer to her heart, while her heart whispered, "Can anything happen in a month?"

CHAPTER VIII

GOING FOR THE DOCTOR

"In God's name, then, take your own way," said Christian; "and, for my sake, let never man hereafter limit a woman in the use of her tongue; since he must make it amply up to her, in allowing her the privilege of her own will. Who would have thought it?"
PEVERIL OF THE PEAK

Three years and more have passed away since we left Matthew the pikeman counting the stones in Goody Grey's box. Many changes have occurred since then, the greatest of all has fallen on his own cottage—Matthew has grown a sober man.

But we must go back a little.

We left Jane closing the cottage door, after the singular meeting that had taken place between her and Goody Grey, on Marks telling the latter of his sister-in-law's extraordinary fainting fit. When he and his wife returned to the cottage, Jane was carried up to bed, apparently too weak to be able to sit up, and there she remained for several weeks, more crazed than ever to Matthew's fancy, frightening him out of his wits at times, lest his wife should find out anything about the charm, and attribute, as he did, his sister-in-law's illness to it. One night his fears grew to such a pitch, he went and buried the box in the garden, and waited events in an easier frame of mind. Days passed, and at length Jane grew better, but strenuously refused to leave her room, and go below. In vain Mrs. Marks remonstrated, in vain she stormed, Jane was not to be persuaded, and at length was allowed to do as she pleased. But suddenly her illness took a turn; she crawled down stairs to dinner, and one day, to Matthew's intense disgust, resumed her old seat in the chimney corner.

As the months rolled on the scrubbing and scouring within the cottage went on more mildly, while Mrs. Marks' strong stout arm grew thinner and weaker; the brush fell less harshly and severely on the ear, as it rushed over the table; the high pattens clanked less loudly in the yard; while the voice grew less shrill, and was no longer heard in loud domineering tones. The change was gradual; Matthew did not notice it at first, until just a few weeks before Amy returned to Brampton with her husband; then the change was unmistakable, the scrubbing and scouring ceased altogether. Mrs. Marks gave in, and acknowledged she was ill.

How Matthew's conscience smote him then! He knew he had never had the courage to face Goody Grey with the box still filled with the small gravel, as when she gave it him, neither had he dared throw the stones away, lest, in offending the giver, worse disasters would follow; and he was too superstitious to think Goody Grey would know nothing at all about it, and believe as he might tell her that he had done as she had directed. No; he was certain that one word of distrust in his story, and he should break down altogether. He tried to reason with himself, and think that the tramping about in all weathers long ago had made his wife ill; but it would not do, his mind was not to be persuaded, and always reverted with increased dismay to the box, while his eye invariably rested upon its snug resting-place under the laurel, as he passed it on his way out to the gate. Many a time he determined upon digging up the box, and restoring it to its owner, just as it was: but when the time for action came, and he drew near the spot, his courage failed him, and he would pass on, cursing the hour when he had been tempted to ask the wise woman for the charm which he believed had done so much evil; while his fear of telling the secret in his tipsy unconsciousness had done what all Mrs. Marks' storming had failed to do—made him, for the time being, a sober man. He shunned the "Brampton Arms" as if the plague dwelt there, and sat in the chimney corner opposite Jane, gloomy, and fearful almost of his own shadow, while his sister-in-law's eyes seemed to pierce him through more keenly than ever.

Mrs. Marks had steadily kept her promise, silently and secretly working with a will to seek out Hodge's son. Like most energetic women, a first failure did not daunt or dispirit her, it only roused her energies the more vigorously. She was not to be defeated. The more difficult of accomplishment the more determined was she, and in the end successful. She dodged Hodge's "wide-awake" friend, and found Tom; nay more, she spoke with him, tried to reclaim him; but there she failed—she was not the sort of woman to win him over. A kind word might have done much, but that, Mrs. Mark's heart had not for such a reprobate as he. She told him the truth, the plain hard truth, heaping maledictions on his head unless he gave up his evil ways, forsook his godless companions, and returned home. She used no persuasion, no entreaty. Had she spoken to him kindly of his mother, perhaps his heart might have softened; but Mrs. Marks' voice came loud and strong, words followed one another fast and indignantly, so that ere she had well-nigh exhausted all the scorn she had, his mind was made up, and he obstinately refused to return home, simply because she desired, nay, commanded him to do so. What! become the laughing-stock of the whole of Deane? be known and marked in the village as the vile sinner she denounced him to be? He laughed at her threats and taunts, and left her, feeling perhaps more hardened than ever.

Matthew was not far wrong when he tried to persuade himself the walking about in all weathers—so mysterious to him—had ruined his wife's health. A pouring steady rain was falling the day of her interview with Hodge's son, but true to her purpose, she had walked for miles along a heavy road, and across still damper fields to find him; then, flushed and heated with her passionate words and subsequent defeat, had started back again through the same rain, and reached home thoroughly wet through; then came a violent cold, and from that time her strength seemed to fail, although unacknowledged to herself, while her limbs lost their power, and pained her strangely; still she worked on, with the will to get well, but alas! the strength to do so was gone.

She wrote to Mrs. Hodge advising her to have nothing further to do with such a good-for-nothing son, but forget him as fast as she could. Mrs. Marks' letter was not meant unkindly, but she never attempted to lessen Tom's fault or palliate his conduct; the truth stood out in all its glaring hideousness. Having no children herself, she knew nothing of a mother's strong, steadfast love. The knowledge that her son, her first-born, was with a gang of poachers who had wounded the Squire's visitor and killed one of the game watchers, threw dismay into the mother's heart and broke it. She died, begging her husband to still look for Tom, and reclaim him if possible—a promise her husband felt impossible of fulfilment, as he, like Mrs. Marks, thought badly of his son's heart.

Mrs. Marks could scarcely move her limbs at all now, except to creep down the narrow stairs of a day into the small parlour, where she sat and scolded to her heart's content, Sarah, the girl who came as a help now the mistress was ill, following her every movement with her eyes, if she could not with her feet.

As her sister grew worse, Jane roused herself wonderfully, becoming as active as before she had been idle, and apparently as sane as she had been crazy; while as to Matthew, he turned into a model husband, helping in the work to be done as far as lay in his power, and nursing his sick wife with a tender solicitude quite foreign to his nature, while she grumbled at everything and everyone in turn, her eye, as I have said before, finding out their shortcomings in a moment, and denouncing them without mercy. But she was ill, must be ill to sit there so quietly and allow others to scrub down the table or be up to their elbows in the washing-tub; she deserved their pity and their silence, and they gave her both.

"There, that will do," said she one day, as Matthew tried to settle the pillows more comfortably at her back. "I don't think it's near so easy like as it was before you touched it, but it wouldn't be you if you didn't want always to have a finger in the pie. Sarah, leave off that racket among the cups and saucers; what on earth are you at, girl? Are you trying to break them all? What are you after?"

"I was a-dusting of the shelves, Mum," was the reply.

"Fine dusting, upon my word, and with a corner of your apron, too; be off and fetch a cloth this moment, such slop-work as that'll never do here; let me catch you at it again, that's all, or that clatter of the crockery either, when my head aches and buzzes like as if a thousand mills was at work in it."

"There, rest quiet, Missus," said Matthew; "it'll be all right by-and-bye."

"That's as much as you know about it. I tell yer I never felt so bad, like, in all my life."

"Ain't it most time to take the doctor's stuff?" suggested Matthew, meekly.

"I'm sick of the medicine, and the doctor too. What good has he done me? I should like to know. I can't walk no better than I could a month ago. My limbs is as stiff as ever, and just every bit as painful."

"That comes of them mad walks yer took in all weathers; yer would tramp about, and it's been t' undoing of yer altogether."

A torrent of words followed this, of which Matthew took no heed, until she leant back, apparently exhausted, saying, "I feel awful bad. I wonder whatever in the world ails me?"

"How d'yer feel?" asked her husband, compassionately.

"My head whizzes, and I'm all over in a cold sweat, like; only feel my hand, don't it burn like a live coal?"

"It do seem as though it were afire," he replied.

"Seem!" cried Mrs. Marks. "Is that all the pity yer have in your heart for maybe your dying wife?"

"Lord save us!" exclaimed Matthew. "I've been a deal worse myself, and got well again; don't be a frightening yourself in that way, or belike you'll think you've one foot in the grave."

Then he poured some of the medicine in the glass, and held it towards her.

"Here," said he, "here's what'll make you think different, and send away the dismals."

"I won't take none of it," she replied; "not one drop. It weren't given to me for the fiery pains I've got about me now."

"Come, Missus, come, don't'ee quarrel with the only thing that can do'ee good," said Matthew, coaxingly.

"Do me good!" she exclaimed, with a sudden return of energy. "It's my belief yer trying to pisin me. Be off and fetch the doctor!"

The doctor! Matthew stared in astonishment.

"What are you gaping at? Do you take me for a fool, or yourself, which? Be off, I tell yer, and don't let yer shadow darken this door again without him. Maybe he'll be able to say what's ailing me."

Away went Matthew, in a ludicrous state of bewilderment. His wife must be bad indeed to send for the doctor; why he had never known her do such a thing since they married. What a trouble he had had only a few months ago to get her to see young Mr. Blane, and now she wanted him to come at once. Matthew began to think his wife was crazy, as well as Jane; perhaps she had sent him on a fool's errand.

He insensibly slackened his steps as he neared the village, and bethought him what he should say, as he suddenly recollected he had received no instructions whatever.

The more he thought the more perplexed he grew, and seeing some boys playing at marbles, Matthew drew near, and leaning against the railings, watched them, and turned over again in his mind what he should say; but loiter as he would, he could think of nothing save his wife's angry face, as she had bade him begone; so, after a short delay, Matthew faced the danger by boldly ringing the surgery bell.

"Is the Maister at home?" asked he, fervently wishing he might be miles away.

Yes, Mr. Blane was in, and Marks followed the boy sorrowfully.

"Good morning, Mr. Marks. Come for some medicine? Where's the bottle?"

"No, thank'ee, Sir," said Matthew, twirling his hat about uncomfortably. "My wife's took worse, and wants to know if so be ye'd make it convenient to come and physic her?"

Yes; Mr. Blane could go at once, having no other call upon his time just at present.

"And what's the matter with Mrs. Marks?" asked he, when they were fairly on their way.

"That's more nor I can tell, Sir. She's all over like a live coal, and 'ud drink a bucket full if ye'd give it her."

"Has she taken the medicine regularly?"

This was a poser. Matthew scratched his head, took off his cap; he was in no way prepared for such a question. What should he say?

"Well," said he presently, in a conciliating tone, "Well, you see, Sir, when folks is ill they takes queer fancies sometimes, as I dare say yer know better nor I can tell'ee. Now my wife's got hers, and no mistake; she says you've gived her pisin."

It was Mr. Blane's turn now to be astonished, this being an answer he was not prepared for. "Poison!" he echoed.

"Yes, just pisin, and nothing else; but there, Sir, there's no call to be frightened, her head's that dizzy she can't scarce open her eyes, much less know what she says."

"Has she taken a fresh cold?"

"Not that I knows on, Sir, t'aint possible now: her legs is so cramped she's 'bliged to bide in doors."

"Poor thing! She seems patient enough under it all."

"Lord bless yer, Sir! Patient? Why she lets fly more nor any 'ooman I know on; I can't say but what she do look meek enough when yer'e at the 'pike, but as soon as she's the least way riled she'll find more words at her tongue's end than any other 'ooman in the parish. It's my belief that's all that's the matter with her now; she've bin rating the whole on us roundly one after t'other and has just worked herself into a biling rage, for nothing at all."

"If that is all; the mischief is soon healed," said Mr. Blane, entering the cottage.

Mrs. Marks sat just where her husband had left her, but her eyes were closed and her face strangely flushed. She looked up wearily and languidly, with not a trace of the temper her husband had spoken of, and said not a word as the doctor took her burning hand in his and felt its quick pulse.

"You had better get your wife to bed, Marks it will be more comfortable for her than sitting here."

"Yes, Sir," said Marks, wondering how it was to be accomplished. However he drew near and said, "Dont'ee think, old 'ooman, yer'd best do as the doctor 'vises yer."

"In course," was the feeble reply, so different to the loud angry one Matthew expected that he was staggered, and still more so when she attempted to stand, but could not, and he and the young doctor between them had to carry her to bed.

"What ails her, Sir?" asked Matthew, as Mr. Blane was going away. "D'yer think it's the tongue's done it?"

"That may have increased the fever but not caused it," was the reply.

"The faiver! Oh Lord; what's to be done now?"

What was to be done, indeed?

Jane gave up the house-work and tended her sister night and day, leaving Matthew and the girl to do as best they could without her, while for days Mrs. Marks struggled between life and death; then she grew better, the fever left her, and she lay weak as an infant, but otherwise progressing favourably.

One evening Jane came downstairs and took up her station opposite her brother-in-law, who, instead of rejoicing at the change, viewed her presence with a rueful face. When his wife was present he could sometimes forget Jane, but all alone it was impossible; move which way he would he was sensible her eyes were on him as she plied her knitting needles at her old work. How he hated that constant click, click!

"Did yer think t'was time for supper?" asked he presently, driven to say something to break the silence, becoming every moment more intolerable.

"No."

"How's the Missus this evening?"

"Better. She's asleep."

"That's all right. I'm glad on it," he said, "for she've had a hard time of it upstairs. When is it likely she'll be about again?"

"What did the doctor say? Didn't he tell you when?"

"He don't trouble to say much. I'm sure I'm right down glad when he don't say she's worse, for that's been the one word in his mouth lately."

Jane made no reply, but the feeling that her eyes were fixed steadily on him exasperated him beyond control.

"What d'yer see in my ugly mug?" he asked. "Have you fallen in love with it?"

"No."

"Then may be yer sees som'ut to skeer yer?"

"It's bad to have anything on the mind," she replied.

Matthew winced a little. "I'll tell you a piece of my mind," he said, throwing his half-smoked pipe into the fire, "I'll take Mrs. Marks' sauce and welcome, but I'm d—d if I take any other 'ooman's living."

"I wonder whatever ails you?" said she, quietly.

"Ails me? D'yer want to make believe I'm going to be knocked down with the faiver? I'm not such an ass, I can tell yer, yer looks a dale more likely yerself; and as to yer mind? yer look as though a horse couldn't carry the load yer've got on it. A terrible bad load too, I'll take my oath on it."

Jane shivered from head to foot.

"I'll take up the broth," she said, "most likely Anne's awake before now."

But her hands trembled so she could scarcely take hold of the saucepan to pour it out, while the cup and saucer rattled and shook as she went across the room.

Matthew sat sulkily by, and never offered to help her.

"Well!" said he, as soon as she was gone, "it's my belief she'd have stuck me, if she'd only laid hold of a knife instead of a spoon. How trembly she was; her hands was all of a shake. She'll 'ave spilt all that 'ere stuff, whatever 'tis, afore my wife tucks it down. Well, if she 'aint crazed, I don't know who is."

He lit a fresh pipe, and smoked away in contented solitariness. Presently, he looked thoughtful, knocked the ashes out of his pipe and said, "she's a-going to 'ave the faiver, or else she 'ave done som'ut bad in her day, and that's what's crazed her."

Matthew was right as to the fever. Not many days passed before Jane was taken ill with it.

CHAPTER IX

"But ever and anon of griefs subdued,
There comes a token like a scorpion's sting,
Scarce seen, but with fresh bitterness imbued;
And slight withal may be the things which bring
Back on the heart the weight which it would fling
Aside for ever: it may be a sound—
A tone of music—summer's eve—or spring—
A flower—the wind—the ocean—which shall wound,
Striking the electric chain wherewith we are darkly bound.

And how and why we know not, nor can trace
Home to its cloud this lightning of the mind,
But feel the shock renew'd, nor can efface
The blight and blackening which it leaves behind,
Which out of things familiar, undesign'd,
When least we deem of such, calls up to view
The spectres whom no exorcism can bind,
The cold—the changed—perchance the dead—"
CHILDE HAROLD

Can anything happen in a month? How often this question was in Amy's mind; how often in her thoughts. What could happen? Her heart suggested many things, strive as she would to think otherwise, and ever reverted with fear to her boy, whom she so passionately loved; old Hannah was surprised sometimes at the injunctions she received and wondered what her young mistress was so nervous about. The boy was well enough and hearty enough in all conscience: there was no occasion to make a "molly coddle" of him.

Bertie had taken a fancy to Frances, and would sit on her knee in preference to others, or hold up his little face to be kissed, when he was shy at being caressed by anyone else. Amy viewed the liking with distrust; she disliked Frances, and could not bear to see her and the boy romping together, and would have checked it, if she could have found some reason for doing so; but Robert countenanced it, and often joined in their play, while Amy alone looked grave and sorrowful.

Why had Frances come to Brampton? Had her stubborn heart at length given way, and did she regret the misery she had caused Amy and come to make atonement? To ask forgiveness and be forgiven? Were they to be reconciled at last? No. Not so. Frances came expecting to find Amy miserable, married to a man she could not love, and weeping the remembrance of the lost love. In that she would have gloried. But she came to find it otherwise; and how great was her disappointment, how bitter became her thoughts, how more than ever determined was she to pursue Amy and make her in the end utterly miserable. It wounded her to the quick to see Amy happy and contented with a husband who seemed to worship her and a child of whom she might well be proud. Was this to be the envied lot of her who had weaned the one heart away, so that harsh, bitter words had fallen on her ear as she had knelt in despair at his feet. Could she ever forget that? or his scorn? No! never! Amy's happiness must be undermined; had she not sworn it on that terrible, never-to-be forgotten night; sworn that Amy's sufferings should some day equal hers! There was little difficulty in accomplishing this if she went cautiously to work: haste alone could bring a failure.

Amy saw little of her husband now; of a morning he rode with Mrs. Linchmore and Frances, or walked miles with Mr. Linchmore: there was always something to draw him from her side. Of an evening it was music and chess. At first Amy had ridden with the rest, but latterly she and Bertie had spent their mornings together; she could see no pleasure in riding by Frances' side, and Mrs. Linchmore was so timid she claimed all Robert's attention.

Doubts fast and thick were springing up in Amy's heart. She shunned being alone with her husband, and insensibly grew cold and constrained. How seldom her eyes looked brightly on him, or her lips spoke loving words! while he never seemed to heed the change, or say aught of his love for her now, but grew colder too.

They were both changed, husband and wife; the one had begun to doubt his wife's love; the other feared her husband's love was fading away, and she without the power to stay its flight. Ah! Frances had already wrought wondrous harm, although only a week since she came to Brampton.

Amy stood at the window one morning, and watched the horses as they were being brought round, Frances's fiery one evincing his hot temper by arching his proud neck and coming along with a quick short trot, while the more sober Lady Emily pawed the ground with impatient hoof. Presently Frances came in ready for her ride, and then Vavasour.

"Are you not going with us, Mrs. Vavasour?" asked Frances. "I thought I heard you say you would."

Amy glanced at her husband. Would he, too, ask her? No; he stood quietly on the hearthrug, apparently indifferent as to her reply.

"Thank you; I am rather busy this morning."

"Busy? What can you find to do?"

"I and Bertie are going for a walk."

"Ah! I thought Bertie had a great deal to do with it. How fond you are of Bertie," and she laid an uncomfortable stress on the name as each time it passed her lips.

Robert spoke at last. "Bertie is Mrs. Vavasour's loadstar," he said, quietly.

Amy felt this to be unjust; not so would her husband have spoken to her a month ago.

"My heart is large enough to hold more than the love for my boy," she replied.

"I expect he holds by far the largest share of it," said Frances.

Amy said nothing until she met Robert's gaze fixed inquiringly on her face. "My love for my child is a sacred love, and scarcely to be called in question, Miss Strickland," she answered.

Frances's eyes flashed; then she laughed and struck her riding-habit with her whip. "Don't look so much in earnest, Mrs. Vavasour. I dare say you have lots of love in your heart for everybody."

"Not for everyone," replied Amy, gravely.

"Ah! you never fall in love at first sight, then; but when once you love, your love lasts for ever. Is it so?"

"I have never asked myself the question."

"But perhaps Mr. Vavasour has. What say you, Mr. Vavasour, you who are supposed to know every thought of your wife's heart?"

"A woman's heart is too difficult a thing for us poor men to fathom."

"Not always. I am going to call Isabella. You can ask your wife while I'm gone."

Amy stood close by her husband, yet dared not raise her eyes to his. Would he ask her if he knew every thought of her heart, and if she said "no," sternly demand what she had to conceal? Now, more than ever, she wished she had told him all long ago. She knew the question must come. It came at last.

"Amy, is it so? Do I know every thought of your heart?"

"You ought to," she replied, tremblingly.

"True." He sighed, then paused, as if expecting her to say more, but Amy was silent.

"Do you love me better than all others, Amy? better than your boy?"

"Nay, what a question. You know I love you, Robert."

He strained her passionately to his heart: had he held her there a moment longer, Amy might have told him all, for she felt strangely softened; but Frances' voice sounded; he drew away from her without a word, and was gone.

"I will ride to-morrow," thought Amy, "perhaps it will please him;" and Robert did look pleased the next day as she came out on the terrace—where he stood with Mrs. Linchmore,—in her riding habit and hat.

"You are going with us?" he cried.

"Yes, the day is so pleasant, I could not resist the temptation."

Ah, yes! The day! His brow clouded, and he turned away.

"I am glad you are coming," said Mrs. Linchmore, "as Frances does not ride."

Frances not ride! For a moment Amy felt glad, then sorry. Would they think she had come purposely to prevent a tête-à-tête?

"I did not know Miss Strickland was not to be of the party," said Amy, as her husband lifted her to the saddle.

"Nor I," he replied.

"You are not sorry I am going with you, Robert?"

He looked at her in surprise. "Sorry, Amy?"

"I mean; that is, I thought yesterday that perhaps you would like me to go."

"Of course, not only yesterday, but to-day and every day," and then he mounted, and went on with Mrs. Linchmore.

So the ride did not begin very auspiciously.

Amy was a good rider, a graceful and fearless one, although perhaps not such a dashing horse-woman as Frances, and her husband looked at her with pride and pleasure as she cantered along on her spirited horse at his side. The exercise soon brought a glow to her cheeks, and a bright light to her eyes, while she laughed and chatted so joyously that Robert thought he had never seen her look so lovely, and forgot the dark lady at his side and riveted his attention on his wife.

"Take care, Amy," said he, as her horse gave a sudden start, "tighten the curb a little more."

But Amy only laughed. "I like him to jump about," she said, "it shows he is in as good spirits as his mistress."

"I certainly never saw Mrs. Vavasour in such spirits," remarked Mrs. Linchmore, feeling herself neglected.

But Amy was not to be checked by a grave look from her rival. Since yesterday, when she had stood at the window with her eyes filled with tears watching her and her husband ride away, she had determined on standing her ground as Robert's wife; she would not fall away from his side at the first danger that threatened, and quietly without an effort allow another to wean his heart from her, but would win back his love to where it had been; and then, not till then, open her heart—as she ought to have done long ago—and tell him all.

Had Frances known of Amy's determination, or even of her contemplated ride, she would not have been walking so quietly along the lane rejoicing in the success of her stratagems. As she emerged into the road she met Bertie, who clapped his hands, and sprung out of his perambulator before Hannah's vigilant eye perceived him.

"I'll go with you," he said, taking Frances' hand.

"Come back, Master Bertie, this moment," said his nurse.

"Let him come," exclaimed Frances, "you are a very naughty boy, all the same, for being so disobedient."

"Please don't take him far, Miss, for it's most time for us to be turning home."

"No; only to the turnpike gate and back."

She took the boy's hand and away they went, Bertie chatting pleasantly until they reached the gate, where he made a stand and began climbing it, notwithstanding Frances' remonstrances. The continued talking brought Matthew to the window.

"There's some folks from the Hall," said he to his sister-in-law, who was busy peeling some potatoes.

Jane dropped the knife and turned sharply round. "Go out to them," she said, "we don't want them in here."

"It's only a young gentleman a-climbing the gate," he replied.

Jane picked up the knife and after a moment went on with her work; but Bertie had seen a cat with its kitten on the door-step; and had run into the cottage before Frances could prevent him.

"Go away! don't come in here!" screamed Jane.

"Put down the knife and hould yer oncivil tongue, yer dafty!" exclaimed Marks. "What the devil d'yer mean by it! Walk in, young gentleman, y'ere welcome to play with the cat as long as yer like. Take a seat, Miss," and he brought forward one of the chairs and dusted it.

But Frances took no heed of the invitation. "I am very angry with you, Bertie," she said, "What will Hannah say? Come away?"

But Bertie would not, but went up to Jane with the kitten in his arms.

"Very well," replied Frances, "I shall call Hannah," but in reality she went outside and waited for him, while Matthew, hat in hand, followed and talked to the young lady.

"I wish pussy was my very own," said Bertie presently, after playing with it for a few moments.

Jane had seated herself in a chair with her face half turned from him and paid no heed to his remark.

"Will you give it me?" he asked in his childish way, pulling at her dress to attract her attention.

"It isn't mine," she replied.

Bertie put the kitten in her lap. "Isn't it pretty?" he said. "Don't you love it?"

"No."

"Do you love the big cat?"

"No."

"Don't you love anything?"

"No. Nothing."

"What's your name?"

"Jane."

"You're a naughty, cross woman, Jane, and I shan't love you."

"You don't need to," she replied. "Go away!"

But Bertie continued playing with the kitten still laying in her lap. As he stooped his little face over it, his soft, dimpled cheek touched Jane's hand, while his fair, curly hair waved almost across the other. Presently Jane raised her hand, took off his cap and stroked his head gently.

Bertie looked up half surprised. "Do you think it pretty?" he asked.

"I don't know." But she did not take her hand away.

"Would you like to have some of it?" he asked again, as Jane passed her fingers through one of the silky curls. "Cut it. Where's the scissors?"

"There on the table over against the window," she replied.

Bertie ran and fetched them, and presently a curl shiny and bright fell in Jane's lap.

"There, that's my present," he said, "now won't you give me kitty?"

"She's too small; she mustn't go from her mother," said Jane, lifting the curl and smoothing it softly.

"Would her mother cry?"

"Oh my God!" exclaimed Jane, burying her face in her hands, "you'll break my heart!"

"But would her mother cry? Would she cry very much?" persisted Bertie, striving to draw her hands away.

"Yes," replied Jane, "cry and go mad, and curse those who took him. But curses don't kill, ah no! they don't kill; they only wear the heart away."

The child drew away, half frightened.

"Bertie! Bertie! are you coming?" called Frances.

"Good bye," he said, shyly. "You'll send me kitty by and by, won't you?"

"Yes,—for the sake of the curl," she replied, wrapping it in paper, and placing it in her bosom.

But Bertie only heard the "Yes."

"Send it for me; only for me," he said.

"Yes, for Master Bertie."

"Bertie Vavasour," he said.

"What?" screamed Jane, starting to her feet with a shriek that startled even Mrs. Marks, asleep in the room above. "Don't touch me! Don't come nigh me! Stand off! I'm crazed, I tell you, and don't know nothing. Oh! I'm deaf, and didn't hear it! No, no, I didn't hear it! I won't hear it! I'm crazed."

"That yer are, yer she devil!" exclaimed Matthew, striding up to where she stood, as it were at bay, before some deadly enemy. "Are these yer manners, when gentry come to visit yer?" and he half thrust, half threw her out on the stairs.

"She's crazed, Miss," said Matthew, returning, "and has got one of her fits on her; but she's as harmless as a fly. Don't 'ee cry, young Master," said he to Bertie, who with his arms clasped round Frances' neck, was sobbing violently. "She ain't well neither, Miss," continued he, "I thought, days ago, she were a-going to have the fever."

"The fever!" exclaimed Frances, "what fever?"

"I don't know, Miss, my wife have been sick of it for days past."

"And how dare you!" cried Frances, passionately, seizing him by the arm; "how dare you let the boy come in. Don't you know it is murder. Oh, if he should get it! If he should get it!" and she flew from the cottage, leaving Matthew bewailing his thoughtlessness and folly.

Frances disliked children, and had made up her mind to thoroughly hate Amy's child, long before she saw him; but the boy's determined will, so congenial to her spirit, and then his partiality to herself, overcame this resolution. Her object had been to conciliate the father through the boy; but in attaining this object she had taken a liking for the child, which she in vain tried to surmount; Bertie wound himself into that cruel heart, somehow, and held his place there in defiance of all obstacles.

Her heart sank within her at Matthew's words, and felt strangely stirred as she drew away the little arms so tightly encircling her neck. "For Heaven's sake, Bertie, don't cry so, you'll make yourself so hot," and then she felt his hands and forehead to assure herself he had not already caught the fever.

"She's a naughty woman," sobbed Bertie.

"Yes, yes, she's a naughty woman;" and then by dint of coaxing and persuading there was little trace, when they reached Hannah at the further end of the village, of the fright or violent cry he had had; still, his nurse was not to be deceived.

"What's the matter with Master Bertie?" she asked.

"A poor idiot in one of the cottages frightened him," replied Frances; but she said not a word of the fever, or that the cottage was the one at the turnpike gate, and Bertie's version of the story was a great deal too unconnected to be understood, and merely seemed a corroboration of the one Frances had given.

"At length within a lonely cell,
They saw a mournful dame.

Her gentle eyes were dimm'd with tears,
Her cheeks were pale with woe:
And long Sir Valentine besought
Her doleful tale to know.

'Alas! young knight,' she weeping said,
'Condole my wretched fate;
A childless mother here you see;
A wife without a mate'"
VALENTINE AND URSINE

Frances was nervous and anxious for days after her walk with Bertie; the sudden opening of a door made her start and tremble lest it should be some-one come to announce the boy's illness. Sometimes she watched and waited at the window half the morning to catch a glimpse of him going out for his daily walk, or if he did not come would seek him in the nursery, and bring him downstairs. She became Bertie's shadow, and he, in consequence, fonder of her than ever. But the days crept on and there was no symptom that he had taken the fever: so by degrees Frances forgot her fears—or rather they slumbered—and went back to her old ways. But it had become more difficult to deal with Amy now, she appeared to have changed so entirely; there was no making her jealous, even if she could manage to make Robert devote himself half the evening to her hostess. Amy seemed just as happy; she either was not jealous or was jealous and concealed it, and rode with her husband, let who would be of the party, or deserted Bertie and walked with him, even learnt to play billiards when she found Robert was fond of it; so that it was rarely chess now, but all, even Mr. Linchmore, joined of an evening in the former game.

Still Robert's love was not what it had been. His wife felt that it was not; he loved her by fits and starts, while some days he was moody and even touchy; but Amy did not despair. How could she when she felt he still loved her? In another fortnight they would be back at Somerton, and away from Frances, who, Amy feared, was fast weaning her boy's as well as her husband's love from her, though how she had managed it she knew not.

"I have just been talking with Mr. Grant, your head keeper," said Robert to Mr. Linchmore about a fortnight after the memorable walk to the turnpike, "he tells me the poaching goes on as sharp and fast as ever."

"Worse," was the reply, "they are the same set we have always had, that is to say, we suppose so from their cunning and rashness."

"You got rid of two or three of them at the Sessions, if you remember, when I was here nearly four years ago."

"Yes, but the example does not appear to have done much good."

"You want Charley here," said Frances, "to excite you all into going out in a body again and exterminating them. Do you remember your fears, Mrs. Vavasour."

Amy looked up to reply, and meeting Frances' gaze, she grew confused and coloured deeply. "I should be more afraid now," said she with an effort at composure.

"I was sorry to hear you had never succeeded in tracking that man?" said Vavasour, with his eyes fixed on his wife's now pale face.

"You mean the man that wounded you? No, several were taken up on suspicion, but we were unable to prove anything against them, and the watcher, the poor man who was so frightfully bruised and otherwise ill-treated, swore, that none of them resembled his or your assailant."

"I could have sworn to the man, too, I think."

"You were abroad, and so I did not press the matter, and in time the affair blew over altogether."

The conversation ended, and was perhaps forgotten by all save Robert Vavasour, and he could not forget it, but snatched his hat and strolled out hastily into the Park. What had made his wife's face flush so deeply? Had it anything to do with Charles, whom Frances was so constantly throwing at his teeth? He began to hate the very name, and was daily growing more madly suspicious of his wife, and yet had his thoughts framed themselves into words he would have shrunk from the bare idea of suspecting his idol. That she had not loved him with all her heart when he married her he knew: she had told him so; and how easy he had thought the task of winning the heart she had assured him none other had ever asked to have an interest in; but then had she loved none other? perhaps this very man of whom for one half hour he remembered being jealous long ago. When she told him the first, why if it was so, had she not told him the second? Why give him only half her confidence? Perhaps she loved him still? Perhaps the remembrance of him had called the guilty blush to her cheek? "Ah! if it is so!" he cried with angry vehemence, "he shall die. I will be revenged!"

"Vengeance! who talks of vengeance?" said a voice near, and, looking up, he saw Goody Grey leaning on her staff. Involuntarily he tendered her some halfpence.

"I want them not," she said. "It does not do for the blind to lead the blind."

"What mean you, woman? I am in no mood to be trifled with."

"Don't I know that?" she replied; "don't I know the bitterness of the heart? Do you think I have lived all these years and don't know where misery lies?"

"Where does it lie?" he asked.

"In your heart. Where it wouldn't have been if you hadn't been there;" and she pointed in the direction of the Hall. "'Tis a gay meeting, and may be as sad a parting."

"Why so?" asked he again.

"Do the hawk and dove agree together in the same nest?"

"The dove would stand but a poor chance," said Robert.

"True." She turned upon her heel and went into the cottage, and seating herself in a low chair, began rocking it backwards and forwards, singing, in a kind of low, monotonous chant,

"When the leaves from the trees begin to fall   Then the curse hangs darkly over the Hall."

"That must be now, then," said Robert, who had followed her in, "for the leaves are falling thick enough and fast enough in the wood."

"Darker and darker as the leaves fall thicker," she replied, "and darkest of all when they are on the ground, and the trees bare."

"What will happen then?"

"Ask your own heart: hasn't it anger, hatred, and despair in it? Did I not hear you call aloud for vengeance?"

"And what good can come of it?" continued she, seeing he made no reply; "like you, I've had all that in my heart, until curses loud and bitter have followed one after another, heaped on those who injured me, and yet I'm as far off from happiness as ever. I began to seek it when I was a young woman, and look! my hair is grey, and yet I have not found it; while the fierce anger, the strong will to return evil for evil, have faded from my spirit like the slow whitening of these grey hairs. There's only despair now, and hatred for those, for her who did me wrong."

"Do we all hate as mercilessly as this? I feel that a look, a word of love would turn my heart from bitterness."

"Then the injury has not been deep. I've lived here a lonely woman twenty years, and a look, a word, will sometimes call the fierce blood to my heart. When the injury is eternal and irremediable then the hate must be lasting too."

"The injured heart may forgive," said Vavasour.

"It may forgive. But forget its hate! its wrongs! its despair! Never, never," said she, fiercely.

"It may be so," said Robert, half aloud.

"May be so? It is so. Hate is a deadly enemy; don't let it creep into your heart; tear it out! cast it from you! for once you have it, it is yours for ever; even death cannot part it from you."

"I doubt that. We know that even a dying sinner's heart may repent and be softened; the thought that he is perishing from the earth nursing a deadly sin at his heart would do much; he would never dare die so."

"Prayers, the pleadings of an agonised, breaking heart may be vain—in vain—was vain, young man, for I tried it," replied Goody Grey, her voice suddenly changing from fierceness to mournful sadness.

"Surely there could not be a heart so hard, if you pleaded rightly."

"Don't tell me that!" she exclaimed, raising her voice, "don't tell me there was anything I might have done. Did I not kneel and pray? Did I not take back my curses and give blessings? Did I not plead my broken heart and withered youth? But death came, even as I knelt; the hate was too strong, and the words I panted to hear were unspoken. What have you to say to that?"

"Hope," replied Robert; "what you have done at a death bed, I have done during life, and been refused; death has come since, and I am seemingly as far off as ever; and yet I hope on."

"Hope on, hope ever," said she, sadly, "yes, that's all that's left me now, but it doesn't satisfy the cravings of my heart; never will!"

"Have you no relations? You must live but a lonely life here," said Robert.

"That is the only living thing that loves me," she replied, pointing to the parrot, sitting pluming his feathers. "He's been with me in joy and sorrow. Don't touch him; he is savage with strangers."

"Not with me," said Robert, smoothing his feathers gently.

"Then he knows friends from foes, or his heart's taken kindly to you like mine did, when I saw you with the bad passions written in your face."

"I once had a bird like this," he replied, thoughtfully, "but it must be years ago, for I cannot recall to my recollection at this moment when it was."

He passed from the cottage, while Goody Grey again rocked herself to and fro' and began her old song.

"When the leaves from the trees begin to fall
Then the curse—"

The rest of the words were lost to his ear, but the sound of her voice was borne along by the breeze, and sounded mournfully and sadly as it swept through the leafless trees.

Robert thought much of Goody Grey as he walked homewards. Here was a woman whose very life had wasted away in the vain search for what for twenty years,—perhaps more,—had eluded her grasp. Would it be the same with him? Would years,—his life slip by, and the mystery of his birth be a mystery still? Would hope fade away, and he, like her, grow despairing in the end? He felt a strange interest in that lone, unloved woman, with nothing in the world to love but a bird. Then his thoughts reverted to his wife, and his love for her. Why had she married him if her heart was another's? Why had she done him this wrong? Why make not only herself, but him miserable for life? But could deceit dwell in so lovely a form as his wife's? only a month ago he would have staked his life; nay, his very love upon her truth. And now—now—

"Where are you going so fast, Robert? Are you walking for a wager? I have been vainly trying to come up with you for the last five minutes," said Amy, taking his arm.

"Have you been out walking without Bertie?" he said.

"Yes, I meant to have gone with you; and ran upstairs for my hat, when I saw you preparing to go out."

"Why did you not come then?"

"I was too late; when I came back you had disappeared, Miss Strickland said down the long avenue: so I followed, and went through the village, and home by the lane, but somehow I missed you."

"Miss Strickland was wrong. I went across the fields into the wood, as far as Mrs. Grey's cottage. What a singular being she is!"

"Have you never seen her until to-day?"

"Yes, several times, but never to speak to. She must have been very handsome in her youth."

"What, with that dark frown on her brow?"

"That has been caused from sorrow," replied Robert, "she has had some heavy, bitter trial to bear; besides that frown is not always there, once I noticed quite a softened expression steal over her face. I feel an interest in the old lady; she tells me she is alone in the world,—like myself. I feel alone sometimes."

"You, Robert!" said Amy, in a tone of sadness and reproach.

"I feel so sometimes, Amy."

"What, with your wife's love?"

"You have the boy to care for. You love him so much, Amy."

"Yes," said she in a tone of disappointment.

"See! there he comes up the walk."

"Yes," she said again, but never turned her head or heeded Bertie's "Mamma!" "Mamma!"

"I love you better than Bertie, Robert," she whispered softly a moment after.

He did not reply; but she felt his arm tighten on her hand and press it slightly to his side. She did not return the pressure, she was only half satisfied as she left him and went up the terrace steps, while Robert's eyes followed her wistfully, until even the skirt of her dress swept through the door out of sight.

Ah! had she only remained with him a little longer.

Robert passed on down the terrace, and stood at the further end. Just then a window was flung open, and Frances Strickland called to his boy. They talked for a few moments, then Hannah passed on with her charge, while Robert still leant against the abutment of the window. Presently it closed gently, a voice saying at the same instant, "Poor Charley! Mrs. Vavasour will break her heart."

Robert sprung to his feet and strode past the window at which Frances still stood, his shadow falling upon her darkly as he went on into the house,—into the room.

Alone! and ready for a walk? That was well, he would not question her there; no, it must be away, far away, and safe from interruption.

"I would speak with you, Miss Strickland," he said sternly, vainly striving to appear calm, and stay the fierce hot blood rushing to his heart and mounting to his brow.

Frances followed him at once without a question; away into the Park, along the very road he had so lately traversed with his wife; she could scarcely keep up with his stride, or heavy iron-sounding step, that seemed as though it would crush every stone and pebble in his path to powder: still he went on; on through the trees and walks, startling the birds from the branches, but striking no dismay into Frances' breast; on, even down to the lake slumbering so peacefully and quietly. Here he stopped, and pointing to the clump of a tree, bade her be seated. Then he stood sternly before her.

"Can you wonder I wish to speak with you?" he asked in a thick, harsh, almost agitated voice, which grew steadier as he went on.

"No," she replied.

"Nor why I have brought you thus far?"

"No," she said again.

"Then speak!" he cried, "and if you speak falsely I will hold you up as a scorn and shame amongst women."

"I am not afraid," she said, "and can excuse your harsh words; but—"

"I will have no buts," he said sternly, "you have slandered my wife, her I love more than my life; you shall either say you have lied falsely, or you shall make good your words."

"Shall I begin at the beginning? Do you want to know all?"

"Begin, and make an end quickly."

And she did begin, even from the time when Amy had fainted, that memorable night, unto where Charles Linchmore had told her he had met Amy on her wedding day; and as she went on he buried his face in his hands, while his whole frame shook and trembled like an aspen.

"Girl, have some mercy!" he cried.

But she had none; no pity. Was not this woman his wife; and had she shown pity. So she never stayed her words, never softened them, she gave him what appeared the hard, stern, agonising truth, and he groaned with very anguish as she spoke.

"Is that all?" he asked at last.

"All."

"And you will swear it. Swear it!" he cried hoarsely.

"I will. But you need not believe me. Ask your wife? See what she says."

He moved his hands from his face. It looked as though years had swept over it. "You have broken my heart," he said, in a quivering voice. And then he left her.

Amy had gone to her room, sad and thoughtful, with the feeling, at last, that her husband doubted her love; and yet, she did love him better than she ever thought she should.

As she turned his words over in her mind, she determined on delaying no longer; but now, at once, tell him all. She dreaded his anger and sorrowful look; but that, anything was better than the loss of his love. So she sat and listened, and awaited his coming. But he came not.

The luncheon bell rang, and she went downstairs wondering at his absence.

"I am sorry to say Mr. Linchmore has heard some bad news, Mrs. Vavasour," said Mrs. Linchmore.

"My husband! Where is he?"—exclaimed Amy, panic stricken.

"It has nothing to do with him," replied Mr. Linchmore, "my brother has, unfortunately, been wounded." And he looked somewhat surprised at her sudden fright.

Then Amy was glad Robert was absent. "I am sorry," she faltered. "I hope it is not serious;" and her pale face paled whiter than before.

"No, I trust not. He has been out with General Chamberlain's force."

"He was very foolish to go to India at all," said Mr. Linchmore. "I dare say he would have had plenty of opportunities of winning laurels elsewhere; but he always was so impetuous,—here to-day and gone to-morrow."

Then the conversation turned upon other subjects, and still Robert came not. Just as they rose from the table Frances came in.

"Have you seen Mr. Vavasour?" asked Amy.

"No. Has he not been in to luncheon? I thought I was late."

Amy passed on up to her room again, and for a short time sat quietly by the fire, as she had done before; then, as the hours crept on, she rose and went to the window.

The sun sank slowly, twilight came on, and the shadows of evening grew darker still; Amy could scarcely see the long avenue now, or the tall dark trees overshadowing it; and still she was alone. Then the door opened; but it was not her husband—it was Hannah, who stood looking at her with grave face.

"If you please, Ma'am, I don't think Master Bertie is well. There is nothing to be frightened about; but he has been hot and feverish ever since he came home from his walk."

CHAPTER XI

REPENTANCE

"Whispering tongues can poison truth,
And constancy lives in realms above;
And life is thorny, and youth is vain;
And to be wroth with one we love,
Doth work like madness in the brain."
COLERIDGE

"My thoughts acquit you for dishonouring me
By any foul act; but the virtuous know
'Tis not enough to clear ourselves, but the
Suspicions of our shame."
SHIRLEY

Robert came back at last, and years seemed to have swept over his head and gathered round his heart, since only a few hours before he had stood in his wife's room. But he looked for her in vain, she was not there, but away in the nursery, hushing, with tearful eyes and frightened heart, poor sick Bertie in her arms to sleep. Robert longed, yet dreaded to see her. Through all his misery his heart clung to his wife, and hoped, even when his lips murmured there was no hope. He took up the work on the table, a handkerchief Amy had been hemming, marked with his name, and sighed as he laid it down, and thought duty, not love, had induced her to work for him.

So he waited on—waited patiently. At length she came.

"Oh, Robert! I am so glad you are here. I have been longing for you, and quite frightened when you stayed away such a time."

The mother's fears were roused, and she clung at once to her husband for help and support. Her trembling heart had forgotten for the moment all she had been braving her heart, and nerving her mind to tell him. The great fear supplanted for the time the lesser and more distant one.

She had seated herself at Robert's feet, leaning her head on his knee. He let her remain so—did not even withdraw the hand she had taken, for the fierceness of his anger had passed away, and a great sorrow filled his heart. Did he not pity her as much as himself? she so fair and young. Had not she made them both miserable? Both he and her.

But Amy saw nothing of all this—nothing of the grave, sorrowing face—her heart was thinking of poor Bertie's heavy eyes and hot hands, and how best she could break it to her husband, so as not to grieve him too much, for did he not love the boy as much as she did? and would he not fear and dread the worst? But even while she hesitated, her husband spoke—

"Amy! Have you ever deceived me? I, who have loved you so faithfully."

The cold, changed tone—the harsh voice struck her at once. She looked up quickly. There was that in his face which sent dismay into her heart, while her fears for Bertie fled as she gazed. Was she too late? Had her husband found out what she had been striving so hard for months to tell him? Yes, she felt, she knew she was too late; that he knew all, and waited for her words to confirm what he knew.

"Never as your wife, Robert," she replied, tremblingly.

"And when, then!"

"Oh, Robert! don't look so sternly at me—don't speak so strangely. I meant to tell you, I did indeed. I have been striving all these months to tell you."

Alas! there was something to tell, then; every word she uttered drove away hope more and more from his heart.

"Months and years?" he said, mournfully.

"No, no; to-day, this very day have I been watching and waiting. Oh! why did you not come back? Why did you not come back, Robert, so that I might have told you?"

"You dared not," he said, sternly.

"Oh, yes! I dared. I have done no sin, only deceived you, Robert, at—at first."

"Only at first. Only for ever."

"No, no; not for ever. I always meant to tell you, I did, indeed, Robert." She began to fear he distrusted her words already—she, whose very "yes" had been implicitly believed and reverenced. Alas! this first sin, perhaps the only one, into what meshes it leads us, often bringing terrible retribution.

"Did you not fear living on in—in deceit?" he said. "Did you not feel how near you were to my heart—did you not know that my love for you was—was madness? that, lonely and unloved, I loved you with all the passion of my nature? If not, you knew that all my devotion was thrown away—utterly wasted—that your heart was another's, and could never be mine."

He stopped; and the silence was unbroken, save by Amy's sobs.

"Had you told me this," he said again, "do you think I would have brought this great sorrow upon you? put trouble and fear into your heart instead of love and happiness, and made your young life desolate—desolate and unbearable, but for the boy. He is the one green leaf in your path, I the withered one,—withered at heart and soul."

"Robert! Robert! don't be so hard, so—so—" she could not bring to her lips to say cruel, "but forgive me!"

He heeded her not, but went on.

"And the day of your marriage," he said, "that day which should have been, and I fondly hoped was, the happiest day of your life; upon that day, of all others, you saw him."

"Not wilfully, Robert, not—not wilfully," sobbed Amy.

"That day, your marriage day, was the one on which you first learnt of his love for you, and passed in one short half hour a whole lifetime of agony. Poor Amy! poor wife! Forgive you? yes; my heart is pitying enough and weak enough to forgive you your share in my misery for the sake of the anguish of your own."

Amy only wept on. She could not answer. But he, her husband, needed no reply; her very silence, her utter grief and tears confirmed all he said.

"Amy, did you never think the knowledge of all this—the tale would break my heart?"

"Never! I feared your anger, your sorrowing looks, but—but that?—Never, never!"

"And yet it will be so. It must be so."

"Oh, no, no! Neither now nor ever, because—because I love you, Robert."

"Amy! wife!" he said, sternly, "there must never be a question of love between us, now. That—that is at an end, and must never be named again. I forgive you, but forget I never can," and then he left her, before she could say one word. Left her to her young heart's anguish and bitter despair, tenfold greater than the anguish he had depicted being hers long ago, because hopeless—hopeless of ever now winning back his love again. And what a love it had been! She began to see, to feel it all now, now that it had gone, left her for ever.

"God help me!" she cried, "I never, never thought it would have come to this. God help me! I have no other help now, and forgive me if I have broken his heart."

Then by-and-by she rose, and with wan, stricken face, went back to her boy.

Mr. Blane was bending over Bertie, who was crying in feeble, childish accents, "Give me some water to drink. Please give me some water."

"Presently, my little man; all in good time."

"But I want it now—I must have it now."

"My mistress, Mrs. Vavasour, sir," said Hannah, as Amy entered, and stood silently by his side, and looked anxiously into his face, as she returned his greeting.

"Dr. Bernard usually attends at the Hall," she said; "but he lives so far away, and I was so anxious about my boy. Is there much the matter with him?"

"Ahem," said Mr. Blane, clearing his throat, as most medical men do when disliking to tell an unpleasant truth, or considering how best to shape an answer least terrifying to the mother's heart. "No—no," he said hesitatingly. "The child is very hot and feverish."

"I hope he isn't going to sicken for a fever, sir," said Hannah.

"I fear he has sickened for it," he replied.

"Not the scarlet fever?" said Amy, in a frightened voice.

"No. There has been a nasty kind of fever going about, which I fear your boy has somehow taken. I have had two cases lately, and in both instances the symptoms were similar to this."

"Is it a dangerous fever?" asked Amy.

"The old lady, my first patient, is quite well again, in fact better than she has been for the last six months, as the fever cured the rheumatics, and from being almost a cripple, she now walks nearly as well as ever. And," he said, rising to leave, "I should advise no one's entering this room but those who are obliged to—the fewer the better—and by all means keep the other children away, as the sore throat is decidedly infectious. Good-bye, Sir; take your medicine like a little man, and then we'll soon have you well again," said he to Bertie.

"My boy, my poor Bertie," said Amy, as she sat by his side, and held the cool, refreshing drink to his parched lips. Did she need this fresh trial coming upon her already stricken heart?

"Don't let the boy see you crying, Ma'am," said Hannah, "or perhaps he'll be getting frightened, and I'm sure that'll be bad for him."

"No," said Amy. But though no tears were in her eyes, the traces of them were weighing down the heavy swollen eyelids; but tears she had none to shed, she had wept so much.

So she sat by the side of her sick child's little cot with aching heart, all alone and lonely, with no one but old faithful Hannah to sympathize and watch with her; he, her husband, she dared not think of, or if she thought at all, it was to almost wish he would not come; so stern and grave a face might frighten her boy.

"Are you not going down to dinner, Ma'am?" said Nurse at last, in a whisper, for Bertie had dropped off into an uneasy slumber.

"Dinner? Ah! yes. I forgot. No, I shall not go down to dinner to-day. I shall not leave my boy."

"I can take care of him, Ma'am, and then shouldn't you tell the Master? Haven't you forgotten him? There's no use keeping the bad news from him."

Forgotten him? How could she forget? Were not his words still fresh at her heart?

But Nurse was right, he ought to be told; there was Mrs. Linchmore, too, she—all, ought to know about Bertie.

So Amy rose and went away in search of her husband. Where was he? Should she find him in his room? She hesitated ere she knocked, but his heavy tread a moment after assured her he was there. She did not look up as the door opened, but said simply, "Bertie is ill, Robert, very ill. Mr. Blane has been to see him, and says he has caught some fever, but not a dangerous one."

All traces of sternness and anger fled from his brow, as he listened and caught the expression of his wife's face. He wondered at the calmness with which she spoke. His boy ill, little Bertie, in whose life her very soul had seemed wrapt? and she could stand and speak of it so coldly, so calmly as this? He wondered, and saw nothing of the anguish within, or how the one terrible blow he had dealt her had for the time broken and crushed her spirit. Only a few hours ago, and she would have wept and clung round his neck for help, in this her one great hour of need. But that was past, could not be; he would not have it so, her love had been forbidden.

"I will go and see the boy," he said, gently.

She turned and went on her way downstairs to the drawing-room.

"Good gracious, Mrs. Vavasour! what is the matter?" cried Frances, her heart beating savagely, as she looked at the poor face, so wan and still, telling its own tale of woe long before the lips did.

Amy took no notice of Frances, but passed on to where Mrs. Linchmore sat with the children. It was Alice's birthday, and Bertie was to have come down too, and as Amy remembered it, her heart for the first time felt full; but she drove back the tears, and said—

"My child is ill. He has caught some fever; but not a dangerous one."

How fond she was of repeating this latter phrase, as if the very fact of saying that it was not a dangerous fever would ease and convince her frightened, timid heart.

The words startled everyone.

"I am extremely sorry," said Mrs. Linchmore, drawing Alice away. "I trust, I hope it is not infectious?"

"I very much fear it is, at least, Mr. Blane thinks the sore throat is, and advises the children, by all means, being kept apart."

"They must go away, shall go away the very first thing to-morrow morning. It is as well to be on the safe side. Don't you think so, Robert?" said Mrs. Linchmore.

"Decidedly. They can go into the village for the time or to Grant's cottage."

"There are cases of the same fever in the village," said Amy.

"Then they must go away altogether," said Mrs. Linchmore, hurriedly. "We must send them to Standale."

"I am so sorry for Bertie, he'll have such lots of nasty medicine," said Fanny; "but won't it be nice to be without Miss Barker?"

"Be silent, child!" said her mother, "Miss Barker will of course go with you."

"Oh! how horrid!" returned Fanny. Even Mrs. Linchmore's frown could not prevent her from saying that.

Amy passed out again even as she had come, almost brushing Frances' dress, but without looking at her, although, had she raised her eyes, she must have been struck with the whiteness of her face, which equalled, if not exceeded, her own.

"Master has been here, Ma'am," said Hannah, as Amy returned, "and bid me tell you he had gone to fetch Dr. Bernard."

Again Amy sat by her boy watching and waiting. What else was there to be done? He still slept—slept uneasily, troubled with that short, dry cough.

Later on in the evening, when Dr. Bernard—whose mild hopeful face and kind cheering voice inspiring her poor heart with courage,—had been, and when the hours were creeping on into night a knock sounded at the door.

"Miss Strickland is outside, Ma'am, and wants to come in. Shall I let her?" asked Hannah.

Amy went out and closed the door behind her, and looked with unmoved eyes on Frances' flushed and anxious face.

"How is he? May I go in?" she asked, eagerly.

"Never, with my permission," was the chilling reply.

"Only for five minutes; I am not afraid of the fever, and my looking at him can do him no harm. I will promise not to stay longer than that."

"No. You shall not go in for half a minute, even."

"You cannot be so cruel," said Frances; "you cannot tell how frightened and anxious I am. Oh! do let me see him."

"I will not," said Amy, angrily.

"Cruel, hard-hearted mother," cried Frances. "I know he has asked for me. I know he has called for me!"

"I thank God he has not," replied Amy, "for that would break my heart."

"Then he will ask for me; and if he does, you will send for me, won't you?"

"Never!" said Amy, as she turned away.

"Oh! Mrs. Vavasour, I love the boy; don't you see that my heart is breaking while you stand there so pitilessly."

"Had you loved the boy," said Amy, "you would not have crushed the mother's heart. What had I done to you, Frances Strickland, that you should pursue me so cruelly, first as a girl, when I never injured you, and then—now you have taken my husband's love from me, and would take my boy's also? But I will stand between him and you, cruel girl, as long as I live."

"Don't say so. Think—think—what if he should die?" said Frances, fearfully.

"Ah! God help me!" said Amy; she could say no more. But Frances clung to her dress.

"It is I who should say, God help me!" she cried; "don't you know I took Bertie to the cottage where he caught the fever? Oh! Mrs. Vavasour, you don't know half my agony and remorse, or what I suffered when I found out what I had done."

"My boy's illness, my husband's scorn, broken hopes, and grieving heart, my crushed spirit, all—all I owe to you. May God forgive you, Miss Strickland."

"Yes, yes; God forgive me. I deny nothing. But, oh! will not you forgive me, Mrs. Vavasour? I will try, I will, indeed, to make amends."

This abject appeal from the proud Frances? But Amy scarcely heeded it.

"You cannot make amends," she said, despairingly. "It is past atonement—this great wrong you have done."

"Oh! do not be so harsh and cruel to me; your heart was soft enough once."

"It was. You have changed it, and are the first to feel its hardness. I am no longer what I was; but for my boy I should turn into a stone, or die."

"And I? What am I to do? If—if anything should happen to Bertie. Oh! I shall go mad," she cried. "Think of my grief then. I, who unwittingly gave him this fever; think what my heart would feel, what it even feels now; and be not so merciless."

"No, not half so merciless as your bad heart has been. I can give you no greater punishment than your own guilty remorse, and frightened heart. I will remain no longer, Miss Strickland. You shall not see my boy!"

And Amy left Frances weeping, perhaps the first genuine repentant tears she had ever shed.

Robert sat at his boy's bed-side all that night, cooling his burning forehead and heated head with the cold wet cloth dipped in vinegar and water, or holding him up in his arms while his poor parched lips feebly yet eagerly drank from the cup his mother held so tremblingly before him, while Frances alternately walked her room despairingly, or crouched away in the dark on the stairs near, her ear vainly trying to catch the words of those mournful watchers and nurses who stepped about so softly in the sick chamber beyond.

CHAPTER XII

A FADING FLOWER

"The coldness from my heart is gone,
But still the weight is there,
And thoughts which I abhor will come,
And tempt me to despair.

"Those thoughts I constantly repel;
And all, methinks, might yet be well,
Could I but weep once more;
And with true tears of penitence
My dreadful state deplore."
SOUTHEY

The long hours of night wore away, and the morning broke, bright, fresh, and frosty. Then the long corridor and passages echoed with the sound of hasty footsteps hurrying through them, while the quick, sudden opening and shutting of doors betokened an unusual stir in the Hall. The children were preparing for their journey.

Half an hour later all was silent and still, more so than it had been for days. The children were gone.

Again we enter the sick room. Bertie is no better, but, if anything, worse; his little face more flushed and heated, his burning hands wandering restlessly about, to and fro, as he tosses and turns upon his little cot, his anxious eyes no longer looking mournfully, and as it were imploringly in his mother's face for help from his pain, for Bertie is delirious, and does not even recognise her; his thoughts ramble, and he talks incoherently and strangely.

Mrs. Hopkins often came to see him, bringing, as was her wont, in cases of illness, broths and cooling drinks she had prepared with her own hand; but Bertie was too ill to heed them, and Amy could but look her thanks—words she had none.

It was on returning from one of these visits, with cup and saucer in hand, that she met Frances Strickland.

"Have you been to see Master Bertie?" she asked.

"Yes, Miss," replied Mrs. Hopkins, with a sigh.

"And how is he? Do you think he is any better this morning?"

"No, Miss, I don't. It's my belief he couldn't well be worse; but the doctor'll know better than me. I suppose he'll be here presently."

"What makes you think him so ill?"

"I've been the mother of four, Miss, and lost them all, and none of them looked a bit worse than Master Bertie, poor, innocent lamb."

"But you had not two doctors," returned Frances.

"No, nor half the nurses to wait on mine; but I'd the same loving, craving mother's heart and the same God to look up to and hope in," and the housekeeper passed on, as the rebuke fell from her lips.

"Oh! I wish I could hope, I wish I could pray," cried Frances, as she went once more into the solitude of her own room; not only did she grieve for Bertie, but the terror lest through her means he should die had at last brought repentance to her unfeeling heart; she had been so wicked, so relentlessly cruel to his mother, that perhaps the boy's death was to be her punishment; and she could think of, scarcely look forward to, anything else.

Dr. Bernard stayed at the Park all that night; he whispered no decided hope to Amy's heart. There was only a very grave look on his face as after bending over Bertie and feeling the quick, sharp pulse beating so fiercely against his finger, he said, "While there is life there is hope," and Amy was obliged to content her poor heart with this, and repeat it over and over again to herself all through that long sad night; the second of Bertie's illness, and of her own and her husband's watch, for Robert scarcely ever left his boy, but remained through the weary hours of night patiently by his side; only old Hannah snatching every now and then a moment's sleep.

Towards the morning Bertie grew more composed, the hands tossed about less restlessly, and the weary, anxious eyes closed in sleep: so calm and still he looked that Amy bent down her head to catch the faint breath.

"It is not death?" she said to Dr. Bernard, who had been hastily aroused.

"No. The crisis is past I hope. The fever has left him. It is weakness, excessive weakness," but he did not add that that was as much to be dreaded as the fever; while Amy only prayed that when he awoke he would recognise her, so long it seemed since his little lips had said "Mamma."

Just before luncheon, Anne with her husband drove up to the Hall. She was rushing into the morning-room with her usual haste and merry laugh, when she was checked by Mrs. Linchmore's grave face.

"Has anything happened, Isabella? How grave you look."

Yes a great deal had happened; she had a great deal to hear, and Anne sat herself down to listen to it all patiently—or as patiently as she could to the end. As soon as it was told, she was rushing impetuously from the room.

"Is the boy in the small red room?" she asked.

"Yes. But Anne, the fever is infectious; you had better stay away. Mrs. Vavasour can come and see you here."

"As if she would leave him?" she cried, "not a bit of it, I know her better, besides I am not afraid of anything. I shall go." Anne was right, there was very little indeed she was afraid of.

"But Anne, think of your husband; he might not like it."

"Ah! true; how tiresome it is sometimes to have a husband! I suppose I shall have to wait a whole hour before he thinks of coming back."

"Did he drive in with you?"

"Yes, and has gone on in the pony carriage to call at the Rectory. Isn't it provoking. I have a great mind not to wait for him."

"It might have been a great deal worse; suppose he had not driven in with you?"

"Then I should have braved his anger and been at the boy's bed-side long ago," and she walked to the window, and strained her eyes impatiently down the drive.

"Have you seen the child today?" she asked presently.

"No, not since his illness; but Dr. Bernard tells me the fever left him early this morning."

"It did? Oh! then he'll soon get better."

"But he is so excessively weak, that he holds out small hopes of his recovery."

"Poor dear Amy, how sad for her. Ah! there's the carriage at last; how delightful! Mr. Russell could not have been at home." And away she flew down the stairs, and stood impatiently on the terrace.

"My dear Thomas," she exclaimed, "how slowly you drive. I always tell you you indulge the pony fearfully when I am not with you."

Mr. Hall looked in surprise at his wife's anxious face. "Why, Anne," he said, "I had no idea you were in such a desperate hurry to return home, or I might have driven a little quicker."

"Return," she cried, "I am not thinking of such a thing. I want to stay for a week, if you will only let me, and Isabella does not object; you can go and arrange it with her presently," said she, in her impetuous way.

"But I have yet to hear why I am to do all this," returned her husband.

"Ah, I forgot! It's because poor Amy Vavasour's child, that little boy we saw when we were last here, is dying of some fever. They say it's infectious, but you will not mind that, will you? I am not a bit afraid, and I do so want to comfort Amy."

Mr. Hall looked very grave.

"Oh, don't consider about it," she said, "you can stay, too, you know; there is no reason why you should go home before Saturday."

"It is not that," he replied, "but this fever is infectious, Anne, and you will be running a great risk."

"Do not think about it, Tom. I shall fret myself into a worse fever at home, and besides, think of poor Amy. I do not believe you can be so hard-hearted as to refuse me."

So in the end, much against his wish, Mr. Hall yielded, and while he went to propose the plan to Mrs. Linchmore Anne went off on her mission of mercy, and was repaid by the sad smile, and almost glad light in Amy's eyes as she greeted her.

Anne was shocked at the change in the boy; shocked too, with the mother's wan, haggard look.

"My Mistress hasn't been in bed for these two nights past, Miss," said Nurse, interpreting Anne's thoughts.

Not for two nights? It was absolutely necessary she should have some repose; so Anne set herself to work to accomplish it.

"Why not lie down, Amy, while your boy is asleep?"

"Impossible!" was the firm reply, "I could not."

"But you will wear yourself out, you cannot possibly be of any use while he sleeps. I will sit by him for you, and call you the moment he wakes."

"No, I must be by him when he wakes, I could not bear to think he looked at anyone else first; he has not known me for so long, that my heart is craving for some sign to show that he recognises me."

This was conclusive, and Anne urged no more, but Robert said, "I think Mrs. Hall is right, Amy, in advising you to rest."

"But I cannot leave the room, indeed I cannot."

"There is no occasion for your doing so, you can lie on Hannah's bed."

Anne expected a fresh expostulation, but no, Amy moved away at once, and did as her husband wished.

"Where can I find a shawl for Amy, Mr. Vavasour?" said Anne, presently, "she will be frozen over there, without some wrap."

He went away, and returned a moment after with one, which he spread over Amy as she lay, but without, to Anne's astonishment, one loving word or even look.

"Try and sleep," he said, gently, "I will call you in an hour."

She thanked him, and closed her eyes.

But long before the hour had passed away, she was at Bertie's bed-side, with the little head nestled in her bosom, and the soft, thin hand clasped in hers; he was too weak to say much, but he had named her, had recognised her; that was enough, he would not die now, without giving her one loving look. Die? Yes, she felt he would die, so thin and wasted, so hollow his cheeks, so weak, so utterly weak; and then the sorrowing faces of those around, the still graver one, and pitying words of the old doctor. Ah! there was no need to tell her; her boy, her beautiful boy, must die. Oh! the anguish of her heart, surely if a fervent prayer could save him, he would be saved yet.

Anne stole away by and by to her husband, and found him busy unpacking a carpet bag.

"I have been home and back again, Anne," he said, "and made Mary put together the few things she thought you might require. I hope you will find them all right."

"Oh! Tom, I do believe you are the only devoted, kind husband in the whole world; how fortunate it was I married you when I did."

"Why so?" he asked.

"Because I see so many bad specimens of married life, that if I had waited until now, I would not have had you at any price."

"Oh, yes, you would," he said.

"Don't be so conceited," she replied, "remember you have never been drilled yet."

"I have my wife to be conceited of," he said, fondly; "and now Anne, tell me what news of the child?" She was grave in a moment.

"There is no hope. None whatever. Dr. Bernard gives none."

"And the mother?"

"She is very quiet, very submissive under it all."

"She knows the worst, then?"

"She guesses it, and bears up wonderfully. How it will be by-and-by, when the worst is over, I don't like, cannot bear to think of; you must come and talk to her then?"

"I?" he said, "no, that will never do; she has her husband."

"He's a wretch! I have no patience with him. As cold as an icicle."

"My dear Anne," he said, reprovingly.

"Oh! my dear Tom, I am so glad you are not like him," and then she burst out crying, a most unusual thing for her, "and I am so glad now I have no children: it must be dreadful to lose them. After this I will be the most contented little mortal going."

And she went back again to Amy, leaving her husband somewhat surprised, and regretful that he should have consented to have allowed her to remain in a scene evidently too much for her.

Bertie had roused again. "Where's Missy? I want Missy?" he said, feebly.

The cry went like a sharp knife through the mother's heart. She brought him toys and pictures, telling him the history of each, and quieting him as well as she could. At first he was amused and interested, but he soon wearied, and said again, "I want Missy."

"Is it Alice he is crying for?" whispered Anne, as Amy moved away, and sent Hannah to take her place by the bed.

"No, not Alice. Oh! Anne, he will break my heart. I had so hoped he had forgotten her."

Again the little fretful cry sounded. "Tell Missy to come."

"I must go," said Amy, "there is no help for it."

Frances had thrown herself despairingly on the bed, shutting out Jane, her maid, who had tried to comfort her, and even Mrs. Linchmore. At one moment she would not believe there was no hope—would not,—the next she wept and moaned with the certainty that there could be none; as she saw Amy enter, she covered her face with her hands, and groaned aloud; thinking there was but one reason the mother could have in coming to see her, and that was to upbraid her for having caused the death of her boy.

"Miss Strickland I said you should not see my boy, but I cannot refuse his,—" Amy faltered,—"perhaps last request. He is asking for you. Will you come?"

"Come!" exclaimed Frances, springing from the bed, and tossing back the hair from off her throbbing temples, "do you think I could refuse him—you, anything? and oh! forgive me, Mrs. Vavasour, for having caused you all this utter misery."

"It is a fearful punishment," said Amy, looking at the ravages grief and remorse had made in her beautiful face.

"Fearful!" she replied, "it will haunt me through life. Think of that, and say one word of forgiveness, only one."

"I cannot forgive you, Miss Strickland. For my poor Bertie's illness I do; that was an unintentional injury, but his mother's misery—broken heart, no; that you might have prevented, and—and, God help me, but I cannot forgive that."

"How could I hope you would," said Frances despairingly, as she prepared to follow Amy.

"You must control your grief, Miss Strickland; be calm and passionless as of old. My boy must see no tears."

"I wonder I have any to shed," she replied, "and God knows how I shall bear to see him."

Anne looked bewildered as the door opened and Amy returned with Frances, and still more so when she saw the child's face light up with pleasure, and he tried in his feeble way to clasp her neck.

"I cannot bear to look at it," said Amy, as she softly left the room.

"Naughty! naughty Missy," he said as he kissed her.

Frances felt as if she could have died then, without one sigh of regret. For a moment after he released her she did not raise her head.

"My dear,—dear Bertie," she said, struggling with her tears. Then presently she sat down and fondled and stroked his thin small hand, soothing and coaxing him as well as she was able. If her heart could have broken, surely it would have broken then.

"Ah! he's thin enough now, Miss," observed Nurse, "even that sour stiff-backed lady would have a hard matter to call him fat. He's never been the same since she looked at him with those sharp ferret eyes of hers;" and then she moved away and went and seated herself by the fire, recounting the whole history to Anne, of not only her dislike for Miss Barker, but the reason of Bertie's apparent partiality for Frances; while the latter sat and listened to Bertie's talk, he wounding and opening her heart afresh at every word he uttered.

"Naughty Missy not to come to Bertie!" he said; and Frances could not tell him why she had stayed away; she could only remain silent and so allow him to conclude she had been unkind.

She took up some of the books Amy had left.

"Here are pretty pictures," she said, "shall Missy tell you some of the nice stories?"

"No, you mustn't. Mamma tells me them; I like her to, she tells them so pretty."

"Is there nothing Missy can do for you? Shall she sing you a song?"

"Mamma sings 'Gentle Jesus;' you don't know one so pretty do you?"

"No, Bertie, I am sure I don't."

Presently his little face brightened. "I should like you to get me kitty," he said.

"Yes. Who is kitty though?"

"That's what Master Bertie cried for the very day he was taken ill. It's the kitten he saw in the village, Miss," said Hannah.

"Bertie shall have kitty," said Frances, decidedly. "Missy will fetch her."

"Yes, she's big now, her mother won't cry," he said, as if not quite satisfied that she would not.

It had come on to rain, since the morning but what cared Frances for that; she scarcely stayed to snatch her hat and cloak before she was hurrying through it. What cared she for the rain or anything else? Her whole soul was with Bertie—the child who through her means was dying, and yet had clasped her neck so lovingly as she bent over him dismayed and appalled at the ravages illness had made in his sweet face.

There was only Matthew in the little parlour as she entered the cottage.

"You'd better not come in, Miss," he said "no offence, Miss, but my sister-in-law's been ill with the fever these days past."

"It can make no difference now," she said, bitterly, "that little boy I brought here only ten days ago is—is dying of the fever he caught here."

"Lord save us! Miss, dying?" said Matthew regretfully.

"He has just asked for the kitten he saw here. Will you let him have it? It may be," she said despairingly, seeing he hesitated, "only—only for a day, or for—a few hours, you would never have the heart to refuse a child's last wish." In days gone by she would have abused him for the hand he had had in causing poor Bertie's illness, and her misery. But it was different now.

"No, Miss, you're right, I haven't the heart to. What's the kitten's life worth next to the young master's. Here take it and welcome; though what the Missus'll say when she finds it's gone, and the old un a howling about the place I don't know, but there, it can't be helped," said Matthew philosophically, as Frances wrapped the kitten up carefully in her cloak, and hurried away.

The evening had closed in by the time Frances reached the Park again. She hastily changed her wet things, and went at once to Bertie's room, but her heart misgave her, as, going down the long corridor, she saw Anne seated on the ledge of the large window, with the traces of tears on her face.

"I am not too late?" she asked.

"I don't know," replied Anne. "He is very, very weak. I could not bear to stay."

Frances went on, Robert, as well as Amy, was in the room. He moved a little on one side to allow Frances to come near. "Bertie, my boy," he said, "Missy has brought you Kitty."

Frances leant over, and placed it beside him.

He opened his eyes feebly, then took the kitten so full of life, and nestled it to his side.

"Bertie is very sick," he said, weakly, as he tried to murmur his thanks.

This was the first time he had spoken of feeling ill. How pitifully his little childish words smote upon the hearts of his sad, sorrowing parents.

"Bertie is very sick," he said again. "I think Bertie is going to die. Poor Bertie!"

His mother's tears fell like rain. "God will take care of my boy for me," she said. "My boy, my precious Bertie!"

"Yes; but you mustn't cry, you and Papa, and Hannah."

Robert's face was wet with tears, while old Hannah sat away in a corner, with her face covered up in her apron, sobbing audibly; but she stifled her sobs upon this, his—might be—last request.

"God bless you, Bertie," said Frances, in a broken voice, ere she went away.

"Good night," he said. "You may have my top, for bringing me Kitty. Papa will get it for you."

And then he turned his head away wearily, and begged his mother to hush him in her arms to sleep. Robert lifted him gently, and laid him close to Amy. She drew him near, nearer still to her poor breaking heart, but she dared not press her lips to his, lest she should draw away the feeble breath, already coming so faintly, growing fainter and fainter every moment.

"Kitty must go back to her mother," he said. "Take care of Kitty—pretty Kitty."

But soon he grew too weak to heed even Kitty, and could only murmur short broken sentences about Papa, Mamma, and sometimes Missy.

Presently he roused again. "Don't cry, Papa, Mamma—Kiss Bertie—Bertie's very sick. Tell Hannah to bring a light—Bertie wants to see you."

Alas! his eyes had grown dim. He could no longer distinguish those he loved best, those who could scarcely answer his cry for their tears. They brought a light, old faithful Hannah did.

"Can you see me, my own darling?" asked Amy.

"No—no," he murmured, and his eyes closed gently, his breathing became more gentle still; once more he said, lovingly, "Dear Papa,—Dear Mamma," and then—he slept.

"Don't disturb him, Robert," sobbed Amy to her husband, who was kneeling near.

But Bertie had gone to a sleep from which there was no awaking.

Bertie, little loving Bertie, was dead.

"Softly thou'st sunk to sleep,
From trials rude and sore;
Now the good Shepherd, with His sheep
Shall guard thee evermore."

CHAPTER XIII

JANE'S STORY

"An old, old woman cometh forth, when she hears the people cry;
Her hair is white as silver, like horn her glazed eye.
'Twas she that nursed him at her breast, that nursed him long ago.
She knows not whom they all lament, but soon she well shall know;
With one deep shriek she through doth break, when her ear receives their wailing,
'Let me kiss my Celin ere I die—Alas! alas for Celin!'"
LOCKHART'S SPANISH BALLADS

The news of the sad death at the park spread like wildfire through the quiet, little village, and soon reached the turnpike gate, where Jane was fast recovering from the fever that had proved so fatal to poor Bertie. She, like Frances, moaned and wept when she heard of it; like her, her heart cowered and shrank within her; and for three days she could scarcely be persuaded to eat or drink, or say a word to anyone. Day after day she lay in her bed with her face steadily turned away from her sister, who as usual, tried to worry her into a more reasonable frame of mind, but finding it useless, left her to herself, and called her sullen; but it was not so, Jane's heart had been touched and softened ever since the unfortunate day of Bertie's visit; he had done more towards bringing repentance to that guilty heart than years of suffering had been able to accomplish; for Jane had suffered, suffered from the weight of a secret, that at times well-nigh made her as crazy as Marks imagined her to be. It was this terrible secret that had made her so silent and strange, this that had driven her neighbours to look upon her as half-witted. But she wanted no one's pity, no one's consolation, had steeled and hardened her heart against it, and let her life pass on and wither in its lone coldness. As she had lived, so she might have died, smothering all remorse, driving back each repentant feeling as it swept past her; might have died—but for Bertie's visit. Since then, the firm will to resist the good had been shaken; she was not only weak from the effects of the fever, but inwardly weak; weak at heart, weak in spirit. She battled with the repentant feelings so foreign to her, fought against what she had been a stranger too for so long, but it was all in vain; she resisted with a will, but it was a feeble will, and in the end the good triumphed, and Jane was won.

One morning, the fourth since Bertie died, Mrs. Marks took up Jane's breakfast as usual, and placed it on a chair by the bed-side.

"Here's a nice fresh egg," said she, "what you don't often see, this time of the year, I wish it might strengthen your lips, as well as your stomach. I'm sick of seeing you lie there with never a word. I'd rather a deal have a bad one, than none at all," and she drew back the curtains, and stirred up the freshly-lit fire.

"I'm ready and willing to speak," replied Jane, "though God forgive me, it's bad enough, as you say, what I have to tell."

Mrs. Marks was startled, not only at Jane's addressing her after so long a silence, but at the changed voice, so different to the usual reserved, measured tone, and short answers given in monosyllables. But she took no notice, and merely said,—

"What's the matter? Ain't the breakfast to your liking?"

"It's better than I deserve," was the reply.

Mrs. Marks was more amazed than before. "You don't feel so well this morning, Jane," said she, kindly, "the weakness is bad on you, like it was on me; but, please God, you'll get round fast enough, never fear. Here!" and she placed the tray on the bed, "take a sup of the tea, and I'll put a dash of brandy in it; that'll rouse you up a bit, I'll be bound."

Jane made no resistance, but as Mrs. Marks put down the cup, she placed her hand on hers, and said, "You won't think me crazy, Anne, if I ask you to send and beg young Master Robert to come and see me?"

"Don't you know he's been dead these four days past? There—there, lie still, and don't be a worriting yourself this way; your head ain't strong yet."

"It's stronger and better than it's been many a long day. Anne, I must see Master Robert, not the dead child, but the young Squire. I've that to tell him that'll make his heart ache, as it has mine, only there's sin on mine—sin on mine," said she, sitting up in bed, and rocking herself about.

"Then don't tell it. What's the use of making heart aches?"

"I can't bear the weight of it any longer. I must tell. Ever since I saw that child I've been striving against it; but it's no good—no good. I can't keep the secret any longer, Anne. I dare not. If I do it'll drive me clean out of my mind."

"Just you answer me one question, Jane. Is it right to tell it? Can any good come of it?"

"Yes, so help me God. It can! It will!"

"Then," replied Mrs. Marks, "I'll send Matthew at once; mother and I always thought there was something had driven you to be so strange when you left your place up at the Park fifteen years ago."

Jane laid herself down and covered up her face, while with a troubled sigh Mrs. Marks went below to seek her husband.

Matthew was surprised and confounded when bidden go up to the Hall and fetch the Squire.

"What!" he said, "are yer gone clean crazy as well as Jane! It's likely I'll go and fetch the Squire at the bidding of a 'dafty.' How do I know, but what it's a fool's errand he'll come on?"

But reason as he would, his words had no weight with Mrs. Marks, and Matthew had to go in the end, though with a more misgiving heart and rueful countenance than when he had gone to the young doctor's.

There was little occasion for misgivings on Matthew's part, Mr. Linchmore received him kindly, and promised to call at the turnpike during the day.

What setting to rights of the cottage there was when Marks returned with the news! It was always tidy and clean, but now for the especial honour of the Squire's visit all its corners were ransacked and everything turned topsy-turvy. Mrs. Marks was still unable to help much in the work, but she dusted and tidied the cups and saucers, and knick-knacks, although they had not seen a speck of dust for days, and certainly not since she had been downstairs again; Sarah's arms ached with the scrubbing and scouring she was made to do in a certain given time, while her mistress stood by, scolding and finding fault by turns. Nothing was done well, or as it ought to be done; but then, as the girl said, Mrs. Marks was so finicking, there was no pleasing her, she should be glad enough when she was able to do the work for herself, and she could go home to her mother.

When Mr. Linchmore came, he scarcely rested in the newly swept parlour at all, but desired at once to be shown to the sick woman's room. With many apologies from Mrs. Marks at her sister's inability to rise and see him, she preceded him up stairs.

Jane was sitting propped up in bed with pillows, her pale face looking paler and more emaciated than usual. Mr. Linchmore's heart was touched with pity as he noted the care-worn, prematurely old face, with its deep lines telling of sorrow or sin. Sin! Surely if this woman's life had been sinful, what had he, with his strict principles of right, to do with such as her? What had she—as Marks assured him—to tell, that nearly concerned himself? His heart reverted to his mother. Was it of her she would speak? of her whose ungovernable temper had driven his father to seek with his children that happiness abroad that had been denied him at home? But then his mother had been mad, at least he had been taught to think that the one excuse for her strange conduct. How severe and tyrannical she had been, not only to his brother and himself, but to that sweet, uncomplaining sister, whose life had been, he truly believed, shortened through her violence, and yet again, when the passion was over, how fiercely loving, how vehemently passionate in her cravings for her children's love, which she alienated from her more and more each day. No; others might love and reverence the name of mother, but Mr. Linchmore's heart was stirred with no such feelings; only a vague sense of fear, a nameless dread of evil came across him as he fancied it might be of her Jane had to speak.

He drew near, and bent down kindly. "I fear you have been very ill," he said, "with the same fever that has wrought such desolation in my home."

"Yes, sir, I have been ill—am ill; but now it's more from remorse; from the guilt of a wicked, cruel heart, than this same fever you speak of."

There was a pause. Jane spoke with difficulty, her breath came quick and short, as though her heart laboured heavily under the load of sin she spoke of.

"Turn more to the light," she said, "so that I may see your face. So—that is well. Still like your mother, strangely like, with none of her hard passions or cruel hate. Your love might be fierce, burning, and strong, but unlike her you would sacrifice your own happiness to secure the well being of the one you love. Had she done so, what misery to her, what misery to me might have been spared?"

"Did you know my mother?" asked Mr. Linchmore.

"Tell him, Anne," said Jane, as Mrs. Marks held some wine and water to her pale lips, that seemed too feeble to utter another word.

"If you please, sir," said Mrs. Marks, dropping her deepest curtsey, "this is Tabitha, my sister 'Tabitha Jane,' who was brought up so kindly by your lady mother; but there, I don't wonder you don't remember her. I had a hard matter to myself, when I went over to Dean to fetch her, come four years ago this next Christmas."

"Tabitha! This Tabitha! The pale, meek girl, who bore so uncomplainingly what we boys resented. Can this be Tabitha?"

"Yes," replied Jane. "It can. It is. The weight of a guilty secret has ploughed my face with these deep furrows. Call me not meek; I was anything but that, I was a sinful, wicked woman. Oh! I have much to tell: much that has been locked up in my heart for more than thirty years. How I have suffered under the burden that at last has grown too heavy for me to bear, and I sink under its load, must divulge it; must have her forgiveness, ere I die!"

"Your words fill me with a foreboding of evil," replied Mr. Linchmore. "Think well before you speak, Tabitha. Is it necessary that this secret, sinful as you say it is, should be divulged. Does it concern, does it benefit those living?"

"If it did not, I would never speak it, but struggle on with its sorrow, till I died. No hard, and cruel as my mistress was, not from Tabitha should come the tale that will denounce her and her evil ways."

"She was my mother, Tabitha," said Mr. Linchmore, as if reproaching her harshness.

"True, she was. I do not forget it; still I must speak, must tell of her sin and mine, for it is sin, fearful sin. I would, for your sake, Master Robert, that it were otherwise; but when I tell of my wrong-doing, with mine must come hers. It must. Justice must be done. The mother's craving, broken heart must be healed."

"God forbid that I should be the one to stand in the way. Speak, Tabitha! but be as merciful as you can; remember you speak of one whose memory ought to be dear to me. I will steel my heart to hear—and bear."

"Do so," she said. "It is a long story. I must go back to the days when I was a child, and your mother, Miss Julia, took me away from my home to hers. She was of an imperious will and proud nature; her mother had died at giving her birth, and her father had never controlled her in any way. She was as wild and wayward as the trees that grew in the forest near here, when they were shaken by the wind. With her, to ask was to have, and when she brought me home and declared her intention of bringing me up, and making a companion and plaything of me, no objection was raised, and she petted and scolded me by turns, as it suited her haughty will. At first I disliked her, then feared, and at length loved, worshipped her, as some beautiful spirit. Her father died; but then it was too late to save his child, or let others teach her wild spirit lessons of meekness and obedience; then your grandmother came and took us both away to live in her own home. She was a widow, with two sons, the eldest not quite so old as Miss Julia.

"A change came over your mother. She loved. Loved the eldest of the two, your father; loved as only she could love, with all the wild, impetuous passion of her nature. It would have been strange had he not loved her in return—so beautiful, so wayward, so bright a being as she was then. They were engaged to be married, and, I believe, had they married then all would have gone well, and perhaps the evil that followed been averted. But they did not marry, they tarried—tarried until another girl, a niece, was left desolate, and she too came to Brampton."

Jane, or Tabitha, paused for a moment, then went on more slowly,

"She was, I believe, an angel of goodness, as pure as she was fair, and as meek and gentle as your mother was ungovernable. From this time nothing went right. Your father and my mistress had words together oftener than formerly; but while she wept and lamented in secret, he would seek Miss Mary, and pour out his wounded heart to her. By degrees Miss Julia grew to learn it, and became jealous. Then, with the fierceness of her nature, she would storm and rave if she but saw Master Robert speaking to her; and yet, when the angry fit was over, be as humbly loving, as passionately sorry.

"Things could not go on like this for ever. I believe her temper was fairly wearing out your father's love, and that he would gladly have turned over to Miss Mary if he could; but I, who was set as a watch and a spy over the poor young thing—she was eighteen years younger than your mother—saw that her heart was another's, even young Mr. Archer's, who was part tutor, part companion to your father's younger brother. How I hated her then—for I had dared to love him myself—and determined on her ruin! How I hid the secret that would have made Miss Julia so happy in the deepest recesses of my heart, and urged my mistress on to believe that Miss Mary loved Master Robert!"

Again Jane paused, then continued as she turned her face away from Mr. Linchmore, who was listening intently to her,

"One morning, I remember it well,—I had quietly wrought Miss Julia up to such a pitch of frenzy, that I believe she would have stopped at nothing to accomplish the removal of her hated rival,—the door was suddenly flung open by your father; his face was pale, and he was evidently labouring under strong excitement. 'Julia,' he said, 'do you still wish to be my wife?'

"There was no need of a reply, could he not see the sudden light in her eyes, the quick bright flash that spread like wildfire over her face.

"That day week they were married, and went away from Brampton for a time.

"I remained behind with my enemy, watching and waiting; but I could do her no harm. Your grandmother loved her as the apple of her eye. I could see Miss Julia—now Mrs. Robert Linchmore,—was as nothing to her. Then I tried to cause a quarrel between her and young Mr. Archer; in vain; they loved too well, my arts were useless, my plans and wishes powerless.

"Your parents returned. A year passed away, and then you were born; but I could see your father was not happy. He still loved Miss Mary, strive as he would against it, while your mother treated her like a dog.

"Another year, and your sister was born; but things went worse. Your mother was no sooner up and about again than your uncle's health failed terribly, and he and Mr. Archer went abroad.

"Six months passed, during which your mother grew more insanely jealous of Miss Mary, and more tyrannical. She bore it all uncomplainingly; but I saw that she worried and fretted in secret, and grew thinner and thinner every day.

"One morning I went hastily into her room, and found her working a baby's cap, which she hurriedly thrust on one side as I entered; but my suspicions were aroused at her evident confusion, and glancing at her, her sin—if sin it was, became evident to my eyes, and I flew, rather than walked to my mistress's room. The scene that followed between her and Miss Mary I will not describe; but through it all—although she did not deny the imputation we cast on her,—she vowed she was innocent, and Mr. Archer's lawful wife. I believed her then. I know she told the truth now.

"That night she fled from the Park, while your father left soon after to join his brother, declaring he would never live with his wife again until she had done Miss Mary justice. Your grandmother never recovered the shock of all these terrible doings, she took Miss Mary's sin to heart. I don't think she believed it: but she sorrowed, and refused to be comforted, and soon after died. Then news reached us of Mr. Archer's death."

Jane stopped again, and lay back feebly against the pillows.

"With the news of his death came a letter, addressed, in his handwriting, to Miss Mary. I recognised the writing, and kept the letter, mad as it made me to read those loving words of his written to another. She never had the letter, or her marriage lines, which were with it."

"Wretched woman!" said Mr. Linchmore, sternly. "Had you no heart—no mercy?"

"No, none. And now I must hasten to close, for I am weak and faint. I told no one of the letter, but tracked, by my mistress's order, Miss Mary. I found her at last. She had heard of her husband's death, for she wore widow's mourning, and looked heart-broken. She was poor, too, with only the small annuity old Mrs. Linchmore had been able to leave her; for her husband, Mr. Archer, had not, I believe, a farthing to give her at his death; but what cared I for that. I took away the one tie that bound her to this earth—I took her child."

"That was not my mother's sin," said Mr. Linchmore, interrupting her. "Thank God for that!"

"Stop! Don't interrupt me! I did it, because she bade me do it. I don't think then I should have done it else, because he was dead, and my heart did not feel so hard as it had done, and I should have told my mistress how I had belied Miss Mary to her, had I dared summon the courage to do so; but I dreaded to think of her anger at being deceived. Well, enough, I took the child. He was a lovely, sweet infant, gentle and fair like his mother had been, and I could not find it in my heart to do the evil with him my mistress wished; for her heart could not but feel savage at the thought of his being her husband's child. So I kept him hid away till long after I had stolen him; then I carried him to Mr. Vavasour, a kind, mild looking, middle-aged gentleman, who had often visited the Park at one time; but now, ever since Mrs. Robert had been left in possession, never came.

"Mr. Vavasour refused to take the child at first, but I pleaded so hard; I told him what the boy's fate would be if he turned a deaf ear to my entreaties; that the mother hated him as a love child, and that the knowledge of his birth would bring sin and shame upon her, and much more beside, and in the end he consented to adopt him,—and did. Four years after this, your father returned home, and things went on more smoothly; your brother Charles was born, and my mistress seemed at last happy, and her restless spirit satisfied; but her temper, at times, was as bad as ever, and I don't believe, at heart, she was happy with the weight of the sin she thought she had been guilty of, on her conscience. How Miss Mary came to guess we had aught to do with her boy, I know not. But about a year after your brother's birth she came and taxed us with the theft. How altered she was! Grief and the mother's sorrow had done their work surely, and I scarcely dared look on the wreck I had helped to make.

"She told us that the loss of her child had driven her mad, and that for months she had been watched and looked after. She conjured us—implored—all in vain; my mistress denied our guilt, and defied her; but your father believed the poor, sorrowing, frantic creature, and never spoke to his wife after, but left her, taking his children with him.

"He never saw your mother again.

"My mistress bore up bravely after he was gone. None guessed of her desolated heart, or that it still loved so passionately. During the five years that followed, I scarce know how she lived; I could see her heart was fast breaking, and that all her hope in life was gone. She grew more tyrannical than ever; there was not one of the few servants we had but did not fear her and think her mad. She would go down the small staircase that led from her room out into the park, and roam for hours at night. As she grew weaker and weaker, and I felt she would die, my heart relented more and more. I could not bear to witness her misery. Then I owned the boy was alive, and begged and implored her to let us find him and restore him to his mother; I dared not say I knew where he was, or that he was not her husband's child; but she resisted my entreaties with violence, and made me swear I never would tell what we had done. She grew worse and worse; but struggled on, defying every thing and everyone. I had a hard matter to get her to see the young doctor even.

"One night she was so weak she would lay on a mattress on the floor, not having the strength to get into bed; as I sat by her side and watched, she fell into a deep sleep. Soon after, I heard steps coming up the secret stairs; I needed no one to tell who that was—my heart whispered it was Miss Mary long before she stood before me. She never said a word, but sat away on the other side of my mistress. My heart shuddered as I looked at her; she was more altered than ever; her hair was quite grey, such lovely fair hair as it had been!—the softness of her face was gone; the sweet gentle look had gone too, and a painful frown contracted her forehead. While I gazed, I forgot Miss Mary, and could think of nothing but the angry, bereaved, half-crazed Mrs. Archer. I knew then, that those who had injured her had no mercy to expect at her hands, and I felt afraid of her, and yet I dared not bid her go, but wished my mistress would tell her the truth when she awoke from that death-like slumber. I prayed she might,—for what harm could that angry mother do to a dying woman? But my prayer was not answered. I forgot, when I breathed it, my own sinfulness,—forgot, even, that if vengeance came at all, it would fall on me; and, if I had thought of it, I would not have stayed the truth from being told then. I swear I would not. I was too miserable. God knows, I would have told, myself, but for the sake of my oath, and that angry look on Mrs. Archer's face; it tied my tongue.

"When my mistress roused, I shall never forget her anger at seeing Mrs. Archer. She heaped a storm of abuse on her head, while Mrs. Archer prayed and wept by turns; promising even to bless those who had robbed her, if they would only give her back her lost treasure. 'Give me back my boy!' was the ever repeated, fervent, agonized cry of her heart."

"She did not, could not plead in vain," cried Mr. Linchmore. "No, no, my mother was not so bad as that!"

"Nerve your heart to bear the rest, it is soon told. Tears streamed from her eyes in vain. She pleaded in vain. My mistress was obdurate. 'I die,' she said, 'but I die with the knowledge that you, who have been the one stumbling-block of my life, and have made it miserable, and a curse to me, are even more wretched than myself, for I will never speak the word that will make you happy. The secret shall die with me.' When Mrs. Archer saw that all her pleading was vain, she grew frantic, and scarce knew what she said in her madness. My mistress grew even more angry than she. I strove to quiet her, to stay the torrent of words, but her whole frame shook with angry passion as she sat up unaided on the bed. I saw it was too much for her, tried to avert it, but, before she could utter a word, she fell back again. 'God have mercy upon me!' she cried, and with that one prayer on her lips she died. I know no more, I fell insensible, as Mrs. Archer, seeing her last hope gone, gave one terrible fearful cry of despair."

Jane paused. "I have no more to tell," she said feebly, "I thank God I have told it; I never would, but for the sake of the curl. I daren't let it lie in my bosom else."

It was many minutes before Mr. Linchmore could speak, and then his voice quavered and shook, and his hands trembled as he drew them from his face, and asked, "Where is the mother—the child?"

"Mr. Vavasour, up at the Park now, is the child. Mrs. Archer, the mother, lives down in the wood, yonder. I have never seen her but once since I came here; I have fled the sight of her. You know her as Mrs. Grey. You will see her, tell her what I say; she will believe it fast enough."

"Your sin has been fearful; God knows it has," said Mr. Linchmore, trying to speak composedly.

"I have been a sinful woman; humbly I acknowledge it, but if my sin has been great, what has been its punishment? Look in my face, you will read the traces of suffering there; but my heart, you cannot read that; and that has suffered tenfold."

"What proof have you of all you say?"

"Mrs. Archer will need none," she said, "if you tell her Tabitha swears it's the truth. But here's the letter with her marriage lines," she added, taking one from under her pillow, "many's the time I've been tempted to destroy it, but somehow daren't do it; and here's another old Mr. Vavasour gave me to keep, stating when and how we had received the child; in it you'll find the beads he wore round his neck when I stole him."

"Are these all the proofs you can give?"

"No. I've a stronger one than this. The child had a dark mark on his arm, it could not have escaped his mother's eye; it can't have worn away, it must be there now, and that'll tell who he is plainer and better than any words of mine. "Are you going?" she asked, as Mr. Linchmore rose.

"Yes, the sooner I tell the dreadful tale the better, if my heart does not break the while. Have you anything else to say? Would you wish to see Mrs. Archer?"

"Oh! no! no!" she said, "don't send her; I know I've no mercy to expect at her hands, I showed her none. She'll hate and curse me, may be."

"You have little mercy to expect from one you have so deeply injured," replied Mr. Linchmore, "but I will see you again, or send another to speak with you. My thoughts are in a whirl, and I cannot—I feel incapable of talking to you today."

"And must I be satisfied with this?" said Jane, "well, I submit; I have not deserved a kind word from you. Still I loved your mother."

"She would have been better for your hate," he replied, moodily, "but in case I should not come again, I leave you my forgiveness for the evil you have helped to work, though it goes hard against my heart to give it; but you have a higher mercy to ask for than mine. I trust you have implored that already—humbly and sincerely."

"God knows I have," replied Jane, feebly.

Mr. Linchmore went slowly from the cottage, scarcely heeding Mrs. Marks' curtseys and parting words, and struck across the fields towards the wood.

It was a sinful, grievous tale, the one he had just heard, and a bitter trial to him, not only to listen to it, but to know that from his lips must come the words to denounce his mother,—proclaim her guilt. It went bitterly against him, although he had no loving reverence for his parent; still, it must be done, his misery must make another's happiness, must restore the son to his mother. He hesitated not, but walked firmly on, perhaps angrily.

At the corner of the wood he met Marks, but his heart was too full for words with any one, and he merely acknowledged the passing touch of his hat, as he turned off into one of the by-paths, a nearer cut to Mrs. Grey's cottage. Just as he was about to emerge again into the broad beaten path, scarcely a dozen yards from the cottage, he stopped for a moment to collect his thoughts. A slight rustle in the bushes near attracted his attention. He looked up, and saw a man, gun in hand, creeping cautiously out of the underwood.

At another time Mr. Linchmore would have confronted him at once, but now he allowed him to pass on unmolested. The man crossed the path, reached the opposite side, and was about plunging again into the bushes, when Robert Vavasour's hand arrested his footsteps.

"What do you here with that gun, my man?" he asked.

It was growing dusk, almost twilight in the wood; still, as the man suddenly turned his face full on Vavasour, the latter exclaimed,

"Ah! it is you, is it? You villain! you don't escape me this time."

A short quick scuffle, a bright flash, a loud report, and Robert Vavasour dropped to the ground.

With a great oath, the man sprang up, but ere he could stir one step, Mr. Linchmore's hand was upon him. A desperate struggle ensued; but a stronger arm, a more powerful frame, contended with him now, and in a few moments he lay prostrate, but still struggling, on the ground.

"Could you be content with nothing less than murder?" asked a voice, sternly.

Mr. Linchmore shuddered as he recognised "Goody Grey."

"For God's sake, Mrs. Grey, go and seek help for the wounded man yonder."

"Why should I?" she exclaimed, fiercely. "I will never stir a finger for you or yours. I have sworn it."

"It is your son, your long-lost son! Tabitha bid me tell you so."

Goody Grey,—or rather Mrs. Archer's,—whole frame trembled violently; she quivered and shook, and leant heavily on her staff, as though she would have fallen.

"Fly!" he continued. "For God's sake, fly! Rouse yourself, Mrs. Archer, and aid your son."

"My son!" she repeated, softly and tenderly, but as if doubting his words.

Again Mr. Linchmore implored her, again she heard those words "It is your son!" which seemed to burn her brain. But the power of replying, of moving, seemed taken from her.

A minute passed, and then the weakness passed away. Her eyes flashed, her face flushed, then blanched again, while with a mighty effort she drew up her tall figure to its utmost height, and proudly, but hurriedly, went over to where Robert lay.

She staunched the blood flowing from the wound, and tenderly knelt by his side and lifted his head gently on her bosom.

There was a slight break in the branches of the trees overhead, so that what little light there was, streamed through the gap full down on the spot where Mrs. Archer knelt.

She raised his coat sleeve, and baring his arm, bent down her head over it.

A moment after a wild cry rent the air, and rang through the wood.

"Oh! help! help!" she cried; "Oh! my son! my son!"

There was no need to cry for help; the sound of the gun had been heard, and the keepers came crowding to the spot, and with them, Marks.

A litter was soon constructed for the wounded man, and once more he was mournfully and sorrowfully borne away towards the Hall.

Marks drew near the captured poacher, now standing sullenly and silently near.

"Ah!" said Marks, as he was being led away, "I thought no good had brought farmer Hodge down here, four years ago. You'll may be swing for this, my lad; and break your father's heart, as you did your mother's, not so long ago."

With which consolatory remark, Marks went back to his cottage.

CHAPTER XIV

DESPAIR!

"Ah! what have eyes to do with sleep,
That seek, and vainly seek to weep?
No dew on the dark lash appears,—
The heart is all too full for tears."
L. E. L.

"The world's a room of sickness, where each heart,
Knows its own anguish and unrest,
The truest wisdom there, and noblest art,
Is his, who skills of comfort best,
Whom by the softest step and gentlest tone,
Enfeebled spirits own,
And love to raise the languid eye,
Where, like an angel's wing, they feel him fleeting by."
CHRISTIAN YEAR

Anne sat in the solitude of her own thoughts; not alone, for her husband was at a table near, busy with his morrow's sermon; but Anne, for once, did not mind the silence, she had many things to think of, many things that made her sad. First, the little dead child lying now so cold and still; then his poor, sorrowing, heart-broken mother, whom she had tried, but ineffectually, to comfort; and then the father, who ought to be the one earthly stay on which the wife's heart might lean, and whose love should wean away the sad remembrance, or soften the blow. But Anne had found out that a great gulf lay between husband and wife, though what had separated them baffled her utmost skill to discover.

Robert must love his wife passionately, else why had he lifted her so tenderly in his arms, as she lay insensible when the truth of her great loss broke upon her; why had he carried her away, and as he laid her on her own bed, bent so lovingly over her, murmuring, as he chafed her hands, "My poor, stricken darling. My own lost love;" and yet, when consciousness returned, how self possessed! how altered! kind and considerate as before, but the loving words, the loving looks were wanting. And Amy, who had seemed so happy only a month ago, surely more than grief for her boy had fixed that stony look on her face, and caused those tearless, woeful eyes.

Anne's thoughts grew quite painful at last; the eternal scratch of her husband's pen irritated her.

"Do put down your pen for a minute, Tom. I feel so miserable."

"In half a moment," he said. "There—now I am ready to listen. What was it you said?"

"That I was miserable."

"I do not wonder at it, there has been enough to make us all feel sorrowful."

"Yes, but it is more than the poor child's death makes me feel so."

"What else?" he asked.

"Why Amy herself, and then her husband."

"Let us pick the wife to pieces first, Anne."

"Oh! Tom, it is no scandal at all, but the plain truth. I wish it were otherwise," she said with a sigh.

"Well, begin at the beginning, and let me judge."

"You put it all out of my head. There is no beginning," she said crossly.

"Then the end," he replied.

"There is neither beginning nor end: you make me feel quite vexed, Tom."

"Neither beginning nor end? Then there can be nothing to tell."

"No, nothing. You had better go on with your sermon and make an end of that."

"I have made an end of it," he said, laughing, "and now, joking aside, Anne, what have you to say about Mrs. Vavasour?"

"If you are serious, Tom, I will tell you, but not else," she replied.

"I am serious, Anne; quite serious."

"Then tell me what is to be done with that poor bereaved Amy,—who has not shed a single tear since her child's death, four days ago now;—or her husband, who I verily believe worships her, and yet is as cold as a stone, and from no want of love on her part either, for I can see plainly by the way she follows him with her eyes sometimes, that she is as fond of him as—as—"

"You are of me," he said.

"Nonsense, Tom. They were so happy last time we came over to see them, that I cannot understand what has caused the change. Can you make any guess at all so as to help me? for oh! Tom, I would give the world to know."

"Curiosity again, Anne?"

"No, not so," she replied, "or if it is, it is in the right place this time; as I want to help them to make up the difference, whatever it is but do not see how I can manage it, when I am so totally in the dark. One thing I am certain of, Amy will die unless I can bring her to shed some tears, so as to remove that stony look."

"She has one hope, one consolation. Surely I need not remind my wife to lead her heart and thoughts gradually and gently to that."

"I have tried it, tried everything; but, Tom, there is no occasion whatever for preaching.

"Anne! Anne!"

"Yes, I know it's wrong to say so, but it is the truth notwithstanding; I feel something else should be tried. She is too submissive under the blow, too patient; not a murmur has escaped her lips, if there had, I should stand a better chance of seeing tears; but as it is there is no need of consolation. I verily believe she wants to die. And then that Frances, I sometimes think she has had something to do with it all; you know I always disliked that girl, and never thought she had a spark of feeling in her, until I saw her coming away from poor Bertie's room that sad evening, and a more woe-begone, remorseful face I never wish to see; and then see how distracted she has been since. Isabella tells me it is dreadful to be with her."

"Poor girl, I pity her with all my heart, she feels she has been mainly instrumental in bringing all this misery upon Mrs. Vavasour."

"I am sure," said Anne, more to herself than her husband, "she has a great deal more than Bertie's death to answer for; she nearly broke his mother's and Charley's heart four years ago, and I half believe she has had something to do with the husband's now."

"Be more charitable, Anne, and do not lay so many sins to her charge. That last is a very grievous one."

"Well," said his wife, rising, "after all my talk, Tom, you have not helped me one bit, I do believe I am going away more miserable than ever to that poor Amy."

"Things do look dark indeed, Anne," said he as he kissed her, "but we must hope in God's mercy all will be better soon; may He help you in your work of love with the poor heart-sorrowing mother."

As Anne went out she met Frances Strickland's maid, "If you please Ma'am, where shall I find Mr. Hall, my young mistress wishes to see him."

"I will tell him myself," said Anne, and back she went.

"Tom! Frances Strickland wishes to see you."

"To see me!" he exclaimed. "I have promised to walk as far as the turnpike with Linchmore. That woman from whom the child caught the fever sent to beg he would call on her some time this morning; he named two o'clock, and it is close upon that now. Will not Miss Strickland be satisfied with you as my substitute?"

"I never thought of asking, and, indeed, I should not like to. She might think I was jealous." Mr. Hall laughed outright.

"You are in such a dreadfully teasing mood this morning, Tom; I have no patience with you! Perhaps Frances is going to clear up all this mystery? I told you a moment ago I suspected she had had something to do with it, and now her remorse may be greater than she can bear; repentance may have come with her grief for poor Bertie. I only hope, if it is so, that she is not too late to make amends."

"Then I must make my excuses to Linchmore, and give up my walk," he said, with a sigh; "and go and hear what she has to say?"

"Yes, do, Tom, that will be so good of you. I will wait here, but do not be long, as this is your last day with me, you know."

As soon as Mr. Hall had gone, Anne half regretted that she had not done as he suggested, and seen Frances instead. Suppose she should try and sow dissension in his heart? Anne's face flushed hotly at the bare idea, then again she consoled herself with the thought that he would be sure to come and tell her if she did, for the sake of the love he bore for her; still Anne passed a fidgety, uncomfortable half hour ere he returned.

Mr. Hall's face was grave; graver than Anne ever remembered to have seen it, and she waited for him to speak first, and checked the impatient question already on her lips.

"It is worse than I thought, Anne, much worse. Your judgment did not lead you astray. She has separated husband and wife."

"Then she has told you all, Tom. Oh! how glad I am, not only for Amy's sake but for her own; it would have been so dreadful for her to have lived on upholding the falsehoods she must have told to work her ends."

"That is the worst part of the business, Anne, she has unfortunately told the truth, and, as far as I can see, the chance of reconciling those who ought to be heart and soul to each other is remote indeed. Time and the wife's love—you say she does love him—may, by God's grace, do much. I see nothing that you or I can do."

"Wretched girl! What has she told?"

"What Vavasour ought only to have heard from his wife's lips. Of her previous love for another and of their unfortunate meeting the day of her marriage."

"I always hoped she had told him," said Anne, clasping her hands despairingly. "The concealment was no sin on Amy's part, only weakness. But as for Frances, there can be no excuse for her. She has been cruelly, shamefully unkind, and revengeful!"

"She has; there is no denying it, but all through your friend's own fault; she nursed in her heart—which should have been as clear as day to her husband—a secret; and that one sin has brought in the end its own punishment, and while we blame Frances' culpable revenge, we must blame the wife's breach of faith and disloyalty."

"Oh, Tom, what hard words!" cried Anne, "poor Amy's has not been a guilty secret."

"No, but appearances are sadly against her, and we know nothing of what the husband thinks; even if he does believe her guiltless, he must naturally feel wounded at his wife's want of love and trust."

"Yes," replied Anne, sadly, "what you say is very just and true. Can nothing then be done? Nothing at all?"

"Frances is ready to make what atonement she can for her fault; it may help us a little, but very little, I fear. She has promised to tell Vavasour that her own jealousy and grief at being supplanted in another's love by his wife, determined her on being revenged; she cannot unsay what she has said, because it is the truth; but she who caused the breach may be allowed to plead for forgiveness for herself and the wife she has injured. The repentance is no secret, Anne; she desired me to tell you all, and beg you to plead for her with Mrs. Vavasour."

"Do you think I shall plead in vain, or that she will with Mr. Vavasour?"

"I trust not," he said, doubtfully; "the knowledge that his wife has not intentionally sinned, but only through fear of losing his love, and the conviction that she loves him may soften his heart."

"May; but I see you think it will be a long time first, and in the meantime Amy will break her heart. Oh! Tom, I don't believe he can be so cruel if he loves her; just now, too, when she is so heart broken, so sadly bereaved. Do make Frances tell Mr. Vavasour at once."

"I intended to have done so," he replied, "but Vavasour has gone out, so we must wait as patiently as we can until he returns. In the meantime, Anne, I will give you something to occupy your time and thoughts. I have promised Miss Strickland that you will ask Mrs. Vavasour's forgiveness for her. She says it is hopeless; but that cannot be," he said, as Anne thought, somewhat sternly; "you had better go at once and ask it; she who has sinned herself, and knows the repentant heart's craving for forgiveness, what hope can she have of pardon if she withholds hers from one who has sinned against her even seventy times seven."

Anne said not a word, but with desponding heart prepared to go.

"I have only an hour to spare," said Mr. Hall. "It is now three, and at four I must get ready to start home. I have ordered the pony-carriage at half-past."

"I shall be with you long before that," replied Anne, as she closed the door.

Amy sat just where Anne had left her only an hour ago; the same hopelessly despairing, fixed, death-like look on her face, which was as white as the shawl wrapped round her. As Anne looked, she wondered if Frances alone had wrought the sad change, while her heart sank within her at the apparently hopeless task her husband had imposed upon her, and she hesitated and faltered slightly ere she went at once, as was her wont, to the point in view. Her sister Julia would have brought the subject gradually round to Frances, but that was not Anne's way; she was, in fact, too impetuous, rushing headlong into a difficulty, facing the danger, and braving it with that strong, true heart.

"My husband has been to see Frances Strickland to-day, Amy."

There was no reply; Anne hardly expected any, but Amy raised her eyes, and looked hastily and inquiringly in her face. Anne took courage; perhaps the very fact of Amy's knowing another held her secret might open the floodgates of her heart.

"She hid nothing from Tom; told him all, everything, and is desperately sorry, as well she may be, for all the misery she has caused you."

"As well she may be," repeated Amy.

"She is repentant—truly repentant, Amy."

"I know it; have known it for days past," was the cold reply.

"She begs your forgiveness most humbly."

"I know that also, and have given it."

"She says otherwise, Amy," said Anne, rather puzzled.

"I have forgiven her for my darling's loss. But for the other; if she has dared tell you of it—of her cruelty, I never will. I have said so. Let us talk of something else."

"No, Amy, I must talk of this—only of this. Does not the very fact of her having owned her fault show how sincerely sorry she is. Think of Frances, the proud Frances, sueing for forgiveness; think how miserable, utterly miserable, she must be to stoop to that. How, almost broken-hearted! Surely, Amy, for the sake of her prayers—all our prayers, for the sake of the love your poor Bertie had for her, you will forgive her."

"No. Had my boy lived he would have avenged his mother's wrongs, and hated her, even as I do."

"Alas, Amy! You hate her. Your heart never used to be so cruel as this."

"No, it did not. She has made me what I am. Has she not pursued me with her revengeful cruelty for years? Has she not taken my only earthly hope from me, even my husband's love? And yet you wonder that I am changed—can ask me to forgive her."

"No, Amy, not taken your husband's love; he loves you still."

"If he did, I should not be sitting here, broken hearted and alone, with nothing but my own sorrowful thoughts, and—and you to comfort me."

"He will forgive you, and take you to his heart in time, Amy."

"Never! How can I convince him that I love him now? His very kindness chills me—so different to what it was; the changed tone of his voice tells me I have lost his love. He lives; yet is dead to me,—is mine, yet, how far off from me; and she who has wrought me all this misery, done all she has it in her power to do, now sues for forgiveness. Is it possible I can forgive, or clasp her hand in mine again?" The stony look was gradually relaxing, a slight, colour mantled her cheeks, and she concluded, almost passionately,— "No, Anne, I will not forgive her! Will not! Urge me no more. I cannot speak to her, much less see her again."

"And yet think of her kindness to your boy. He remembered it, and gave her his top when he was dying."

"You are cruel to remind me of it," said Amy, taking some fresh flowers off the table she was wreathing into a cross for Bertie; her last sad, mournful, but loving work.

Anne drew near, and passed her arm lovingly round her waist.

"This," said she, touching the cross, "is the emblem of your faith; and what does it not teach? It tells you that He who died on it to save us miserable sinners forgave even his murderers. 'Forgive them, Father, for they know not what they do.' Not only forgave them, but excused their faults, and interceded for them. Amy, if this is your belief, if you indeed take Him as your model, then forgive, even as he forgave; if not, never dare to lay this sweet white cross on your dead child's breast; would he not now, a pure and immortal spirit, sorrow at his mother's want of faith, and hardness of heart."

Amy's head drooped; every particle of angry colour fled from her face, while the hard, unforgiving look gradually died away as Anne went on.

"Spare me, Anne! Spare me!" she said.

"No, Amy dear, I must not, although it is as cruel to me to speak to you so harshly as it is for you to listen, and believe me when I say that your child, your little Bertie, was never further off from you than now, when you forgive not another her trespasses, even as you hope your own will be forgiven. Oh, Amy! think—can you kneel night and morning, and repeat that one sentence in your prayers, knowing how utterly you reject it? Can you press a last loving kiss on your child's pure lips, knowing how you are hugging one darling sin at your heart? Amy, Amy! listen to my warning voice, and forgive even as you hope to be forgiven," and Anne bent forward and lovingly kissed her forehead.

The spell was broken: as Anne gently withdrew her lips, tears welled up from the poor overcharged heart, and Amy wept,—wept an agony of tears.

"Oh, Anne!" she said presently, "Stop! stop! You will crush my heart. I will forgive her, for the sake of my boy, my darling Bertie."

"God bless you, dear Amy," replied Anne, delighted at not only having gained her wish, but at the sight of the tears she was shedding. "These tears will do you good. My heart has ached to see, day after day, your cold, calm, listless face."

Anne could have cried herself for very joy, to think how nicely things were coming round; as for Robert Vavasour, of course, with Frances to plead for forgiveness, and his wife to throw her arms round his neck, and vow she loved him better than all the world beside, his stubborn heart must give in; so Anne sat quite contented and happy by Amy's side, and let her weep on. Then, as her watch told her the hour for her husband's departure drew near, she soothed and comforted Amy's weak, quivering heart, as well as she was able, and went—for Amy would go at once—as far as Frances Strickland's room door with her, then flew, rather than walked, to her own. Mr. Hall, carpet-bag in hand, was just coming out, and nearly ran over her as she burst open the door.

"Is it you, Anne?" he said, as he staggered back, "I thought, at least, it was a cannon ball coming."

"It's only my head," she said, laughing, "I was in such a hurry. I felt I should be too late. I ought to have packed up your things before I went to Amy."

"Ought is a very fine word, but it is generally a late one."

"I am so sorry," said Anne in a repentant voice.

"My next wife shall never say she is sorry," he said smiling.

"What a hardened wretch she will be!"

"Not so," he replied, "she shall be the most gentle, submissive creature in the world; everything shall be in its right place, and there shall be a right time for everything."

"Yes, Tom, I know I do try you dreadfully; but, all the same, you will never get another little wife to love you better than I do."

"True, Anne," he said, "or one that I could ever love as I love you."

"And now, Tom, do put down that horrid carpet-bag, I hate to feel you are going to leave me here even for a few days all by myself; and for the first time too. I can't think what I shall do without you."

"But it is more than half-past four," he replied.

"But not railway time, only the poor old pony's, and I am sure he will not mind waiting just to oblige his mistress."

Mr. Hall sat down, and placed her by his side. "And now, Anne," he said, "tell me what success you have had with Mrs. Vavasour? but do not make a long story of it, as I really must be away in another ten minutes."

"I had a hard matter to persuade her, Tom, but I managed it at last, and she is with Frances now. I feel so happy, because I am sure all will be right; poor Amy! how she did cry."

"She cried at last, then?"

"Heartily; and I know it will do her a world of good; she looked far happier when I left her than she has done for days."

"And now, Anne, I really must go and see after the pony, and settle the carpet bag, but I will come back once more, and say good-bye."

Ten minutes, twenty, slipped by, and Anne began to fear her husband had forgotten his promise; she wondered at his delay, and looked round to see if he had forgotten anything. His sermon, blotting book, small ink-bottle, all had gone. She turned to the chest of drawers and was ransacking them hurriedly, when she heard him come back.

"Why, Tom," she said, without turning round, "Here are all your handkerchiefs, every one of them! Don't talk of my carelessness after this," and she laughingly held them up as a trophy.

But her husband's face was white, so very white, that Anne's heart turned sick, and almost stopped beating.

With a faint cry she crept up to him, and with a timid, frightened look, gazed into his face.

"What is it?" she whispered, "are you ill? Oh! tell me! Tell me!"

"No, no. It's worse, Anne, worse," he murmured hoarsely.

"Oh! for God's sake tell me, Tom! or I shall die."

"It is Vavasour," he said, as he took her in his arms and held her to his heart. "Forgive me for having frightened you so, Anne. But Vavasour has been shot."

"Thank God you are well?" said Anne, bursting into tears, "But, oh, Amy! my poor darling Amy!"

CHAPTER XV

THE LAST OF LITTLE BERTIE

"She put him on a snow-white shroud,
A chaplet on his head;   And gathered only primroses
To scatter o'er the dead.

She laid him in his little grave—
'Twas hard to lay him there:
When spring was putting forth its flowers,
And everything was fair.

And down within the silent grave,
He laid his weary head;
And soon the early violets
Grew o'er his grassy bed.

The mother went her household ways,
Again she knelt in prayer;
And only asked of Heaven its aid
Her heavy lot to bear."
L. E. L.

On leaving Frances Strickland, Amy went to poor Bertie's room to lay the fair white cross in his coffin, and was bending down over her lost darling in an agony of tears which old Hannah vainly attempted to check, when the sudden, hasty gallop of a horse away from the stables struck her ear. It was the groom going for Dr. Bernard.

Amy's mind, already unnerved and unstrung, was easily alarmed.

"Alas! Hannah," said she, drawing near the darkened window "has any accident happened that some-one rides so furiously?"

"My dear Miss Amy," replied Hannah, forgetting in her tender pity Amy's new tie, and thinking of her only as the wee child she had so lovingly nursed on her knee, "you must not be frightening yourself this way. What should have happened? God knows you've had enough to worry you. There, don't tremble that way, but let go the blind, and come away from the window."

But Hannah's persuasions and entreaties were alike useless. Amy, with fluttering anxious heart still looked out through the deepening shadows of the day, now fast drawing into evening.

Her husband was away. Oh! how she wished she could see him or hear his firm, yet for the last few days mournful step. Her heart had taken a strange fear, which she could neither shake off, nor subdue; a trembling nervous dread of some fast-coming evil.

Mr. Linchmore came up the drive, and for a moment a joyous thrill crept through her as she thought it was her husband; but no, he came nearer still, then disappeared up the terrace with Mr. Hall, and only the groom with the pony carriage was left, standing quietly as it had stood ever since she had so eagerly strained her eyes from the window.

Then once again—as it had done long, long ago—that strange, dull tramp from without smote her ear.

Meanwhile, Anne had nerved her heart as well as she could, and gone sorrowfully enough to break the sad news to Amy.

Not finding her either in her own or Miss Strickland's room, she guessed she was in poor Bertie's: besides, she missed the white cross.

"Oh! Tom!" she said, going back to her husband, "What can I do? She is with her poor dead child, surely I need not; and indeed I feel I cannot go there and tell her."

"No," replied Mr. Hall, after a moment's consideration, "perhaps it will be best to try and get Vavasour into his room without her knowledge. I think with caution it might be done. Go and remain near the nursery door, Anne; they will not have to pass it on their way up, and I will go and enjoin silence and caution."

Anne sped away, and took up the post assigned her, listening eagerly, yet fearfully for the sound of the muffled footsteps, and straining her ears in the direction of the stairs, so that Amy stood before her, almost ere she had heard the opening of the door.

Anne saw at once Amy guessed at some disaster, for she gently but firmly resisted Anne's endeavours to arrest her footsteps, and said, while she trembled excessively,

"My husband! Is he dead?"

"No. Oh no! Amy darling."

Then as Amy would have passed on, she whispered, in a voice she in vain attempted to steady,

"Don't go there Amy! pray don't!"

But Amy paid no heed, but went and stood at the head of the stairs on the landing.

In vain Mr. Linchmore and Mr. Hall gently tried to induce her to leave; she was deaf to reason.

"I must be here," she murmured, with pale compressed lips, "I must be here."

There was no help for it; so they bore him up slowly past her on into his room, and laid him on the bed, and there left him.

"Do you think he will die?" asked Amy, fearfully, as she grasped old Dr. Bernard's arm tightly, some time later as he sat by the fire.

How he felt for her, that old man, she so young, and so full of sorrow. He drew her hand in his, and stroked it gently and kindly.

"Trust in God, and hope," was the reply.

"I do trust," she replied, firmly. "I will try and hope. But, oh! I love him! I love him!" she said.

And this was the one cry for ever, if not on her lips, at her heart.

She sat by the pale insensible form day after day; she knew no fatigue, heeded not the lapse of time. Once only she stole away to imprint a last loving kiss on her dead Bertie's lips ere they bore away the little coffin to its last resting-place in the cold churchyard; then silently she went back to her old place by her husband's bed-side. Would he die without one word? without recognising his wife who loved him so entirely? Oh! surely he would speak one loving word if but one; give her one loving look as of old. She felt that her boy's death was as nothing in comparison to this.

As the love deep and strong welled up in her heart, she felt half frightened at its intensity, while it crept with a great fear as she whispered over and over again, "He will die." If he would but speak; or say one word.

Alas! the words came at last, but only incoherent murmurings, indistinct unmeaning words. His eyes opened, and wandered about without knowledge, and though they rested on her, knew her not. His burning hands returned not the soft pressure, the loving touch, of hers. Would he die thus, and never know the deep love she had for him; the tenderness, devotion of her heart? She groaned in utter anguish and misery; but patiently sat on.

In vain they tried, those kind friends, to draw her away; or if they did succeed in persuading her to lie down on a mattress on the floor, her large mournful eyes never closed in sleep, but still kept watch on the one loved form; her heart ever fearing he would die—praying that he might not.

And Mrs. Grey, or rather Mrs. Archer, the newly-made mother; where was she? She kept watch, too, over her long-lost son, but without being the slightest help to the poor heart-broken wife, having apparently no thoughts, no words, no looks for anyone but the son who had been lost to her for so long. Fear mingled with her joy; fear like the wife's lest he should die.

Amy was told part of her story by Mr. Linchmore, and made no objection to the poor mother sharing her watch; she was her husband's mother, that was enough. What he loved, she would love.

Very silent and motionless Mrs. Archer sat. Amy sometimes wandered about restlessly, or gave way to passionate weeping now; but very patiently, very sorrowfully, the mother sat. They exchanged no words with each other, those two mournful watchers; Mrs. Archer had been told the young girl's relationship to her son, and sometimes her eyes rested lovingly on the pale, beautiful face.

When Amy went to take a last look at her boy, she took Mrs. Archer's hand, and drew her away with her, and together they had stood and gazed at the little white marble face. Amy said no word, but as Mrs. Archer moved away, she murmured,—

"Better thus, than lost. Lost for years."

The shock of all these events proved too much for Anne, and when her husband returned on the Tuesday morning he could not but notice how wan and pale she looked, and so excitable, that the least thing in the world upset her. Instead of the glad, but perhaps sober welcome he expected, she threw her arms round his neck, as she had done at parting, and burst into tears, which she had a hard matter to prevent ending in hysterics. Mr. Hall's soothing, gentle manner soon calmed her; but she was very nearly giving way again that same evening, when he urged her immediate return home.

"What! leave Amy, Tom, in all her trouble? Oh, no, never!"

"The worry and excitement is too much for you, Anne, I cannot shut my eyes to that fact, and must not allow you to sacrifice your health for the sake of your friend."

"My dear, dear husband, do let me stay?"

But the look on her husband's face convinced her that his resolution was taken, and inflexible. She ceased to coax and persuade, and bethought her what could be done. Frances Strickland was still weak and ill; besides, her companionship was not in any way to be desired for Amy.

"Have I not heard you, Anne," said Mr. Hall, as if answering her thoughts, "speak of some kind old lady, a great friend of Mrs. Vavasour's mother? Surely her aid as a companion, though not as a nurse, might be called upon now."

Of course. Why had not Anne thought of it?

In a few moments, with her usual haste, she was speeding away in search of Mrs. Linchmore, to beg her permission, before she invited Mrs. Elrington. It was given, though with Anne thought anything but a good grace, and the letter written and despatched, and Anne tried to appear content and satisfied that she was leaving; and doing right; and that Amy might not think it unkind. As she packed her box, she was forced to confess she was weak, and that it was perhaps as well she had a husband to look after her some times, and that Mr. Hall was right, as he always was, in wishing her to have rest.

The next few days passed much as the former ones to Amy, being, so to speak, a misery of doubt and hope; but on the morning of the third there came a change—a change for the better. Robert Vavasour slept. Not that dull, insensible sleep, a hovering between life and death, such as it had been when Amy first watched by him, but a soft, natural sleep; the breathing came faint, but regular; the face wore none of its former set, rigid look, but gradually grew into the old, old expression she loved so well. Then Amy knew her husband was better; God had been very merciful; he would not die and leave her desolate and alone; she knew it long before old Dr. Bernard's anxious face wore that pleasant, cheery smile, or Mrs. Archer had thanked God so fervently on her knees.

Robert Vavasour slept, slept for hours; and during that long sleep Amy and Mrs. Archer arranged their future plans; her husband must not be told of his mother's existence yet; in the first place, he was not strong enough to bear any excitement, and in the next, the poor, fond mother hoped to win a little of his kindly feeling, if not his love, before she held him to her heart.

"I hope to win his love in time," she said quietly to Amy, "to feel he loves me before he knows he is bound to do so. I cannot hope now for the first strong love of his heart—that deep earnest love with which he loves his wife; but I feel nevertheless that I shall be satisfied with my son's love. His face is like his father's, and he must be as noble and as good, to have won such love as yours."

Then Mrs. Archer went away to seek Mr. Linchmore, and hear the story of her wrongs, leaving Amy to watch sadly and alone for her husband's awaking. Sadly, for how would his eyes meet hers? Would they have the same stern, severe look that had shivered her heart for so long? Would he still think she loved him not? But she would tell him all by-and-by. She could not live as she had lived: he must hear and judge whether she was as guilty as he thought her.

Robert awoke to consciousness: awoke to see the soft eyes of his wife, looking mournfully, doubtfully, but oh! how lovingly at him. As his eyes met hers, a tender light played in them; he even pressed the hand she held so tremblingly in hers; but only for a moment, the next, as she bent down and pressed her lips to his, he gave a deep sigh, and turned his face away wearily.

"He has not forgotten!" murmured Amy mournfully, as she rose and went to seek Dr. Bernard, "He has not forgiven!"

CHAPTER XVI

THE CLOUDS CLEAR

"Nor could he from his heart throw off
The consciousness of his state;
It was there with a dull, uneasy sense,
A coldness and a weight.

It was there when he lay down at night,
It was there when at morn he rose;
He feels it whatever he does,
It is with him wherever he goes.

No occupation from his mind
That constant sense can keep;
It is present in his waking hours,
It is present in his sleep."
SOUTHEY

Mrs. Elrington could not resist Anne's pleading letter, but decided on going at once to Brampton; her heart was too compassionate to refuse to aid those in distress, and especially one who had ever held, as Amy had, a high place in her esteem and love.

As soon as Anne received the answer so favourable to her wishes, she prepared at once to return home, and went to Amy—not with the glad news of the now expected guest, that she decided had best not be mentioned—but to say good-bye, and a very sorrowful one she felt it.

Amy was sitting working in her own room, once poor Bertie's; her mind as busily employed as her fingers, only more mournfully; when Anne burst open the door in her usual hasty way.

"Here I am!" she said, "Did you expect to see me? Did you think I should come to say good-bye?"

"How should I?" answered Amy, "I never knew you were going to-day, and I am sorry to see you cloaked for your journey."

"And so am I; but Tom would not rest quiet without me any longer, so dear, I must go; the pony chaise will be round directly, and yet I should have liked to have sat with you for an hour or so before leaving."

"Then why did you put off coming to see me until the last moment, Anne?"

"I did not know I was going until half an hour ago. How is that wretched Frances? Will you say I had not time to stay and see her; I should so hate—although, mind, I pity her with all my heart,—giving her a sisterly embrace."

"But," said Amy, "What occasion is there for such a warm farewell?"

"Ah! thereby hangs a tale. The fact is I don't wish to see Frances Strickland."

"Poor girl! She has suffered so much."

"I wonder you can find it in your heart to pity her; but you were always an angel of goodness."

"You are wrong, Anne," sighed Amy, "and I think you should go and see Miss Strickland."

"You are evidently in the dark, Amy; I thought Julia would have written to you, and told you, as—she has me,—that she has been so stupid, so foolish, as to engage herself to cousin Alfred, Frances' brother. Is it not tiresome of her?"

"But the marriage will scarcely affect you, Anne?"

"Oh, but it will, though; for I had made up my mind Julia would be an old maid; she always said she would, and come some day and look after my children, if I ever have any," said Anne, blushing; "for I am sure I should puzzle to know how to dress them, much less understand how to manage them. Mamma says Aunt Mary—Mrs. Strickland—is very angry about the marriage, so I really do think Julia ought to give it up."

"Why does your Aunt dislike it?"

"Because Julia is penniless and a nobody; meaning, I suppose, that Alfred should marry some high born girl, who would, I have no doubt, snub him in the end. But then it would be so nice for Aunt to say, 'My daughter-in-law, Lady so-and-so-that was,' or the Earl of somebody, my son's father-in-law. Instead of which she will only have to recall the plain and poor Miss Bennet, that was. Fancy Alfred coming to stay with us in our nutshell!"

"I never thought Mr. Strickland gave himself airs," replied Amy.

"Nor does he. But it is disagreeable to see a man sitting over the fire all day; or in summer time basking lazily in the sun."

"But Julia will probably change all that laziness and inaction. She is full of life and work herself. I think he has chosen well."

"Of course he has; but I consider Julia to have sacrificed herself. And now, do come down and see me off."

Amy put down her work and went.

"I shall see you again soon, Amy dear," said Anne, with tearful eyes, as together they stood on the terrace. "Tom has promised to drive me over some day next week, not entirely for his dear wife's sake though; but because he has taken a great interest in some dreadful sinner in this parish, and she as violent a liking to him. The old rector has given Tom permission to visit her whenever he likes, glad enough, I dare say, to be rid the trouble of it himself. Poor woman! she cannot live long—a breaking up of nature, or something of that sort; but Mrs. Archer knows more about it than I do."

"Anne! Anne! What are you talking about?" asked her husband, catching a word here and there, of her rambling speech. "Come! jump in, the pony is quite impatient to be off."

"And so is his master," laughed Anne; "we shall drive off in grand style, and then dilly-dally for half-an-hour, or more, at the turnpike, while he chats to his heart's content with Jane; that's the name of his new friend, dear. There, I really must say good-bye, or perhaps Tom may go without me." And almost smothering Amy with kisses she sprang down the steps and in another moment was seated by her husband, and they drove off.

A few hours after, Mrs. Elrington arrived at the Hall; but as she had truly said, long ago, it was pain and grief to her to look on Mrs. Linchmore's face again; and she leant heavily on Mr. Linchmore's arm, as she passed from the carriage.

She paused a moment, as he would have led her into the drawing-room to his wife; and pointing through the half-open door, said simply, "We meet as strangers."

And so they did—the once adopted daughter and fondly-loved mother; but it cost them both an effort; for while Mrs. Elrington's hand trembled and shook like an aspen on the top of the stick with which she steadied her footsteps, Mr. Linchmore thought he had never seen his wife look more proudly beautiful and magnificent.

Anne's letter represented Amy as heart-broken, not only with the loss of her child, but sorrow stricken with the anxiety caused by the fresh trial of her husband's illness. Anne said not a word of the living grief consuming her heart, but Mrs. Elrington had not been many days at Brampton ere she suspected it; that pale, sweet anxious face, so thin and care-worn, told its own tale, with the faltering, uncertain step; the mournful yet loving way with which she tended her husband now rapidly approaching convalescence. How she anticipated his every wish. Yet there was a hesitation, an uncertainty about it, all too evident to a watchful eye; it seemed as though with her anxiety to please, there was an evident fear of displeasing. Surely the wife needed the most care and tenderness now: the first she had, but the latter, where was that? Where the nameless attentions and thousand loving words her husband might speak?

Mrs. Elrington saw with sorrow the coldness, and estrangement, that had crept between the two. Was that fair young wife so recently afflicted—so loving, so doubly bereaved at heart—to blame? or Robert?

Mrs. Elrington loved Amy, and could not sit silently by without risking something to mend matters, so one day, when she and Robert were alone, she spoke.

"I trust you are feeling stronger this morning, Mr. Vavasour?"

"Thank you. Yes, I am I believe, mending apace."

"I am glad of it, as I think your wife needs change, she is looking far from well; the sooner you take her home the better."

"Bertie's death was a bitter trial; and she felt it deeply."

"Bitter, indeed, it must have been, to have changed her so utterly. She is greatly altered since her marriage."

Robert Vavasour sighed.

"You are right," he replied. "I myself see the change, but without the power to remedy it now."

"How so?" she asked.

"You say altered since her marriage. It is true; for when Amy married she wilfully shut out from her heart all hopes of happiness."

"You speak in riddles, Mr. Vavasour, which I am totally unable to comprehend."

"I am a rich man, Mrs. Elrington, and that alone might have tempted many a girl, or led her to fancy she loved me."

Mrs. Elrington drew up her head proudly. "But not Amy Neville," she replied, "no amount of wealth would have tempted her to marry a man she did not care for."

"Care for," he repeated bitterly, "caring is not loving."

Mrs. Elrington had arrived at the bottom of the mystery now; he fancied Amy did not love him! Amy who was devoting herself to him day after day, never weary of, but only happy when she was in his sick room, nursing and tending him as few wives would, treated so coldly, giving him all the loving worship of her young heart; while he refused to believe in it, but gloomily hugged the morbid fancy to his heart that she loved him not.

Mrs. Elrington could have smiled at the delusion, if Amy's happiness had not been at stake; as it was she replied gravely, "You are mistaken, Mr. Vavasour, wilfully blind to what is openly apparent to all others who ever see you and your wife together. Why I verily believe Amy worships the very ground you stand on; but I fear no words of mine will convince you of the fact, while the indifference with which you are treating her is well-nigh breaking her heart."

No, Robert Vavasour was not convinced.

"She did not love me when she married me; her oath was false, she—" but no, his pride refused to allow him to tell of her love for another.

"I cannot listen to this," replied Mrs. Elrington, rising, "whatever her love may have been in the days you speak of, I am convinced Amy has never acted falsely towards you since you called her wife; neither do I believe there lives a man who now claims or holds one thought of hers from you. I am an old woman, Mr. Vavasour, and have seen a great deal of sorrow, and one heart broken through the cruelty of another; let not your wife's be so taken from you, but believe in her, trust in her, watch over her as the apple of your eye, for indeed she needs and demands all your love and tenderness; crush not the love that is even now struggling in her heart, at your hardness and neglect, or take care lest you build up a wall that you will find it impossible hereafter to knock down, or when falling, will bury her you love beneath its ruins."

Robert's heart was strangely ill at ease and stirred by these words of Mrs. Elrington's. Perhaps he began to fear that even if his wife loved him not, he had been unnecessarily hard and severe, and pitiless, very pitiless and unloving. Might he not yet succeed in winning her love—the only thing in the wide world that he coveted? But then again, the thought that she had loved another, had cruelly deceived him, when he had loved and trusted her so entirely, was gall and wormwood to him, and turned his heart, when he thought of it, to stone. No; even allowing that she might love him, he could never love her so passionately again. So Vavasour thought, and so men and women have thought, and will think again, as long as the world lasts, and yet, do what they will, the old love will come again, with all its old intensity, overthrowing all their wise and determined resolutions.

Deep in thought, Vavasour sat, until the minutes crept into hours, and then Mrs. Archer came, looking very different from the Mrs. Grey of old. The frown had not, it is true, disappeared, but it had faded and given way to a mild, happy expression pervading every feature of her face. There was still a mournful look—how could it be otherwise?—the mournful remembrance of the past; but even that was growing dim beside the ever-living presence of her son, and of her love for him. She had gained her wish, too, for Robert loved his mother, and, I think, was somewhat proud of her. There was nothing to be ashamed of, nothing he need blush for; she was his mother, he her son, acknowledged to be so by all the world.

She was dressed in black silk, and grey-coloured ribbons in her cap; her glossy, almost snow-white hair, still beautiful in its abundance, rolled round her head. She had grown quiet and gentle, and had none of the wild passions or fits of half-madness now. As Robert sat gazing at her, he thought she must have been very beautiful in her youth, when that mass of hair was golden.

"Amy is not here," she said, looking round.

"No. I am alone, and rather tired of my solitude, with a don't-care feeling of being left any longer by myself just creeping over me."

"I thought Amy had been with you, or I should have been here before. Ah! I see she has been, by the fresh flowers on the table. She is always thinking of you, my son; her love always in her heart."

Robert moved impatiently. Had every one combined together to din his wife's love into his ears? Was he the victim of a conspiracy? So he replied, touchily.

"Amy is kind enough, and I dare say I am an ungrateful wretch."

"Not ungrateful; but you might be a little, just a little, more loving to her sometimes. She is such a loving, sweet young wife."

"You think she loves me?"

Mrs. Archer laughed. "Are you in earnest, my son?" she asked.

"Never more so in my life," was the reply.

His mother looked at him almost reproachfully.

"Can anyone doubt it?" she answered. "I believe her whole soul is wrapt up in you, and I thank God that it is so, my son."

Robert was silent,

"She is a fragile flower," continued Mrs. Archer, "one that the slightest cold breath might crush, yet withal strong in her deep love for you. It must be that, that has enabled her to bear up as she has, for she has had enough to try the strongest of us, and, I fear, looks more thin and shadowy every day."

"Mother!" cried Robert, in alarm. "You do not think Amy really ill?"

"I don't know what to think. She suffered an agony while she and I sat watching those dreadful weary hours by your bed-side; and I know Dr. Bernard now prescribed a tonic; but she does not gain strength, and seems more feeble than ever. Forgive me, my son, but I sometimes fear there is a coldness, a nameless chill between you, which makes my heart tremble for the future of both. For hers—because she will die, loving you so intensely, and—" Mrs. Archer hesitated a moment, "and with little return; for yours—lest, when too late, you will see your error, and the remorse may break your heart. Oh! my son, if she has erred, it cannot have been wilfully, and surely she has been sufficiently punished. Think," she added, laying her hand on his, as she was leaving the room, "think well on my words, for I can have but one wish at my heart, and that is my son's happiness."

And Robert did think—think deeply all the rest of that day. He seemed never tired of thinking, while his eyes rested oftener on his wife, and he watched her intensely.

What if she did love him? Ah! if only she did. His heart leapt wildly at the thought, and his jealous hatred seemed to have no place there now, but to be a far-off dream; or if it did intrude, he set it aside as a bugbear, or felt less savagely inclined than heretofore.

Could it be for him—she, his wife, brought fresh flowers for those already fading? How graceful she looked as she arranged them; not hurriedly, but slowly and tastefully—as though her heart was with the work,—in the glass. Was it for him she trod so softly over the room, while everything she touched assumed a different look, and slid quietly into its place, as though under the influence of a magic wand.

Hard and cruel! How chill those words of Mrs. Elrington's fell, like a dead weight on his heart, and had been ringing in his ears ever since. If Frances Strickland had told him a lie, then he had been hard and cruel. But his wife had never denied the facts, hideous as they appeared; but had Frances exaggerated the story, and why had he refused to listen to Amy's explanation? Might she not have cleared away half its hideousness? His heart surged like the troubled waves by the sea-shore, and his breath came quick and hot, as he felt that he might have been mistaken in fancying his wife loved him not. If all this long time it had been so, then, indeed, he had been hard and cruel; and would she ever forgive him? or could he ever forgive himself? Tormented with doubts and fears, he watched and waited, and gave no sign to his wife that he did so, while she grew paler and paler, fading imperceptibly.

The days crept on—three more slipped by, and found Robert still undecided, still undetermined. Again Amy brought fresh flowers, and stood at the table arranging them as before, and again her husband's eyes watched her, and had she only looked up as the last flower was being placed in the glass, her heart would have found its rest, for her eyes must have seen the love trembling in her husband's; but Amy never looked, but went and sat over by the fire, without a word. Then Robert spoke—

"Those flowers are very beautiful, Amy."

The words themselves were nothing, but the tone was the tender tone of old. Had he spoken coldly she could have answered at once, but the old, old loving tone, smote on her poor overcharged heart, and she could not answer a word, while the heavy tears gathered under her eyelids, and trembled as they fell. But her face was from her husband, and as yet he did not see them. Then some one came in, and they were interrupted. But the time Amy sighed for was not far distant, it was only delayed awhile.

Again they were alone; and again Robert spoke.

"Were the flowers gathered for me, Amy?"

The words were even more tenderly spoken than before; still there was no reply, and Robert half raised himself, and stooped forward to look into his wife's face; but she kept it steadfastly hidden: she dared not look until she could control some of the emotion, which seemed as though it would suffocate her.

They were both silent now. Robert grieved at her silence, while Amy sat striving and fighting with her sobs; yet so very still that none could have guessed the pent-up agony she was enduring.

By-and-bye she grew more composed; had conquered and mastered her emotion, and turned her head towards her husband; but he was reading, and if he saw her, never raised his eyes from his book.

Unconsciously her thoughts wandered, wandered away to the days at Somerton when she had been so happy. Ah! what a world of woe had overtaken her since then. Her boy dead, her only one; her husband worse than dead, his love estranged, perhaps gone for ever! and yet if he had only allowed her to speak,—not to attempt to palliate her fault, but only to tell how dearly she loved him! she felt she had rightly forfeited some of his esteem, but scarcely deserved all the bitter misery his coldness had cost her.

Would he ever trust her again? Ever believe her love? Yet if she died for it, she must tell it him; the weight of it was killing her, and she clasped her small white hands tightly over her knees as she thought that perhaps the time for her to speak had come. Only a few moments ago he had spoken almost tenderly to her, and more like his former self, and he was better, almost well now, and able to bear what she had to say. The excitement of her sad tale would not hurt him half so much as the telling it would grieve her.

He was no longer weak, but gaining strength every day; there was scarcely any trace of his illness now, save that ugly scar near his temple, and that was gradually fading away.

How should she begin? What should she say? As she essayed to think, the suffocating feeling arose again in her throat; again the large heavy tears dropped one by one; but her face was turned full on her husband now, his eyes on hers, yet she knew it not; knew not that his book had been laid down long ago, and that he was watching eagerly the various emotions flitting over face.

As the tears sprung from her eyes, he said, hastily reaching out his hand,

"Come here, Amy! Come nearer to me."

She saw him then. Their eyes met, and that one glance told him his wife's love was his; told her she was trusted and forgiven. In another moment she had tottered forward and was gathered to his heart, her tears falling like rain on his breast.

"Oh! Robert! Robert!" she wailed.

But loving words poured impetuously in her ears, loving arms were round her.

"My wife! my own! My darling Amy. Hush! hush, love!"

But she could not hush; but lay weeping, weeping passionately, nestled close to him; clasped tightly in his arms, as though he feared to lose her.

He thought those tears would never cease, and almost grew frightened at their intensity, but they stopped at last, subsiding into sobs; and presently they were gone altogether, and she rested gently and quietly in his arms while she told him the tale that had nearly broken her heart and his; and if he thought her to blame, as without doubt she was, he forgave her now from his heart, and bitterly accused himself of being hard and cruel indeed; and thanked God he had not been too late in breaking down the wall that had severed them, and nearly buried them both in its ruins.

Mrs. Elrington came in, but was moving softly away again when Robert called her back.

"She does indeed love me," he said proudly and humbly; while he resisted Amy's efforts to free herself from his grasp, "Your words, dear lady, were severe but well timed. I deserved them and can thank you for them now; while all my life long I will strive to make amends for what my wife has suffered."

Amy looked up, her bright face flushing with smiles, but her husband covered her mouth laughingly with his hand as she attempted to speak; possibly he thought she would, like a true woman, strive to hide his fault by exposing her own. But she struggled to free herself and said,

"I am more happy than I deserve to be, dear Mrs. Elrington, my one sin so bitterly repented of having taught me the value of my husband's love, and how dear, how very dear, he is to me."

"Heed her not! heed her not!" cried Robert.

"God bless you both, my children," said Mrs. Elrington fervently.

SUNSHINE

"Here may ye see, that women be
In love meke, kynd and stable:
Let never man reprove them then,
Or call them variable."
THE NUT BROWN MAID

Then only doth the soul of woman know
Its proper strength when love and duty meet;
Invincible the heart wherein they have their seat.
SOUTHEY

Mrs. Elrington did not remain much longer at Brampton, she and Mrs. Linchmore parting as distantly as they had met, Mr. Linchmore grieving that the visit from which he had hoped so much had failed in reconciling those who had once been bound together by the strongest ties of affection. They were severed utterly and for ever: the remembrance of the old tie only bringing sorrow to the hearts of each.

Mrs. Linchmore never once relaxed from her pride and haughtiness but seemed to her husband's sorrow to bear herself more proudly and stormily every day; whatever her inward sufferings,—and she did suffer acutely,—she gave no outward sign, deceiving her husband into the belief that she was the injured one, who would not make one step forward to mend matters or heal the old wound, lest it should be construed into an acknowledgment that she, having done the wrong was anxious to make atonement.

Mrs. Linchmore knew did she implore or even plead for Mrs. Elrington's love, it would not be given: forgiveness unasked had been granted her in that letter received long ago; but love the old love, could never be hers again. The injury was too deep wherewith she had injured her; the deceit too cruel and wilful. Her son's broken heart could never be forgotten; how could she love her who had broken it? It was a lasting injury; one neither could forget. It had well-nigh broken the mother's heart as well as the son's, leaving broken hopes; lonely, sad, even painful recollections: it had changed Mrs. Linchmore more sadly still.

Mrs. Elrington apparently gave no heed to the contemptuous indifference with which she was every day greeted, but behaved as a guest who now sees her hostess for the first time, and only to Amy did she ever say—and that but once,—how changed, how sadly altered she thought Mrs. Linchmore.

Jane never recovered from the weakness consequent on the fever, but gradually grew more feeble every day, weaker each time Mr. Hall went to see her; her one sorrow being the misery she had in her wickedness caused others; her one fear lest so grievous a sin could never be atoned for or forgiven; but a visit from Mrs. Archer—which she had never dared hope for, although she had over and over again begged her forgiveness through Mr. Hall, and been assured of it from him—served to calm and tranquillise her troubled spirit, and led her to look—to hope for a higher forgiveness still. Jane died thoroughly, sincerely repentant; the last few days of her life being the only peaceful happy ones she had known for years. Mrs. Marks regained the use of her limbs, and stormed at Matthew, and held her own sway in the cottage as much as ever, if not more so; but Marks said he did not mind it now, and was right down glad to hear his old woman's tongue going at it harder and faster than ever; it was dead-alive work enough when she was ill, and as he had ceased to frequent the "Brampton Arms," and was satisfied with his wife, why should we find fault with either her or her tongue?

Tom Hodge did not fulfil Marks' prophecy, either as to the hanging, or breaking his father's heart; William Hodge came down to Standale to see his son, and left it an altered, almost an aged man. Like his wife, he took his son's crime to heart, and although Mrs. Marks said, in a sympathising way, Tom was only in jail awaiting his trial for an attempt to kill, yet Hodge could not shut his eyes to the fact that he might have been heavily ironed for murder, and the thought crushed him. A change imperceptibly crept over him from that time, and although he struggled with the shame he felt for his eldest son's evil doings, and held his head as high as ever, the old hearty good-humoured manner had fled, and not many months passed ere he gave up the smith's business,—that had once been his pride and pleasure,—to his other and younger son.

Tom Hodge's crime was proved; his reason for shooting at Robert Vavasour the second time being, that the latter had recognised him as the man who had wounded him four years ago. The act was not premeditated, but the momentary impulse of the surprise and sudden recognition. He was sentenced to penal servitude for a lengthened term of years; let us hope he returned a wiser and a better man.

Frances, anxious to make all the amends in her power, and atone for the fault that had cost her so much, begged—when strong enough, and recovered from her illness, which was more of the mind than body—to see Mr. Vavasour; but he was obdurate.

"Tell her," he said, "that I believe in my wife's faith and love so entirely, I need no assurance of it from one who tried to injure her so deeply, no explanation of what I ought never to have doubted."

So Frances left Brampton, carrying with her the life-long remembrance of poor little Bertie's death, which she could not but be persuaded was mainly attributable to her, and sent as a warning and punishment for her pride and revengeful wickedness. Perhaps, had the child lived, her bad, passionate heart might never have been touched, and she might have lived on still in her sinful revenge, working, if it were possible, more and more misery; but Bertie's sad early death wrought the change, bringing to her stony, unfeeling heart both sorrow and remorse, while the end for which she had so wickedly striven she never attained, losing in time all interest, all kindly, cousinly feeling even, in the heart, to gain which she had wrought so much evil, and brought all the worst passions of her nature into play.

And Charles Linchmore? What need to say anything of him? He has ceased, perhaps, to hold any place in my reader's interest; but in case some care to know of his well-being, I may mention that he recovered from his wound, and when last heard of was talking of returning home to England.

Mrs. Archer's days glided peacefully on, calmly, happy at last in her son's love, in witnessing his and his wife's happiness; and when another little Bertie, almost rivalling the first in beauty and spirits—in all save his mother's heart—played about in the old house at Somerton, the frown had faded away more visibly still, though the remembrance of the anguish of mind and miserable days she had passed, consequent upon her deceit and one false step, could never be forgotten, or cease to be regretted. Her mind could scarcely ever be said to have entirely recovered from the shock it had sustained, though all angry fierceness and bitter fits of half madness had fled, never to return.

The mysterious light that had so troubled Amy, and been a source of superstition to the servants and villagers, was fully accounted for, as Mrs. Archer, in touching upon her previous miserable life to her son, mentioned, that having a key of the door leading up the secret stairs into old Mrs. Linchmore's room, she had sometimes been seized with an uncontrollable desire to revisit the scene where with the closing of the life of one, had died out so she thought, her sole cherished hope, the hope of ever finding her son. She had never divested herself of the idea that old Mrs. Linchmore had stolen the child; through all her wild dreams she had held to that, and fancied that at Brampton only should she ever hear of him again; and when, on his wife's death, Robert Linchmore's father had searched for and found her, she would accept nothing at his hands, poor as she was, but the cottage which, at her own earnest request, he built for her, while the secret of her relationship with those at the Hall had, she hoped, died with him, she having asked him never to divulge it; and he who had loved her once, nay, loved her still, and had been the unwitting means, through his wife's mad jealousy, of causing her so much misery, granted, though unwillingly, even that. At his death Mrs. Archer changed her name, and came to Brampton, fearing no recognition from those still living. How could they recognise in that broken-hearted, wild-looking woman, the once fair, gentle Miss Mary of the Hall.

Anne came to see Amy as she had promised, and spent the day at Brampton, her heart feeling really rejoiced at the happy change in her friend. There was still a shade of sadness on Amy's face, but the weariful look was gone, and she appeared almost as bright and youthful as on the day when Anne had first made her acquaintance; while as to Robert Vavasour? Anne wondered how she ever could have thought him an icicle or indifferent to his wife, so fond of her as he seemed now, so anxious that she should not over exert herself; for she was anything but strong or recovered from the shock of the severe trials she had gone through.

"I do think," said Anne, as Amy was busy putting together a few last things—a work which she either did not wish, or would not trust her maid to do for her; "I do think your husband is a most devoted one, Amy; there is only one other that excels him, and that's—my own!"

Amy laughed. "Are you quite satisfied with your husband, Anne?"

"What a question!" answered Anne indignantly.

"Opinions formed hastily easily change," replied her friend, "Did not you say you would only marry a man with fierce moustaches and whiskers!"

"I did," said Anne consciously, "and—and—well you have not seen Tom lately, or you would not say that, because a beard does improve him so much; and between ourselves, dear, I am nearly fidgeting myself to death, lest he should grow a moustaches, for I have changed my opinion, and don't like them!"

"The carriage is at the door, Amy," said her husband, entering the room.

"Oh, Mr. Vavasour! how sorry I am you are going to take Amy away. It may be years before we meet again, as I know Mrs. Vavasour will never come to this odious place if she can help it."

"Brampton," replied Amy, sorrowfully, "will always hold one little spot of ground towards which my heart will often yearn. As the resting-place of my boy, Anne, I think I shall—must revisit Brampton."

"True. I am always wrong, and speak, as Tom says, without considering in the least what I am going to say. Forgive me Amy, I quite forgot for the moment your grief."

"I hope," said Robert, as he drew his wife away, "you and Mr. Hall will soon come and see us, at Somerton. Amy and I will give you a hearty welcome."

"I accept the invitation with pleasure, that is," said she correcting herself, "if Tom can find anyone to do his duty during his absence."

As Amy drove away with Mrs. Archer and her husband, Anne waved a tearful adieu until the carriage turned the drive, and was out of sight.

As they drove through the park Amy sat very silent; her husband did not interrupt her thoughts, perhaps he guessed her heart was too full for words: but as they passed through the large gates her eyes looked wistfully towards the—churchyard, little Bertie's last resting place, and as she pictured to herself the small white marble cross, looking whiter still with the sun reflected on it, and the little mound almost green now, and covered with the early primroses she had strewed there that morning,—her eyes filled with tears, and she sighed involuntarily.

Robert drew her gently, but fondly, towards him.

"Our boy is happy, Amy, darling. And you?"

"I?" she replied, smiling and struggling with her tears. "I, Robert, am happier than I deserve to be, with you to love and to take care of me."

"Not so, Amy," he said. "We have been both to blame. Perhaps, had it been otherwise, we should never have found out how dear we are to each other. Is it not so, my own dear love?"

Amy did not reply, save by the loving light in her eyes, as she nestled closer to his side.

If she had been greatly tried, she had indeed found her safest and best earthly resting-place now and for ever!

MRS HENRY WOOD (aka ELLEN WOOD) – A CONCISE BIBLIOGRAPHY

Danesbury House (1860)
East Lynne (1861)
The Elchester College Boys (1861)
A Life's Secret (1862)
Mrs. Halliburton's Troubles (1862)
The Channings (1862)
The Foggy Night at Offord: A Christmas Gift for the Lancashire Fund (1863)
The Shadow of Ashlydyat (1863)
Verner's Pride (1863)
Lord Oakburn's Daughters (1864)

Oswald Cray (1864)
Trevlyn Hold; or, Squire Trevlyn's Heir (1864)
William Allair; or, Running away to Sea (1864)
Mildred Arkell: A Novel (1865)
The Argosy (1865)
Elster's Folly: A Novel (1866)
St. Martin's Eve: A Novel (1866)
Lady Adelaide's Oath (1867)
Orville College: A Story (1867)
The Ghost of the Hollow Field (1867)
Anne Hereford: A Novel (1868)
Castle Wafer; or, The Plain Gold Ring (1868)
The Red Court Farm: A Novel (1868)
Roland Yorke: A Novel (1869)
Bessy Rane: A Novel (1870)
George Canterbury's Will (1870)
Dene Hollow (1871)
Within the Maze: A Novel (1872)
The Master of Greylands (1872)
Johnny Ludlow (1874)
Bessy Wells (1875)
Told in the Twilight: Containing 'Parkwater' and nine short stories (1875)
Adam Grainger: A Tale (1876)
Edina (1876)
Our Children (1876)
Parkwater: With four other tales (1876)
Pomeroy Abbey (1878)
Lady Adelaide (1879)
Johnny Ludlow, Second Series (1880)
A Tale of Sin and Other Tales (1881)
Court Netherleigh: A Novel (1881)
About Ourselves (1883)
Johnny Ludlow. Third Series (1885)
Lady Grace and Other Stories (1887)
The Story of Charles Strange (1888)
Featherston's Story. A Tale by Johnny Ludlow (1889)
The Unholy Wish and Other Stories (1890)
The House of Halliwell. A Novel (1890)
Ashley and Other Stories (1897)
Victor Serenus (1898)
Johnny Ludlow. Fifth series (1899)
Johnny Ludlow. Sixth series (1899)

Translations
Les Channing. Traduit de l'Anglais par Mme Abric-Encontre (1864)
Les Filles de Lord Oakburn: Roman traduit de l'anglais par L. Bochet (1876)
La Gloire des Verner: Roman traduit de l'anglais par L. de L'Estrive (1878)

Le Serment de Lady Adelaïde: Roman traduit de l'anglais par Léon Bochet (1878)